W9-BDM-306

A SEDUCTIVE CALL

"Come here, darling—" Her voice came from just out of sight, the voice that had trembled on the fringes of his consciousness every night just before he fell asleep, deep and sensuous, promising things men dreamed of at that hour. "You need to let me hold you."

Rexford froze in place, knowing no power on earth could make him take the final steps that would bring him into view and end the illusion that she was talking to him.

"I can feel you trembling. Don't be afraid. You will learn to love the way I touch you."

Oh, yes. Rexford pictured her long fingers moving over his body, her strokes as smooth as her words.

"That's better. You're not afraid anymore. You like the feel of my hands. You like it when I touch you right here. So soft."

A tiny voice of reason told Rexford she was talking to a bird. His body chose to believe she meant the words exclusively for him. The mirage of her touch was an almost physical sensation. He closed his eyes and surrendered to the fantasy.

Flight of Fancy

Judy Veisel

LEISURE BOOKS   NEW YORK CITY

To Sam, who was, is, and always will be
the prototype of all my heroes.

A LEISURE BOOK®

February 1998

Published by

Dorchester Publishing Co., Inc.
276 Fifth Avenue
New York, NY 10001

If you purchased this book without a cover you should be aware
that this book is stolen property. It was reported as "unsold and
destroyed" to the publisher and neither the author nor the publisher
has received any payment for this "stripped book."

Copyright © 1998 by Judy Veisel

All rights reserved. No part of this book may be reproduced or
transmitted in any form or by any electronic or mechanical means,
including photocopying, recording or by any information storage
and retrieval system, without the written permission of the
Publisher, except where permitted by law.

ISBN 0-8439-4351-3

The name "Leisure Books" and the stylized "L" with design are
trademarks of Dorchester Publishing Co., Inc.

Printed in the United States of America.

Flight of Fancy

Chapter One

"Damn pigeons."

Even as he muttered, Marcus Blackerby, Earl of Rexford, knew the words came from habit rather than from the black mood that had possessed him since learning of his mission. The exhilaration of finally being outdoors after the week of rain lifted his spirits so that even the ominous sky and up-coming confrontation seemed a minor annoyance.

Still, a man had to do his cursing when he could.

He pulled his hired mare to a halt in front of the modest stone manor house built sometime in the last century. "No offense, Tillie, but I will be glad to see the last of you." He drew his fingers in a caress along the animal's drooping neck, but stayed in the saddle for one last grumble.

He was a soldier, for God's sake. With Napoleon on the march again, he belonged in Brussels with Wellington. In-stead, fate and a stray musket ball had condemned him to bird duty, the only enemy an obstinate spinster who raised

7

carrier pigeons and thought the war too dangerous for her precious birds. He arched his neck and fingered the board-stiff cloth at his chin. "Wretched thing." A man wearing one of these cravats could get shot in the neck three times and never lose a drop of blood. Nevertheless, impeccable dress could be as effective a weapon as a pistol under the right circumstance.

Pleased to have worked himself back into a foul and therefore intimidating mood, Rexford dismounted and looked for a groom to hold the reins. When none appeared, he dropped the reins. The reluctant Tillie would not go much further than the shrubs at the edge of the drive. "Somebody will be with you soon, girl." He straightened his shoulders, approached the elaborately carved wooden door, and knocked.

A pink-cheeked serving girl responded. "Good day, sir." Her face and the lilt to her voice said Ireland, and not long ago at that.

"I am here to see Miss Amanda Langley."

"I'm sorry, sir. Miss Langley is not here at the moment."

Fresh from the country, but well-trained enough for a polite evasion. Rexford doubted Miss Langley had gone out, with the roads just barely passable. More likely the eccentric daughter of the house rarely saw anyone not sporting feathers. He drew himself up to his full height. "I am Lord Rexford and I need to see your mistress. Fetch her, please."

"It doesn't matter who you are, sir. She ain't here. You could come in and look but you would just see she ain't here." The natural blush of the girl's cheeks deepened when she realized she had lost some of her carefully assumed poise, but the rattle of her words gave them the unquestionable ring of truth.

Rexford waited with his eyebrows raised, knowing patience would draw forth an explanation faster than a question.

"She rode out early. She made the butler and everybody else go with her. She left me in charge." The girl gave him a proud smile. "You will have to come back."

Rexford would have to do no such thing. He had taken advantage of the brief hiatus in the week-long rains to ride four miles on the only horse that, according to the innkeeper, could sludge through the mud on the water-logged roads. He wasn't leaving—not now, and if he could obtain the necessary invitation, probably not for weeks. Miss Langley would not be riding long in this weather. "I will wait." He took a step forward, satisfied to see the girl melt back though she did not actually retreat a full step. "I assume the rain will send the lady home within the hour."

"If you assume that, you don't know Miss Langley. She's like to spend half the day in the rain, the way she did yesterday." The girl nodded in unbridled admiration for the lady with the curious habit of riding in the rain.

Two minutes later, having received from the loquacious colleen directions for locating her mistress, Rexford swung into the saddle.

The placid mare, who fortunately had dined only sparingly on the shrubs, moved better on the less well-traveled ground across country. Only occasionally did Rexford hear the slurping sound that signaled her hoof had sunk deep into the water-saturated earth. The rapid beat of a pigeon's wings overhead drew his gaze and reminded him of his mission. He tried to conjure up some affection for the creature, but managed only a mild indifference.

Until the previous week he had been behind a desk, sorting through the conflicting masses of information from the Continent. His years on Wellington's staff had given him the ability to evaluate not only the messages but the senders, an ability unmatched, at least by anybody willing to stay behind in London while Wellington was screaming for experienced troops in the field.

A week ago, London had seemed a safe distance away from any possible battlefield. Then an unknown traitor had revealed the London location of the military carrier pigeons to the enemy. The birds had been slaughtered and the building burned to a hollow shell. While the battle on the Continent might not come for a month, the vital communication link with Wellington had to be restored as soon as possible.

Initially the task appeared simple. For years the Langleys had been exchanging crateloads of birds with Albert Gully, a Brussels breeder, so they could carry on a purposeless but efficient aerial correspondence. The message route might not have been established for Wellington, but it was better than anything the army could establish on short notice.

Unfortunately, Dalton, the young blockhead sent to explain the situation to Miss Langley, had chosen to describe the London massacre in vivid detail. Not only had the lady failed to volunteer her birds, but she had told Dalton if she ever caught him near her place again, she would feed him to the pigeons. While Dalton had not exactly said he believed her, he had asked for a transfer to an infantry regiment.

Rexford himself had visited two other pigeon trainers the day after Dalton's debacle. One breeder had said he could probably have some birds trained to fly that distance within the next six months; the other had referred him to someone in Scotland whose birds regularly flew to Antwerp. Both had acknowledged that Miss Langley not only owned the best birds, but knew more about training them than anyone in England. Rexford had reported his findings to the head of British military intelligence, and been only mildly surprised when the old man said, "Charm the lady or force her, Rexford, but we must use those birds."

Rexford considered the problem simple enough. He planned merely to solicit an invitation to visit, cultivating a one-bird-fancier-to-another friendship until he knew Miss Langley well enough to discuss the situation rationally. He cast an upward glance at the threatening sky. That plan was conceived, of course, before he learned the lady did not have wit enough to come in out of the rain.

Tillie plodded to a stop at the crest of a hill overlooking the steel gray water of a swirling river. Rexford stared at the frenetic activity below. Miss Langley had obviously come out for more than a comfortable ride in the rain. Twenty or more people scurried back and forth along the riverbank, waging a desperate battle against the swollen river. On the far side the water meandered in splotchy fingers across a narrow spit of land. On the near side, where the land dipped into the hollow, people were fighting gallantly to prevent the water from taking its obvious course toward a solid-looking stone building about two hundred yards from the bank.

The structure looked as if it could survive a dozen floods. Someone needed to tell the workers simply to save the contents, evacuate the people, and wait for the water to go back where it came from. He nudged his mare forward.

People raced back and forth to reinforce a mud-caked, thigh-high wall built across the path nature dictated the water would take. Water already lapped at the top of the wall, spilling over crumbling areas in tiny surges. He glanced at the sky and winced. They had fought a good fight, but lost. The workers' grim expressions said they knew it. A few more minutes . . .

Rexford rode forward faster, hoping to persuade them to save what they could. As he drew within shouting distance, he saw the only person who had not accepted defeat, a woman wearing a muddied riding habit whose color could only be described as drab. She had the trailing skirt tied up around her waist like an improvised apron, and wielded a shovel. An absurd hat of the same indescribable color as the riding habit clung precariously to the back of her head, threatening to drop into the mud with each step. A white curved feather grew from the hat and swiveled with every abrupt movement like a compass needle to point at some random place behind her.

The lady, Miss Langley he presumed, bounded everywhere, seeking out the weak spots in the makeshift wall. When she found one, she barked orders to grown men, who should have known better than to listen. They trudged toward her dragging two-wheeled carts filled with dirt. On command they shoveled the muck where she pointed. When they did not move quickly enough, she grabbed the shovel and demonstrated—demonstrated she had more vigor than brains. A dozen more workers and a miracle and the defense might have worked.

11

Thunder rumbled in the distance. It was time he told the energetic commander that water like this generally went where it decided to go. If she wanted to save anything from inside the building, she had to do it soon.

He arrived at her side just as she discovered a new spot where water trickled over the barricade carrying granules of precious mud with it.

"Here! Here!" she shouted. "Somebody over here!" She turned to grab a shovel from the soft mud, then saw Rexford. "Help me." Without waiting for a response she slapped two half-full shovels of mud onto the lapping water, and watched for a moment to be sure she had effectively stopped the flow.

She twisted around to look up at him, her feet remaining mired in mud. "What are you just sitting there for? I asked for help." Her eyes flashed her impatience at Rexford.

He almost smiled. She had actually asked him to dismount and begin shoveling mud. "I am sorry, Miss Langley. I just want to suggest—"

She waved a muddy hand to block his words. "That is not important now. You can see we need everybody to help stop this water. Hurry, please." She reached up and brushed at a tangled hank of hair that had escaped from the tie at the back of her head to fall over one eye. She pinned him with a gaze that almost insisted he salute rather than protest.

He chose to protest. "It is not going to help. More rain—"

"Of course it is not going to help if you just sit there. Now, please." She thrust out the shovel, her message unmistakably clear.

Rexford looked around for a servant to set to the task. He might consider humoring her, but surely his new coat deserved some consideration. "I am not attired for—"

"Oh, bother your clothes. You can always get more."

He should have guessed she would not care passionately about his clothes. Her riding habit had probably been fashionable the year the old king took the throne, and the color, darkened by mud and water, undoubtedly looked better than the dull gray or green of the original garment.

He inhaled. His tailor would never forgive him, but given

12

his mission, he needed her cooperation. Even if they failed here, this madwoman would remember his effort. With a mental shrug of resignation, he swung his leg over the mare's neck and sprang down. Huge gobs of mud spattered in all directions. "Here, give me that."

He stomped the shovel into the soft earth and lifted. The tight shoulders of his coat effectively bound his arms to his body. He managed a weak thrust with his elbows, which got the shovel about a foot off the ground before it twisted and dumped its contents.

He bit his lip and kept his curse inaudible. The lady's impatient look said he had about two seconds to redeem himself. "Call me Macaroni," he muttered, and tore at the sleeves of the offending coat, tossing it over the saddle of his compliant mare. With a friendly nicker she backed up, dislodged the coat, and worked it into the mud with one oversized hoof, answering for all time the question of whether the coat could be salvaged. Rexford toasted her success by hoisting several shovelfuls of earth to the crumbling wall. Tillie snorted.

"Good. Good. Good." The lady nodded her enthusiastic praise. With a shrill whistle, as unfeminine a sound as he had ever heard, she attracted the attention of a plodding worker. "Jeb, over here." The huge man trundled over, dragging a cart of earth behind him. "Well done, Jeb," she said in a voice that almost patted the man on the head. "Now bring us more."

Jeb gave an open-mouthed nod and trudged off. His huge feet left six-inch-deep prints in the mire behind him.

Rexford began shoveling from the cart Jeb left behind, surprised to find himself invigorated by the physical activity after days of tedious confinement. "Do you mind telling me why we are doing this?" He glanced around at the solid-looking stone building. "Not that I mind," he added quickly to ward off the words her imperious expression promised.

His improbable companion pointed to the building. "We have to keep the water from getting over there." She clenched her teeth, and her pointing finger bounced several times to emphasize the point.

Rexford reached up and ripped off his neckcloth. This was obviously a very informal party. "That is the sturdiest-looking building I have ever seen in my life. This little river is not going to do it any harm at all." He wadded the white cloth, threw it toward the standing horse, and hoped she would enjoy stomping the wretched thing into the ground.

"You can't see from here. The fourth side is open—for the birds." Her face tightened as if she were lifting the shovelfuls of water-saturated dirt. "If the water gets high, we will lose too many birds."

"What—" Rexford's lower body froze while he looked around for somebody playing an elaborate joke on him. He was standing with England's foremost expert on birds and should not have to be the one to tell her the creatures could fly. "Correct me if I am wrong." He turned the shovel and let the dirt he had just lifted fall back to the ground. "These birds are supposed to come home. You can just let them go and tell them to come back after the flood." He wondered if she would pay for a new pair of Hessians in gratitude for the suggestion.

Her brow furrowed. She leaned forward as if she might grab the shovel. "This is no time for levity. If the water reaches that building I may lose half my flock, Mr.—who are you, by the way?" If she directed that imperious look at the river, the waters might go right back where they belonged.

Rexford, however, could out-imperious just about anyone. He drew himself up to his full height. "I am—"

"Oh, no." She shrieked, and Rexford followed the direction of her gaze. Another low spot. Water, a miniature stream, spilled over the wall about twenty feet away. "Stay here and keep shoveling." She turned and ran.

Rexford had never taken orders from a woman, but he kept shoveling. Her conviction that the birds were in danger made their defense top priority. A large raindrop splattered against his cheek. It would not be long before another deluge. He piled more dirt on the crumbling wall because for the moment he could not think of what else to do. He paused to watch Jeb lumber toward him. He would wait for the cart's dirt rather than take any more from the ground at his feet.

For the first time he looked across the swollen stream to the spit of land beyond, a flat stretch about thirty feet wide. On the far side it sloped down to what appeared to be an old riverbed.

Jeb plodded to a stop next to Rexford. His brow furrowed. "Did Miss Langley want me to bring this here? Where did she go?"

"This is good, Jeb. We can use it right here." Rexford found himself speaking slowly as Miss Langley did. He pointed. "What is that over there, Jeb?"

The rain began falling in heavy slapping drops. Jeb turned his head very slowly and looked at Rexford from the corner of his eyes. He hesitated. "The other side?" He made the words a question and waited to be corrected.

"No, not right there. Beyond that. Where it starts going down."

"That's where the river used to be. Am I supposed to go and get more dirt?"

Rexford felt the rain drip off his hair and down the neck of his shirt. "Not now. Tell me about where the river used to be. Did you do something to make it come over here?"

Jeb opened his mouth and nodded. "Mr. Barrows, who has the house there"—he pointed upriver—"made us build a dam and put the river over here. He said he needed the water for more fields." He straightened. "Miss Langley let me help him because I'm strong. I give the money to my da'. I didn't know it would make the water do this."

"Probably nobody did until the spring rains. When did you build the dam, Jeb?" He ignored the nagging throb in his recently healed shoulder and continued shoveling, faster now because the rain washed away about half of every shovelful.

"In the summer because it was hot. I remember. I liked getting wet."

Rexford scooped the last dregs of dirt from the wooden cart, and knew it would not be enough. He looked along the river to the curve about a hundred feet away. "Where is your dam?"

Jeb shook his head impatiently. "Up there, of course." He pointed up the river. "Don't you know nothing?"

Rexford winced. It had been a fool question. "I am going to take a look." Possibly he could turn the water back into its old bed. Grasping the shovel and a discarded ax, he mounted Tillie.

No one bothered to look at him as he passed. Water began to slosh over the wall in a dozen places. One by one, men turned away. Everyone looked tired and defeated except Miss Langley. She stood, her hair plastered to her face, the hat long since lost in the mire, shaking her clenched fist at the blackened sky. If he could hear her silent words, Rexford suspected he would discover she could curse as eloquently as he.

The promised dam stood fifty yards upstream. A water-covered bridge provided access across the swollen arm of the river. Tillie, undaunted by the swirling water, trotted across the wooden bridge. Rexford sat in the driving rain, studying the construction. He did not know much about dams, but this did not look like any great engineering feat. Two wooden walls, spaced about a foot apart with a layer of earth between them, turned the water from its original course. A little effort might divert it back.

As Jeb promised, the dam was better than the fragile earth wall, but not a great deal better. Toward the center, a heavy log carried by the current pounded against it, rebounded, and pounded again. The dam shuddered with each thump.

He looked back toward the stricken workers who gathered around Miss Langley. He could hear no words, but saw her gesturing toward the stone building. Not a good time to discuss his plan.

Ignoring Jeb, who had followed on foot, Rexford dismounted and tore off his boots. "Damn things pinch anyway." If he kept this up he would wind up stark naked with his clothes strewn all over the county. Barefoot, the rain plastering his shirt to his body, he edged along the top of the dam, headed for the center to the board that seemed to shudder most when the log slammed into the shaking wood.

Facing downstream, he took a minute to test his footing, unsteady but not impossible, then started swinging. Wind drove the rain directly into his face nearly blinding him. The ax slammed into the board at an angle. Pain tore through his injured shoulder. He wrenched the ax free, swung again. On the fourth swing he heard the board splinter and split down the center. He reached down, ripped the loose flap free, and let it fall to the old riverbed.

"He's breaking it," Jeb shouted. "Come quick everybody, he's breaking it." In the background Jeb's voice faded into the distance as he raced to inform the others.

Rexford slashed at the boards. Each time he tossed aside a section of wood, the water surged forward between the upstream boards and slurped away at the packed earth separating the two frame sections. He concentrated on only one side. Once he began on the other, the water would help him.

For sure he would take a dunking, but the water did not look too deep or wide. He just could not predict how much flying debris there would be. He had divested himself of his senses when he divested himself of his coat, so he settled for whispering a silent prayer to the god of flying debris.

He sensed the crowd assembled on the bank, heard their ragged comments.

"He is breaking it!" That tortured cry must be Jeb. The dam was probably his finest accomplishment.

"Whadda's he wanna do that for? Stop him."

"How do we stop him?"

"He's a madman. Stop him."

"Stop that right now." Miss Langley's voice rang out above the crowd. "Do you hear me? You are destroying the dam. All that water will . . . Lord-a-mercy! Why didn't I think of that? All that water will just go back where it belongs. Hurry!"

If Rexford could have stopped gritting his teeth with the

effort, he would have smiled. Didn't she know any word but *hurry*? At least she understood what he was trying to do.

He turned and started to attack the boards behind him. Three strokes and the first board shattered. Water surged through and the dam trembled. Rexford danced to hold his balance.

"Yes, yes, yes." Miss Langley cheered. "Look, it is going." Then the inevitable "Hurry."

"Yes. Look." A chorus of voices picked up her cheer.

Rexford felt like the hero who had ridden in to save the town. The exhilaration of the physical exercise and the unabashed adulation of the crowd made it possible to ignore the fire in his shoulder and added strength to his swing. Then a tremor more violent than any before reminded him he should be planning his escape.

With luck he might be able to smash a few more boards and dash to the far side before the entire dam collapsed. He did not dare look up to see if the earth wall protecting the birds still held, but the admiring murmurs led him to assume it had. The structure on which he stood swayed and threatened to buck him into the growing puddle below.

Shrieks of the tortured wood drowned out all other sounds. Time for his dash to safety. He made it three steps before the entire wall swayed again, then gave way with a series of gunshot cracks.

With a final quick prayer, Rexford surrendered to the swirling water. Everything would be luck now.

He tumbled, making no effort to fight the water. He raised his arms to protect his head and face from the jagged wood he knew surged about him. A sudden flow bounced him to the surface. He opened his eyes to see a thick board rushing toward him. It slammed into his temple. Something jagged slashed across his shin.

Time to fight, he thought weakly, get out of the current. Feebly he forced himself to stroke for the shore. The one with the people. People would help.

Strong arms grabbed him around the waist, lifted. Rexford's chin struck his chest with bone-jarring force. He

18

should walk. He let the arms carry or drag him. Dimly he saw Jeb's angry face. Jeb was big enough to carry him. Rexford tried to help, took one step, and surrendered to the blackness.

He slowly became aware he was lying in the mud, face-down, a solid foot planted on his backside.

"He broke it." Jeb's anguished voice came from above him. "I told you he was breaking it. Why didn't you stop him?"

Rexford opened his eyes. Through a haze he saw a sea of muddy boots. His tongue passed over gritty sand on his lips, but he could still form words. "I saved your bloody building," he muttered. "The least you can do is tell him to get his damn foot off my arse."

Back at the house Amanda stopped to remove her boots, then hurried to catch up with the men carrying the stranger. Kitty, the thoroughly breathless housemaid, stopped her before she could follow the thumping procession up the stairs. "Is that the lord, miss? Have you killed 'im?"

Amanda resisted the temptation to brush past Kitty. Jeb and the others would need some time to undress the man, and Kitty obviously knew more about him than anybody else. "No, I have not killed him." Detecting the hint of disappointment on Kitty's face, Amanda smiled and added, "I just dumped him in the river and hit him with a plank. Who is he?"

"Oh, mercy, miss. Your mother's going to have a twiddle fit if you dumped a perfectly good lord in the river." Kitty loved nothing as much as a little drama to brighten the day, but she clapped her hand over her mouth. Her wide-eyed look gave evidence that several months of training had at least produced the realization she had been behaving in a grossly inappropriate manner—again.

Amanda repressed a smile. Kitty's gesture could not conceal the spark of unholy delight in her eyes.

"Begging your pardon, miss. I'm sure you didn't . . . I'm sure your mother . . ."

JUDY VEISEL

Would have a twiddle fit, Amanda finished mentally, *particularly if he is a perfectly good lord.* Aloud she said, "Never mind that. Who is he?"

"He is a lord. I'm not exactly sure what he's the lord of. He said it fast. 'I'm Lord Something.' But I was too busy thinking what to tell him so I don't exactly remember."

Amanda breathed a silent prayer for patience. She should never have left Kitty in charge in the house. But when she asked Prescott to come out and help hold back the flood-waters, she never considered Kitty might have to assume his duties. "I trust you can at least tell me what he wanted."

"I remember that exactly. He wanted to see you. He made me tell him where you were. I hope I didn't do wrong. I didn't know you was gonna drop him in the river."

Amanda decided against any more futile questions. She could think about the stranger once she got rid of her sodden clothes. In the meantime, Jeb's mother would take care of him until the doctor arrived.

During her hasty bath Amanda thought of little else but the stranger and the fact that he might be *a perfectly good lord,* which by her mother's definition meant unmarried. In this house even the lowest parlor maid knew her mother would never approve of dumping any gentleman, titled or untitled, in the river without finding out first if he had a wife.

The visitor would be a blasted nuisance if he did not. Her mother simply would not accept that at twenty-five Amanda had little interest in finding a husband.

Amanda bit her lip and tried to picture the man as she had first seen him, as if that might answer the critical question of his marital status. Well dressed, because he had ripped off a handsome coat. On a horse, because he had dismounted in a great splash of mud. But other than that, she could not remember much else except that he possessed hands to take a shovel.

The picture engraved indelibly on her brain was of him standing barefoot in the center of the dam, his white shirt plastered to his taut body by the driving rain. Of course, the fact that he looked like Hercules changing the course of a river didn't necessarily mean he could not be married with six pasty-faced children. Still . . . the safest plan would be to get him out of the house before Mother returned and discovered his presence.

Amanda scrubbed at her fingernails and tried to visualize the conversation that feat would involve. *Thank you very much for breaking the dam. I am sorry about your head. You must stop by again sometime.* That did seem a little hasty even for her. Hasty and perhaps unnecessary. She tried again. *Thank you very much for breaking the dam. By the by, are you married? Yes? Splendid. Feel free to take all the time you wish to recover from your unfortunate injuries.* She smiled. A much more compassionate conversation, though the question might seem a bit out of place.

Amanda stepped from the tub into the towel held by her maid, regretting the fact she was hardly dressed to go down and box Kitty's ears for not recalling the visitor's name. How much simpler it would be if she could walk into the sickroom armed with the knowledge of his marital status and a plan for dealing with him. She stopped. Kitty's oversight could be remedied.

She turned to her waiting maid. "Lily, please go and inquire about the condition of the man we just brought in. And while you are there, find out his name."

Minutes later Lily returned with the name, and Amanda settled at her dressing table to stare at her mother's bible, Burke's *Peerage*. The book contained a wealth of information, including the unhappy fact that, unless he had done so recently, the current Earl of Rexford appeared not to have had the good sense to get married before showing up on their doorstep. The only question remaining for her mother would be whether she could keep the eligible earl captive in one of the spare rooms long enough for him to develop an insatiable passion for Amanda. Never mind that insatiable passions tended to be excessively tedious and time-consuming.

Never mind that Amanda had more important things to do than catering to the tiresome demands of the visitor or arguing with Mother about who should serve as ministering angel. She needed every minute between rainstorms to train and exercise the birds for the race. The wretched weather had already mangled her carefully formulated schedule. That would mean nothing to Mother. Once she discovered the visitor was unmarried *and* had a title, she would scheme to have the Earl of Rexford linger on for weeks.

Naturally she would expect Amanda to entertain him every hour of every day. Birds could wait. A potential husband could not. And if the earl saw Amanda at her best and just happened to fall madly in love, her mother would be in ecstasy.

Amanda bridled. She had let her wild imagination make a tempest of a slight breeze. Lily said the earl was conscious. Conscious men could take their leave and depart. "Never mind drying my hair, Lily. Just braid it. We can deal with it later." She smiled. "Right now I must go delicately suggest the Earl of Rexford might want to be on his way before Mother returns from the village."

Chapter Two

Conscience forced Amanda to show enough concern to go downstairs and hear the doctor's assessment of the earl's injuries before going in to bid the unwelcome visitor farewell.

The butler, scrubbed clean of any trace of mud, met her at the foot of the stairs. "The doctor has left already, miss. He had to get back to Mrs. Green, who is in the final stages of her delicate condition. He asked me to assure you that Lord Rexford's injuries are uncomfortable but not serious. Mrs. Carter is with his lordship now."

Amanda noted Prescott's careful use of the earl's name. He might only have heard it once, but he, unlike the featherbrained Kitty, would remember it until the day he died.

Uncomfortable, but not serious, Amanda mused. Prescott's concise summary of the earl's injuries meant the man could travel. She decided against asking any more questions, which might rouse her sympathy and weaken her resolve. "Why don't you rest this afternoon? You were a great help this morning. I am sure we can manage for a few hours without you." She turned and hurried up the stairs.

She stopped at the door of the sickroom. Even now the

visitor might be dressed and preparing to take his leave. She knocked softly.

Jeb's mother pulled open the door with a whisper-soft movement, slapping her lips fiercely with her index finger. "Shhhh."

Not a good sign. Mrs. Carter, ordinarily the humblest woman in the county, became fiercely protective when nursing the sick. Amanda's glimpse of the wide bed confirmed her fears. Lord Rexford lay covered to the shoulders by a hand-embroidered quilt. His dark hair stood out starkly against the white pillow and his eyes were closed. Dark lashes lay softly against his cheeks as if carefully arranged there by Lily in one of her often-frustrated frenzies of curling everything in sight. Nothing about him suggested plans to move in the immediate future.

Amanda suppressed an urge to go in and shake him. Instead she whispered, "How is he, Mrs. Carter?"

"He's—"

"You need not whisper. I am merely resting my eyes." Lord Rexford's eyelids fluttered, but stayed open for only a few seconds. He produced a wince so genuine Amanda could almost feel the pain.

"How are you, my lord? You did get a bad knock on the head."

With a grimace he sat up. The quilt dropped to his waist.

Amanda congratulated herself on suppressing a maidenly gasp, and continued to look him in the eyes because to turn away seemed ridiculously missish. A fresh white bandage crossed his body like a shoulder sash. The material should have given the illusion of clothing. It merely emphasized the masculinity of his exposed muscles.

"Forgive me if I don't get up. I don't appear quite dressed for formalities." The earl's forced smile did not quite banish the pain lines around his eyes. "This visit has been rather hard on my wardrobe. Mr. Carter insisted on cutting off my breeches, so at the moment I have noth— Take my word for it. It is better if I don't get up."

Amanda had no intention of admitting her runaway mind

had already drawn the same conclusion. "You have not answered my question. How do you feel?"

With extreme care he turned his head to the side. "I have had worse headaches, but generally I have had the pleasure of earning them with a fine bottle of port. Other than that . . ."

Mrs. Carter moved to the bed and tucked two more pillows behind him. "Here, your lordship, lean back." She accompanied the words with a firm hand on his shoulder.

He yielded to the pressure. Most of the pain lines melted from his face as the pillow assumed the task of supporting his head. "Ah. That does feel better."

Some of the tension left Amanda's body. She had not been aware of her physical response to his pained expression. She had planned to be much firmer.

"You should not be sitting up," Mrs. Carter scolded.

He should be leaving. Realistically, even without the evidence of his physical discomfort, Amanda had given up that notion with the news of his cut breeches. Most earls would probably be a bit persnickety about riding off clad only in a green embroidered quilt. She added obtaining suitable clothing to her list of things to deal with later. In the meantime, she could at least find out why he had come, though first he deserved some show of gratitude. "I must thank you for your help this morning. Though I am sorry about the shovel. If I had known who you were, I would never—"

His smile seemed genuine. "You would have done precisely the same thing."

"I would n—" Amanda laughed. She would have put a shovel in the Prince Regent's hand to avert the disaster. "In any case, thank you. Without you . . ." She shuddered, thinking of the birds, particularly the hatchlings.

"Please finish. Without me what? This morning I asked why the birds did not just fly away, but you went dashing off before you could answer."

"Many of them could have done exactly that, but there would have been the most frightful mess with the others. Some of the babies have not learned to fly yet. Most of the

25

young ones are only partly trained. Who knows where they might have gone in the confusion. I am also keeping birds here for other people. They would probably have tried flying hundreds of miles through the storm.''

''Couldn't you have moved them to some other place? Perhaps the stable?''

Oddly pleased, Amanda smiled. He was the only person other than her cousin, Margaret, who had ever given serious thought to her birds' welfare. That made him even more attractive than the acres of bare chest he continued to expose. ''Just what we were preparing to do. But that would have been almost as bad. Some eggs would never hatch. The young birds without mature feathers could not survive the drafts. Worse, it would have meant dumping all the birds in together. There are dozens of reasons why some must be separated.''

Amanda flushed. She had been going on about the birds, something she tried hard to avoid because people generally yawned and looked for the nearest escape. Men preferred talking about themselves. This man particularly should be talking about himself. He had showed up on her doorstep for a reason and had yet to state it. ''My lord, you certainly did not come all the way out here for a lecture on birds. I do go on if given the slightest encouragement.''

''But that is precisely why I have come.'' His head nodded to confirm his words. The pain lines on his forehead deepened again.

Amanda's hand fluttered with the need to provide some comfort, but she could think of nothing the doctor or Mrs. Carter had not offered.

''You look surprised,'' he said. ''You are the foremost authority in England on raising pigeons. I should expect people come to consult with you all the time.''

''Yes, but . . .'' But what? Never an earl? Never a naked earl with black curls? Without time to speculate on why he had come, Amanda could not imagine why his reason astonished her. ''I . . .''

''Do sit down, Miss Langley. This conversation is not going exactly as I planned, and your hovering makes me feel even more the supplicant.''

Amanda turned and reached for the straight chair set against the wall. The distraction gave her a moment to gather her thoughts. An earl had as much right to be curious about birds as anyone else. Before she could move, Mrs. Carter dragged the chair over and placed it behind Amanda with an imperative nod. Only she had the right to hover.

Amanda sat.

Rexford's eyes gleamed his approval, but he had learned the wisdom of keeping his head still. ''That is better,'' he said. ''Now, let us talk about the birds and their remarkable ability to carry messages. I have a number of distant estates and have decided to set up my own loft. Naturally I wish to learn from the best, and you, I am told, are that.''

''You want to learn about birds?'' Amanda pictured him in his wide-legged stance balanced on the shuddering dam.

''Does that surprise you?''

''About as much as the image of Hercules raising radishes.'' She realized she had spoken the words aloud, and flushed.

Rexford laughed. ''I like your analogy. Hercules, I mean, not the radishes. But I assure you I spend only a small fraction of my life smashing things.''

His oversized hand curled over the quilt. Perhaps the power of that hand explained why her tangle-witted brain refused to accept his words. ''I am sorry. You just seem so . . . so large.''

''Unfortunately a man's size is determined at birth and he cannot possibly have established all his interests by then.''

''Of course not.'' Nor would Lord Rexford's size matter. Earls generally hired people to handle everything for them, even their hobbies. Amanda relaxed. The earl's request was really quite simple, and there were few things she enjoyed more than teaching a novice about her hobby. ''Forgive me, I am not alert today. I will be happy to talk with your game-keeper. Perhaps we could even arrange to have him stay here for a few weeks.''

"Splendid. That is precisely what I hoped you would offer. A few weeks' instruction on the sport."

Amanda basked in the earl's approving smile, pleased to be able to pay him back so easily for his earlier rescue.

His dark eyes invited her to share a pleasant surprise. "But I am sure you will find me much more delightful company than my gamekeeper. He is a surly old codger."

"You?" Amanda's thoughts swirled like the swollen river. "You wish to stay here? For a few weeks?" She had heard him, but still could not believe he meant the impossible words. She faced not just a few lost hours, but days of catering to an earl and dealing with her mother's madcap schemes. "You?"

"Of course me. That is who we have been talking about. At least until two seconds ago when you mentioned my gamekeeper."

"But . . ." *You're an earl. You're too large. Mother's going to drive us both crazy if you stay even twenty-four hours.* She said the only thing that made any sense at all. "I don't understand."

Rexford's smile had the faintest touch of chagrin. "To be honest, I came hoping for precisely the invitation you just issued."

"But I invited your gamekeeper." She had not even invited the gamekeeper, just mentioned he might stay for a few weeks. There was a difference.

"You wouldn't like him at all. John doesn't bathe more than once a month. I on the other hand—"

"Cannot stay!" Amanda clamped her lips, then decided maybe she did not want to call the words back. She had not meant to be rude, but she had stated her position quite concisely. In spite of her brave thoughts, she waited for lightning to strike.

Lightning struck softly in the form of almost imperceptible flickers in the small muscles of his face and the half-inch lift to his eyebrows. His dark eyes held a cool hint of amusement. "John will be delighted to learn of your preference. I, however, am concerned. Is there some difficulty I should be aware of? Other than my size, of course, which we have already established I can do nothing about.''

The mocking words had the desired effect. Amanda found herself mentally backstepping, fighting the urge to say *Of course not,* to assure him that he was most welcome. Which he was not, she reminded herself sternly. At least not now when she needed every spare minute. ''Nothing personal, my lord, and I am shocked you would even consider it so. There is simply an enormous difference between finding a spare cot for a gamekeeper and entertaining a earl.''

''I am relieved to hear that.'' He gave an exaggerated sigh of relief. ''Since that is the only problem, let me assure you I am quite capable of entertaining myself. My interest really is in the birds.''

''You are not serious.''

''Completely. I would not have sought you out otherwise. I assure you I will be no more trouble than my gamekeeper.''

Amanda nearly laughed aloud. No more trouble than his gamekeeper—only if his gamekeeper had elaborate social events organized in his honor every hour. The village would be ablaze with plans the minute word of his presence leaked out.

Amanda forced herself to rein in her racing imagination. The situation called for a firm no—or at worst a postponement. The ton was so easily bored, the earl would probably forget the whole notion in a month's time. She spoke calmly. ''I am extremely flattered by your interest, my lord, and I wish I could oblige you. But for the next month I have an extremely busy schedule.''

''With your birds?''

''Several of us have gone to a great deal of trouble to organize an international competition in June. We intend to establish once and for all the superiority of our English birds. You have no idea of the details involved. Judges. Travel arrangements. Simply establishing what timepieces to use. I must devote every spare minute—''

''I certainly would not interfere. In fact I cannot think of a more exciting time to watch and learn.''

"But you don't understand—"

With a grimace Lord Rexford put his hand to his head. "Please, could we continue this discussion another time? I am afraid I am not at my best right now."

Mrs. Carter stepped from behind Amanda's chair and put her hand on the earl's head. "Please, miss. He should rest."

Amanda rose. To do anything else would have been inhumane, but she refused to leave the length of his stay open to debate. "Perhaps we can work out some satisfactory alternative tomorrow—before you *go*." She turned and walked to the door with what she hoped appeared to be unshakable resolution.

"Miss Langley, if you could do me a favor?" The earl seemed determined to have the last word.

She turned and raised her eyebrows at least as high as his. "Yes?"

"I spent last night at the rather dubious inn in the village. My valet is there now. Perhaps you could send for him." He gestured at his naked chest. "I seem to be lacking a few essentials."

A firm knock on the chamber door awakened Rexford. A moment later his best friend and cohort, Viscount Taggart Elmgrove, entered.

"A little late to the rescue," Rexford said sharply. "I have been lying here stark naked all afternoon while half the village wandered in and out."

"To admire your amiable disposition, I'm sure." Tag grinned and strolled to the bed. "I haven't come to rescue you, merely to congratulate you on a novel method of securing an invitation." He cocked his head to the side and studied Rexford. The intensity of his gaze belied his light tone and casual manner. "Was it really necessary to strip off all your clothes? I would not have predicted that would be particularly effective in your case."

"Dammit, Tag, you are pretending to be my valet. Act like one and find me something to wear."

Still smiling, Tag ignored the snarl. He circled the bed to

study Rexford from the other side. "I see you have opened your shoulder wound again. Probably not the wisest idea." He pointed. "And we will have to buy you an extra hat for that knob on your head. Is that the extent of your injuries?" He was eyeing the quilt with the obvious intention of completing his inspection.

Rexford secured the covering with both hands. The last shreds of his dignity compelled him to answer hurriedly. "A slight scratch on my leg. The doctor bandaged it and is confident I will survive."

Tag nodded and exhaled. His smile finally included a twinkle in his blue eyes. "You always did have a penchant for the dramatic." He rounded the bed again, reached back with his foot to pull the chair closer, and sat. "Tell me, was your self-mutilation successful? Has the formidable Miss Langley invited us to stay and use Gully's messenger birds for communicating with Wellington?"

"We are still negotiating the matter."

"Then the lady is the dragoness Dalton described?"

Rexford smiled at the memory of the firm thrust of her chin. "That and then some. She would make a splendid general. Apparently she has some problem with my presence, though I am not certain of the precise nature of her objection."

"Curious. According to the tales I heard on my way from the village, I assumed she would have presented you with half the estate out of simple gratitude for saving her birds."

"I plan to suggest something of the sort in the morning. Frankly, I was not at my best this afternoon. Now some clothes, if you please." Rexford closed his eyes, actually looking forward to the next encounter with Miss Langley, which he would approach forewarned and forearmed.

The next morning, a servant escorted Rexford downstairs to the sitting room, where Miss Langley stood next to a gold brocade sofa. Though he had noted her height the previous day, it still surprised him. He generally looked down at most people, but she could not be more than four or five inches shorter than his own six feet. Hardly a fashionable size for a woman. Not that it appeared she had any serious concern about fashion.

Her gown, the color of wet clay and no more fashionable than her riding habit of the previous day, drooped carelessly over a frame that had put more effort into height than curves. Her hair, the color of iron left in the rain long enough to turn wild shades of amber, red, and ginger, might have been interesting, but she pulled it back so tight her ears must be aching.

High cheekbones and strong features gave her a haughty air, but a splash of freckles across her nose totally ruined the classical effect. Probably somewhere in her mid-twenties. Obviously a born spinster. She would not look much different at ninety.

She smiled, and he found himself staring directly into her eyes. He must have been dead not to notice them before. God had made up for a whole host of defects by giving her a pair of spearmint green eyes that could make a man forget to breathe.

"Lord Rexford, I trust you are feeling better this morning."

Choosing to take his opponent's measure before revealing any of his own tactics, he kept his answer short. "Considerably."

"Good. Please sit down." She led him to a winged chair a few feet from the sofa and sat facing him. "I apologize if I was less than gracious yesterday. I can only plead exhaustion and some surprise at your request to visit. I believe I have worked out a satisfactory compromise."

Rexford repressed the urge to smile. He should have guessed she would not waste a great deal of time on civilities. He needed to begin as he meant to go on, so he maintained a stern expression. "A compromise is rarely satisfactory, but I should be interested to hear your idea."

She showed no inclination to shrink from his cool tone. "As I mentioned, for several reasons an extended visit would not be convenient this month. However, I have no objection to taking an hour or so before you leave to introduce you to the birds and explain the essentials. If you wish to know more, we could meet again in a few months." She sat back with the air of one who has successfully resolved a minor problem.

Rexford noted the somewhat unnecessary emphasis on the word *leave*. As a compromise her suggestion amounted to a total rout. Time to bring in the artillery. "May I assume the reasons you mention have something to do with the birds? Yesterday you mentioned something about a race."

"An international race, but I don't see how that is any concern of—"

"I am reluctant to remind you, but according to what you told me, the fact you have any birds left to concern you is due to my efforts."

"But . . ." Her face hardened and her green eyes lost their placating softness.

Rexford moved in for the kill. "To put it very bluntly, Miss Langley, you owe me a debt. You look like a woman who always pays her debts."

"And you look like a man who always gets his way." She squeezed the words out through tight lips.

Rexford relaxed. He did not need her straight back to inform him she was a proud woman. She would not ignore a debt.

"Why are you so intent on staying?" she asked.

"Call it a whim if you will, but for now, I believe I have earned the right."

She leapt to her feet, strode across the room, then turned and spoke. "You are quite impossible."

"No. I am quite reasonable. If social obligations concern you, you may put it about that I am as reclusive as my game-keeper. I promise not to take up any more time than is absolutely essential."

Her fingers flexed as if toying with the idea of throttling him. "The larger problem is Mother. Oh, bother. I need some time to think." She paced for several turns about the room without speaking. "I am sorry. I cannot think confined in

33

here.'' She paced some more. "Suppose we do this. Come with me. I will introduce you to the birds. Perhaps you will find they are not as charming as you anticipate. After that, if you still wish to stay we will . . . I don't know what we will do."

She turned and left by a door opening to the garden, giving Rexford the opportunity to follow or remain seated. She showed no interest in which he chose.

She ignored him during the quarter-mile walk toward the river, a much shorter route than he had taken on horseback, but ending at the back of the building he had seen the day before. The fresh smell of spring air gave him time to contemplate the fact she intended to show him through a structure full of repulsive-smelling birds. He struggled to think of anything he could like about the creatures. Overhead a hawk glided across the empty sky. A man could respect a hawk, master of the world, circling endlessly. He seized the opportunity to make an amiable comment. "Nice bird." He pointed to the now tiny speck in the sky.

She bridled and looked at him as if he had just canonized Beelzebub. "That, Lord Rexford, is a hawk. The most deadly enemy of the pigeon."

Rexford grimaced. Obviously he had not made quite the friendly comment he intended. "I meant the color, naturally. Only the color." He crossed his fingers and prayed someone had remembered to make some pigeons the same shade as a hawk.

They arrived at the clearing he had seen from the river. He studied the cote she intended to tour, a long, narrow, stone building with a rounded tower on one end. It was walled on three sides, and the angle protected the open side from the river winds. The front faced a net-covered aviary, which already looked sufficiently crowded. Birds scurried about the fenced area, nodding and bobbing like pompous theatergoers at intermission.

Rexford forced himself to focus. If Miss Langley had her way, this might be his only chance to visit the birds by invitation. Her stubbornness could force him to devise an alternate plan, and he would need everything he could learn in these hours. The ten-foot-high slat and net roofing seemed ten feet too low. He thought longingly of the parks of London where flocks of birds roamed free, certain to melt into the atmosphere when humans approached.

Miss Langley walked across the open area, confident he would follow. He did, slowly. A soft cooing from many throats mocked his reluctant progress. A dozen protests formed on his lips.

At the wooden door of the aviary, she stopped and studied him. "I don't suppose you have had the good sense to get married recently, have you?"

A frantic flutter of wings in the net-covered area kept him from even looking at her to see what might have prompted the bizarre question. "No."

"I rather thought not. Well, pay it no mind." She made a shooing sound and tugged on the metal handle. "Mind the door now." She slipped through an opening hardly wide enough to admit her slender frame. Her entrance set off a wild slapping of wings.

Rexford minded the door, but from the outside. The rains had intensified the tangy odor one associated with bird cages. She never bothered to look down and watch her step. His stomach lurched with the inevitable squish. Rationally he had known it was too much to hope these supposedly remarkable creatures had found some more pleasing way of disposing of nature's waste. Maybe she would not notice if he did not follow her.

As quickly as it began, the flurry settled, and Miss Langley turned toward him, a pigeon on each shoulder and several pecking at her toes. "You may come in. In spite of what you see, these little creatures enjoy company. They will flutter around for a moment, but then I am sure they will regard you with the same affection you regard them."

The same affection you regard them! He suppressed the temptation to observe that her birds must be picturing him swimming in broth and surrounded by potatoes. With a barely controlled sigh he sacrificed his body and his second-best pair of Hessians for the good of the Crown. His entrance produced the chaos he anticipated. Birds flew so close he could feel the brush of their wings against his ear. Despite every scrap of battlefield training, he closed his eyes against the onslaught. His earlier uneasiness intensified a hundred-fold.

He acknowledged an irrational fear of birds.

The frantic flapping ceased. He opened his eyes and exhaled the breath he had not even been aware he held.

Bird feet danced on his left shoulder. Even rolling his eyes to the left as far as possible, he saw only a blur of white. You will face the enemy, he commanded, mentally addressing himself as he would a subordinate whose nerve seemed ready to snap. He turned his head a fraction of an inch at a time, and found himself staring into a miniature pair of black eyes.

"That is Grace." The soft female voice came from somewhere beyond his field of vision.

He dared not turn toward it to see if she was laughing at his discomfort. He could do nothing but stare at Grace.

"Actually, it used to be His Grace, the Duke of Something. But then we discovered His Grace was female. Everyone forgot what she was supposed to be the duke of and just took to calling her Grace. I believe she likes you."

Rexford heard footsteps in the background and the female voice whispering something softly to a bird. He remained locked in place, wondering how deeply he dared to breathe.

"You may speak, Lord Rexford. Whenever you wish." This time there seemed even less effort to conceal her pleasure at his discomfort. "Just speak softly."

Rexford discovered the possibility of whispering through clenched teeth. "Does Her Grace like eyes—for dinner, I mean?"

"Your eyes are quite safe." Miss Langley moved so he could see her without sacrificing his view of the ubiquitous Grace, who watched him with a curiously cocked head. "You will get used to it. Later, when she gets to know you, Grace will probably nibble on you in various places if she wants attention. But somehow all the birds know to leave your eyes alone.'' The sole consoling aspect of her appalling statement was the implication that he would have time to get used to it. Perhaps his reminder of her debt had been effective, and there would be a *later* for him and Grace to deepen their acquaintance.

Miss Langley took another step toward him and held out her hand with the index finger slightly curved. ''Come here, Grace.'' She spoke softly, but her voice held an unmistakable command. ''The nice gentleman thinks you excessively forward.''

Instead of obeying, Grace took several scurrying steps, which brought her body to rest against his chin. Rexford instantly envisioned legions of vermin transferring themselves from the vibrating body to his unprotected face and hair. He couldn't speak without getting a mouthful of feathers. Could he call for help without opening his mouth? ''Go away, Grace,'' he mumbled, probably the most ineffectual command he had given in fifteen years. The bird didn't move.

Grow up, Rexford, you are a soldier. Now act like one. He had a mission. If Miss Langley remained adamant in her refusal to let him stay, then he would have no alternative but to ''borrow'' the birds he needed. Without moving his head, he ignored Grace to study the chaos around him. Partitions on both the right and left segregated some birds, which kept the entire flock from attacking him at once. No one had expected his visit, so perhaps the partitions had a more practical purpose. He stored that information for a time when he could think rationally.

First he had to get rid of Grace. ''Go away, Grace.'' He probably would not get a medal for actually moving his lips, but he deserved one.

''Come along, Grace.'' The feminine finger jabbed more insistently toward his shoulder. The voice held a teasing firmness. ''If you do not care what the gentleman thinks of you, at least consider that he might want to move his head sometime today.'' Grace stepped onto the extended finger, but the baleful look in her black eyes clearly said Rexford had disappointed her.

Miss Langley waited until Grace settled in her palm, then caressed her tenderly in long smooth strokes. Her face looked much younger, or perhaps the uneven light had softened it. "Grace needs some extra attention right now. She just lost her husband."

"Her husband?" Rexford looked around.

"Her mate. Grace lost her husband."

He tried to estimate the numbers. "How in heaven's name does she know?" The cote contained at least a hundred birds. Colors varied, but about half were white without an iota of difference between them.

She smiled. "I assure you, in no time you would be able to call each of these birds by name. They are as distinct as people—fortunately without some of our worst failings." She looked down at the bird in her hand. "I know it hurts, dear. But he truly does not understand." She looked up and met his gaze again. "Pigeons generally mate for life. They grieve deeply when they lose a spouse."

Rexford's mind leapt ahead to the potential disaster, a lost bird. He strove for a casual tone. "What happened to Mr. Grace—her husband? I thought these birds were absolutely reliable." He scanned the skies as if he might will Grace's errant spouse home.

"That is one of the heartbreaks of raising racing pigeons. We seldom know exactly what happens." Heedless of the birds perched on each shoulder, she bent from the waist and set Grace gently on the soft earth. Her feathered shoulder decorations adjusted to her movement with rapid, mincing steps. She straightened and spoke in a discreet whisper. "However, one thing we can be certain of. A bird who does not return is dead."

"Dead? Don't you send out only young birds? How do they die?"

"Hawks generally. Good birds never stop on short flights, but hawks are vicious. They can snatch a pigeon right out of the sky."

"Hawks! Don't you warn the pigeons—" Now he was truly ready for Bedlam. He had just asked a woman wearing live birds for shoulder padding why she didn't warn a creature with a brain the size of a pebble about hawks, and that only moments after proclaiming the hawk his favorite bird.

He looked down to watch the grieving Grace happily pecking the shine from his boots. He could not risk arousing Miss Langley's suspicions by asking how many birds they would have to send out to insure getting a message through. The bird people he had met had seemed so proud of the creatures, so sure they would come home. This was not the time to learn he would have to steal five birds to get one message through. "But some flyers are superior to others, are they not?"

"Absolutely." Her face glowed with pride. "I have any number of champions right here. Those particular birds will come home unless they are struck by lightning."

He could not tell if her sweeping gesture meant he should admire all the birds or just the champions. In either case, except for color, they all looked alike. The white ones were slightly more attractive, but obviously Grace's husband had not been a winner.

She nodded with satisfaction. "Within a month, everyone will recognize my champions as the finest in Europe."

A few of the creatures had settled on perches, but most milled about the ground, indifferent to the presence of intruders. He studied the flock and tried to identify the strongest. Since he needed to identify the birds belonging to Albert Gully in Brussels and those capable of making the flight across the channel, the isolated birds seemed a good place to start. He pointed. "Why are those birds kept apart?"

"Various reasons." She did not even bother to glance in the direction he indicated. "These are the ones you would be interested in, the young ones still in training."

Not terribly informative, but at least she had told him which birds he had no interest in. A few more questions should narrow down the search. "I assume you have to keep your racing birds separate?"

"If you are just starting a loft, you will not be ready to think about racing for a long time. You have to start with young birds first, and train them to return home." She bent and picked up a small bird.

He dutifully smiled at the bird she held out, but looked about with what he hoped appeared to be casual interest. "You mentioned birds you were holding for other people. Would those be over there?" He made a guess and pointed left.

She gave a look that might have been impatience or suspicion. "Some of them. Now these—"

Another question would be pushing too hard for idle curiosity. Time to retreat and regroup. He donned his most engaging smile. "I completely forgot to mention that Albert Gully asked me to give you his regards."

A pleased smile warmed her face. "You know Albert?"

"He is a most particular friend of mine." He saw no need to mention theirs was a rather shallow friendship based on the fact that someone in Brussels had browbeaten Gully into cooperating with this scheme. For now he still needed to identify Gully's birds. "He told me you have several of his birds. I promised I would admire them. Perhaps you would be good enough to point them out."

"I don't—" She hesitated. "Of course." She turned and walked not to the left as he expected, but to the partitioned area on the right, hurrying him through a wooden door. She began to speak, pointing rapidly. "That red speckled one, the blue checkered one over there, the blue bar, that silver one, and the white one with the funny tilt to his neck." Her finger bobbed faster than Rexford's eyes could follow.

Of the twenty or more birds in the area, he succeeded in finding the white one with the funny tilt. "Excuse me, that might have been just a shade too rapid." Not only had she spoken quickly, but except for the white, he could not find a single one of the colors she had mentioned. "I am afraid I don't see any red birds at all."

"There." She pointed to a singularly unattractive creature

40

whose body appeared to be spattered with the dull rust of dried blood. "That is Bacchus."

Rexford redefined red as dried blood and nodded. "Now blue?"

"Two in that corner are blue." That corner had six birds in varying shades of gray and black.

Rexford mentally identified three birds somewhere between the two extremes. They could be blue—if one chose not to be a purist. "Which one is Albert's?"

"Oh, he is not part of that group any more. Helios is right here." She laughed and gestured at a bird who had scurried over to scratch dirt onto Rexford's boots.

Rexford succeeded in not mentioning the cost of those boots, or totaling it with the cost of the pair he had lost twenty-four hours ago.

As a color, silver had nothing to do with gleaming candlesticks. It proved to be a shade much lighter than gray and not quite white—but only as long as the silver bird stood next to Athena, the white hen, giving Rexford the chance to make the comparison. He eventually identified Persephone, the silver hen, and waited patiently while Miss Langley located Albert's other two prize flyers.

Finally he relaxed, confident he had accomplished his mission. "Let us review. That is Bacchus." He pointed to the bird pecking the wooden board. He refused to let himself flinch when Grace, who had scurried through the door behind them, flapped her way to his shoulder again.

Miss Langley shifted impatiently, but let him point and name each bird. He and Tag could return after dark for Bacchus and company if necessary. Later he could figure out some way to intercept the messages carried by Miss Langley's birds from Brussels.

She seemed as relieved as he that the exercise had ended. "They are splendid creatures, but not nearly as fine as mine. Let me show you."

Rexford smiled tolerantly. She could show him anything she wanted now that he had accomplished what he had to.

She took three rapid strides into a flock, reached down,

and scooped up a plain gray bird. The remainder of the flock took to the air, as did every other bird in the aviary.

"Wait." He gave an involuntarily shudder, ducked his head, and buried the rest of his protest in a string of silent oaths. He had identified the creatures solely by position. He snapped his head from side to side to follow the incredibly rapid movement. It was hopeless. Bacchus and his friends disappeared into the horde as surely as if they had donned cloaks of invisibility.

Rexford searched frantically for another way to identify Gully's birds. Have her repeat the lesson and nail the birds in place this time? Cut his finger somehow and mark the birds with blood? Perhaps her servant, Jeb, could . . . ? Could do what? He simply could not think with all the creatures weaving about him. He would have to . . . He would have to do something. But right now he could think of nothing but getting out of the cote.

An hour later, after a glowing Miss Langley had introduced him to a host of irrelevant young birds, Rexford succeeded in easing her toward the entrance. At the door he removed Grace from his shoulder and listed for her eight reasons why she could not accompany him to the house. To show his confidence in the assumption he could change his hostess's mind about the length of his stay, he even gulped down his distaste and promised the sad-eyed bird she could ride in the same spot tomorrow.

Miss Langley waited for him to latch the wooden door. "Thank you for being so gentle with Grace. She needs all the tenderness we can offer right now." She studied him questioningly. "Now that you have met the birds, are you still certain you want to stay?"

He was certain he would prefer facing two columns of artillery with Wellington, but no one had given him a choice. He rotated the shoulder everyone refused to believe had healed. "I am still as committed as ever." Since he could think of nothing else to say, he waited in silence for her to renew their discussion of his request to visit. He did not plan to make it easy for her to refuse.

She bit her lip and studied him thoughtfully. "I have reconsidered, Lord Rexford. I admit it is somewhat difficult having you here, especially at this time, but as you so bluntly pointed out, I owe you a debt. I believe we can deal with it—if you cooperate."

Relief flooded him. It did not matter what had changed her mind. He would cooperate with anything. "You may count on me."

"I shall hope so." She smiled with a challenging gleam in her eye. "Perhaps you will meet me in the library in half an hour to discuss your betrothal."

Chapter Three

In her bedchamber Amanda shifted from one foot to another. How much more time would she need to settle on a delicate way to explain the situation to Lord Rexford? Probably a century. At twenty-five, a woman should not have to explain a scheming mother. But so far she had not been able to invent anything better than the simple truth.

The entire debacle could have been avoided if Lord Rexford had only had the good sense to get married before throwing himself in their river. Since it was his fault, he could just take some responsibility for dealing with the situation. She nodded at the reasonableness of that statement. He should not have any major objection to becoming engaged. If he did, she could simply order him to leave.

Amanda set her chin at its firmest angle and headed for the library.

It might not be quite the thing to ignore the fact that he had risked his life to save her birds, but better to be slightly uncivil than hounded for days to bat her eyes and listen to his inane opinions on everything in the universe.

She hesitated to admit her mother's silly schemes were not the entire problem.

If Rexford were not an earl, perhaps . . . Not that the title itself made a difference. It was his manner. Even lying in bed naked he managed to dominate the whole room, as if the air itself should obey when he raised an eyebrow. His very insistence on staying made her uneasy. She hoped she wasn't making a mistake.

Her crisp footsteps clicked against the marble floors. She must wait and see how he responded to her plan. If he were compliant enough to agree, perhaps they could deal well enough to manage for a few days. Yes, she thought, taking a firm grip on her control, by the time this interview ended, Lord Rexford would be betrothed—or he would be taking his leave.

She flung open the door to the library. It made a satisfying thunk as it hit the outside wall. That should inform Rexford he could not intimidate her just by being an earl.

He sat hunched over the massive oak desktop, his valet, who had arrived with Rexford's clothes, hovering at his shoulder. Rexford sprang to his feet. "I hope you do not mind my using the desk while I waited."

He gathered the notes that had been spread over the desk into a neat pile. Without looking, he placed them facedown on the map he had been studying. "This is Taggart, my valet, but also an invaluable help with my research. I am preparing a dissertation on the topography of France and the surrounding countries."

Amanda nodded to acknowledge the introduction, and privately hoped Taggart made a better research assistant than he did a valet. Her fingers itched to straighten the knot in Lord Rexford's cravat. "You are welcome to use the room. However, there is something we must discuss immediately."

"I have merely been using the idle time." He folded the map over the assorted papers and placed the bundle in Taggart's already outstretched hand. "Perhaps you can just take care of those things we discussed."

"Yes, sir. About the other?"

"Later." A very clear dismissal.

Amanda waited until the servant firmly closed the door. It

might be silly to feel Lord Rexford had assumed the imperious manner just to make her feel even more awkward about her mission, but in this setting he did look very much the earl. She hardened herself against the uneasiness.

Title or no title, he was in *her* house.

"I am afraid there is no delicate way to phrase this, Lord Rexford. Shall we sit?" She circled the desk and seated herself in the chair he had just vacated. His right brow raised a fraction of an inch, and she wondered if the admiring gleam in his eyes recognized the significance of her choice. Lord Rexford moved gracefully around the desk and lowered himself into the red leather armchair, the one with the seat worn smooth from the countless hours she'd spent with her cousin, Margaret, consulting on breeding programs. Margaret, who had taught her everything about independence, but who in the end had proved as conventional as everyone else.

Even there he looked as if he had only temporarily ceded possession of the more powerful position. He studied her with eyes that held a hint of wariness, and she wondered what had happened to the unstinting cooperation he had promised an hour earlier.

Since she still had not come up with a delicate way of phrasing the primary problem, she plunged directly into the truth. "You have not yet met my mother. The rains obliged her to spend the night with a friend after her garden club meeting yesterday, but I assure you, she would have swum the channel had she known of your presence here."

"I am most flattered."

"You needn't be. Mother is a bit of a problem. She has been married four times and—"

Amusement danced in his eyes. "And you felt I would need this hour to determine how to address her?"

"Fortunately she is the daughter of an earl, so Lady Harriet has always worked nicely. That is not the—" Amanda exhaled, impatient to deal with the matter at hand. "Mother spends a significant portion of her life luring eligible gentlemen down here for me to inspect. Nothing I can do will convince her to give up hope I will find one of them interesting enough to marry. When she discovers you almost literally washed up on our doorstep . . ."

"I see." Only the hint of a furrow between his brows hinted at his difficulty in coming up with an adequate response. "And you—"

"You need say nothing. It is my problem, and generally I deal with it quite well. For now, though, it may be an annoyance to both of us unless we agree on a plan."

"I am naturally at your service." A look of suspicion in his eyes suggested "at your service" had some limitations.

"There would not be any problem if you were not so wretchedly eligible. You have no idea how troublesome that will be. Mother will follow you around every hour you are here listing all my virtues. And I warn you, she will include quite a number I have no hope of possessing."

His polite smile disappeared behind an incredibly correct mask. "I am sure anything she might say would be the most feeble understatement."

Annoyance exploded with a puff of air from her lips. "That kind of attitude will make matters infinitely worse. Not only would she persist in telling me every five minutes that you are sufficiently young, and not hideously ugly, but she would prattle on for hours about your excessively fine manners."

Mischief flickered in his eyes and made his face look years younger. " 'Not hideously ugly?' Is that the best she will be able to do in extolling my virtues?"

"Please. This is serious, and if you are to stay, we must deal with it." His lingering amusement told her she had failed to communicate the gravity of the situation. "She will have me changing my gowns eleven times a day and wearing flowers in my hair. To say nothing of her elaborate schemes to leave us alone together."

Rexford smiled and gave an exaggerated shudder. "Then we positively must deal with her." His manner became more tentative. "I believe you mentioned something about . . ."

"I have considered a variety of things and am willing to discuss anything you might suggest." She waited for him to speak. When he didn't, she continued. "We simply must come up with a sure plan to cause even Mother to declare you totally ineligible. I had considered declaring you a rake." She narrowed her eyes to debate the matter again. "A dreadful lecher. A seducer of innocent females. Someone whose terrible reputation puts him quite beyond the pale." She shook her head. Despite a certain rugged good looks, she could not mold a man seeking information on her birds into the picture forming in her head. "No. Mother would never believe that."

He bristled. "I beg your pardon."

Amanda almost laughed at the smoldering look his eyes assumed. Why did men always want to be rakes? Even Tommy Cosgrove, with his protruding teeth and face full of boils, had confessed he planned to be a rake when he grew up. She smiled at the picture of Lord Rexford arguing with Tommy Cosgrove over who would be the more notorious rake. "Very well. You may be a rake, but we shall need something else for Mother. At this point she is less concerned about my virtue than my marital status."

"I see."

"I also thought your fortune perhaps . . . You might be completely done up, hiding here to avoid your creditors." Pictures of herself carrying baskets of day-old bread to Old Bailey tumbled through Amanda's mind. "For all her faults, Mother would not have me spend the rest of my life visiting you in debtor's prison."

"Regrettably, my fortune is quite adequate, and I should detest becoming a parsimonious nob just to prevent you from changing gowns eleven times a day."

No one could say she had not given him a choice. "Then it must be an engagement."

His lips tightened. "Don't you think this is a bit precipitous? We have known each other less than an—"

"Don't be a ninny." Men were so predictably arrogant. It never occurred to any of them that a woman might not be spending her entire life scheming to trap some male into declaring his intentions. "You may be engaged to anyone you want. Mother would never expect you to be such a scapegrace as to cry off from an engagement to marry me.''

''I see.'' A hint of amusement glinted in his eyes. ''Do I actually have to marry this person, or will a betrothal suffice?''

Amanda relaxed. He would cooperate. They merely had to work out the details. ''An engagement will do quite admirably. It must be to somebody quite believable so when Mother says, 'Tell me about your fiancée,' you will not just stand there mumbling.''

The corners of his mouth twitched. ''You are absolutely certain she will ask?''

''Most definitely. Now about your fiancée . . .''

''I assume I can leave that in your hands.''

''Stand up.''

''Pardon me?''

Amanda made a mental note not to make his fiancée terribly quick-witted. ''Stand up. We must design a female for you to marry.''

Still studying her uncertainly, he used his arms to push himself out of the chair. His fingertips brushed against the sides of his coat, then seemed to flap about looking for a place to land. Amanda decided she was too nice a person to take a grim satisfaction from the image of a man on display at the marriage mart. She studied him thoughtfully. ''Clarissa,'' she said. ''I think she is to be Clarissa. Do you like that name?''

He gave an almost imperceptible shrug. ''I am sure you will tell me if I don't.''

''You are too tall,'' she said, then remembered his annoying inclination toward male vanity. ''Not that that is a bad thing in a man, but your daughters would never thank you for marrying somebody too leggy. Turn around.''

He obeyed, turned a little too rapidly on one foot, and arrived back in place with a face threatening rebellion. ''Must you look at me as if I am one of your pigeons?''

''If we are going to do this thing, we may as well do it right. It may even help you when you are truly ready to select

49

a bride." Amanda walked around him rather than setting him to twirling again. "Definitely Clarissa must be short. About up to here, I think." She held her hand a few inches lower than his shoulder to let him visualize the height. "And blond. Not that you don't have frightfully nice hair." Her hand involuntarily moved up to test the texture of the tumbling locks. She checked the movement before he could object to being handled like a pigeon. "Shiny and dark as a blackbird's wings. But I do think your daughters would rather have blond hair. It is so much more fashionable." She felt obliged to make some concession. "Perhaps you could give the black hair to the boys."

She shifted her gaze to his face. "Too bad about your eyes."

"Dammit it, madam." He murmured a hasty apology, but his face remained fierce. "What is wrong with my eyes?"

The offending black eyes bore into her with an intensity and an accusation that urged her to retreat a step. "Not a thing. They are really quite magnificent."

"But . . . ?"

"But we really cannot give Clarissa dark eyes. Blondes must be blue-eyed, so some of your children will probably inherit her washed-out blue eyes." Really quite a pity, she decided. "Oh, well, it cannot be helped."

He folded his arms across his chest and settled his weight on his back foot. "I believe I can live with that. Since they are only imaginary children, they can just imagine themselves content with washed-out blue eyes. Are we quite finished with my breeding potential?"

His movement drew Amanda's attention to his well-shaped front leg, an extremely attractive leg for posing, but slightly undersized for real endurance. "Almost. Your legs are a shade thin. Should you mind terribly marrying a woman with thick legs?"

He straightened, jolting the offending leg beneath him. "I should mind prodigiously." He looked shocked she had even suggested such a thing, equally stunned he had responded

50

seriously. He laughed. "In fact, I shall refuse even to look at Clarissa if she has thick legs."

"Very well. You may design the legs, but it is a point you might want to keep in mind for the future."

"I certainly shall. Now may we sit?" He gestured with his hand toward the chairs they had abandoned, then hesitated. "Unless there is something else you object to. My features perhaps?" If he could have read her thoughts he would not have sounded so hostile.

"Oh, no. Your features are quite attractive. Quite rugged, craggy even . . . most attractive . . ." Discretion urged her to put a period to her words and sit, but this might well be the only time the gentleman with the mildly ruffled feathers ever gave a thought to the coming generation. "Distinctly attractive . . . for a man . . . but . . ."

"But . . . ? But my daughters . . . ?" He arched his eyebrows.

"Since you mention it." She hesitated long enough to be certain he recognized the criticism as his rather than hers. "We should probably give Clarissa very tiny features. You know. A little rosebud mouth, a tiny button nose. Whatever appeals to you so long as it is small." Amanda took the seat he had indicated. She had done what she could, helping him not only design a temporary fiancée, but possibly select a future bride.

He sidled to the chair he had just vacated, as if by turning and approaching it directly he might expose another defect. Just as tentatively he lowered himself into the seat and studied her expectantly with his head cocked to the side. After a moment he broke the silence. "Well?"

"Well what?"

"Surely you have not finished."

Amanda studied his face for signs he was teasing. "I believe we have covered everything. Nothing else occurs to me at the moment."

"Why, you have scarcely begun. What about the fair Clarissa's accomplishments?" He made a sweeping gesture. He expected his intended's accomplishments to fill the room.

"I believe I can leave that to you. You are not likely to be asked about her accomplishments in any case."

"Nonsense. A young lady's accomplishments are surely her most important aspect."

Amanda shook her head. He seemed a trifle naive, even for a man. "Perhaps at some very late stage they become important to the gentleman involved. But you forget our purpose. You only need to cope with questions from my mother and her friends."

He frowned. "And they will be interested only in appearance?"

"Absolutely. In fact, most women when they inquire about a gentleman's fiancée are secretly wishing she will be quite plain. It leaves some hope to those of us not so well favored." Amanda hurried on before he could tax himself with a tedious string of insincere assurances. "When describing Clarissa, see that you do not wax too eloquently on her beauty. It will only depress Mother even more."

She glanced toward the window, a little sorry to have finished with the intriguing topic of finding him a proper mate. "May I assume then that you have no objection to being engaged for the next day or so?"

"Are you quite certain this scheme is essential?"

"Most definitely. If we do not do this, Mother will follow you around, begging you to cancel all your appointments and stay on for weeks in order to become better acquainted with my charms."

His eyes widened. "Say that again." Something in her words pleasured him enough to want to hear it again.

"I said this is essential. I need your assurance that you will feel comfortable being betrothed for the next few days."

His eyes took on a determined look. She steeled herself for a refusal. Instead, he agreed readily enough. "I assure you I always do what I must." His brows drew together in a frown. He did not look as if he planned to enjoy his new status.

Amanda rose, and the ever-gallant Lord Rexford rose with her. "Thank you for understanding about Mother. Both our lives will be much easier now that we have Clarissa. I believe we can cope with your remaining time here. I shall see you at dinner in an hour.''

Rexford returned to the room Miss Langley had assigned him to find Tag sprawled on the bed.

The young blond man looked up, studied Rexford from head to toe, and grinned. ''I neglected to mention it in the library, but I am not cleaning those boots. And at this rate, you will be barefoot in a week.'' His grin widened. ''I can't say the rest of you looks much better.''

''Dammit, Tag, if you are going to be a valet, you can at least be respectful. And get your feet off my bed.''

Tag slowly peeled himself off the bed. ''A little prickly this afternoon, are we?'' He ducked the glove Rexford threw. ''You can have a respectful valet, or you can have a second in command. And I am still not cleaning those boots—I am not even sure I want to be in the same room with them.''

''Forget the boots. I have already rinsed them in the kitchen.'' He followed Tag's gaze to the milk-white film that covered his boots to the ankles.

''And a splendid job you did, if I may say so. Did you have a problem with Miss Langley? You look like you have been wrestling with the devil himself.''

Rexford winced. ''We all pay for our sins.'' He could be saving thousands of lives by being here. He had no reason to feel so shabby about planning to betray a rather eccentric lady into changing her gown eleven times a day.

''This whole business is not your fault, Marc.''

Rexford swatted his hand angrily across the dust on his breeches. ''Of course it is. I should have thought to set a guard on the carrier pigeons in London. I would have if I had not been so angry about being left behind to sit in the intelligence headquarters and shuffle stacks of messages about a desk.''

''They were birds, for God's sake! No one could have anticipated anyone would know enough about the operation to consider destroying the network by killing the birds. Hell, only a few people knew we were planning on using the blasted creatures.''

"I should have done something. Now we will pay by spending the next weeks humbugging some flighty spinster. She does not deserve that.''

"We are at war, Marc.'' Tag's impatience showed in his voice. "She could have cooperated when Dalton approached her. She has the perfect arrangement. She keeps some of Gully's birds, he has some of hers, and they fly their little notes back and forth. God knows what kind of messages those two send, but it would take months to set up anything half as adequate.''

"Is that brandy on that table?'' Rexford asked. Tag might be a little casual about some things, but he knew enough to take care of the essentials. Rexford poured, drank, and waited until the amber liquid cut a river of warmth through his tension.

He had to remember Tag had not seen the expression on the lady's face when she handled those birds. Most people did not love their families the way she loved those silly creatures! "Why they had to send that cow-handed Dalton to talk with her I will never know. Only he would feel obliged to give a complete graphic description of the butchering. That bloody fool probably used exactly that word, probably enumerated every blood-covered feather, and threw in all the gory details for effect.''

Tag raised his eyebrows and studied the glass in Rexford's hand. "Not your usual time for brandy. Is she that much of a thornback?''

A spinster maybe, Rexford thought, but he smiled at the memory of her pacing around him, her hand rubbing thoughtfully at her chin. "She is an interesting lady.'' She certainly did not share her mother's eagerness to snag him as a husband, not with his unacceptable height and too-thin legs. He kneaded the muscles in his thigh and found them quite adequate. *A shade thin indeed!*

What did she know about such things? She needed a pudgy little husband who would keep her in bed all day. He recalled the way her gown had swirled around her legs as she turned to leave. She decidedly did not share Clarissa's defect of thick legs.

Though Rexford promised himself he wouldn't, he turned to study his reflection in the looking glass. "Would you call my features craggy, Tag?"

Tag gave the matter proper consideration, then answered with a chuckle. "Not as fast as I would call your neckcloth a fright. Have you managed to identify the birds we can use to send messages from this end?"

Rexford shuddered at the memory. "Oh, yes. I identified them, all right. Miss Langley obligingly pointed them out this afternoon."

"Splendid. Then if we should need to send an urgent message, you can just stroll into the loft, select the appropriate carrier, and Calquohoun Grant will have your report in a matter of hours."

"Not precisely."

Tag's eyebrows rose. "Would you care to elaborate on 'not precisely'?"

Either Tag or the brandy had restored enough of Rexford's usual good humor that he could offer a self-deprecating grin. Though he expected little sympathy, he described the scene in the cote, beginning with Grace taking up residence on his shoulder and ending with the point where he could finally identify all five birds.

Tag clutched his stomach as if that might contain the laughter. "I swear I would have given my entire fortune, and all I could borrow, to witness that. But I can tell by your face there is more."

Rexford sighed and confessed the rest. "I had everything memorized, then Miss Langley strolled into the flock to pick up some damn fool creature. She set the whole regiment flying. Five seconds later I could no more pick out the birds who could fly to Brussels than I could fly there myself."

Tag wiped a tear from the corner of his eye and had to try twice before he could speak. "And Miss Langley would

55

not point them out again? Seems a trifle uncooperative of her.''

It seemed a trifle unimaginative of Tag to find it so amusing. ''I am sure she would have pointed them out, as many times as I asked. What she would not do was agree to have them nailed in place.''

''So we have no choice but to stay here until you learn to tell blue from black. Have you succeeded in getting her to invite us for a few weeks?''

''Not yet, but I will before the evening is out.'' Rexford considered another brandy, then decided he ought to stop reeking of pigeons before he began reeking of alcohol.

He and Tag spent the next hour analyzing the reports from the Continent. Finally, he stood and stamped across the room. ''What a tedious task.''

Tag looked up from where he sat cross-legged on the bed. The paper in his hand rustled as he shook it at the air. ''Don't look to me for sympathy. Even my father is over there.''

In spite of his frustration, Rexford smiled. ''That is from him? We should have predicted he would manage to be in the thick of it.'' Until he had met Tag's parent, the word *father* had always called up images of a dark-coated man with stiff movements and a perpetual scowl. But Winston Elmgrove gave new definition to the word. An older version of Tag, he could be on intimate terms with a king or a chimney sweep before most men could even think of a greeting. From their antics when father and son were together, one would need church records to tell which was older. Tag worshipped him.

''He's in the thick of it, all right. Having a bang-up time galloping around between Brussels and Paris.'' Tag's smile held as much admiration as envy. ''I can see him now, passing through those French lines with his 'Good morning, mates, got time to chat about where you're marching to this morning?' '' He gave a resigned sigh. ''I can't wait to swap war stories. He can tell me about being a spy, and I can tell him about being a valet. Forgive me if I am not too sympathetic with you for being wounded out of the thing.''

56

"Speaking of being a valet, why don't we discuss the rest of the preparations while you help me get dressed for dinner."

Tag's grin announced the return of his good humor. "Sure I'll help." He shuffled the papers aside with his legs and stretched out on the bed. "Your coat is over there. And I think it's wrinkled."

Rexford rolled his eyes. "At least tell me what arrangements you've made in the village."

"Very much what we discussed. Peter and Chumley are in place at the inn. Any non-urgent communication will go directly to them. The tavern has a fine ale house and no one will take it amiss if I make it a habit to drop in every night for a glass or two. There should be no need for anyone to contact you here except in an extreme emergency."

Rexford finished dressing. Automatically he stepped to the glass to check his appearance. "By Jove, one of us must learn to tie a neckcloth or figure out some way for my useless valet to employ a valet." He bent and removed his milky boots to replace them with evening shoes. "Have the next man to go to London order me half a dozen more pairs of boots from Hoby's—and send the bill to the Crown. As for you, do not come back tonight without at least three more of these wretched coats. You should be able to find something in the village." He matched the comment with a grimace. "I refuse to go about in a coat that has been used as a pigeon roost."

"Anything else, sir?" Tag's delighted chortle ruined his attempt at a subservient nod. "A nice tall hat, perhaps. With an extra wide brim, of course, to accommodate any number of your feathered friends."

"Your resignation would do nicely." He could think of nothing more to postpone his appearance at dinner. "I am off. When I return I shall have secured us a definite invitation."

Amanda looked across the table at Lord Rexford. He sat behind his soup, amiably describing a play he had seen in

Drury Lane as if he had not had a more important thought in his head since Christmas. This would be the ideal time for him to mention how much Clarissa had enjoyed the play. She lifted her toe to give him a gentle nudge, but the wide table prevented any contact.

Her mother cleared her throat and smiled. She turned her attention back to Lord Rexford with a look she should have reserved until God came to visit. Amanda could almost see the cogs and wheels of her mother's brain totaling up the earl's advantages. A title. A fortune, though the limited time since her mother's return home had probably prevented her from determining the precise size of his income. Presentable-looking. Personally, Amanda considered him quite hand-some, but since even "presentable-looking" was far down on her mother's list of priorities, she probably had not even noticed. By now her mother was probably adding "exces-sively charming" to her list.

Amanda shifted impatiently. She wished Rexford would mention his fiancée before Mother became so enthralled that even Clarissa would not be a sufficient impediment.

Fifteen minutes in the drawing room and ten minutes at the table. Would these two never get on with it?

Her mother turned to speak to a footman, then dismissed the man with a gesture. "Thank you." She turned her glow-ing face to Amanda. "I forgot to mention, I met Lord Bat-terton in the village. Down from London after all this time."

Rexford's lips curled as if he had tasted three-day-old fish. "Lord Batterton is here?"

"Oh, yes." Mother smiled coyly. "He was a particular friend of Amanda's. Visited the neighborhood several times after the season we met him in London." She turned to Amanda. "He particularly asked if he might call on you."

"And you told him—"

"That you would be delighted, of course."

Amanda decided she could deal with only one potentially bothersome suitor at a time. "Of course." Now that Mother had established that other suitors existed, those two could get to the business at hand. "Clarissa," she mouthed soundlessly at Lord Rexford.

He nodded. "Charming place you have here, Lady Harriet."

Mother turned her coaxing charm on him. "It must have been terribly difficult to tear yourself away from London at the height of the season." She gave a patronizing smile. "Unless this year's crop of beauties is as mundane as usual."

Amanda mentally applauded. Mother had finally begun. It had just taken longer than usual. Now if Lord Rexford would take his cue and begin singing Clarissa's praises, they could all relax.

Lord Rexford gave a casual shrug. "Quite ordinary, as you say."

Amanda's spoon clattered against her bowl. She glared across the table. *Clarissa,* she shouted with her mind.

Lord Rexford nodded to her and smiled at her mother. "There is one young lady . . . a rather charming young lady . . ."

He would never accomplish this on his own. "You are betrothed," Amanda said. She hoped her words sounded like a question to her mother and a command to the recalcitrant lord.

"In a manner of speaking. We have an . . ."

Amanda gave an emphatic nod. "You have an understanding. Of course. Quite to be expected at your age." She decided reaching for her wine glass to toast the couple's happiness might be too much. "We wish you every happiness, don't we, Mother?"

Mother's spoon hesitated halfway to her mouth. "I have seen nothing of this in the papers."

"Naturally not. The young lady and I want to wait until we are absolutely sure. I dare not even mention her last name until—"

"But you have declared yourself." Amanda bit out each word. He had to understand, nothing short of total commitment would satisfy Mother. "You are—"

Mother interrupted. "Tell us about this lady you are considering.'' She drew out the word *considering,* as if even the duration of the word might give Lord Rexford time to avoid an unfortunate mistake.

Amanda allowed her shoulders to relax. He should be on comfortable ground here. Lord knows they had spent enough time on the subject.

''Her name is Clarissa. She is short and blond, with rather washed-out blue eyes.''

Amanda rolled her own eyes and caught a glimpse of the soft blue ceiling—the same color as Clarissa's sorry blue eyes. Why had he chosen to remember that particular detail? She had little hope her mother would overlook such uncomplimentary phrasing.

''She sounds quite lovely.'' Mother's tone said she sounded exactly the opposite. ''Except for the eyes,'' she added. ''Is she not attractive, Lord Rexford?''

He let too much time pass. An ardent lover should not have to consider such a question. ''Oh, she is very attractive.'' He paused with an unreadable look in Amanda's direction. ''Except for her legs. She does have rather thick legs.''

Amanda gasped her horror. She could not possibly attack him with her dinner fork, though the idea had a certain appeal. How could anyone be such an idiot?

Her mother's mouth rounded at the impropriety of mentioning a lady's extremities, particularly at the dinner table. Then her expression melted into a patronizing smile. ''I am sure your Clarissa's accomplishments make up for what she lacks in physical beauty.''

''I trust you are correct, madam. Though to be honest, our relationship has not advanced to the point where I am familiar with her accomplishments.'' He kept his gaze so firmly fixed on her mother that Amanda realized he was deliberately avoiding looking at her.

The room shrank around Amanda as she struggled to understand. Everything he said seemed right, but so terribly wrong. Why would he . . . ?

Her mother nodded, all gentleness and understanding. ''I

think I understand why you might have retired to the country at the height of the season. Perhaps you needed time to consider. . . . One cannot be too careful when making a decision like this.''

Almost from a distance Amanda watched. Comprehension dawned even as she watched the two speak out their predictable lines.

''Precisely, madam. And this is a charming place to consider such a serious decision.''

''Such serious decisions should not be rushed.''

''That would be a dreadful mistake.''

''Please, my lord, I hope you will regard our home as your own while you decide if someone else might not suit you better.'' Her mother did everything but stand up and point to Amanda. Surely Lord Rexford should have gagged on his soup.

He did not. He nodded and smiled and thanked her for the splendid suggestion.

''Stay as long as you like. I am sure . . .''

Amanda did not even listen to the rest. Nor did she eat.

The betrayal sat on her stomach, leaving no room for the meal that followed. He had done it deliberately. He had used all they discussed, the eyes, the legs, the accomplishments. But he had twisted everything to his own purpose.

She remembered his face when, like a fool, she had told him her mother would invite him to stay for months. He must have been making his plan even then.

Now he might not stay for just a few days. He could stay as long as he wanted.

Amanda could understand what had happened. What she could not understand was why he had gone to such lengths to deliberately manipulate the situation. She had no illusions he had already fallen under her spell. But he insisted on staying, and he insisted on questioning her very intensely on the birds. She might not understand why yet, but she would. And he would find her not quite so easy to manipulate as he expected.

61

Chapter Four

Lord Rexford scowled at his reflection in the mirror. "Harden up, man. You did what you had to. Now stop whimpering." He turned away before his own eyes could accuse him of treachery. He had done nothing more than let some young lady's mother coax him into visiting for a few weeks. If that slightly inconvenienced the young lady, his reasons were more than adequate.

Why then did he still feel like swamp water?

The question answered itself in a series of mental images of Miss Langley at dinner. Though he had avoided facing her directly, he had seen the play of expressions across her face. Impatience, annoyance, disbelief—and finally horror. He could not recall a single thing he had eaten, but he had only to relax his guard to feel again the ice of every contemptuous look that accompanied the remainder of the meal.

"Bah." The word did not banish the plaguing thoughts, and he began mentally to justify his actions for the tenth time that morning. He might not have to reveal his real purpose, but he certainly had to find some way to make peace with the woman who knew more about birds than anyone in England.

Lady Harriet looked up and smiled when he entered the breakfast room, where she lingered over a final cup of chocolate. With an approving nod, she informed him he would find Miss Langley in the pigeon cote.

Men probably walked to the gallows faster than he walked toward the dusky stone building he could just see through the trees, but the rich spring air banished his dark mood, substituting distant memories. The heavy breeze in the damp woods carried the seductive scents of late May. Fecund springtime aromas conjured up another spring and a pleasure-to-the-point-of-pain walk through similar woods with his hand dangling carelessly over the breast of a willing milkmaid. His first time had been in a woods such as this. They had dropped onto the ground in a secluded glade and she had guided his fumbling hands, slowing him until he thought he would go mad, then welcoming him to the wonder of it all. Twenty years, and the remembered combination of loam and green and early violets could still bring an ache in his loins.

"Ahhh! There you are, sweetheart. Come to me now." The indescribably sensuous voice came straight from his fantasy. A woman's voice. A hair-spread-on-the-pillow, body-already-writhing voice. Rexford froze. The voice was too real.

"I have been waiting all morning for you. Come to me." Too close and too breathy to be anything but corporeal. "You know how I love to hold you."

Blood rushed to Rexford's cheeks. Heat broiled his ear lobes. The voice was real, worse than real. It belonged to Miss Langley. He had stumbled on an assignation. How could this have happened?

He couldn't walk on. He would intrude. If he retreated they might see or hear him.

"Yes. Yes. That's it. Just like that. Everything is all right now." The low husky tones came with the trembling note of a ready woman. Rexford could picture her hungry lover sliding his hand under her skirt. What would those long legs look like parted, waiting?

"Yes." Miss Langley could have any man she wanted if she beguiled him in that voice.

Surely the couple had heard his approach. He remembered the crunch of the small branches under his feet. Surely they would hear a retreat. They would think he had been watching. He could not accept that humiliation. Better to announce his presence and suffer the embarrassment.

He coughed.

"Quiet, Lord Rexford, I know you are there." She drew the words out in the slow languorous voice she had used to her lover. If anything, she had added even more gravel to the words. "Please don't move." She spoke softly and slowly despite the undeniable urgency of the command. "For the love of God, don't move."

He obeyed. In spite of the strange order, he obeyed because he could think of no better alternative.

A rustle of leaves to his left made him realize how close they were. "No, no, no. Don't go." The words came in a desperate rush. Then the soft seductive voice assumed control. "That's it. I know you are frightened. But it will be all right. That's it, sweetheart, come to me now."

Understanding hit Rexford like a cuff to the head. She was talking to a bloody bird. If he had dared to move he would probably have strangled her for his own thoughts. But the underlying note of desperation in her voice nailed him in place. By the time he had finished calling himself every kind of fool known to man, she still had not given him permission to move. He had no choice but to stand there watching the sky and listening to the provocative voice.

Out of sight, she spoke in the most blatantly suggestive images. "That's it, sweetheart, come to me. Remember how softly I can hold you. I can make you feel better. I can stroke away the pain."

Against his will the bedroom images returned. The voice breathed naked female, and he mentally put the naked female in his bed where she belonged. There she would wake him up with sleepy stroking words. Her tangled hair would be spread on the pillow between them. Perhaps he would wake with his lips only inches from her swollen nipple, his hand already between her silken thighs.

"Come to me." The words promised she would arch toward him with the first movement of his hand against her skin. He mentally matched his smooth strokes to her caressing words. Her thighs parted. "Yes. Yes." She arched toward his searching fingers, urging him on. He rolled over, savoring the warmth of the—

"Lord Rexford." Miss Langley's normal voice brought him crashing back to reality. He opened his eyes to see a distant bird streak across the blue sky. "Lord Rexford, you may move now." The soft voice was pleasant enough, but nothing that could beguile a man into humiliating himself completely. Despite the permission to turn, Rexford took several deep breaths and continued to stare at the sky, fiercely ignoring the ache his thoughts had created.

"Shhhh, you are all right now." Again her words held the indescribable roughness of sex. "It is all over, sweetheart. I can take care of you now." She was talking to the damn bird again.

Rexford turned before the blood could begin pounding in his veins once more. He saw what he knew he would see, not a breathless, naked woman, but a plain spinster in a drab brown dress, staring at him anxiously. She held a motionless gray bird crushed to her breasts. Her index finger stroked the creature's curved head. She looked down occasionally to breathe tender words on her prize.

"Tha . . ." Her lower lip trembled, and she had to try twice before she could control her voice enough to speak. "Thank you for staying so still. I almost lost her."

You almost lost more than a bird. Someday he would have to inform her of the devastating effect of that bedroom voice on a man. "What happened?"

She closed her eyes, tightened her lips, and shook her head against the unthinkable. "Come. We must hurry." More murmuring, but blessedly soft enough that when he dropped two paces behind, the throaty voice had no power over him.

He followed her through the remainder of the wooded area

and around the stone loft they had visited the previous day. She led him to a shed at the far end of the building and gestured for him to open a door secured with a wooden bar. They walked into a room about ten feet square with a wide waist-high shelf extending from three of the sides. More shelves lined the two side walls, shelves filled with amber bottles, jars, and large earthenware containers.

"Please open the other door as well."

Rexford threw back the second half of the double door, and light flooded the room. Miss Langley gave no appearance of hurrying, but still crossed the room in three long strides. Her movements were smooth and sure. "Could you look outside, please, and see if you can find Jeb." She had used *please* twice now, but there was no *please* in her tone, just a clear instruction that she expected would be obeyed.

Rexford stepped out, looked around, and called. "Jeb. Jeb." He circled the building and called again, "Jeb!" Full voice this time.

"Enough, Lord Rexford." Miss Langley poked her head out the door, still cradling the birds in her hands. "He must have gone to his mother's to eat. You will have to help me." She nodded toward the far wall, indicating he should move over there. "It will be good for you." A hint of ice in the words told him she had more to say on the subject of what might be good for him.

He moved quickly to follow her directions. Fate had given him an opportunity to soften her attitude. He could not afford to waste it. "What happened?"

"A hawk," she said crisply. "Your hands, please."

No question she meant him to cup his hands and take the bird.

"My courier must have released the birds earlier than I instructed, or perhaps Elizabeth just came faster than I expected. I looked up just as she landed." She looked at the cupped hands Rexford extended, but did not immediately hand him the bird. Instead she lifted her fragile burden to her face and rubbed her cheek against the feathered head. She murmured words that seemed so private Rexford shifted his gaze to the far corner of the room, only looking back when he could tell from her tone she was addressing him again.

"I could tell from the way she landed she was hurt, but before I could get to her, another bird flew over, casting a terribly large shadow on the landing platform. It terrified Elizabeth. She flew away. I followed her to where we met you, but by then she was in a panic." Her voice trembled as she relived those moments. "She would not let me near her, hopping and fluttering away every time I came close enough to touch her. I almost lost her." Unshed tears caught in her voice. "I knew she was hurt and I couldn't get to her. I almost lost her." Another stroke of her cheek against the bird's head, then she extended the tiny creature.

Rexford realized his hands were shaking. He had no fear of the helpless bird, but he had a mortal terror of squeezing too hard and hurting not only the bird, but this vulnerable woman. She lowered her hands into his open palms. He felt warmth and love in her touch, but a reassuring steadiness too. She lifted her gaze to his face as if searching for signs of weakness.

He fought to put a lifetime of knowing he could do what he had to into his expression. Whatever she saw heartened her. "When I draw my hands away, you are going to have to close your thumbs over her wings. Ready?"

A thousand internal demons shouted no. He nodded. She withdrew her hands and he imprisoned the trembling creature with his thumbs, praying the pressure would not be too much. The fragile wings beat two or three times against his hands, then stilled. An incredibly rapid heartbeat throbbed against his fingers. The heart kept beating and he did not hear the half-expected crunch of bones too fragile for his rough, soldier hands.

"Good." Miss Langley had already turned from him to gather materials from the side wall. Seconds later she was again standing so close he could feel the soft puffs of her exhaled air on his cheek. "Her wing is slightly injured, but I am more concerned about this." She pointed with her index finger to a darkened area on the bird's neck where the feathers were matted with blood. "I have done this a dozen times. It never gets easier." She drew her lips into a thin, tight line and nodded her readiness to begin.

Difficult or not, she approached the task with crisp, sure movements. She washed and clipped away the mangled feathers, exposing a gaping gash that left Rexford wondering how the fragile bird had ever managed to keep her head upright. Occasionally the helpless creature would stir to life to batter softly against his palms, but mostly she endured in silence. Rexford had to consciously keep from tightening his grip when he saw Miss Langley turn and thread a needle. He had held enough soldiers while battlefield wounds were stitched to know he would rather be anywhere else.

"It is all right. It will all be over in a minute." Rexford realized with surprise he had spoken those words. *Insanity is contagious,* he thought, searching for his customary air of studied indifference.

It is only a bird. His stern reprimand could not diminish his concern. Only he and the woman opposite him would ever know of his weakness. Only she would ever know he cared. He needed to ease the pain of the trembling creature in his hands. He gave a mental shrug and released the lock he had clamped on his tongue. He let the reassuring words tumble out, and fought to keep from clenching his hands as Miss Langley took the first stitch.

She worked without hesitation, drawing the ragged skin together and stitching as she might on any piece of needlework. So intent was his concentration, she had half completed the task before he even raised his head to look at her. The sight of her face reached him as few things ever had. Her teeth had bitten a white line into her lower lip, and silent tears ran down her flushed cheeks. He had seen hundreds of women fawning over pets they claimed to adore, but he had never seen such undisguised love. Only the beating heart in his hands kept him from reaching up to brush away the unacknowledged tears. Words of reassurance would only have belittled the emotion. He kept silent and mentally willed her to hurry.

She finished the task with a sigh that came from her toes, and seemed to lose an inch of height with the completion. She put the thread aside and rinsed her fingers in the large basin of water on the bench. "I will take her now." The softness of her words contrasted dramatically with the abruptness of her reach for Elizabeth.

He surrendered the bird, and watched her raise the limp creature to her cheek with a long possessive exhale. In her raspy love-voice she whispered words of unity and understanding, so private that Rexford, for the second time that day, had the experience of intruding on an intensely intimate scene.

"I will be outside if you need me," he said.

She looked up with a start as if only now seeing him as a living human being. Her eyes engulfed him in the tenderness that had filled the room. "Thank you, Lord Rexford. You are a very gentle man."

The sharp glare of the sunlight brought back reality. *A gentle man.* Rexford tried to recall the last time someone had called him gentle. Numerous women had batted their eyes and called him a "splendid gentleman." He gave a mirthless chuckle and recalled that far more had feigned shock at his roaming hands and giggled, "I fear you are no gentleman, sir." But *gentle*.

The word stirred vague memories of his childhood. He ran his fingers through his hair, a gesture he should have abandoned with adolescence. He had been gentle as a boy, with a stable full of pets. Where had that gentleness gone?

A war, a slaughter of innocents, a lifetime spent in seeking out those who would betray their country and their friends. That kind of history did not leave much room for softer emotions. He tried to remember when he had felt anything but cold anger or bored indifference.

He shook his head and admitted he had felt something today. He had watched men die on the battlefield with less emotion than he felt watching an uncomely woman stitch up the neck of an unattractive bird. He took several heavy steps to adjust to the novel thought. He told himself he had only been trying to win forgiveness, but he could not banish the memory of tightening every muscle to help a fragile bird cling to life. It had mattered in some way he did not completely understand.

Inside the surgery shed, Amanda said a whispered good-bye to Elizabeth and turned to the door to find Lord Rexford. She checked her step before she could go out and inundate him with her appreciation. Elizabeth's plight had blotted out everything else. She had forgotten his treachery, forgotten her anger, forgotten everything but the need to save Elizabeth. Now he would expect . . .

It did not matter what he would expect. Anyone could have held the bird. He probably did it just to win her gratitude. Well, it would not work. She paced the hard dirt floor of the room until she felt the anger at his betrayal build again. Then she stepped through the door, far less grateful than she had been a moment earlier.

He had wandered across the yard and looked up apprehensively as she came out. "Is she . . . ? She didn't . . . ? Did she . . . ?"

"No. She did not die, though she still may."

"You love her very much, don't you."

She paused and tried to think of a bird whose passing she wouldn't mourn. With an effort she banished the recent scene from her mind. She looked at the green tree beyond him to stoke the anger she had so carefully rekindled moments earlier. "I do not believe whom I love or don't love need concern you." She could feel it now, the coldness that had engulfed her with his chicanery. "Right now I want to know why you are here."

His face assumed the amiable expression she had sense enough now to distrust. "I explained, I want to learn about birds so I can—" She knew in a minute he would begin babbling about how he loved the darlings and how he wanted to set up his own loft, when it was quite obvious he could barely endure their presence. Whatever his reason for insisting on staying, it was not affection for the birds.

"And I don't believe you," she said.

"I assure you I love—"

"And I assure you, you barely tolerate the birds. You flinch every time one comes near you." She had the satisfaction of seeing a crimson flush color his cheeks.

"I am sure I could learn—"

"Perhaps. The question is, why would you want to?"

"I hope to set up—"

Amanda shook her head. His words said he wanted to keep a loft of birds; his manner said he would rather keep a nest of spiders. She would continue shaking her head until he decided to stop treating her like a fool.

"You don't believe me?"

"No, my lord, I do not."

"Well . . ." He turned and took several insistent steps to the right, a man who could think better in motion. He arrived back at the spot he had previously occupied. "I am—was a soldier. The army is aware of the value of carrier pigeons for communications. I have been asked to set up a loft of birds for the military. Naturally, I want to learn everything I can for the assignment." He did not look particularly pleased, and the words had the ring of truth.

"That still does not explain why you need to impose yourself on me."

"You are the best, Miss Langley." He gave a half smile and a nod that conveyed his compliments to her reputation. "Where else would I go?"

The subtle flattery did not change the fact he had originally lied about his reason for coming. "You could have confided this the moment you arrived."

He took two steps to close the distance between them and lowered his voice to a confidential whisper. "The less one talks about military communication, the better. At that point you had no need to know my intentions." His confidential tone might have been more effective if he had not two minutes before announced his military status to the entire neighborhood. His candid tone increased her wariness.

71

Amanda gave her head an impatient shake. "There are many kinds of intrigue, Lord Rexford, and they are not all military. I would know a thing or two about that."

He gave a patronizing lift to his eyebrows and cocked his head questioningly.

Amanda found his posture altogether maddening. "Pigeon breeders are some of the most conniving people in the world," she said. "Not so much in England, but on the Continent. Some of them would do anything to win this race in June. It is a very prestigious event." A biting desire to strike the patronizing expression from his face compelled her to continue. "You may not be aware of it, but that is why you are here, you know." She could tell from the stiffening in his posture she had his full attention now.

His lips narrowed into a thin line. "What would you know of why I am here?"

"Perhaps more than you do. With all the secrecy you mentioned, you may not know that the army already had a loft. Somebody viciously murdered those birds two weeks ago. That is why they need you to set up another one."

He concealed any horror he might have felt under a stony, soldier expression. "You seem very well informed."

Amanda's skin turned cold at the memory. "An officious little man came to tell me about the incident just after it happened. I assure you, I knew more about it than he did."

He leaned forward, his eyes focused on her face. "How so?"

She shook her head in remembered annoyance. "He tried to convince me the French were responsible. But he obviously knew nothing about the community of pigeon breeders. The murdered birds probably belonged to General Stonehaven. He almost won a similar race two years ago. Naturally anyone intent on winning would want to get rid of his birds."

Rexford blinked. "Then you don't believe the French—"

"Of course not. One of the Belgian breeders figured he could get rid of the competition and blame it on Napoleon. Anything that goes wrong in the country today, we just blame it on Napoleon. Believe me, the French have too much to do to worry about a few pigeons.''

Rexford smiled for the first time. ''I should have guessed you would have an interesting perspective. Did you share this opinion with the messenger?''

In spite of the seriousness of the topic, Amanda found herself responding to the smile. ''He scarcely gave me a chance. He was a real ninnyhammer, carrying on about plans to move half a regiment of soldiers here and use my birds for flying back and forth to Brussels. As if I would be daft enough to let any strangers near my birds before the competition.''

Rexford's straightened into a military stance. ''If you will give me his name, I will report that he is not a particularly astute judge of character. I assume you sent him packing.''

Amanda nodded. ''I most certainly did. We may look very casual here, but Jeb has a musket in that shed over there and orders to shoot any suspicious strangers.'' Of course, if that suspicious stranger happened to be an unarmed earl, one could not very well shoot him. She needed time to decide how to deal with the situation.

Rexford gave a most innocent smile. ''Remind me to do my best not to look suspicious. I trust you do not suspect an inoffensive fellow like myself.''

She could not simply send him on his way after Mother's specific invitation, but until she knew more, she could be as canny as he. She smiled back with equal artlessness. ''Frankly, I considered it, but you did save the birds. And . . .'' For now she could appear every bit as credulous as he expected.

He nodded. ''And?''

''Villains are not usually very bright, you know. And . . .''

A hint of amusement in his eyes acknowledged the mild compliment. ''You have given this matter a lot of thought. And?''

''You may not like my last reason quite as much.''

''I am sure I can handle it. Though I hope it is not another of the wretched faults I displayed when you were trying to marry me off to Clarissa.'' His self-mocking tone did not quite conceal his irritation at the memory.

Amanda noted the vulnerability and tucked it away for future reference. ''And if someone wanted to send in an assassin to kill the birds, I doubt he would choose one who is so uneasy with them.''

Rexford winced. ''I thought I hid that quite well.''

''Only if you always walk with your arms or legs as stiff as fence posts. In any case, it makes you quite above suspicion. In fact, now that I understand your job, I can even be mildly sympathetic.'' She hoped her look appeared more reassuring than her thoughts.

''So you will help?''

He would not expect too easy a victory. ''And if I refuse?''

''Why would you refuse?''

She could think of several reasons, but had no intention of stating them yet.

He interrupted before she finished compiling her mental list. ''Certainly if you can send the British army scurrying off with its tail between its legs, you can deal with your mother.''

She had dealt with her mother all her life. She had not dealt with gentlemen of questionable motives, but for now . . . ''Of course. But I give you fair warning, she will be a nuisance.'' Amanda laughed as if she had no concern but her mother. ''And I vow, if you give her the slightest reason to hope you might be developing a tendresse for me, I shall turn Grace loose on you.'' Until she had time to think, she would give him every appearance of cooperation. They could discuss everything but the racing birds. She could even enjoy watching his discomfort.

She led him into the aviary and waited while he hurried to latch the door behind them. On this second visit he seemed better able to control his near-panic at the flurry of activity their entrance produced. He scarcely jumped when Grace claimed possession of his shoulder. Lucifer, a thunder-dark bird who regarded the aviary as his own personal preserve, made a sortie at the earl's left ear, but settled for merely an offensive brush. The attack ended so quickly, Rexford might have put it down as just part of the general turmoil if Lucifer had not settled on his high perch to stare down with venomous eyes.

"Did that bird just attack me?"

She smiled, not the least averse to letting Rexford suffer for his high-handed treatment at dinner. "I am afraid so." She reminded herself to give Lucifer an extra treat.

"What did I ever do to him?" Lucifer made another swooping dive. Rexford ducked just in time, and the bird glided harmlessly over his head. Grace scampered to maintain her perch on his shoulder.

Amanda knew the muttered oath was not meant for her ears.

"What did I do?" he repeated.

"Keep your voice down. You will upset every creature in here." Amanda knew she had only a minuscule fraction of his attention.

He glared at Lucifer with a promise of violence that would have intimidated a lesser bird. "What did I ever do to him?" he asked again.

"From your point of view, nothing." She felt a twinge of guilt for enjoying this small vengeance so.

"And from his point of view?" His eyes watched as Lucifer launched himself into flight and circled overhead.

Oh, please, yes, Amanda thought. "You fell in love with Grace."

"Dammit, I am not in love with—" Lucifer launched his only weapon. With lightning reflexes, Rexford jumped back. The sodden projectile landed on the ground with an explosive splat. "Dammit, tell me he didn't just—"

Amanda fought to control her laughter at the shock and indignation of his face. "I am afraid he did."

Lord Rexford whirled and took three pounding steps with Grace bobbing on his shoulder until he stood beneath Lucifer's perch. He slapped his ungloved hand against his thigh. "I take that as an insult. You will—" Lucifer took flight and landed somewhere on the dirt behind Amanda.

Lord Rexford turned, his face an unhealthy crimson color. When he saw the grin on her face, his mouth dropped open and his eyes widened. "Please tell me I did not almost challenge a bird to a duel."

Amanda surrendered all hope of controlling her laughter. It burst forth, and she could only stand there shaking her head. "It is . . . you . . ." Every placating thing she thought to say made her only laugh harder. Slowly his face lost its bewildered expression and he joined her, an uneasy self-conscious laugh. When she finally regained control, Amanda realized he had crossed the enclosure to stand next to her.

"You are not angry with me?" He stood too close, and Amanda realized that it was his nearness that had caused her to stop laughing. Her awareness of him made it difficult to recall what had happened.

She retreated half a step to where the lighter air made breathing easier. "Angry with you? Why should I be?"

"I promised to learn to be rational around these birds but"—he shook his head and the incredulous amusement returned to his voice—"but I almost challenged one to pistols at dawn."

"Like people, some birds are more difficult to love than others." He still seemed too close because her hands kept thinking of reasons to touch him. Lucifer offered a safe reason to retreat. "Let me put Lucifer away and we can continue with your education." She located the abusive Lucifer at the far side of the enclosure, captured him, and put him in one of the breeding pens.

She returned to find her guest wandering around studying the birds at his feet, the ever-present Grace contentedly settled on his shoulder. He looked up and smiled. "I am making progress. I can now identify two birds, Grace because she persists in nibbling on my ear, and Lucifer because he wants to do unmentionable things on my head. Now about the others, I do not suppose you will agree to let them wear name cards?"

The breeze had ruffled the fringes of his gleaming hair.

An errant lock had tumbled over his forehead. She resisted the impulse to cross the hard-packed dirt and brush the dangling curl back into place, surprised at how often her hands moved to touch him. She remembered the itch to straighten his skewed neckcloth, the way her fingers had automatically moved to test the texture of his hair when she decided to mate him to a blonde. He looked like a fine cock that no one had taken the time to groom adequately.

She focused on the birds to cover the sudden rush of awareness. "The other names will come just as easily. Hannibal likes to climb mountains. You will usually find him walking up something. His favorite is that board over there. We leave it because he sulks if he does not have anything to climb."

"And Gully's birds? I promised him I would get to know them. I know you pointed them out yesterday, but if you would not mind . . ."

"His birds are really quite ordinary. Though please do not tell him I said so. That one . . ." Amanda started to point out one of her own birds in the main area, but stopped to watch with satisfaction the flurry of activity a few feet away. The coupling took only seconds.

Lord Rexford followed the direction of her gaze, and watched with somewhat less interest. "I am surprised you did not stop that. They might have hurt each other."

"Hardly. I never leave them together unless I am here to observe. Come, we must record it, though." She started toward the wooden cabinet where she kept her writing materials.

"Record what? He only fluttered at him for a minute. Surely that must go on all the time with so many birds."

His question halted Amanda. She felt herself flush. She had not considered she might have to explain. "You have no idea what you just witnessed?"

"No more than the obvious. A little scuffle. Should I have seen more?"

Amanda tried to analyze her odd reluctance to speak. She had discussed breeding all her life, not only with Margaret,

JUDY VEISEL

but with men as interested in the subject as she. But suddenly she could not find the proper words, possibly because she did not know how much she would have to explain. Surely he knew some basic facts. "My lord, if we are going to deal together, we must learn to speak frankly, don't you agree? Without embarrassment."

"Naturally." His puzzled expression said he still had not stumbled on the nature of the topic.

"Those birds, the ones you watched . . . they were not two males."

"Ahhh. Some kind of a courting ritual. I should have guessed."

"Not courting ritual. They were . . ." She had never stumbled like this, nor felt so cow-handed. He was doing it to her, with his nearness and his eyes that made her wonder . . . Instead, she imagined hitting him over the head with the information, and proceeded to do a verbal version of precisely that. "They were breeding." She had spoken louder and more emphatically than necessary, but at least he could not question her meaning.

"You mean they were . . . they did . . . They certainly did not seem to enjoy it very much."

"One is not supposed to enjoy breeding."

He muttered a comment she could not hear, raised his eyebrows, and looked at her as if waiting for her to correct that statement. "Of course they don't," he agreed. "Perhaps that is where the expression 'bird-witted' comes from."

Amanda decided the comment was just the kind of unrefined thing males tended to say in their obsession with reproduction. She would not think too long about it. Instead she treated him to a lecture on the necessity to know as closely as possible when the act occurred so that you could be prepared for the egg and be reasonably certain when it would hatch. The pair they had just witnessed, she informed him, had already prepared an adequate nest. If they had not, she would have had to encourage them by laying out extra materials, or even taking the egg if necessary.

He listened with apparent interest, and even managed to

78

produce a question at the end of her discourse. "You spoke of selecting mates for your birds. I cannot imagine anything more random than the coupling we just witnessed. Are these two just a promiscuous pair?"

"Hardly, and that was hardly a random event. I arranged that weeks ago."

He dismissed her words with an impatient hand gesture. "Now I know you are teasing. How could you have arranged weeks ago for a two-second meeting to take place?"

Amanda found she was quite enjoying herself. Men always thought they knew everything about mating. "Precisely as Mother would arrange the same thing for you if she could." She ignored his disbelieving snort. "I simply put those two in a pen next to each other, separated by just a thin barrier of wire. Within a few days the male began cooing and strutting, ruffling his feathers and fanning his tail until the female began to notice him. Once she began to bob her head and swell her neck, I knew it was only a matter of time." Amanda had to clamp her lips to control a giggle at the look of outrage on his face.

"Are you saying that within a few days I will be strutting and cooing?" The small vein in his right temple throbbed so rapidly, Amanda wondered if she should warn him it might burst.

"Calm yourself, my lord. You are perfectly safe in the bedchamber next to mine. I am, after all, not an adorable little blonde. However, if I could arrange to settle you in a room next to Clarissa . . ."

The vein pulsed back into action. His words came with the subtlety of a bludgeon. "*I* would be cooing? *I* would be strutting?"

Amanda found herself torn between appeasing his offended dignity and making her point. She did deserve some revenge for his deliberate manipulation at dinner. "You would assuredly be mouthing pretty compliments and posing in the most uncomfortable-looking positions." She turned sideways and extended a foot in what she considered an excellent imitation of a gentleman posing. "Admit it now."

79

"I admit you have a most warped view of the entire situation. May I remind you, we do not lock our males and females in a room, separated only by thin barriers."

"Only at house parties, though I admit you use walls and chaperones instead of wooden slats."

"But that is not the usual case."

Amanda winced at the memory of her only season in London. "Oh, no, the usual case is far worse."

"I cannot imagine what might be worse."

"At least my birds have the privacy of a sheltered cage, so the entire world does not need to watch them strut and perform. The system you champion would put them on display at Almack's for all the world to watch—and criticize every breath."

"Most people enjoy the display."

Amanda remembered some of the painful expressions she had noted on the young girls in unguarded moments. "Often I have wondered how many truly do."

Distracted, she missed the instant when Lord Rexford took the step that brought him far too close to her. He took her chin between his thumb and index finger. He looked directly into her eyes, deep enough to cause the breath to catch in her throat. "I believe you have missed the most critical ingredient of the process. How about the simple physical attraction between a man and a woman?" He exhaled as if his warm breath on her face might add credence to his argument. For a heart-stopping moment he looked as if he would kiss her.

For an equally terrifying moment, she wanted him to. She stepped back, freeing her chin from his hand. "Biology, sir. That is nothing more than the same biology you witnessed a moment ago—and a trap as sure as any my mother would set for you."

She spun away so he would not see the flush that burned her cheeks. Distance brought rational thought. A frightening rational thought. All of her superior knowledge did not explain how she could suspect a person of being an enemy and still be so intensely aware of him as a man.

Chapter Five

The next morning Amanda released the birds for their morning exercise. For the first time in memory she failed to feel the familiar excitement as they surged toward the sky. She had postponed any decision until dawn, her best thinking time, but her eyes felt gritty and her arms ached as if she had been lifting heavy boulders. Rexford, with his drooping curl and indolent smile, had walked stiff-legged in and out of her dreams all night.

Her thoughts swirled back and forth, mirroring the random patterns the pigeons traced across the sky. The man made no sense. A supposedly wealthy, highly respected earl who would use any method to secure an invitation to an unprepossessing country estate. A polite request, an insistent reminder of a debt, and finally the deliberate twisting of their plan, which procured for him precisely what he wanted.

Only the birds made Langwood different from the thousand other estates he might have chosen to foist himself upon.

Try as she would, Amanda could not cast him in the role of villain. He walked too straight, met her eyes too directly, and his smile . . . *Anyone can smile.*

Grace traced a figure eight across the red-tinged sky. Amanda exhaled her tension and let her thoughts drift with the white bird's graceful glide. Anyone can smile, but a slow smile that lit a room like a thousand candles? Dark eyes that teased and flattered, then melted into a liquid softness. Could a villain—

Could an honest man lie about his reason for coming, then turn around and replace that lie with another tale that might be equally untrue? Only a child believed all villains lived in dank castles and carried blood-dripping daggers.

Amanda stood at the aviary door and whistled the seven melodious notes that called the birds home. They arrived in a rush with a whoosh of air and a cacophonous flutter of wings. She whistled again to hasten the stragglers. They scuttled about at her feet with an occasional peck at her toes to remind her the whistle promised breakfast. She hand-fed as many as she could without making them all too wildly impatient. While the rest ate, she walked among them, talking all the time, lifting and caressing those who needed to become accustomed to her touch.

She reached for Grace and smiled. The grieving bird had flown with more enthusiasm this morning than she had in weeks. Amanda's smile stiffened. She rubbed her index finger along Grace's soft neck. "Rexford might be bad, darling. Don't let him matter too much."

He might be bad. He might have come with unsavory intent, but for all the reasons she had listed to him, that did not fit either. He had saved the birds from the flood when he might have just let the chaos happen. Not only did he not have a strong personal interest in the birds, but he virtually cringed every time one came near him. If he did intend mischief, he had to be acting for somebody else. But somebody could not just go out and hire a wealthy earl as a bird-slayer or kidnapper. Again, it made no sense.

Amanda completed her morning routine and congratulated herself on spending two hours carefully analyzing the situation, only to arrive back at exactly the same spot as when

Rexford had first mentioned a visit. Whether he was a threat or merely an annoyance, he had to leave.

She glanced at the hazy yellow sun. The easiest course would be to persuade Mother to do a little uninviting. She would be awake and at her most reasonable, maybe willing to trade this one earl for some unspecified future cooperation.

Amanda smiled at the picture of Mother standing at the door, pointing the eligible earl on his way. It would certainly be a first. She brushed the lingering traces of grain from her hands and started for the house.

Amanda entered her mother's bedchamber without knocking. Mother looked up with a beatific smile. Against the abundance of pink pillows, the gold curls that ringed her face made her look rather like a cherub reclining on a sea of dawn-drenched clouds. "Amanda. Come in. I have not just been lazing about. See what I have been doing." She held up a rustling piece of paper in each hand. "One for me and one for you." Scattered books and newspapers shuddered on the coverlet, which enveloped her from the waist down. "A list for me, and a list for you," she repeated.

Amanda ignored the papers and kissed her mother's cheek. "Good morning, Mother. You certainly are full of energy this morning."

"I have been in the doldrums too long. We cannot afford to waste any more time. I have always thought the summer the best time to look for a husband. Other women simply melt away as if husbands only come out in the spring and shrivel up for the rest of the year. I have been making lists." She forced one of the papers into Amanda's hand. "This one is for you. What do you think?"

Amanda glanced at her list. Names, some familiar, many new. "I am sure—"

Mother smiled patiently. "I am sure I know what you are going to say. None of them suit. But you have not even looked. And this time you simply must cooperate. Notice, I put Mr. Royston on your list. He is too young for me, but not too old for you any more."

"He is a gaseous old windbag."

"I admit he talks a bit too much, but so kind. And a splendid family. Please don't cross him off just yet. Now, about Lord Mendenhall, do you want him? Or shall I keep him?"

"You may keep them all." Mother had buried her fourth husband more than a year ago. She had waited a full month longer than Amanda expected before beginning her search for a new one. "You have my permission to do all the marrying for both of us."

"I wish I could, but this time I am resolved. I will not marry before you." She tightened her lips and nodded her head emphatically. As if that physical punctuation would make that a believable statement! "Now we need to go over the lists, because what we do will depend on whom we choose. I know Cecil Fanshaw will be in Brighton for the summer, Lord Mendenhall as well."

"Please, Mother, I will help you choose, but—"

"But nothing. This time we will be together. I do believe I am quite ready." Mother let her list flutter to the coverlet and patted her hair. "I had Yvette put a little something in my hair to brighten the color. I think it is much better, don't you?"

Amanda thought her brightened looks had more to do with the sparkle in her eyes than the color of her hair. Mother was never happier than when rummaging for a husband. "You look lovely." Impulsively Amanda squeezed her hand, moving aside a crumpled newspaper to sit on the edge of the bed.

"I had her take away my black and gray gowns. I am sure it is time to move into lavender. Maybe even some lighter shades as well. Now, what do you really think of Mendenhall? Shall we go to Brighton?"

Amanda started to protest, then realized this might be just the bargaining chip she was looking for. "You have forgotten Lord Rexford. If we are going to be making plans, perhaps you need to suggest that he consider scheduling his visit for another time."

Mother clapped her hands with the enthusiasm of a seven-

year-old. "No. I hadn't forgotten him at all. Isn't he splendid? I am sure he is quite the reason I am in such fine fettle
this morning. So clever of you to lure him here all on your
own."

"I did not lure him here," Amanda said dryly. "I merely
fished him out of the river." She mentally regretted she had
not had sense enough to consider throwing him back. "In
any case, his timing is most inconsiderate."

"Oh, not a bit. We cannot leave for at least a month, what
with your tedious race. And of course, I cannot go anywhere
with gowns in only the dullest shades or two years out of
fashion." She crossed her arms across her chest and shuddered as if the imagined garments caused physical pain. "My
plan is for you to practice on him here for a month. Then,
if for some reason you deem him unsuitable, we shall go
wherever you choose."

Amanda almost smiled at the prospect of informing the
toplofty Rexford that Mother had declared him merely a
training exercise. "I have already decided he will not suit.
Not for a month. Not even for a day." She lowered her voice
to communicate her suspicion. "Mother, I think he has designs on—"

Mother's mouth had already rounded in delighted horror.
She liked nothing better than delicious gossip about who had
designs on whom.

"The birds," Amanda finished.

Titillated enthusiasm changed to impatience. "Oh,
Amanda. I knew those wretched birds were a mistake. But
you and Margaret would have them." She buried her face in
her hands. "It is all my fault. Leaving you for her to raise.
But my own sister's daughter. How could I have known?"
She produced the expected tears, just enough to make her
blue eyes glisten. This was a scene Mother did exceedingly
well, no matter how many times she replayed it.

Amanda settled back. She could let her mind wander while
she endured ten minutes of Mother's self-castigation.

"How could I have left my only child, left her with the
daughter of that . . . that barbarian . . ." To mother, civiliza-

tion ended at England's northern border, and she had never forgiven her sister for marrying a wealthy Scottish rake. He had remained "that barbarian" until the day he died.

The barbarian was, of course, Margaret's rollicking, horse-breeding father whose only crime had been to allow Margaret to grow up at his side rather than in some stuffy drawing room.

Margaret, Amanda's surrogate parent, mentor, and friend, had come from Scotland to stay for a few months when Amanda was seven, and stayed for eleven years. While Mother talked of the horror of Amanda's childhood, Amanda pictured morning rides across dew-drenched hills, late night talks in front of a roaring fire with Margaret, who in the end married her Rodney.

Amanda drew her gaze from the window. Mother would finish soon. She had reached the what-else-could-I-do stage.

"I had just gotten married. We could never have traveled the places Charles wanted to go. Not with a child. You don't blame me, do you, dear?" She searched Amanda's face for the forgiveness she sought. "No, of course you don't. You refuse to believe there is anything wrong with all these in-dependent notions of yours." As quickly as it began, the storm ended. Mother lowered her hands from her face and smiled. "But I am sure we can fix all that. A month with Lord Rexford, then we can . . . What were you saying about Rexford? Something about the birds. Tell me again. I prom-ise not to get upset."

"I said I think he is here only because of the birds. He is much too interested in them."

"How wonderful. That should make it doubly nice for you. To be perfectly honest, that is the most difficult part of finding you a husband. If Lord Rexford likes the birds, why, the deed is half done."

"But he doesn't like the birds. He may even want to harm them." Even to Amanda, the suspicion sounded absurd when spoken aloud. She pictured how gently Rexford had held the injured bird. He could not have feigned the compassion on his face.

Mother patted her hand. "Why would an earl come all the way from London to hurt your birds? The best I could hope for would be that he might not notice them."

Amanda would have given up if she had not been so certain things were not as they seemed. "The race. Maybe he does not want me to win the race."

"That is absurd."

Part of Amanda agreed, the other part remembered. "No, it is not. It is just like when I sent my best birds to Canterbury two years ago. That time somebody talked Jeb into giving my prize birds to him. I never saw them until two weeks after the race when they finally came flying home. I will not let that happen again. Rexford is just too eager to ask after them. I want you to tell him to leave. Today."

"Now, dear, you know I cannot do that. Especially not after I just finished asking him to stay. It would be so . . . so . . . just not the thing."

"But the birds—"

"Oh, bother the birds, Amanda." Mother shook her head impatiently. "This is a splendid earl we are talking about. Certainly a match like that is worth a few birds." Her voice softened. "Think how many birds there are in the world. And only a very few eligible earls."

"But—"

"Please, don't be difficult. If you are so concerned about the birds, send them to Margaret. She would not mind a bit, and her charming husband is so patient about things like that."

"But I need them here these last few weeks."

"Not as much as you need Lord Rexford." Mother rang the bell next to her bed, summoning Yvette. "Now run along, dear. I need to get into the village today and order some new material to be sent from London."

"But—"

"No!" Amanda recoiled from one of her mother's rare sharp noes. "As long as you insist on hiding yourself down here, I cannot afford to waste any gentleman who does not have the pox." Her mother tossed back the pink coverlet,

87

ignoring the books and papers, which tumbled to the floor. ''And you might try putting on a more attractive gown and letting Lily do something about your hair. That way Lord Rexford would have something far more attractive than birds to think about.''

Amanda considered another protest, but her mother's mind had already shifted to the subject of appearance. Once she locked onto that topic Amanda would be lucky to escape with less than a twenty-minute harangue on how she refused to make an effort and would never catch a husband unless . . . She bent and kissed her mother's cheek.

Mother smiled her pleasure. ''Thank you, darling. Please understand, I am only concerned about your happiness.''

Amanda forced a smile and hurried from the room. She wanted to be angry, but Mother was truly only concerned about her happiness. Unfortunately, to Mother happiness and husband were synonymous. How she could still believe that after the wrenching grief she had endured with the death of each husband, Amanda never understood. She herself had been only five at the time of her father's death, but she still remembered the black void left by his passing. She closed her eyes to the memory. She had more important problems to deal with.

Mother would never invite Rexford to leave. Amanda would have to do that in her own way. But she did have a plan. With a smile she turned and headed toward the library.

Rexford sat in a brocade-covered armchair in the library, idly reading a book of old reports on Napoleon's campaigns. If he could learn how the man thought, he would be better able to predict where the wily general would make his stand. The click of heels on the marble floor alerted him to an impending visit.

Furtively he glanced around for a place to hide the book, then stopped himself. No need for stealth. It was just the kind of thing an inactive soldier might read. But the startled reflex alerted him to something he had only been marginally aware of. Miss Langley was a long way from the slightly dotty spinster he had visualized. He found himself guarding every word in her presence, and was still uncertain whether he had aroused her suspicion.

As he expected, she entered without knocking. "Good morning, my lord."

He pushed himself to his feet and bowed. "I am sorry I did not rise early enough to join you with the birds. Jeb told me you had come and gone."

"That is quite all right." She seated herself in an armchair separated from his by a round rosewood table. "I take it that means you do not feel you learned enough yesterday." Still smiling politely, she picked up the book he had set down and glanced at the title.

"Hardly. I have been waiting impatiently." He glanced at the book. "Struggling to find ways to fill the time until we could resume our charming—"

She raised an eyebrow and let the corner of her mouth curl up, but did not precisely call him an out-and-outer.

"Well, perhaps charming is a bit much," he went on. "But I am still terribly committed to learning everything I must." He debated using a ten-guinea smile to convey his enthusiasm, then decided not to waste it. She had already said balderdash to his enthusiasm with her eyebrow.

"Splendid. Shall we begin?" she said.

Obviously he hadn't generated too much suspicion. She was still willing to teach. "Certainly." He rose. "Though perhaps I should change into the coat I wore yesterday. The birds seemed so fond of that one." He gave a wry grin. "As I am of this one."

She stopped him with a raised hand. "That won't be necessary. We can accomplish everything we need right here."

"Here?" He almost ducked, picturing the birds flapping about the closed room. "But the birds—"

"You have seen the birds. What you need now is knowledge, and this library is full of that."

"But I thought . . . the birds . . ." He didn't know what he thought. Or what she thought. He settled for a questioning look.

"To be perfectly honest, the birds were a little erratic this morning. No reflection on you, but they do seem to react to the presence of strangers. I have decided to confine our study to this room."

"They certainly did not seem upset yesterday. In fact one happy couple even . . ." He stopped and gave her time to remember and flush. The notion of handling a slight case of nerves in that particular way even generated a slight tinge of envy. He repressed the thought of the pigeons' unenthusiastic coupling and dealt with the problem posed with the directness she seemed to expect. "What are you suggesting?"

"Well, as I mentioned, you have seen the birds. They are very much the same today as they were yesterday. No need for you to view them, or even go near them again." He might have imagined the hint of steel in her voice, but it seemed to match the flinty look in her eyes. She paused long enough to give him the full impact of tone and look. "You can learn everything you need right here."

"But . . ."

She swept her arms in a gesture that called his attention to the shelves full of books. "It is all right here. Every book of any merit ever written on the subject of birds. And I will be happy to direct you to the best ones." A hint of crimson spread over her face, giving it an almost girlish look. "I have even written . . . a very modest effort, of course, but . . ." She rose and walked toward one of the shelves.

She did not see his fingers curl in frustration. *A very neat flank attack, Miss Langley.* She had just denied him access to the birds and threatened to bore him to death with one . . . two . . . three . . . He kept mental count as she selected five worn volumes from the shelves. By claiming to possess birds subject to the vapors, she expected to chain him to a desk without ever bringing whatever suspicion she had into the open where he could deal with it rationally. "Books are never a substitute for personal experience," he observed.

She offered a smile of challenging innocence and set the tomes on a long narrow table in front of an uncomfortable-looking straight-backed chair. "I am sure you will enjoy these. They are most informative."

He stood, refusing to give her the advantage of looking down at him. "If I wanted to do my learning from books, I could have stayed in London and sent my man out for them."

A hint of triumph flashed in her eyes. "I thought that might occur to you. I do not usually lend my books, but if you wish to take these to London . . ."

"I wish . . ." He did not finish the thought, because a gentleman simply never verbalized a desire to turn his hostess over his knee. He took the four paces necessary to bring him face-to-face with her across the table.

She continued as if he had neither moved nor spoken. "Or if you wish for more practical experience with the birds, I would suggest Michael McHenry in Scotland. I don't believe he plans to race this year, so he should have plenty of time. I could write to him—"

"You are still angry with me, aren't you?"

She met his gaze directly.

At any other time the challenge in her flashing green eyes would have had him circling the table to show her how quickly anger could be turned into far more interesting emotions.

"Angry with you? Why should I be? Simply because you hocus-pocused Mother into inviting you for an indefinite stay?"

"So you plan to punish me by confining me in here with those . . . those—"

"Punish? What an incredibly odious thing to say." She didn't actually smile, but laughter bubbled in her voice and her eyes. The minx was enjoying herself. "After I just confessed to writing a small treatise on the subject." She pulled back the chair. "Here, sit, Lord Rexford, while I see if I can locate my manuscript." Her look challenged him to do anything else.

With halting steps he rounded the table and sat, well and truly a prisoner of his own declared interest.

She leaned over his shoulder and opened the first book to the first page. "This book starts with the eggs. An excellent place to begin."

The illustration at the top of the page showed exactly what he expected. An egg. With a glance he learned all he wanted to know on the subject and wondered if she would notice if he skipped to the next chapter. She drew back. The movement stirred the air behind him. He forgot about skipping to the next chapter.

The hairs on the back of his neck reached out.

Face-to-face, Miss Langley was a perfectly ordinary, even severe-looking female. Out of sight only the woman mattered. His body tingled with the awareness of her behind him. He wanted her to return, perhaps even place her hand over the tingling hairs.

Rexford closed his eyes and savored the sensation. Realistically, if she had this power to rouse him in undefined ways, he needed to be aware of it. He listened to the whisper of her skirts behind him and the soft thunk of the books as she moved them on the shelves. Undefined senses measured the distance between them—less than a foot.

"This is an interesting book." Her voice came from the charged air behind him. "An excellent one, but I don't think you are ready for it yet."

He blocked out the words, and listened just to the alluring sound of her voice. Not the palpable sensuality she used with the birds, but deep and strangely stirring. Experience told him the rising awareness he felt was rarely one-sided. Perhaps she felt a similar attraction for him. He opened his eyes and stored the possibility for future use.

A moment later, Miss Langley returned to his side, close, but not close enough to satisfy the craving he had just discovered. She placed a home-bound book on top of the pile. "This is my contribution." She moved to the other side of the table to face him. "I plan to go into the village with Mother this afternoon." Her smile, which she would innocently call polite, was like a gauntlet thrown between them.

"But I will be certain to reserve some time before dinner to discuss what you have learned."

He bit back his first three replies, which all began with *Dammit*. "Thank you. I shall look forward to it." He would look forward to a renewed encounter, though certainly not to a discussion of creatures crawling out of eggshells.

She turned and walked to the library door. There she paused, her hand on the frame, and twisted to face him. Her dull gown draped nicely over some very interesting curves. "By the way, I have warned Jeb again about letting strangers near the birds. Not that he would ever deliberately harm you, but . . ." She let the picture linger long enough for him to get a clear mental image of Jeb inexpertly fumbling with a musket. "I only mention it because he is still frightfully annoyed about your breaking the dam. He might not be as careful as he should about remembering you are a guest."

He responded with his best parting shot. "Thank you."

After she left, he exercised remarkable restraint and did not sweep the books onto the floor. He sprang out of the chair, which hit the shelves behind him with a crack. Four steps brought him to the far wall. He turned on his heel and paced in the other direction while he reduced the conversation to its essence. *Do not go near my birds or I will have you shot. Here are enough books to bore you into fleeing for the nearest town. If you want to leave, I will lend you a horse.* All couched in excessively polite terms, but nevertheless, unmistakably clear.

He stared out the window to review his alternatives. Ten seconds later he had eliminated his first choice. Even if he could identify the birds that could fly to Brussels—which he couldn't—he still could not pack up and leave. He had to remain on hand to intercept messages coming here from the Continent under the guise of innocent messages from Gully. Even with Miss Langley's hostility, the house was more comfortable than skulking around and watching from a nearby hill.

Almost as rapidly, he eliminated his other favorite choice. English law was incredibly specific about marching one's hostess around at gunpoint to secure cooperation. Jeb had seemed friendly enough earlier and might have been duped into cooperating, but that was before the formidable Miss Langley had reminded Jeb of the dam and given him permission to shoot on sight.

After ten full minutes, Rexford accepted his only option, playing Miss Langley's game and beating her at it. At any other time he would have welcomed the challenge, but now . . .

Her dedication to winning rivaled his own. He straightened his spine and turned to face the door where she had stood moments before. "Choose your weapons, Miss Langley. This should be interesting."

From the corner of his eye he spotted the table laden with books. "Intermittently interesting," he amended.

He listened to the bustle of activity that signaled the departure of the Langley women, then drifted out to test Jeb's alertness. He found the bulky young man whistling tunelessly and raking the clearing in front of the cote. His head snapped up at the sound of Rexford's approach, and he ducked into a shed to trade his rake for a musket.

"Afternoon, Jeb. I am just out for a stroll. I thought we could chat."

"Can't do that." Jeb's big hands grappled with the musket until it eventually pointed to a spot on the ground a few feet to Rexford's left. "Miss Langley said I was to shoot any strangers." His brow furrowed. "She said you was a stranger even though we know your name. That don' seem right, but she said."

"I am sure she didn't mean that. Tell me about those birds there." He pointed to the section of the aviary with the special birds.

"I have ta ask Miss Langley if I can do that, 'stedda shoot."

"No need for that, Jeb."

"Yes." Jeb gave a series of slow nods, the barrel of the musket occasionally touching the ground. "Yes. I have ta ask, or else I have ta shoot you. An' that don' seem right."

Rexford tried a few more questions, but the earnest young man was so distracted by the question of whether or not to shoot that the answers were less than satisfactory.

Four hours later he had changed "intermittently interesting" to fiendishly dull. He wanted nothing more than to be done with the entire mission. He glanced at the clock for the forty-second time. Tag should have returned from the village an hour ago with a packet of messages from the Continent. With all his soul Rexford prayed one of those messages would be his release from bird-bondage. He had sent a very cogent letter directly to the Duke of Wellington listing the dozen reasons why any coxcomb could replace him here.

The sound of the soft shoes Miss Langley had worn to the village informed Rexford that he would have to deal with her first. Feeling like a disobedient schoolboy, he quickly closed the book on Napoleon and opened a worn volume that should have been titled *Birds You Could Learn to Despise*. He pasted a pleasant smile on his face.

Prescott opened the library door, then had to scurry aside before her breezy entrance. She looked far less formidable in a sprigged muslin gown, her hair still pulled back, but much softer about the face.

Her feminine appearance reminded him he had removed his coat and probably tied his hair in knots by running his fingers through it in frustration. "Good afternoon, Miss Langley. I trust you had a pleasant outing."

"Extremely. I hope your time was equally enjoyable. I just stopped by to see if you had any questions about your reading." She offered a smile that on a smaller woman might have been called impish.

"My only question is why I must limit my learning to ancient tomes on such a pleasant day as this."

"Books are excellent teachers."

"They are no substitute for experience."

Her gaze darted to the book he had closed, but neglected to tuck under the open volume. "You seem to be doing quite well with Napoleon."

Rexford shrugged. "I don't have to breed and train Napoleon."

She settled herself in a chair to one side of the table. "I am tempted to doubt your dedication to this project. Suppose you tell me what you have learned."

"I confess to being a bit disconcerted by the information that if I hold a candle to an egg, I can see tiny little bird bones inside. It makes me quite resolved to choose biscuits over eggs in the future."

She gave a disapproving frown. "Not bird bones! The infinitesimal beginning of life. Quite a miracle. Not only is it a privilege to view it, but it is a very important piece of information, in spite of your levity. You would scarcely want a valuable hen to waste seventeen days sitting on an egg that has no hope of producing." She frowned at the appalling thought. "Tomorrow I will show you how it is done."

Rexford bit back a reply that would not have displayed adequate gratitude. Her voice interrupted a rather pleasant mental stream of caustic remarks.

"I trust that is not the extent of your learning. Perhaps there is something else that merits discussion?"

Rexford considered confessing he had skipped to the chapter on the sex life of pigeons and found that even less interesting than holding a candle to an egg. But she had already given him her opinion on levity. "Not at this point. The information is quite sufficient to . . ."

"Quite sufficient to make you ready to return to London?"

"Not as long as there is hope you may get over this silly notion that I deserve to be flogged with a stack of books, when what I am asking is so reasonable."

"Then I suggest you begin packing. If not, then I hope tomorrow's study is somewhat more productive than today's. At your current rate of progress you will probably still be sitting here at Michaelmas." She rose and swept out of the library before he could think of a reply.

Chapter Six

Tag spoke, the butler laughed. Tag spoke again. He could at least have the decency to hurry, Rexford thought. The library door opened.

Rexford waited until Tag stepped in and closed the door behind him before giving rein to his impatience. "You could deliver the dispatches before entertaining the servants." He rounded the desk and held out his hand for the leather pouch.

"And a splendid afternoon to you too." Tag handed him the case.

"What is in here?" Rexford hurriedly undid the buckle. "My message from Brussels?"

"A whole packet from the Dover boat. I assume most of them are from Brussels, but I figured you would have me drawn and quartered if I stopped to sort through them just so I could answer your questions for you."

Rexford muttered his usual curse, shoved the bird books aside, and started to dump the contents onto the table. He hesitated. "I believe we had better take these to my bedchamber. Miss Langley has an annoying habit of bursting in without notice, and I don't want to keep looking over my shoulder while we sort through these."

97

On the short trip upstairs he fought to control his impatience to get at the message that might release him from confinement in the library and give him permission to rejoin his regiment. He belonged with his men, not in East Sussex reading about birds.

In the room, he dumped the contents of the pack on the bed and sorted through the documents until he found one with the Duke's unmistakable stamp. This he opened with impatient fingers. He read and crumpled the paper in his fist. "Dammit, dammit, dammit."

Tag's eyebrows rose. "I take it we need not pack for Brussels."

Rexford tossed the wadded white paper across the bed. The message contained a single line, *I prefer you remain where you are*, followed by the distinctive signature.

Tag's disappointment had to be as deep as his own, deeper perhaps because he had never seen the true horror of battle, but his face remained in his customary nonchalant expression. "Doesn't waste a lot of words, does he?" Tag dropped the paper on the coverlet and reached for another dispatch. "One from Grant as well. Perhaps he is a touch more eloquent." He handed the letter to Rexford and came around the bed to read over his shoulder.

Grant, unfortunately, said precisely the same thing as the Duke, only in a great many more words. He could not take the risk of having his intelligence headquarters buried under two columns of infantry. Anyplace closer than Dover was too close. Langwood was ideal.

Wellington and Grant shared the obsessive fear that Napoleon would deploy his troops between Brussels and the Channel, cutting off both supplies and communication. If that happened, then the birds Rexford spoke so disparagingly of would become the only certain way of getting a message through.

Tag stepped back and nodded. "I can't say he is wrong, Marc."

"Right or wrong, any lobcock can sit and coddle a flock of birds. I told them that. I told them even you could—"

"Oh, splendid. Remind me to thank you for your vote of confidence."

"I only meant—"

Tag grinned. "I know what you meant."

Rexford forced himself to unclench his fists. "You have to forgive me, I have had a rather depressing afternoon. But dammit, Tag, it feels so cowardly to be playing foolish games here. Why me?"

Tag raised his eyebrows and answered with a wordless nod at Rexford's left arm.

Rexford scowled. "There is nothing wrong with me." He rotated his shoulder, ignoring the arrows of pain that shot through his upper body. "Look. Not a twinge."

Tag winced, but his tone held no hint of sympathy. "Good job of controlling your face, but you forget, I can see your eyes. Let that thing heal." He returned his attention to Grant's message. "I assume you noticed his closing line."

The line, *Regarding the problem with the birds—solve it*, had engraved itself on Rexford's brain. "I saw it. I certainly didn't make much progress this afternoon."

"I suspected from your beaming countenance that might be the case. What happened?"

"I spent the day in the library reading about birds. That's what happened."

Tag's face brightened with amused comprehension. "Always your favorite pastime. Ranks right up there with charging into enemy artillery. Now I understand your mood." He chuckled. "Learn anything interesting?"

As always Tag's good humor was contagious. "More than you ever want to know about the sexual preferences of birds."

"Try me. Sex is one of my favorite subjects, you understand."

Rexford laughed. "Now that you mention it, birds are very much like females. More interested in a long-term relationship than in the act itself. You would not believe the things they have those poor males doing."

"At least they don't have them lying around for hours

afterwards thinking up pretty compliments.'' He slapped Rexford on the shoulder. ''Sorry for your troubles, old man, but shall we get to work on this business?'' He dropped down to sit cross-legged on the bed and shuffled through the pile. ''Here is one from my father.''

Rexford watched the younger man's eyes until he stopped reading. ''Does he say anything interesting?''

''He sends you his regards. Said to tell you you're not the only one living in bird dung. Several of Grant's people are carrying a bird when they go into France. In case they have to get a message out in a hurry.''

''How the hell do they do that?''

''He doesn't say. Knowing my father, he probably just tucks in his shirt.''

''Better him than me.''

''Actually he rather likes the idea of the birds. He said to tell you they are going to need a whole bunch more Langley birds over there before this thing is over.'' Tag grinned mischievously. ''The rest of the message might sting a speck.''

''Get on with it.''

''If you don't ship some birds over there soon, he plans to come back here and give you a few lessons in coaxing a lady into cooperating.''

Rexford laughed. ''Encourage him by all means. And I want to be there when Miss Langley sits him down to read about tiny birds coming out of shells. His language should send the library up in flames.'' He dismissed his lingering smile with a head shake. ''I trust his information above the rest of what we are getting. Does he say anything of note?''

''Just says it is impossible to tell which side those country people are on. One day a man is for the king, and the next day he is so hoarse from shouting Napoleon's name he can't even talk at all. Says half the information we are getting here isn't worth the paper it's written on.''

''About what I figured.'' Rexford tensed. ''Does he give you the feeling he is running about behind the lines out of uniform?''

Tag grimaced. "Drat! I hope not. Those Frogs hung a man they caught out of uniform last week."

"Forget I said it. He has better sense. Also too proud of the way he looks in scarlet. Shall we get at the rest of this?"

For the next hour the two read, sorted through the messages from the Continent, made notes, and moved miniature flags about on the map, trying to predict the site Napoleon would eventually choose.

Tag sighed and rubbed his temples. "Too damn much information." He lowered a hand to rest on a ragged pile of papers. "I particularly like these reports of where Napoleon has been sighted. Calais, Ostend, Antwerp, and twice in Ghent. And those are just the ones where the idiot reporting is absolutely certain he saw Napoleon."

Rexford laughed, "You forgot the loose screw who saw him in Dover."

"Do you believe any of them?"

Rexford waved a dismissive hand. "Not unless Napoleon is the devil himself. According to these he was in Paris until two days ago." He pointed to three reports of a celebration Napoleon had held on the first of June. "My guess is he will head toward the border now." He placed his finger on the spot on the map less than one hundred miles from Paris. "He certainly is working hard to make us believe he is going to fight right here."

"But you don't believe it?"

"Half of this information is coming from informants he planted." Rexford combed his fingers through his hair. "But how the hell am I supposed to judge from this distance? Like everyone else, we will just have to wait for more information and hope we can get the word to Wellington in time." He looked at the ceiling with tired eyes. "Who knows? Maybe the damn birds will turn out to be important. Maybe I will be glad I didn't make soup out of the lot of them."

Tag uncurled his legs, unmindful of the smudge of dirt his boots left on the coverlet. He bounced to his feet. "I do have some other news. The cote in Oxford, the one you set up as a diversion . . ."

Rexford nodded.

"Someone attacked it two nights ago. Killed all the birds and two men guarding them."

"Bloody hell." Rexford stomped several paces across the room before turning to face Tag again. "Nobody knew about that cote but . . ."

Tag nodded. "But the people in the War Department. You were right. There is a traitor. It gets worse, though."

Rexford fought to block out a picture of Miss Langley holding an injured bird to her cheek. "What could be worse? Lord Batterton is here. I doubt his arrival in the neighborhood is pure coincidence."

"There is a distinct possibility your suspicions are justified this time. Whoever is passing on the information knows you are involved. Peter got a message at the inn from your butler. Somebody was making very persistent inquiries on your whereabouts. The message didn't say what made your man think it serious enough to inform you, but—"

"Dawson is nobody's fool. If he didn't like the inquiries, he had his reasons." Rexford's fist tightened. It was one thing for a soldier to march off into battle, but something else to lead a man like Batterton to this tranquil place. "We have to set a guard."

"Miss Langley is not going to like that."

"Miss Langley doesn't like much of anything. But she would like it even less if she got herself killed protecting her precious flock." Rexford clenched his teeth and closed his mind to the possibility. "I will simply have to think of some way of setting a guard on them without her knowing."

"No chance of just telling her how badly we need them?"

"No chance of my telling her much of anything today. She has these damn fool notions about how everyone is trying to keep her from winning that idiot race." He paused and gave an amused smile. "Do you know she half believes Napoleon escaped from Elba just to provide a diversion for anyone who might want to attack her birds?"

Tag laughed. "Talk at the inn says she is a bit of a queer duck, but I had a suspicion you liked her."

Rexford struggled to think of an appropriate response. Tag would probably condemn him to a ten-day stay in the nearest brothel if he confessed some of his thoughts about the improbable Miss Langley. "Let us just say, I respect her—hell, if Wellington had her in his headquarters, Napoleon would probably go slinking back to his island and send an apology by the first post."

"I hate to be the one to remind you, but that message from Grant does not leave you much time to come up with a plan for dealing with her."

Rexford's shoulders tensed. "I am aware of that, and I am open to suggestions. Anything short of chaining her and her musket-wielding servant to a post. In the meantime I hope you have someone in place watching from the hills for incoming messages. We cannot afford to miss one."

"Peter and Chumley are sharing that duty. Peter did nothing but complain about it all afternoon. Told me to ask if you have any idea how many birds there are flying around this place."

"Tell him at least they are not flying around his face." Rexford reached for a pen in preparation for the report he had to complete before dinner. "Don't you have something you should be doing?"

Tag laughed. "That sounds suspiciously like a dismissal. And the answer is no. I must remember to ask my valet what he does with all his time when he is not valeting. I sit about my room and can't think of a single thing to do."

"I suspect that is because your valet is infinitely more competent at his position than you are. You might practice tying a neckcloth. My man would break into tears if he saw me today."

"You are not the only one who is tired of looking a fright." Tag paused by the looking glass and gave an exaggerated shudder. "Oh, well, I am off to contemplate the walls."

For Rexford, the next day followed a depressingly similar pattern. He made what he considered an eloquent appeal to join Miss Langley with the pigeons. She assigned more reading. He wore out his eyes learning more than any human being should know about the creatures, had a few pleasant sensual fantasies about his tutor, and ended the afternoon berating Tag for his lack of sympathy. Just before dinner he came up with the ghost of a plan to reunite him with Miss Langley and the birds.

At dinner that night he appealed to his only ally.

"Do I look a bit pale to you, Lady Harriet?" Unfortunately the seating arrangement had him on Lady Harriet's right, but looking directly across the table at her daughter. He could not miss the flare of skepticism in his opponent's eyes.

"Oh, dear. Are you ill?" Lady Harriet looked at him with enough concern to ignite some smoldering embers of guilt. "We must send for a doctor immediately."

He brushed aside the suggestion. "Not ill. Just a bit peaked. Your daughter has been keeping me so occupied with books, I have not had a chance to get out much." He managed to give the glowering daughter a fond glance without actually meeting her narrowed eyes. "To say nothing of furthering my acquaintance with her."

"Oh, Amanda! You have not been *making* him read those tedious books on birds, have you?"

Miss Langley gave him a honeyed smile and turned her beguilingly innocent look on her mother. "Of course not. Lord Rexford is fascinated with the birds. Is that not so, my lord?"

"Naturally. Except when your time with them deprives me so completely of your company."

Lady Harriet glanced from one to the other. "Oh, my, such sparks." She relaxed with a pleased smile.

"Please, Lady Harriet, have some pity on me. Coax her to let me spend some time with the birds—and her."

"Of course. I am sure she never intended to exclude you. Tomorrow, Amanda . . ."

Rexford prayed he managed to conceal the surge of triumph. Not merely pride at a victory for his mission, but a glow from besting a worthy opponent. A calculating glance from the green eyes across the table warned him not to savor his success too quickly.

"An excellent suggestion, Mother. Though you know I am never at my best when I am with the birds. You are forever talking about the plain gowns I must wear." She turned to Rexford and spoke with the air of a patient tutor, but her eyes danced with challenge. "My gowns must be laundered so frequently I cannot have the maids forever picking off the trim and sewing it back on. I do hate anybody seeing me in such dismal attire."

Lady Harriet had begun nodding at the mention of the gowns, and continued nodding even as she spoke. "I quite agree, but . . ." Her head finally stopped bobbing.

Since disagreement about the attractiveness of the gowns would make him look like a nodcock on the subject of fashion, and agreement might foster defeat, Rexford kept silent.

"Perhaps Lord Rexford and I could think of some other activity where I need not appear quite so plain. And the birds are so distracting, Mother. You know that. Perhaps—"

Lady Harriet clasped her hands. "I have just the thing. A picnic. I will have cook prepare a basket and you two can ride. I am sure one groom will be much less a distraction than all those dreadful birds. Amanda, you can wear your new riding habit, and you two can get to know one another."

Rexford finally collected himself enough for a protest. "But I like the birds."

Lady Harriet gave him a benevolent smile. "Of course you do. I do too. But in their place. This will be so much nicer."

Rexford managed a polite smile, though the effort hurt his jaw. "I shall look forward to the outing." *And to a renewed encounter,* he thought. The fire in the eyes across the table could not be merely candlelight.

The hint of laughter in her voice confirmed his suspicion. "Don't worry, my lord, you should have ample time in the morning to continue with your books."

Lady Harriet signaled for the footman to clear the plates, then turned to Rexford. "I am so glad you reminded me. We have been neglecting your entertainment shamefully. I shall also arrange to have some people come in to play cards tomorrow night. Amanda, you can wear the new gold gown if it is delivered on time.''

Rexford bowed to defeat and the prospect of a less than fascinating evening.

Rain canceled the picnic the next day, so Rexford spent the tedious hours in the library, ducking his head into the required books each time the click of Miss Langley's heels announced her approach to check on his progress. By the time the promised neighbors arrived, Rexford was no closer to gaining access to the birds than he had been the morning after he arrived. Worse, he could think of no way the evening would improve his prospects, though he vowed to be on the watch for any advantage.

The group proved an amiable mix, large enough to make up two tables and leave a few women to chat comfortably in the corners of the large drawing room. Lady Harriet, of course, managed to partner him with her daughter. Miss Langley played as he expected, with enormous skill and just a shade too much daring.

In one hand a bold move on her part cost them a modest sum. She grimaced, but immediately had the grace to apologize. ''I am sorry, Lord Rexford. Perhaps I should have opted for caution.''

''Perhaps. But if you had won—and it was a distinct possibility—I would have had nothing but praise. As it is, I enjoyed watching you play.'' The words were an understatement. He had scarcely been able to concentrate all evening. Whether to please him or her mother, she had worn a most enticing gold gown, cut low enough to reveal just the tops of creamy breasts. Even his overactive imagination had failed to visualize such richness. The candlelight and the green baize of the table had her eyes sparkling like emeralds. Loose for once, her hair tumbled over her shoulders like liquid fire. If her rashness had cost them a few points, certainly his distraction had cost more.

Rexford was astonished to find himself muttering a mental protest when Lady Harriet began ushering her guests toward the door. He did not want the evening to end.

Lady Harriet returned to the room, brushing her hands together. "What a splendid evening. I do believe everyone enjoyed themselves. Amanda, did you think Mr. Felspeth was making up to me?"

Miss Langley laughed from where she stood next to the mantel. "Of course he was. He has waited a year to do so." She crossed the room and kissed her mother's cheek. "How could he help himself? You looked lovely tonight."

Her mother preened with the compliment. "He is most unsuitable, what with his gout and all." She laughed, almost a girlish giggle. "But it is nice to know one can still attract." She looked about the empty room. "Well, I must toddle off to bed. But do not let me hurry you. I am sure you young people can stay up much later." She nodded to the expressionless footman standing just outside the door and left.

Amanda shrugged. "I warned you she does not deal in subtleties."

The gesture called Rexford's attention to her breasts—though in truth it had not wandered too far from them all evening—and the sudden awareness that they were alone in the room. Under any other circumstances . . . Under any circumstances he wanted to prolong the evening. "You play an extremely skillful game of cards, Miss Langley."

"Thank you. My cousin Margaret—the woman who raised me—learned a great deal about gambling from her father. We used to play constantly." She looked toward the door and Rexford read *good night* in the glance.

Her words gave him the glimmering of a plan—whether to improve his situation or simply to delay her exit, he did not even try to guess. But as far as his situation in her house was concerned, he could scarcely be any worse off. "Have you ever gambled for any reasonable stakes?"

"Well . . . I . . . only—"

"I thought not. You probably don't have the nerve."

She bristled right on schedule. "Why would you say that? I—"

"No need to be offended. I did not mean you specifically. Most women don't have the nerve to gamble with something important. That is why gaming clubs are for men." He carefully averted his face so she could not read his eyes.

"That is ridiculous. It is not a question of nerve. It is a question of opportunity. Why, I am sure I would match my nerve against any of the men I have met."

He raised his eyebrows and held his breath as he asked, "Against mine?"

"Certainly." She drew herself up as stiff as any man who had ever been slapped with a glove. "My father left me a sizable fortune. Mine to keep or gamble as I choose. Name your stakes, Rexford."

He gave a contemptuous wave to show what he thought of the suggestion and looked about the room. "We could scarcely gamble enough money here to intimidate either of us. I was thinking of something more meaningful—unless you want to change your mind?"

Her eyes narrowed and she turned her head a few degrees off center, but her determined stance did not change. "What are you suggesting?"

He had one moment to retreat and might have taken it, except that retreat left him exactly where he was right now— no place. "We will play for what you want against what I want."

"And that is?"

He breathed a silent apology for putting the fate of England in the hands of the muses of gambling. "I think you know. I want access to the birds. I want you to really teach me. And you want—"

"I want you to leave."

"Precisely. And that is what we play for."

Only her eyes moved, but her mental debate could not have been clearer if she waged it aloud.

Rexford's concern she would say yes changed to a fear

108

she would say no. "Unless you want to tell me now the stakes are too high for you," he said.

With a sudden decision she strode across the room and stood beside the table. Never before had he thought card-table-green a dull color, but the shade finished a dim second in a comparison with her blazing eyes. She picked up the cards. "If I win . . . ?"

"If you win, I leave." He carefully did not add *and never bother you again.* "And if I win, you do what I never expected you to refuse anyway. Teach me about the birds—with the birds."

She gave a tight-lipped nod. "Very well."

Amanda shuffled the cards. She had done it again, let Rexford manipulate her. She had broken Margaret's first rule—never gamble with something you cannot afford to lose—and she could not afford to let Rexford near her racing birds.

Every intuitive feeling insisted he could not be the tool of some cunning breeder, but she could not ignore the evidence. He had lied about his reason for coming, tricked her mother into extending the invitation, tried to gull Jeb into giving him information when she had forbidden it, and probably a host of other things she could only guess at. Always to gain access to the birds. Only the fact that he could not identify the valuable birds had protected her flock so far.

He had inveigled her with the one thing she could not resist, the temptation to see him on his way. Now she could not afford to lose. She grasped at Margaret's next inflexible rule. Never gamble with a rogue unless you are sure you are a better Captain Sharp than he. "We will play Piquet au Cent," she said with what she hoped was believable innocence. "Only one turn, and you will deal."

He arched his brows. "If we played the regulation longer game, you might learn to deal with your tension better," he said dryly.

"I am not tense, merely eager to say good-bye." She exhaled. "We will need a Piquet deck." She waited for his nod before reaching in the drawer for the familiar cards Margaret had used to teach the gambling tricks she had learned from her father. Amanda ignored her twanging conscience and drew them out.

"Allow me." Rexford held out his hand. He smiled when she dropped them into his palm. He drew out a chair and casually sat to shuffle the smaller thirty-two-card deck. He alternated between looking at her face and glancing at the cards as they slapped between his skilled fingers.

Amanda wanted to scream. He should be as impatient as she to get this over with. Instead he sat as casually as if he had just been invited for tea. She wanted to snatch the cards from his hands and deal, but that would give him the opportunity to discard and draw first, her sole advantage. "We do need to finish this game sometime tonight."

"I am confident we will." Too slowly he dealt twelve cards to each of them.

Amanda resisted the impulse to snatch at her cards as he laid them down. Even with the edge of knowing the cards, monumental bad luck could destroy her. She forced herself to move as slowly as he did, and hoped her face mimicked his casual indifference. She spread her cards and almost shouted with relief. Not an exceptional hand, but a good one.

With a start, she realized he had merely fanned his cards once, glanced at them, and closed them in his palm. He sat back watching her with patient amusement.

She refused to let his patronizing look intimidate her into hurrying while she diligently arranged her cards according to suit and value. Her heart had never pounded like this when she played with Margaret, but Margaret knew she needed time to study the cards she would draw from. She wished he would look anyplace but at her face. "Perhaps you would like to pour yourself a brandy, Lord Rexford."

"Not just yet, thank you. I enjoy watching your mind work."

Damn him. With a good imitation of a merely cautious player, she studied her hand and the cards spread between them. The position of the almost imperceptible markings in the decorative border identified them for her. The ace of spades would fill out her sequence perfectly. Twice, because of his unwavering interest, she lost track in trying to calculate his hand from the cards she held and the draw cards. Finally she was satisfied. She would win.

Slowly she discarded and drew exactly the cards she anticipated. He did the same, showing not a hint of disappointment when he picked up the seven of clubs.

"Point?" he asked.

As she expected, they tied on that and neither scored any points. "Quint," she said, claiming fifteen points for the highest sequence.

Without any change of expression, he shocked her by claiming fourteen for a set.

She had miscalculated. She would have only a one-point lead when play began. Her mouth had a dry cotton feel. She licked her lips and calculated again. She would still win if she played correctly. She led and won the first two tricks. He won the third and fourth and led to her strength.

Play continued until they were both down to two cards. Amanda began to breathe easily again. She would win, but only by a single point.

Before she could lead the next card, Rexford relaxed back in his chair. "I believe I will take that brandy now, if you don't mind."

Amanda's fingers tensed around her cards. "Can't you wait until we have finished here?"

He smiled. "And drink it alone? I think not. If you would not mind getting it, I could study my cards."

He had not bothered to study his cards all night, but she could at least fetch him a brandy after what she had done. She crossed the room and poured a single glass from the crystal decanter on the sideboard, grateful for the opportunity to let her face relax, away from his concentrated attention. She returned to the table and placed the glass in front of him.

"Thank you." He crossed one ankle over his knee and sat waiting for her next lead.

She sat and played her queen.

He casually laid an ace on top of it, drew the two cards toward him and put down his final card, a king.

Amanda stared at the card. Her face flushed with indignation. "That is not your card."

He smiled and shrugged. "Of course not. But how would you know, Miss Langley?"

Her face burned. She longed to sink under the table. She had been exposed as a cheat. She who had always been so . . . "You cheated too."

"Ahhh, but there's a difference." He shook his head, his mile warm and amused. "Not until after you did." He looked thoroughly pleased with the situation. "Sorry. You lose, my dear."

"I didn't lose. It was not a fair game. It—"

He continued to sit there, looking smug and tolerant. "That is where your inexperience tells. It is an immutable law of the universe. The person who cheats first loses, and you have well and truly lost. And I will see you at dawn with the birds."

Amanda's mouth flapped in protest, but she could not find words to put with the motion. She stood and stormed across the room. *Surely—there must be a way—surely* . . . She could not find anything to say, because everything she had ever believed told her she was completely in the wrong. Her face still sizzled. She could not get out of the room without facing him directly. She straightened her shoulders and turned toward the door. "Very well, Lord Rexford, you win. Though I find it curious you are such an expert on the subject."

"Well done, Miss Langley." His chair whispered against the carpet and she saw the shadow of his movement. He came to her side and tilted her chin up with his forefinger so she looked into his eyes, which held an unexpected gentleness. "Some day you will discover I am an expert on many things."

A flood of emotions kept her from producing a rational thought. Her knees felt weak. He released her chin and breathing became possible again.

"I have not finished my brandy." He took her elbow and guided her to the chair she had just left.

She sat, and finally remembered she wanted to get as far

away from him as possible. She glanced toward the door.

"I hope you are not thinking of leaving. We still have not had our high-stakes game. You owe me an honest one."

A spark of hope flared. Perhaps she still had a chance.

He must have read the thought in her eyes. "No. You have lost there, but perhaps there is something else we can play for, Miss Langley. I do hate that." He picked up the deck the group had played with earlier and began to shuffle.

"Hate what?"

"Hate calling you Miss Langley." He dealt twelve more cards to each of them. "Perhaps we could play for that."

"For what? My name?" Amanda eyed the cards and felt some of her starch return.

"The privilege of calling you Amanda. Amanda, I like that, you know. I would consider that name on my tongue very high stakes indeed."

"And what is in it for me? I certainly have no desire to call you—"

"Perhaps not now. But in the morning, when you think about tonight, I am sure you will think of all manner of things you would like to call me. If you win, you will have the privilege of calling me anything you like—in private, of course."

Amanda practiced a few names in her mind. He was right. By morning she would surely want to use some of them. She reached in the drawer and drew out a new deck. Ignoring the heat in her face she said, "Perhaps we should play with these."

Five minutes later he looked at her, his dark eyes twinkling. "Thank you, *Amanda. Now* what shall we play for?"

His head on a platter was Amanda's first choice. Her mind suggested a tactical retreat. "I am sure you will think of something."

"I have been thinking of something all night." His eyes challenged her to ask what. The air around the table seemed more alive than it had a moment ago.

Amanda knew better, but of course she had to ask, "What is the wager?"

He glanced significantly around the room, reminding her without words how alone they were. "The only thing any self-respecting lady and gentleman could possibly play for at this time of night. A kiss." His voice seemed to drop a full octave. "I know exactly how I would like to do it."

Amanda's breath caught in her throat. She pictured the wager. No, she pictured losing. She could not draw her gaze from his lips, softer than she had ever seen them. The smoldering look in his eyes told her he would collect on this debt with the same vengeance as on the other two. The thump of her heart said she wanted him to.

Where was her resistance?

From somewhere in the direction of her toes she found strength she didn't know she possessed. Her chin came up and her spine stiffened. "Don't push your luck, Rexford. I'd sooner kiss a toad." She dropped the cards on the table and stood. That was as good a final line as she could come up with. She hurried toward the door before he could say something that demanded a response.

His chuckle followed her. "Lucky toad."

Chapter Seven

Amanda stood in front of the aviary at dawn the next morning looking at the birds with dread in her heart. What had she done? All night she had been tortured with nightmares of Rexford in a black cloak, a dripping dagger in his hand. She brushed aside the other dreams, vivid images of his lips as dangerous as the dagger.

Grace pecked at the side of the aviary, hungry for attention. Rexford would never hurt her. He had shown too many times he was interested only in the finest birds, the racers. He could not tell one bird from another, but she would be pointing out the best that years of breeding could produce.

The obvious solution struck. He could not tell one from another, and she could not point out birds that were not here. She had promised to teach, but she had not promised to show him her racers. Hurriedly she opened the door and stepped inside. She studied the birds in the main area. Some of them were obviously of lesser quality, but others—bred exactly the same—were identical in every way except for the indefinable heart that marked a champion.

If Rexford's objective truly was to learn, he would lose

nothing by studying those birds. She mentally reviewed how she would teach, evaluated the characteristics he had to learn to recognize. They were all here in the general area, and Rexford would never know he was not looking at a bird with the dogged determination to return home first. *Oh, yes,* her mind shouted.

Amanda darted into the separated area that held her racing birds, and matched them one for one against the lesser birds. Only her personal knowledge of the individual birds enabled her to distinguish one from another. It would work. She could protect her birds from Rexford, yet not deprive him of anything unless he had lied about his intent.

She glanced toward the rising sun. She did not have much time. At any moment he might decide to collect on his wager and join her here. With shaking hands she scurried to the shed and dragged out one of the slatted boxes she used for transporting the birds. One by one she gathered each of her twelve strongest flyers and placed them in the case, replacing each with an almost identical bird from the main area.

The task took only moments. When she finished she stopped and looked at the rest of the pigeons in the special enclosure. Most of them belonged to other people, kept separate so they could not fly home until they were needed for a message. She had no right to risk them. Quickly she dragged in another case and loaded in birds from Gully in Brussels, and McHenry in the north. She selected replacements for them, but with less care because she was not as likely to use them to illustrate desirable characteristics. She added two of Margaret's birds, but left the rest, which were of indifferent quality. Margaret would not object to the risk.

In spite of her nightmares, she did not for a minute think Rexford would physically hurt the birds. She could not be that wrong about a person. Kidnap them possibly, but never purposely hurt them.

"Good morning, Miss Langley."

Amanda, stooped by the packing box, had to dig her fingertips into the ground to keep from toppling over. Her heart thudded. *Jeb. It's only Jeb.* She had to reassure herself twice

116

to quiet the pounding. To have come so close and fail would have been worse than no plan at all.

She closed the box and stood, aware of a lingering weakness in her knees. "I am glad you came early, Jeb. I want you to take these birds to your house."

Jeb's brow furrowed in the frown anything out of the ordinary produced. "Those ain't your bad birds." He usually took the birds Amanda culled from the flock and kept them as his own. He hunkered down next to the crate and wiggled his fingers between the slats. "Hi, Regina." A frown replaced the smile he had given the prize flyer. "I don' think I should take Regina."

"This is different, Jeb. I don't want you to keep these forever. Just while Lord Rexford is here." Amanda hesitated. Her reluctance to confess her suspicions made her wonder if she was being overly cautious. The move would all but destroy her training schedule. If Jeb released these birds, even for moderate exercise, they would fly directly back to this loft. Maybe . . . She straightened her spine. She could not take even the smallest risk until she knew more. "I hope it will only be for a few days."

"Do I have to let my birds all go?" His face held sadness, but no reluctance.

"No. These may make it a little crowded, but they will be all right for a few days."

"I'll take good care of them. Honest."

"Don't tell anybody about this. Not even Lord Rexford."

"I won't tell anybody. I won't even tell—" He broke off with a frown and studied her face. "You said he is a stranger. I can tell him I will shoot if he comes near."

"Not any more, Jeb. We are going to let him near the birds. But we don't have to let him near these birds. That's why I want you to take them to your house."

"I like shooting better." He smiled. "You tell me if we change again." He picked up the crates and walked to the door of the enclosure.

Amanda stepped around him and opened the door. "I will send a message to you if I want you to let the birds out for

117

exercise." Surely Rexford would not be about all the time. "But be sure to come right over here so you can take them home again."

"I'll do everything right. I promise."

He disappeared, and Amanda exhaled a sigh of relief. She looked in the direction of the house for some sign of Rexford. If her suspicions were correct, she had just turned last night's defeat into a victory. Better even than if she had succeeded in sending him away.

Whoever sent him had tried twice, once with him and once with the paperskull Dalton, who thought she would let a random regiment of soldiers near her birds. If she had sent Rexford off, she would never know where the next danger might come from. This way she could let Rexford play out his game and try to best him at it.

She smiled. With the birds safe she might even enjoy teaching the earl who liked to win that he could not always have things his way. "You darlings may be going on a vacation," she warned the milling birds. "But it will be fun. It may be we will all have fun."

Rexford added his signature to the page of tightly scripted words. When the alternative had been reading how pigeon tails distinguished good birds from indifferent ones, he had planned to linger over the report. Now he could not wait to be out in the morning air with his contentious Amanda.

He stood, crossed his bedchamber floor, and pounded on the door connecting Tag's room to his. Opening it, he called into the darkened room. "Wake up. You cannot be planning to spend this glorious morning in bed." Only an innocent would expect a reply in less than ten minutes, so Rexford walked to the window to contemplate the day.

Early morning sun threw patches of light and shade across the landscape. Tall trees bent and straightened with the erratic breeze, and everything looked wonderfully clean. The slow padding of bare feet alerted him to Tag's reluctant arrival. Rexford spoke without turning. "Take a look, Tag.

This is what morning looks like. It is magnificent and you've been missing it all these years.''

Tag's groan sounded like a cow giving birth. ''Tell me you did not haul me out of bed to announce the sun had risen again today.'' He stood in the center of the room, his feet wide apart, his hands awkwardly fumbling his shirttails into his pantaloons.

''It is a sight worth viewing.'' Rexford laughed. ''You could learn to appreciate it.''

''God's britches, I prefer you surly in the morning. What is going on?''

Rexford had been grinning all the time he wrote the report, so another grin came as naturally as the morning sun. ''I believe our troubles are over.''

Tag finished with his shirt and dropped down to sit on the bed. ''You got me out of bed to say you talked Miss Langley into going to France and personally defeating Napoleon.''

''Not quite. But she has agreed to give us access to the birds.''

''Well done! How did you accomplish that?'' He sat up straighter on the bed and laughed. ''You've been using a rack. I did hear a rumor she was getting taller.''

Rexford shook his head. ''Nothing quite so crude. Amanda has a weakness for gambling.''

Tag's eyes widened. ''Amanda is it? Sounds like she has a weakness for more than gambling.''

''Same weakness. After we played for access to the birds, we played for her name. The formidable Miss Langley is now the gentle Amanda.''

''And fortunately you are invulnerable.''

Rexford remembered how his entire body had tensed when he suggested the third game. In the cool light of morning it was easy to believe he had merely been responding to the challenge, not to some unbridled passion for a caustic lady past her prime. He laughed. ''I may have a slight susceptibility to women with green eyes and a tendency to play games.''

"Which you always win. Do I dare ask what else you played for last night?"

Rexford's laugh welled up from deep in his chest. "You mean almost played for. The lady said she would rather kiss a toad."

Tag, who never smiled before noon, guffawed. "Can't say as I blame her. Though that certainly explains your high good humor this morning." He pretended to study Rexford's face. "You, of course, are committed to proving her wrong."

"I can scarcely let any lady go through life with such a mistaken impression." He picked up the report on which he had wasted a full hour of a very promising dawn. "Now, if you will see about getting this report to London, I can be about the real business of the day."

Tag's eyes danced with amusement. "I am going no place until you define 'real business.' Would that be identifying the birds and winning the war, or practicing your kiss?"

Rexford walked to the looking glass and grinned at his reflection. "No reason why the two need to be mutually exclusive. I plan to quite enjoy the morning."

Tag crossed the room and stood behind him so their reflections merged in the glass. "Not that I would ever presume to give advice, but you might consider wiping that pleased expression off your face before you meet the lady. Nobody likes a happy winner. I would suggest humble, but I doubt your face would know how to do that. Try for something a bit neutral."

Rexford practiced a series of abject expressions.

On the third try Tag spoke from behind him. "That one is not bad. Except for the eyes. You will have to do something about the eyes."

Rexford had to agree with Tag. He looked altogether too pleased to be truly amiable.

"I'm off." Rexford turned, clapped Tag on the shoulder, and left. On the short walk to the cote, he continued practicing humble expressions. He mentally reviewed Amanda's every expression from the night before, particularly the way her eyes blazed at him when he spoke her name aloud for the first time. Amanda. He savored the taste of her name on his tongue. A few kisses and perhaps she would turn as gentle as her name.

By the side of the moss-covered stone building, he slowed his step to rearrange his countenance one final time before coming into view.

"Come here, darling—" Her voice came from just out of sight. The Voice. The voice that had trembled on the fringes of his consciousness every night just before he fell asleep, deep and sensuous, promising things men dreamed of at that hour. "You need to let me hold you."

Rexford froze in place, knowing no power on earth could make him take the final steps that would bring him into view and end the illusion that she was talking to him.

"I can feel you trembling. Don't be afraid. You will learn to love the way I touch you."

Oh, yes. Rexford pictured her long fingers moving over his body, her strokes as smooth as her words.

"That's better. You're not afraid any more. You like the feel of my hands. You like it when I touch you right here. So soft."

A tiny voice of reason told Rexford she was talking to a bird. His body chose to believe she meant the words exclusively for him. The mirage of her touch was an almost physical sensation. He pictured her hand inside his shirt, moving over his chest with her words. He closed his eyes and surrendered to the fantasy. Across his nipples, down his sides, up again so her fingers splayed out across his flesh. Molten blood coursed through his body.

"Yes. Yes. You will learn to look for my touch, because it's warm and soft. You're so safe here in my hands. Now I'm just going to rub you here. It feels good. You like it. Of course you do. You never want me to stop."

She breathed out the words slowly like the long smooth strokes Rexford could feel across his chest, down over his ribs toward his waist. He trapped his lower lip between his teeth to contain the air, which had begun to come in deep hungry breaths. In his mind he saw his own hands moving over her shoulders toward the neckline of her gown. Saw his hands slipping inside, her breath growing rapid with his touch.

"Yes. Yes. Yes. That's it."

That voice, those hands, belonged nowhere but in bed. They suggested sensual experiences no twenty-five-year-old virgin should have. Perhaps . . . He could decide later how he felt about her having such experiences. For now he could think only of her flaming hair spread out on a white velvet coverlet.

Mentally he took her to bed, not even bothering to remove the gold gown, just raising it above her waist so he could insinuate himself between her legs. So she could touch him as her words promised, sliding her hands slowly between his body and the waistband of his pantaloons. Fire in long, cool strokes. *Yes. Yes. Yes.*

"That's all now." The words in a different but still gentle tone ended the fantasy before Rexford could embarrass himself completely. "It is somebody else's turn. But I promise to hold you every day until you get used to my touch. Until you want to come home to it."

Rexford exhaled a trembling shudder of air and let his body relax back against the cool stone of the building. He drew several long breaths and shook his head. Even now he didn't believe the experience. He had undressed and bedded women without feeling the pounding heat her liquid speech aroused. No question, Amanda was different from any woman he had ever met. Straight-laced and only moderately attractive in person, but possessed of some unimaginable power to arouse him when she reached him with only her voice. Did his body know something he didn't?

Rexford gave a powerful sigh and decided some things were not meant for men to understand.

He began to walk again, this time with heavy steps to warn her of his approach. He passed the corner of the building. A stone crunched under his feet. She looked up from where she crouched in the center of the aviary, a small bird cupped in her hands. "Good morning, Lord Rexford. I expected you earlier.'' If she had any resentment about the lost wager, it did not show behind her bright smile. "Come in."

"Good morning." His voice sounded surprisingly normal for one who should have been hauled to Bedlam in chains only moments earlier. Aware of Tag's warning about gloating, he deliberately did not use her first name.

Rexford forgot until the moment his fingers touched the metal door handle that his gambling victory had some very distinct drawbacks. He had won the privilege of walking through pigeon-squish and having Grace dance out her grief on his shoulder. Perhaps he should let Amanda replay the hand.

He stepped in and Grace claimed his shoulder, from a high perch this time, which involved an infinitely more intense flapping of wings than a simple leap from the ground. The last several flaps took place in the vicinity of his right ear. He resisted the temptation to scrape her resident vermin from his ear with his forefinger. That might have disturbed her again and led to flapping and vermin-scraping ad infinitum.

When all the birds in the area had finished fluttering their applause at his entrance, Rexford found Amanda standing a few feet away, holding a small bird and smiling, probably at his discomfort.

"Actually, you have come at a good time. You will need to spend some time every day accustoming the birds to your voice and touch. It is that more than anything that makes them come when you whistle them in." She held out her cupped hands, obviously intending to drop her quaking burden into his palms.

He darted a glance in the direction of the only birds that interested him.

She followed the direction of his look, and minuscule furrows appeared between her brows.

Rexford spoke quickly to distract her from his interest in the older birds. "I understand the need for handling." He understood that holding the tiny creature would leave him defenseless against any sudden aerial attacks. He kept his

123

hands resolutely at his sides. "But these are your birds. I am sure they would prefer—"

"Only the human touch matters. Just talk to her. It doesn't matter what you say. Jeb does quite as well as I do."

Not in all respects, he informed her mentally. He held out his hands, struck by an interesting thought. Perhaps his voice could have the same effect on her.

He consciously lowered his voice several octaves. "You want me to touch you. You like it when I hold you and stroke you." He continued through several more phrases, combining what he remembered of her words with some stirring thoughts of his own. His voice stumbled to a halt. *This isn't working for me,* he admitted. His fingers knew they stroked feathers instead of soft feminine flesh.

Not quite ready to admit defeat, he shifted his gaze from the indifferent bird in his hand to the human face a few feet away. If she was trembling with unbridled passion, she hid it well.

Her eyes, regrettably not limpid pools of desire, appraised him coolly. "I think you have the idea. Try to concentrate on the younger ones. They need it most." She bent and scooped up another bird without quite enough feathers to be an adult.

For the next hour—or maybe only ten minutes that lasted long enough to be an hour—they moved about talking to birds. Rexford found if he maneuvered to keep her directly in his range of vision at all times, he could control his reaction to her voice, though any time she spoke from behind him, his blood started pounding.

The effect did not appear to be mutual. He made a mental note to confess to Tag that, as activities go, kissing a woman and handling birds might not be quite as compatible as he'd suggested. Grace kept flicking her tail across his lips, producing a desire to wash rather than nuzzle.

"I think that's enough for today, Rexford." Amanda straightened and brushed invisible bird feathers from her hands.

Grace or no Grace, the words promising release produced a desire to kiss the speaker.

Amanda looked around, her air of final inspection promising blessed escape—blessed escape, but also another day without the information he needed. "Shall we go?" But she didn't move in the direction of the door, and something told him she didn't expect him to either.

"Not just yet." Rexford reminded himself to see the Regent about a reward for the effort those words cost. "I believe our wager included all the birds, and so far we have concentrated only on the young ones."

Her shoulders rose with the challenge. "I do not recall we specified anything except 'the birds,' and since the young ones are the ones you will be dealing with in setting up a loft, you should be satisfied."

He had expected the protest. "Put it down to perversity if you wish. I demand more because I can. Because I won. Unless you plan to renege?"

"Of course not." Oddly, her smile held the gleam of triumph he had fought in his own earlier. "I am curious about what you want and why you want it."

"I want to meet your best birds. As to why, the books you have been choking me on for the past days insist that any loft is only as good as the eye of the person selecting the inhabitants. How else can I develop that eye on young untried birds?"

Instead of the argument he expected, she nodded her approval. "Good. You did not completely waste your time in the library. Shall we go?" She might have been a duchess asking to be led into supper.

Rexford's muscles actually tensed with the impulse to offer his arm for the stroll across the aviary. However, his arm extended from a dancing collection of feathers, and Grace showed no sign of abandoning her post. He contented himself with falling into step beside Amanda.

Amanda maintained her gracious air inside the smaller segregated area. She stood back and gave him time to get used to the turmoil their entrance produced. This time Rexford controlled the impulse to rush through the task of identifying the birds. Consciously forcing his muscles to relax, he stood for a long time and studied the milling creatures.

Gradually the flock resolved itself into individuals. To his surprise he found that even the limited reading he had done helped. The birds differed not only in color but in physical characteristics; longer necks, broad or narrow chests, tails that pointed up, down, or straight back. With time they could become individuals.

Finally, when he had learned all he could on his own, he closed his mind to the distraction of Grace hopping about on his shoulder, and turned to the woman beside him. "Ready. Now if you would identify these birds, and help me distinguish what makes them so special, I think we will have made splendid progress for today."

She nodded and began to point to individuals. "That red one is mine. Notice the wide chest. It means strong muscles and the potential for unlimited endurance. Notice how the tail points straight back for much less wind resistance. That one over there . . ." She continued until she had identified six birds.

Rexford carefully memorized two or three characteristics of each. He closed his eyes, visualized the colors and attributes, then deliberately moved, dispersing the flock. When they settled he could pick out the birds she had identified as hers. "Splendid. I can see now how they might eventually become as unique as people. Now, can we do Gully's birds again?"

She stiffened. "We have done enough for one day. I am rather tired."

"Just this. And then . . ." And then he should not have to come near the birds until he needed them.

"You remember, we went through that exercise twice the first day you arrived. It would be most tedious to repeat it."

Something in her posture caused Rexford to look at her questioningly. She could not have guessed his mission, but she seemed more reluctant to identify Gully's birds than the racers she had guarded so jealously to date. He flexed his fingers to release the tension and spoke casually. "I can scarcely tell Gully I remember nothing of that day but masses of wings flapping about my head. One more time and I should be able to report to him that—"

"Very well." She identified birds in colors he vaguely remembered.

He followed her pointing finger, memorizing colors and characteristics as he had before. After they had scattered and settled, he again succeeded in picking them out. Still something nettled at him. "Where is the white one? The one with the funny tilt to her neck?"

Rexford might have imagined the lines of tension around her mouth. If they existed at all, they disappeared with a blink. "Right there." She pointed to the white bird she had identified as Athena.

"But the tilt. I remember that quite distinctly. That one, her neck is completely straight."

Amanda laughed. "Now you are being silly. That day she had her head tilted to the left. Today it is straight. If you want to know why, you will have to ask her. Now, if you don't mind . . ." She didn't wait for his consent, but started for the entry.

The opening door and the prospect of saying good-bye to Grace proved too great a temptation. He followed Amanda with only one more puzzled glance at the white bird with the straight neck.

Amanda sat in the morning room, her sketch pad temporarily abandoned in her lap. Rexford had mumbled a few words of apology and retired to his room to work on some research. Her hands still shook every time she thought of how close he had come to uncovering her deception. She had forgotten how carefully she had identified Gully's birds for him. How could she know he would remember the tilt to Athena's neck?

In the end he had let the question drop, but she still quaked at the memory of the look in his narrowed eyes. He was not an easy man to lie to.

127

She glanced at the pad on her knees where she had sketched his eyes. Not really his eyes. The flat drawing captured only the shape, but not the power to reach out and sear the very skin under her gown. She had only to relax to feel again the heat that had flooded through her when he stepped through the door of the aviary. Heat as intimate as a touch. How had she even been able to speak?

No. She shook her head. She would not recall his hands. The thought set her body tingling with sensations. She had handed him the bird, had felt his fingers curl around hers for the long instant it took her to transfer the creature. Then he had spoken, deep, rich sounds that washed over her more intimately than a caress. His voice had rumbled of stroking and touching, and the soft thrum of the words had made every nerve cry out to change places with the fledgling he handled so gently. Though turning her back had given her time to control the flush and assume a cool expression, it had done nothing to banish the image of his soft stroking hands.

Never before had she understood the power a man could have over a woman. A dangerous power in this case, where the man might well be her enemy. Time, she told herself—she needed time away from him to control these new sensations.

And of course she could not afford the indulgence of time away from him, not if she hoped to discover the secrets those provocative eyes hid. For the fiftieth time since his arrival she wished the author of Mother's favorite reference book on English peers had been astute enough to realize people needed more than cold facts. Perhaps something like: *Lord Rexford. Beware of his sensuous appeal and be aware he hires out to kidnap birds.* She smiled at the fantasy and remembered her morning resolution to discover his intent. She would find a way.

Prescott gave a discreet cough from the doorway. "Lord Batterton is here to see you."

Amanda flicked her head impatiently. Batterton, a tiresome man whose attentions to her five years ago had increased when he discovered the size of her fortune. Discouraged by her lack of interest, he had married a drab young thing from Bath, only to lose her and a babe in childbirth eighteen months later. Perhaps he had lost her fortune as well. "Tell him I am not—"

Lord Batterton. Whatever his faults, he spent most of his time in London, and would certainly know more about Rexford than either Burke's *Peerage* or anyone in the village. And he was as dedicated to dispensing scandal broth as anyone she had ever met. For that she could be the gracious hostess.

She smiled and uttered a silent prayer to keep Rexford in his room for the next half hour. "Show Lord Batterton in, please."

A moment later Batterton entered. He took only a single step into the room and stopped. "Amanda, how delightful to see you again. You look splendid."

Amanda smiled. At twenty she might have believed he paused only to admire her. Now she realized he assumed the self-conscious pose to give her the opportunity to appreciate *his* appearance. Clad in a superbly cut morning coat and fawn pantaloons, he conspicuously displayed the leg he, at least, considered well formed. A twist of blond hair curled onto his forehead in almost the same arc that Rexford's always tumbled in. The difference was that Batterton's curl looked as if his valet had spent hours arranging it. Rexford sculpted his himself by running both hands through his hair when frustrated.

Amanda considered reproving Batterton for his familiar use of her first name, but that would scarcely produce the comfortable exchange of information she needed. "Lord Batterton, how nice of you to call." She permitted him to hold her hand in his cool fingers for several seconds, and indicated a chair next to hers.

They traded the expected pleasantries. Amanda had just begun framing the words to ask about Rexford when Batterton dropped his voice to a confidential whisper. "Amanda, I heard you are entertaining Lord Rexford."

She smiled. "Your face looks rather like his did when Mother mentioned your name. Do you know him?"

"I had a rather unpleasant encounter with him several years ago. I never did like the man, and I cannot say I approve of some of the things he has been involved in."

"I am afraid we are rather isolated here. I had not heard—"

"Rumors. Strictly rumors. Still, I would not expect . . . Why is he here? Has he been asking about your birds?"

"Yes, of course, that's why . . ." Just in time, Amanda remembered Rexford's warning about the confidential nature of his military mission. She wanted to get information from Batterton, not to offer grist for his gossip mill. "Why do you ask?" She leaned forward until she could almost feel his breath on her face. Her half whisper matched his own. "What have you heard?"

"Some very ugly news. I had to come and warn you. Two lofts of pigeons have been completely destroyed. All the birds slaughtered."

Amanda gasped. "Two!" Instinctively she covered her mouth with her hand. "What . . . who . . ." Her fingers dug into her cheeks, and the words were almost inaudible through her clutching hand.

Batterton nodded. "I know. It's horrible. General Stonehaven in London—"

"I heard about that, but who else?"

"A man named Crowley in Oxford. Someone slaughtered his entire flock four days ago. I have no idea why, but . . ."

Amanda clenched her trembling hands in her lap. "I can explain why." Her jaw trembled so she could not complete a coherent sentence. "The race."

"What race?" His face registered confusion.

"There is to be an international competition in June. General Stonehaven's birds might have won. But I cannot imagine anyone thinking Crowley's weaklings had a chance." The frantic pounding of Amanda's heart had slowed. Her thoughts still tumbled over each other, but at least they were beginning to come in phrases rather than in jumbled half-formed words.

"You believe this all has to do with the race?" He angled

his head and narrowed his eyes questioningly.

"Yes, and I am sure they are after my birds as well. A man claiming association with the army did approach me about moving some men here to work with my birds. He tried to pretend it had something to do with the war."

"How frightening, given what has happened. And then Lord Rexford appeared. You must be careful of that man."

Amanda took several deep breaths. "I have taken precautions. My racers are safe." She reminded herself to caution Jeb every day against mentioning those arrangements to anyone.

Batterton scowled. "Are you aware Lord Rexford is with the army?"

Amanda pictured Rexford's face when he made his reluctant confession. "He admitted as much."

Batterton's jaw tightened. "He is a sly one, though not many people realize it. I tell you this as a friend. Be very wary of him."

Amanda's stomach sank. Something inside forced her to protest. "But he seems so . . ."

Batterton gave an exasperated sigh. "You would be much safer to get rid of him."

"I can't." Amanda hesitated. She could get rid of him, but it would mean giving up what she thought of as her best defense—knowledge of her opponent. "I mean, I can, but I cannot understand why he would even consider being part of such a scheme."

Batterton's cautioning look turned patronizing. "Money, of course."

"But he is an earl. He has two or three estates—"

"It means nothing."

"But . . ."

"Half of the estates in England are encumbered for more than their value. Rumor has it Rexford is quite done up."

Amanda shrank back, automatically shaking her head to reject the notion of Rexford selling his pride for the paltry sum such a scheme would involve. "Why . . . why would he stoop to this?"

"The man I know would stoop to anything that promised sufficient funds." "But why does he not repair his fortunes in the usual way and marry an heiress?" She flushed with the memory that Batterton had done precisely that.

"I suspect he tried. The season is coming to an end and rumor has it that the heiress he fixed on chose to bestow her favors somewhere else."

Amanda's mind railed against the words. "But he is so attractive. Surely someone . . ." Not someone—anyone. Anyone would choose Rexford over any of the men she had met in London. "He is so . . . so . . ." She gave up trying to articulate the attributes which should win him any bride he chose. "But such a small sum. Surely he cannot hope to change his situation much with what a breeder would pay to kidnap . . ."

Batterton reached over and patted the back of her hand. "Trust me." His cool fingers curled around her wrist. "He only needs enough to tide him over until next season. You must send him—"

The light in the room changed. A sound drew Amanda's gaze to the door. Her start snatched her hand from Batterton's, and he drew back as disconcerted as she.

Rexford stood in the doorway, leaning casually against the wooden frame. The width of his shoulders blocked all but small patches of light behind him. But those were small details. His eyes made it impossible for Amanda to wrench her gaze from his face. His long lashes shielded pupils as hard and cold as agates. For long seconds she could hear only the sound of her own pounding heart.

"I hope I am not interrupting," he said.

Chapter Eight

Rexford's appearance startled Amanda so, she rocked back sharply against the rigid slats of the chair. Her spine hurt. Batterton probably felt a similar thump. They had leapt apart like two conspirators.

Nonsense. Rexford could shoot all the arrows he wanted with his eyes. She would not feel guilty about talking to anyone in her own home. Ignoring the ice in his words, she smiled. "Come in, Lord Rexford. I believe you know Lord Batterton."

Rexford drew himself even straighter. He made no effort to step any deeper into the room. Batterton stood. Amanda continued to watch Rexford. He could not stand forever like an Elgin marble.

Beside her Batterton's heels clicked. "Rexford."

"Batterton." Rexford returned the courtesy bow with but a hint of motion.

The two men faced each other across the tight air in the room. They obviously felt they had made sufficient contribution to the conversation. Amanda fumbled for a topic. *How much are they paying you to steal my birds?* seemed wildly inappropriate, but various forms of the question kept repeating itself in her mind.

She visualized what her mother would do under similar circumstances. Mother would be oblivious to anything but the fact she had two eligible gentlemen in the room. Amanda smiled brightly. "Shall we sit, gentlemen, and discuss . . . the weather, perhaps?" She gave a carefree toss to her head. "Delightful day, is it not? I was just saying to Lord Batterton—"

"I prefer to stand." Rexford crossed his arms over his chest and leaned against the door frame. Obviously, he preferred to be difficult.

"Perhaps you can think of another topic," she said.

His eyes traded the granite hardness for a sardonic gleam. "I had the impression you had found a satisfactory one before I interrupted."

Amanda looked at Batterton.

He gave a stiff bow. "It has grown rather chilly in here. I suggest we continue our discussion another time. Now if you will excuse me . . ." He took Amanda's hand.

From the corner of her eye, she saw Rexford stiffen. Annoyance at his high-handed interruption caused her to favor Batterton with a far brighter smile than he would otherwise have merited. "Of course."

"Possibly tomorrow, if you would care to go for a ride—"

"I believe the lady has promised to ride with me tomorrow." Rexford's feet didn't move, but he seemed considerably closer. His cold tones filled the room, crowding Batterton out. "If you have no objection, Batterton, I will walk out with you."

A flicker of apprehension danced through Batterton's eyes, replaced immediately by a polite smile. "Until next time, Amanda." He released her hand and turned to face Rexford's glare. Both men left the room before Amanda could declare she would ride with whomever she pleased.

Amanda rose and paced to the window, grateful for a few moments alone. Rexford's appearance had thrown her thoughts into a turmoil. She pictured again the two men confronting each other across the palpable tension. Rexford was so different, but if she could believe Batterton, also a fortune hunter. The notion appalled her, but then she had never known anything but complete security.

How could she imagine what it must be like to be a man with nothing but his wit or charm to depend on? Perhaps she should not judge too harshly.

She resisted the surge of feelings that rose up to protest the comparison. Try as she would, she could not recall even a vague disappointment five years ago when a chance remark confirmed her suspicion that Batterton was courting her only for her fortune. A cloud passed over the sun, stealing the color from the day as surely as Batterton had clouded her pleasure in trying to best Rexford. Rexford, a fortune hunter, and not even a successful one. Why, then, couldn't she feel the same disdain for him she did for Batterton?

Again she tried to doubt Batterton's words. He did enjoy gossip so. But that left her with no explanation for Rexford's interest in her birds. And Batterton had seemed so sure.

She turned around, rested her backside against the window ledge, and crossed her arms. Light spilled through the doorway where Rexford had stood, his presence dominating the room. Batterton's words should have diminished Rexford. Instead, Amanda continued to listen for the sound of his step.

In spite of all the tension of the last few days, she had enjoyed every minute with Rexford. She woke looking forward to the day, and without thinking, knew where he would be at any hour. A dozen times she had manufactured an excuse to seek him out in the library. And always, like now, she listened for the sound of his approach.

"Damn him." Amanda spoke the forbidden words aloud, and realized she meant the curse for Batterton for spoiling everything.

She should . . . She should look at precisely what had changed. Batterton certainly had not produced suspicion where none existed. She had always known Rexford had some hidden motive related to her birds. A small but essential financial gain would explain everything. Now that the birds were safe she could foil his plot, even enjoy doing it. But after that, she could not leave him to the mercy of his creditors. Once she succeeded in besting him, perhaps she could even be magnanimous enough to aid him in improving his fortune.

Since he would not realize any profit from this scheme, she might have to lend him enough money to survive until next season, but that would be a safe enough investment. With a few instructions on curbing his natural arrogance and pleasing a woman, he should have no trouble capturing an heiress.

Amanda pictured his eyes as they had smoldered at her across the card table. A more susceptible woman would have fallen into his arms. Amanda closed her own eyes and thought about how the night might have ended if she had not been so angry at losing the game to him.

A sound from the doorway yanked her from the fantasy. "I hope you do not plan to spend too many days waiting to hear from him. I doubt if he will call again."

She raised her brows. "I gather you were rude." She might object to his high-handed action, but certainly not to the prospect of never seeing Batterton again.

He smiled. "Incredibly."

"It is my house, so I presume I am permitted to ask why."

"I don't like Lord Batterton." He crossed the room and lowered himself into the chair next to her. The chair seemed much nearer than when Batterton had occupied it. "I have my reasons, and they make it easy to be rude to the likes of him. The fact that I came in here and found you practically nestled in his arms is what made it a pleasure." He leaned forward.

The diminished space quickened Amanda's breath. "I was not nestled in his arms. We were talking."

"Let us talk then." He reached across the few inches that separated them and drew Amanda's hand into his. "Like this." His warm palm engulfed hers. "If I remember, Batterton used both hands." He did not settle for Batterton's quick pat, but stroked his long fingers up her forearm, brushing the inside of her elbow with his index finger before gliding again to her wrist. "Now, what were you talking about about?" Tiny puffs of air played across her cheeks with his words.

"I . . . we were . . ." Amanda could scarcely remember who she'd been talking to, much less what they said. Her mind commanded her to pull her arm away. The arm stayed, growing warm under the long smooth strokes. "Please, let go of my arm, Rexford. I can't think while you are doing that." She finally managed to gather enough energy to tug against his grip.

"My point exactly." He released her and straightened so his shoulders almost touched the back of his chair. "Why would Batterton want to distract you so you couldn't think?"

Amanda sprang from her chair and counted out six long steps across the room before she turned to face him again. "Batterton didn't . . ." She stopped herself before she could confess only Rexford had the power to scatter her thoughts to the four winds just by leaning too close. "You forget yourself, my lord. My private conversations are no concern of yours."

"From what I saw, I suspect they are very much my concern. If I know Batterton, he was filling your ears with some very interesting tales about me." He stood.

He had her in such a dither that for a moment she thought he might block the door. A silly thought with a house full of servants, but so typical of the danger she felt from his physical presence.

He rocked back on his heels and rested a hand against the back of his chair. "I don't suppose you would care to sit? You realize you oblige me to stand as well."

Mentally she reviewed the furniture in the room. She would have to select first, giving him the opportunity to settle as close as he chose. "Please, don't stand on ceremony," she said. "Sit down. I merely wish to take a turn about the room." Even if he thought a very close chair would give him an advantage, he could do nothing. He had just expressed a desire to sit and he must sit.

He sat, and Amanda's shoulders relaxed with the minor victory.

She made a mental note for the future. Distance made dealing with Rexford far easier. She took the turn she claimed to want about the room and used the time for organizing her thoughts. She could annoy him by telling him nothing of the conversation. But that would merely prolong the stalemate between them. Directness always worked best for her. Even if she related the entire conversation, she would not be telling him anything he did not already know. She might even learn something from his reactions.

"You are aware I have always been uneasy about your interest in my birds." She chose a chair separated from him by a small table and sank into it. "Batterton confirmed my suspicions."

She hadn't exactly expected him to gasp in shock, but neither did she expect the shrug and the smile. "I suspected as much. Now I deserve a chance to unconfirm them. Tell me what he suggested."

She memorized every detail of his face, so she could note any change. "Something very bad is going on with the birds this year, and I fear you might be part of it."

His face assumed the impassive look she had noted in the early moments of their card game. "You are, of course, going to ask me about it."

"Somebody attacked another loft." She thought she would be able to simply state the facts, but with the words pictures began to form in her mind. Her hands shook. Her face felt cold.

He remained as immobile as the marble bust on the table behind his shoulder. "I see."

"They . . . they killed all the birds . . . he had beautiful white birds." Her face began to tingle.

Furrows appeared on his brow. "Are you all right?" He leaned forward as if he might come to her. "Just take some deep breaths and then we'll talk."

She looked at the floor. "I'm sorry, I cannot get the pictures out of my mind. All those birds . . . they belonged to a dear old man, Matt Crowley." Her eyes stung at the memory of Matt tenderly cradling a cooing pigeon in his hands, but she refused to surrender to the weakness. If she thought of Matt or even of herself, she might miss Rexford's reaction. She bit her lip. "I just wonder how much you know about that."

His jaw tightened and his eyes narrowed. "I have called men out for less than what you're thinking." His knuckles whitened on his knees. "You don't wonder how much I know. You are asking if I slaughtered a cote full of harmless birds, aren't you?"

Amanda managed to nod. Even she could not hear the yes she tried to utter.

"I could swear to you I didn't. For most people that would be enough." A thin vein throbbed at his temple. "But you want more, so let me try to convince you another way. When did this happen?"

She dug her fingers into her palms to control the trembling and refused to retreat from his blazing eyes. "Four days ago. In Oxford."

His quick nod made his jaw seem less rigid. "Now think. Where was I four days ago?"

"Here. You were here." Until this moment she'd refused to acknowledge how badly she wanted to be wrong.

"That's right. It doesn't matter what time it happened. I never left here long enough to get to Oxford and back, did I?"

"No." Amanda's fingers uncurled, leaving white tingling half-moons in her palms. She exhaled deeply and understood her tension had not been fear of his anger, but fear of what she might learn. Every nerve in her body had railed against the thought she could have been so wrong about his gentleness. Whatever Rexford's crimes, he was not vicious. At least she had been right about that.

"So I could not have hurt those birds, could I?"

"No." Amanda remembered his long fingers holding the

wounded Elizabeth, his anxiety when he thought she might die. "I never really thought you did." The clock ticked in the silent room. Amanda gathered her thoughts. Perhaps somebody else had been hired to do that, but Rexford had been hired for something. "But you are here."

His hands, which had begun to relax, tightened on his knees again. "Forgive me for being dreadfully blunt, but now you are concerned about me slaughtering your birds, isn't that correct?"

"Yes." Amanda said the word and knew it was not true. "No, I . . . I cannot believe that."

The air he exhaled sounded like a gust of wind in the silent room. "I truly hope not. I have seen the way you love those birds, and if you think I could—well, I truly hope not." He eased himself back into the chair.

"Kidnap them, perhaps. I do think you might do that."

He laughed. "Certainly not for my own personal pleasure."

Amanda smiled at the memory of his posture in the cote. Even the most dull-witted simpleton could never imagine him coveting Lucifer for his own enjoyment. With the ugliness behind them, she found she could relax, possibly even turn the encounter into something that would benefit them both. "No, but you still might hide them temporarily. As a service to someone else."

"Unfortunately, I can't convince you of my innocence there as easily. But why would I want to take your birds?"

On surer ground now, Amanda leaned forward. "Money."

"Money!" His mouth dropped open and he let out a peal of laughter. "Money. Can you picture me walking the streets trying to sell your birds? Really, Amanda, it would be easier to believe—" His face sobered. "No. I won't even joke about that."

Hard as she tried, Amanda had been unable to detect a false note in his laugh. She checked her natural inclination to join him in his good humor by warning herself that he must be very practiced in the art of humbugging if he could laugh so comfortably when confronted. "I am not joking.

140

Batterton told me you are completely done up."

He smiled, and even his eyes twinkled in amusement. "Ahhhh, we are back to Batterton again. Please enlighten me. How have I managed to fall on such ill times?"

"I know it is embarrassing, but if we can be completely honest about it, I am sure we can deal with it."

"I am sure we can. But remind me to have a pair of dueling pistols handy the next time I meet your good friend Batterton."

"Don't be too hard on him. He only told me about the wretched state of your finances when I could not understand why an earl might be in league with a foreign breeder. You should be grateful to him, because I have the most perfect plan that will benefit both of us."

"I shall certainly remember to thank him appropriately." The corners of his lips twitched. "But right now, I am more interested in your plan, which I assume is designed to improve my current unfortunate financial state?" He crossed one leg over the other and rubbed his chin with his large hand, covering his smile but not the sparkle in his eyes.

"Improve it for a short time. Naturally, you still must marry an heiress. But I am sure I can even help with that." She leaned forward. It was understandable that he would want to cover his embarrassment with amusement, but she did need his serious attention.

He gave an exaggerated wince. "Please tell me this isn't leading to another engagement. I have not yet fully apologized for the failure of the last one."

"Of course it is. You have already faced the reality of that."

He turned his head to the side and regarded her suspiciously. "Haven't we already been through this? And haven't we already established that neither of us has the least interest in marrying? Though I assure you, if I had any interest in marrying, I would consider no one else until you had refused me a dozen times."

Amanda resisted the impulse to reach over and shake him. Embarrassment about his finances was one thing, but if he insisted on being deliberately obtuse they would be here all day. "Would you please forget about marrying for now? We must deal with the other first."

"Ahhh, yes, the other. We certainly must deal with the other." He smiled, then furrowed his brow in overstated confusion. "What is the other?"

"Humph." Amanda gave an impatient toss to her head. "The birds. You cannot even pretend to have forgotten the birds. Now that I understand why you might be willing to work for a disreputable breeder, we can work together." She waited for him to nod his acceptance. He didn't. He would not give up until the last card was played. "At first I thought you should leave once you knew I understood everything. But whoever is behind this terrible thing would just find somebody else, and both of us would lose. Don't you agree?"

"I'm sure I shall. Once I find out what I am agreeing to."

Amanda knew him well enough now to know he was nowhere near as slow-witted as he pretended. She let the comment go, knowing men liked to have things carefully listed in neat columns. "You will stay here, exactly as you wanted to originally. But you won't kidnap my birds or anything annoying like that. And you won't tell anybody you've changed sides. That way they won't have to send anybody else. Now, doesn't that seem perfect?"

"Frankly, I am stunned."

Amanda suppressed her disappointment at his lack of enthusiasm, then realized she had not explained the benefit to him. She leaned forward, now sorry for the table between them, which prevented her from giving him a reassuring pat. "I am sorry. I forgot you would be concerned because nobody will pay you for not kidnapping the birds. But that's not true. I will."

He leaned forward, his eyebrows raised and his eyes shifting rapidly. "Pardon me? I am afraid you lost me with too many nobodies and nots."

"I will pay you for not—the same as anybody else would pay you for doing."

"Not . . . ?"

"Not kidnapping. At least that's what I assume you were planning. It happened once before, you know. Somebody took the birds from Jeb and kept them until after a race. This way you don't have to do anything like that. I am proposing just a loan, but it will be enough to tide you over until next season."

Finally his head began to nod. "I do believe I understand. I am completely under the hatches, so I have hired myself out to an unscrupulous breeder to kidnap your birds. But if I stay here and don't kidnap your birds, you will lend me whatever I would have made from somebody else."

"Exactly."

He regarded her intently. "That appears to solve everything." He held out his hand with the thumb and forefinger two inches apart. "Except for one very small point. The part about my marrying."

"We have already agreed you must marry."

"You have agreed. I am still merely an onlooker. But I am willing to leave that for the moment. Am I marrying you?"

"Of course not."

"Because I am without a feather to fly with?"

"Because you are beginning to annoy me. Please concentrate on the problem."

He turned his palms over. "Believe me, I am doing my best. The problem is to find me a fortune. May I ask one more time why this is necessary?"

The table between them kept her from standing to pace off her exasperation. "Because I cannot support you forever. I am aware earls are expensive, even penniless ones." She noted his frown and added, "Much less expensive as long as you are here, of course."

A smile trembled on the corners of his mouth. "Now I am to stay here. Simply because you always wanted a tame earl running about the house? Or do you have some other motive?"

Naturally a man of Rexford's pride would try to deal with

the situation lightly. "Please, don't be frivolous. I can scarcely deprive you of your income and throw you out on the street. You need not stay here all the time. Just until we can deal with your problem with women."

Rexford threw back his head and laughed. "My problem with women!" His shoulders shook and he rocked forward. "Until this moment I was scarcely aware I had one—though I trust you will explain it to me."

"I am sure you are only laughing because you are embarrassed. But you must stop because it will only distract us both."

"I certainly do not want to be distracted before I learn the precise nature of my problem." Intermittent chuckles slowed his speech, but he finally managed to control everything except an occasional twitching muscle in his face. "Please, tell me more about this difficulty of mine with women."

At least he was willing to listen. That might be all she could expect from a first discussion. "I am sure it is only little things, and I know I can help."

"I am grateful, but I am curious where you got the notion I need help in that particular area. Unless you are referring to something between the two of us. In that case I—"

"Not at all. In fact there are times when I find you quite—" She clamped her lips. He certainly didn't need her to add to his high opinion of himself. "Lord Batterton told me you had spent the season courting an heiress to improve your fortunes. Apparently she accepted someone else, so you had to sell your services to the foreign breeders for money to live on until next season when you absolutely must find someone else."

"Batterton certainly knows how to spin an interesting tale. You believed him, naturally. Would it help if I told you that, if the lie suited his purpose, Batterton could convince you the Thames had decided to flow in the opposite direction?"

Amanda shifted uncomfortably. "I admit he is not the most reliable source. I considered that, but it does explain everything. And quite nicely too, because I am sure I can help you catch your heiress."

Rexford smiled and eased forward in his chair until his knees pressed into the table between them. "In that case, I am willing to set aside the question of truth for the moment. Just out of curiosity to see how you propose to help. While I have enormous respect for you, it had not occurred to me you might be an expert on the subject of snaring a wealthy bride."

Pressure from his knees shifted the light table toward Amanda until it brushed against her skirt. Rexford noticed, and solved the problem by shifting the table so it no longer formed a barrier between them. He leaned forward so his hands rested on his knees, disturbingly close to her legs.

Amanda resisted the temptation to turn sideways. She would not move while she had Rexford's full and serious attention. "I admit I had only one season in London. But I am excessively wealthy, precisely the kind of heiress you need."

"I am deeply honored, but—"

"Rexford, stop." Amanda thrust out her hand, palm forward, almost smacking his nose, and he reared back. "That is one of the first things we must cure you of," she said, "your annoying arrogance."

Rexford's eyes shifted warily before he leaned forward again. "Arrogance? I am not aware of—"

"Of course not. That is what makes it even more annoying. It is excessively arrogant of you to regard every word I say as an attempt to scoop you up in some kind of net. Believe me, if you were a fish, I would throw you right back."

A hint of crimson colored his sun-darkened cheeks. "That is rather a harsh judgment. You did insist I need an heiress. Then you said you are an heiress. What am I to think?"

They certainly could not go through this every time she spoke honestly to him. "Think this. I am quite happy with my state. I am wealthy. I am independent. I have no father who might pressure me into an unpleasant marriage, and I have seen enough of the men who have come and gone in my mother's life to know I want nothing to do with that kind of grief.''

''You certainly cannot blame them for dying.''

''I don't blame them for anything, but I see no need to change my whole life for some man who will stay only a few years, then leave me more unhappy than I was before.''

Rexford's face softened to a tender expression Amanda had never seen before. ''I am sorry, Amanda.'' He reached across the table and rested his fingers on her hand. ''I wonder no one even thought what a wrench all that must have been for you. Each time your mother lost a husband, you lost a man who might have been a father.''

Amanda stared at Rexford, amazed at this perception from a man she had known only a few days. Everyone always assumed because Mother and her husbands had spent so little time here, Amanda had never dreamed of having a real father. Resolutely she blocked out the pictures of the black-draped house from her mind. ''It was not like that. I scarcely knew some of the men. Besides, it does not matter now. I only mention it to be very clear I have no intention of ever marrying.'' She drew her hand away and folded it with the other in her lap. ''That will save you the trouble of proposing every fifteen minutes.''

''I shall do my very best to restrain myself.'' He looked up and gave a smile that would have made even Princess Charlotte's heart flutter. Amanda noted it as one of his strongest assets. ''But why, then, did you mention London, and how excessively eligible you are?''

She mentally praised him for getting back to the topic at hand. ''Merely to establish that I have had ample experience with suitors in need of a well-to-do bride. While I myself did not fall into any of their snares, most of them did very well indeed. Even Batterton, much as you dislike him, came off quite nicely.'' She ignored his dark look. ''I remember enough of their pleasing manners to be quite helpful in pointing out things that might improve your chances.''

His frown melted into a thoughtful expression that became

increasingly brighter. "A tutor in securing a wife. What a novel idea."

How like a man to claim credit for inventing everything. "Not so novel. Women spend most of their lives learning to make themselves agreeable to even the most tedious gentlemen. I see no reason why a man should not have the same advantage."

His eyes began to sparkle with interest. "Nor do I. Precisely how extensive are these lessons you plan?" His voice seemed lower than a moment ago.

Something in his manner quickened Amanda's pulse. "As complete as you require. We cannot take a chance of dragging out our quest for several seasons." Without knowing why, Amanda found her attention focused on his lips. She ran her tongue along her own and watched him do the same.

"I find the idea most intriguing," he said. "When can we begin?"

"Right now, I suppose." Amanda studied him. He would need a new valet, one who could tie a proper neckcloth and keep that distracting curl in place. But that could wait. She needed something he could improve immediately to prove the worth of the scheme.

He exhaled, and she became uncomfortably aware of his nearness. Surely a more timid woman would find that nearness even more disturbing, and he could change that easily. "I would not be surprised if you frighten women just a little bit."

He bridled. "Frighten? I assure you I would never do—"

He had misunderstood. "It is not something you do exactly. It is your presence."

His brows furrowed. "My presence? In a room, you mean?"

She shook her head. "Not in a room. And not all the time." She was explaining badly. "Occasionally you sit or stand too close. It . . . it makes a woman uneasy."

He cocked his head sideways and eyed her speculatively. "Am I too close now?"

"No," she lied. Her fluttering stomach illustrated what she meant. Rationally she knew he had not moved, but somehow she had become acutely aware of his nearness. "It is hard to explain . . . just a danger one senses . . . as if you might . . ."

"Do this?" He drew his chair forward, angling his legs to the side so they brushed past hers.

Amanda drew several quick breaths, conscious of his thighs touching hers, his face only inches from her own. "That is it. A more susceptible woman than me might think . . ." She couldn't finish the sentence. Her mind swirled with all the things a more susceptible woman might think of. She could think only of his hands, that they might reach out and touch her.

"This makes you uneasy? What are you afraid of?" His hands still rested on his knees, but so tentatively.

"I am not afraid exactly, just uncomfortable—like before when you touched my hand. I—"

"Like this?" He reached across and took her hand. She was no more prepared than when he had imitated Batterton. He rested his elbows on his thighs and cradled her hand in his palm, holding it a few inches above his knees.

Amanda's heart began racing. This wasn't the lesson she intended, at least not so vividly. "I think we better stop. I'm not sure—"

"No, please." With his forefinger he tilted her chin up so she looked directly into his smoldering eyes. His hand left her chin and he began running his fingers along her arm, so softly every nerve begged for more.

Gooseflesh broke out all the way to her shoulder. She knew he was toying with her, but couldn't find the will to order him to stop.

"It is important that I understand." His words came in puffs of air across her cheeks. With a will of its own, her chin lifted and let his balmy breath caress her throat.

Amanda resisted the sensation of floating. Words. She needed words to stop him. "This . . . this is most improper. Most women . . ."

"Most women like it." He stood, drawing her to her feet

as well. He tucked her hand under his chin while he continued to stroke her arm.

"Most women would think you mean to kiss..." Amanda knew he would kiss her.

He didn't. He stood there stroking her arm, his voice soft as feathers blown in the wind. "I believe most women like to be kissed when it's done right." He held her arm between them, the back of his caressing fingers almost brushing her breasts.

"Sometimes... but not... there is a time... not..." Amanda's fingers brushed his chin. Words lost their meaning. *Stop*, she thought. *In a minute I will make him stop.*

He tilted his head forward, whispering a kiss onto the back of her fingers. "How is a man supposed to know when a woman wants to be kissed? When she looks into his eyes as you're doing now? When her lips are parted and ready?" With a slow motion that seemed to take an hour, he moved their joined hands aside and bent forward so his lips just rested on hers. "Mmmmm."

Amanda felt the tremor of the sound against her lips. For a full second everything in the world stood still. His lips moved, warm and alive. Hers trembled in response. His hand slid around her waist, pulling her to him. She resisted the sudden hardness of his body, her breasts pressed against his chest. "Stop," she tried to say, but his mouth responded as if she returned his kiss, working against hers. She drew back her head, only to find herself held in place by his hand at the nape of her neck, his fingers just below her ears.

His tongue touched her lower lip. She surrendered to long-forgotten sensations, a tingling that radiated out from her mouth down her throat to harden the nipples of her breasts. Just for a minute she would enjoy it. Her hand crept to his shoulder, to his collar, where his ragged curls tickled the back of her hand. Now she let her lips respond, moving with his to produce waves of heat. His tongue moistened her lower lip.

"Now," he whispered, exhaling the word, forming it with his lips and hers. His arm pressed her even tighter against him until she could feel his taut thighs against hers. His tongue darted between her parted lips, a shocking sensation, gone almost before she could recognize it. His tongue slipped between her lips again, lingering for a fraction of a second this time.

She drew her head back, but this had the effect of arching her lower body even harder against him. He stirred against her. Her knees weakened. She could feel so much of him.

"That's it. You taste like. . . ."

She heard the words, felt him forming them with her lips. For just a moment they had no meaning. Then his tongue came into her open mouth, not a quick dart, but a deep searching probe, staying to light a fire down the center of her body. His hand dropped from her head to cup her buttocks and draw her against him.

Her blood pounded with the rhythm of his tongue. His hands pulled her to him with the same rhythm. She could do nothing but surrender to the roiling sensations.

His lips left hers to puff tiny kisses down her neck, and stopped to suckle at the pulse point in her throat. "Amanda," he whispered, again allowing one of his hands to stroke up her body and come to rest cupping her breast.

Amanda drew two gasping breaths. "Stop," She dimly realized her fingers, tangled in his hair, made obedience impossible. She drew on the little strength she had to lower her hands to his shoulders and push. A feeble effort.

He looked up with liquid eyes. "I knew you would kiss like fire." The words had a raspy sound. His hands slid to her waist.

Amanda's face flamed. "Get away from me." She should have spoken more firmly, but felt grateful to have gotten the words out at all. "Please move away so I can think."

He straightened and looked down at her, still far too close for her to think rationally. "I am not sure I could even if I wanted to. Right now I have to focus on breathing."

She believed him. Her own breath came only in short gasps with far too little air to keep pace with her racing heart.

Still . . . "Then please, stand aside so I can pass." Distance. She could deal with him better from a distance.

He stepped back and angled his body, opening a path. She took a hesitant step. Her knees shook so she had to rest a hand on his shoulder for support. After two deep breaths she found the strength to cross the room and turn to face him. "What happened?"

"I kissed you."

"I know, but I let you."

He smiled. "I think you even helped me."

"But . . ." Amanda remembered the whole incident, not just the kiss but what led up to it. "I remember now. We were talking about how you make women uneasy."

"I'm still not sure I do, but—"

Amanda retreated behind the sofa before he could consider taking a step toward her and making her uneasy again. "Oh, you do. Probably because they sense you might do something like that. Do you . . . do you do that often?"

His face broke into an unself-conscious grin. "Every chance I get."

Her hand tightened on the sofa back. "I see. Well, we'll have to work on that."

His grin widened. "I assure you, it will be my pleasure." He took a step toward her. "Right now, if you have nothing more pressing."

"No!" Amanda thrust out her hand. "Stay right there." She kept her hand extended until she was sure he had no intention of moving toward her. "I mean, we will have to work on your thinking about things like that. Women can sense when men are thinking in that direction. I am sure that must have been what frightened your poor little London miss away. Most heiresses are just out of the schoolroom or they would have been snatched up. So you must make a resolve right now to change."

His laugh echoed through the room. "Are you saying I have to stop thinking about ever kissing a woman?"

Amanda's jaw tightened. "I am not quite as naive as you

think. You were thinking about a lot more than kissing just then. Admit it.''

Rexford stepped toward her. ''Oh, I admit it. What I am thinking of doing right now would have half of London in bed with the vapors.''

152

Chapter Nine

Rexford repressed his chuckle until he could no longer hear Amanda's footsteps as she made her hasty retreat. Did she lie awake nights planning her schemes, or did they just wondrously appear the minute he became too confident? He paced to the mirror to search for any physical trace of his new status. In less than an hour she had robbed him of his fortune and turned him into a pockets-to-let scoundrel.

Mentally he framed a letter to his banker. Hell, why limit it to one banker? He could organize a parade: stewards, solicitors, and bankers carrying long parchment scrolls which they would unroll across the drawing room. Not worth a bean, indeed! He'd list every asset, every farthing, until there wasn't a single place to step. He would show her....

He sighed. None of that mattered. He could show her a world of wealth and still feel as shabby as he did right now, because he could show her everything but his honor.

However wrong her facts, he had come here to rob her of her dream as surely as if he had sold his soul for whatever paltry sum she expected to pay.

"Dammit. Dammit. Dammit." He cursed Napoleon, the

war, and the whole French army. He added another "Dammit" to curse himself for agreeing to the scheme. He had options.

Amanda was neither beetle-headed nor irrational. Occasionally mulish, perhaps, but . . . He smiled. He had never before met a person who simply didn't believe in Napoleon, as one might deny the existence of demons.

She had heard the name, but for her, he existed as some far-off entity that the army would deal with when they found the time. A nuisance, but not one that would ever affect her.

Rexford debated. If he could convince her of the real threat, she would probably personally carry a cannon into Napoleon's camp and expect the self-styled emperor to understand why she had to fire at him. He clenched his fingers into his palms. If he spoke slowly and clearly, he could explain. He should explain.

He found one tiny flaw with the plan. Mathematicians probably hadn't invented numbers small enough to calculate the probability she would believe him. Mentally he rehearsed the conversation. *I am a representative of the Crown, come to urge you to do your duty to king and country.*

Not an innocuous earl, who wants to set up his own loft?
No.
Not a minor functionary for the army?
No.
Not an impoverished earl?
No.
Oh, how silly of me. I should have guessed.

Then she would probably call Jeb, the birds, and her mother to help skin him alive.

For now, he decided, the truth would have to be a final desperate alternative. If she didn't believe him or flew into a rage, he would lose everything.

The role of impoverished earl presented some interesting possibilities. At least she seemed fond of it. It made them allies and gave him access to the birds. He smiled. It also held the potential for a very interesting relationship.

He had never met a human being as fascinating as Amanda

in her I-have-a-plan mood. Her eyes danced. Her brow furrowed when she perceived a problem, and her face glowed with animation when the solution struck.

Which brought him to his problem with women, one woman in particular. Several sharp paces across the room, an equal number in the opposite direction, and a final sharp turn prepared him to face the thoughts he had thrust aside while pretending to debate whether to continue to be impoverished.

The whole scene had been rollicking fun until he had turned it into a potential disaster. Even to himself he could not explain why he had taken her in his arms. Not out of pique at her assumption she knew more about dealing with the opposite sex than he. He had quite enjoyed that. But something in the way she sat had tempted him beyond human endurance.

The minute she began to explain how he made women "uncomfortable," he had been unable to resist the temptation.

A man would have had to be made out of iron to resist a small demonstration. His move had been nothing but an innocent jest.

Even when his lips touched hers he'd been smiling. Her small start of alarm that left her lips parted had caught him off guard. He hadn't been able to resist touching his tongue to her lips, and then the jest had gone up in flames.

She kissed the way she battled floodwaters and devised plans—with every fiber of her being.

Rexford shuddered. Days ago, from the first moment he'd heard her seductive voice, his body had known she would kiss like that. He had fantasized the experience a dozen times, and none of his fantasies had sent his blood rushing as it had the instant his tongue slipped between her lips. If her husky voice said, *Take me to bed*, the passion in her response said, *Keep me there for a week*.

For a hundred practical reasons, the move had been a wretched mistake on his part. He would have to explain and apologize. He would have to pretend it had been nothing more than a cow-handed attempt to illustrate her point.

She might even believe him.

His body hardened again at the memory of fire and innocence. How far would she have let him go? The kiss certainly had not been her first. Her parting words had suggested she knew precisely what he had been thinking. At twenty-five, perhaps she had.

Next time . . . next time he'd kiss her until she begged him to stop—or begged him not to. Next time—

Rexford's fist clenched. *Forget it, Rexford. You don't tumble your hostess on the floor of her own sitting room. No matter how nicely she kisses.*

The clock on the mantel chimed. Tag had probably been waiting none too patiently for the last half hour. Rexford gave one final hungry glance at the spot where he had stood with Amanda, and strode from the room.

He entered the library, and Tag looked up with a reproving frown. "Nice of you to join me."

Rexford grinned. "You will have to forgive me. Life is not easy for me nowadays."

"Problems with the invincible Miss Langley?"

"Let us just say interesting developments." Rexford stopped in the center of the room and turned his palms up. "You see before you a pathetic dished-up simpleton."

Tag chuckled. "I know that, but I assume you are going to explain in more detail. Have we been found out? I would not expect you to find it quite so amusing."

"Not found out. I am all to pieces financially. Not a feather to fly with." He laughed again at Tag's bemused expression. "Console me, Tag. I am penniless."

"Oh, splendid. I will have to remember not to come to you when my tailor becomes impatient." Tag's eyes twinkled merrily, and he ignored the pile of messages he had brought from the village. "May I ask how you managed to dispose of such a healthy sum since dawn?"

"Not only have I frittered away my fortune, but I have found our villain."

Tag eyed Rexford's rather disheveled appearance. "And I

thought you had spent all morning arranging that cravat so it would tickle your ear. Tell me how you found our villain and lost a fortune without leaving the house?''

"Lord Batterton arrived this morning to malign my reputation. I have been expecting him ever since Lady Harriet mentioned him at dinner, and today I found him whispering in Amanda's ear.''

Tag endured two seconds of silence before growing impatient. "So you gave him your fortune, and now want to borrow money from me?''

"Not quite.''

"That is the only scenario I can produce which would have you looking so chipper. The more obvious one, that he told her our intentions and she drove us out at the point of a gun, would have you gnashing your teeth. What did he tell her?''

"As near as I can determine, he told her I am quite penniless, failed to win the plump heiress I hung out after all season, and sold my services to a foreign breeder who wants me to kidnap her birds.''

"Why in blazes would he tell her that? Why not simply tell her that we came to draft her birds into the army?''

"I can only guess. He may have feared that if she knew the truth she might cooperate. The more I see of her, the more I think he might actually have helped us if he had told her.''

"Now you have totally lost me.''

Rexford struggled to put all he sensed into words. "Amanda's problem has never been lack of courage or commitment. She is simply so concerned with her own world here, she can't see anything else. If she could . . . If I could convince her . . .''

"You think she might cooperate?''

"I simply don't know. I think Batterton suspects she might, so instead he fed her suspicions with who knows what lies, and trusted her to send us on our way.''

Tag looked at the ceiling and exhaled a long breath, his brows drawn so tight together they almost touched. He finally looked back at Rexford, all trace of his earlier playfulness gone. "Then I think the time has come for you to tell her the truth."

"I came close this morning. But I am not absolutely certain she would simply hand the birds over to us, and more important, I doubt she would believe me. I've told so many lies already."

Tag laughed. "But on this one, even I am confused. Very slowly now, explain how I have managed to become valet to a penniless earl."

"Batterton's one miscalculation. Amanda could not resist the challenge of turning me from my evil ways." Briefly Rexford summarized the essential facts, mentally labeling "problem with women" and "handling of problem with women" nonessential. "In any case," he concluded, "we are not any worse off than before."

Tag looked doubtful. "If you say so. I can still see some—"

"Difficulties. So can I. But we'll deal with them as they arise. Now let's get to business."

"Right." Tag glanced at the papers on the desk, then back at Rexford. "Batterton first, I'd say. Do you want me to shoot him or just drop him in the river?"

"Leaving aside for the moment the fact we have no right to do either, I think we will borrow Amanda's philosophy here. The villain you know is better than the one you don't. Leave him be. Just be sure somebody is watching him all the time. In addition, we need to guard the birds."

Tag held up his hands, palms outward, mock terror in his eyes. "Don't look at me. I've met Jeb and his musket. I am not about to walk up to him and say, 'I'm your replacement.' "

Rexford smiled in anticipation of a confrontation, not with Jeb but with Amanda. "I told you we could turn this situation to our advantage. Amanda cannot hope to adopt an earl without a bit of inconvenience. Have Wolfe and Brownley deliver my horses to the stables here tomorrow morning.

They can pretend to be grooms for a few days and guard the birds at the same time.''

Tag laughed. ''I hope Wolfe likes being a groom better than I like being a valet. Before this is done you will have the army restaffing you entire household.''

Rexford found it hard to generate any sympathy for the young lieutenant who had probably never brushed a horse in his life. ''Tell him if he prefers, I will be the groom and he can deal with Miss Langley. That should make him pick up the curry brush in a hurry.'' He pointed to the dispatches from the Continent. ''Now, what's in there?''

Tag shrugged. ''It depends on who you want to believe. Wellington is in Brussels and''—he pointed to a stack— ''according to those, having a hell of a fine time with balls and parties every night. Acting as if he never heard the word *war*. He is playing it very close, though he says here he may stroll out to meet Napoleon sometime toward the end of the month.''

Rexford added the unspoken ''But . . .''

Tag picked up a letter he had isolated on the corner of the desk. ''But I trust my father. For all his cavorting, he is not easy to fool. He simply doesn't believe Napoleon is going to wait for Wellington to make the first move.''

''He thinks Napoleon will cross the border?''

Tag nodded. ''Cross the border and gobble up Brussels. That's why my father is screaming for you to send out more of these birds. They are using local birds very effectively, but the loft is right in the middle of where he expects the action will be. Right now they only have four birds that can fly back here. He wants a dozen. Said you may have another week to get them out there, but he'd wager my inheritance you don't have two weeks.''

Rexford held out his hand for the letter.

Tag flushed and did not offer it. ''Some of what he says is not particularly complimentary.''

''I can imagine.'' Rexford gestured more firmly with his hand, and Tag released the letter. Rexford read. He laughed. ''Bumbling twerp, indeed. Serve the old bastard right if I sent Amanda instead of the birds. She would have him trussed and served for dinner before he had a chance to ask her name.''

Tag grinned. "I knew you would be bitter." His face turned serious. "Still, we should think about what he says. Now that you can identify the birds, we could just send them off. Your lady couldn't say much once it is done.''

"I think about that two or three times a day, but always come up with the same problem. Somebody still has to stay here and wait for the messages to come through from the Continent. The minute you volunteer for that job, I will take the birds to Brussels myself and send my condolences to your family.''

Tag raised his hands in surrender and grinned. "That's why I am second in command. If you are afraid of something, I get to hide under the bed.''

Rexford returned the smile. "I am not afraid at this point. In fact I plan to quite enjoy myself—as long as we don't have to steal a bird.''

Amanda woke the next morning with the first hint of gray in the sky. She sent a message to Jeb to release her racing birds, and hurried to the cote to watch them exercise. Jeb, carrying the crate for transporting the birds, joined her only moments after the first bird appeared. "Does this mean they can come back home?" He pointed to a speck in the sky. "Samson is not happy without you.''

"I don't know, Jeb. I think I have found a way to keep them safe. But I am not sure, so I want you to keep them for another day.''

He nodded amiably, picked up a rake, and started cleaning the aviary. His tuneless whistle provided a familiar background for some very unfamiliar thoughts. For the first time in her life she was not sure of anything.

By the time she had been able to think rationally after her encounter with Rexford, he had gone to the village. He had timed his return to coincide with the arrival of the guests Mother had invited for dinner. Instead of asking him, *Who were you working for? Why did you kiss me?* or even, *Why are you looking at me like that?* Amanda had struggled to produce a bright smile and make non-babbling responses to the interminable conversation.

She had not expected morning to find her still nervous. Anyone would think she had never been kissed before. At twenty-five she had had her share of . . . of nothing. Not if what happened yesterday could still be called kissing. She remembered other men. Fleeting pecks on the lips followed by awkward apologies or lingering contacts that produced a brief tingle. Those were kisses.

Rexford had not kissed, he had consumed her. She had only to shut off the warnings her mind screamed and let her body remember, and she felt torn in two.

She closed her eyes and surrendered to the memory. Gooseflesh broke out on her arms and spine. Her toes curled in her boots and her lips pursed. Every nerve reached outward, commanding her to seek out Rexford and beg him to kiss her again.

A sharp peck on her wrist broke the spell. She opened her eyes and looked down. Grace pecked again, calling Amanda's attention to her empty extended hand. "Sorry, darling." Amanda reached into her attached pocket and pulled out a handful of cracked corn. Sanity returned. "It's all right, sweetheart. I know you're trying to warn me. You think I don't realize he kissed me to make me forget everything else."

Grace pecked happily at the yellow kernels, looking up occasionally with enough encouragement for Amanda to continue. "You are worried because I liked his kiss. You think I will forget he's a rogue and a scoundrel." Amanda laughed, grateful she didn't have to make sense when talking to Grace. "And those are probably his good points."

The corn disappeared, and Grace hopped into her open palm. Amanda rose from her crouch, smoothing Grace's white feathers, as whisper-soft as the tendrils of Rexford's hair. "Don't worry, my love, I know how to deal with him." She would keep her wits about her, at least long enough to ask him whom he was working for. "Distance is the key."

She let Grace hop to her shoulder, then moved about feeding and handling the other birds while she planned her next encounter with Rexford.

First she needed the proper setting. The terrace would work. She pictured two stone chairs, completely immovable, each only large enough for one. That would deal with the problem of his coming close enough to scatter her thoughts like fluff. The breeze could absorb the humming vibrations he set off. Even he should have sense enough to know curious eyes might be watching from any of a dozen windows. The terrace would be perfect.

Grace snapped her wings and jumped to the ground for more grain. With a few plump turns she shuffled the other birds out of the way, pecked at three grains, and leapt into Amanda's palm again. Amanda laughed. "I know. You like him too. Don't worry, I won't send him away. If I do, he might get involved in something worse, something dangerous. Neither of us wants that."

Grace pecked her on the cheek. "No. I won't promise never to let him kiss me again. But I won't do it until I'm sure he's on our side. Until then, I'll be as prim and a proper as—" Grace pecked again. "No. Not as prim and proper as you, you hoyden. I have seen the way you are starting to look at Lucifer. For the first time I'm beginning to know how you feel."

Grace flew off.

Two hours later Amanda found Prescott at the foot of the stairs, scolding Kitty for a patch of dust on the leg of a gleaming table. "Would you please ask Lord Rexford to join me on the terrace?" She hurried out the side door to settle in her chosen chair before he arrived.

The sun felt warm on her face and the soft breeze occasionally tickled her nostrils with fine strands of her hair. She inhaled the scent of roses and thought about the silly widgeon who had rejected Rexford's suit. Had that girl ever waited for him in the sunshine, listening for the first sound of his step? What a goose she must have been to let a little thing like lack of fortune trouble her.

The click of boot heels on stone alerted Amanda to his approach. She inhaled and straightened her shoulders. A moment later he bent over her and raised her hand to his lips. She had forgotten how close he would come for a greeting.

"Good morning, Amanda." He released her hand and managed to flit his fingers through the hair at her cheek as he drew his own away. "This is only the second time I have seen you with your hair down. You look lovely."

"Thank you." She pointed. "You may sit over there." She was proud of her voice, polite, but just firm enough to prove she had not summoned him to discuss her hair.

He looked in the direction she indicated. Amanda took his slight frown as her reward for selecting immovable furniture. For a moment she thought he might reject her choice and hover over her, or worse, pace about. But eventually he backed up and dropped into the stone chair. Tying him there would probably be going too far.

His gaze took in the setting, lingering on the windows of the house behind her. "I regret I cannot commend your choice of a place to continue our discussion of my problem with women. Far too public, wouldn't you say?" His eyes twinkled.

Amanda ignored the warm flush that crept to her cheeks. He had obviously decided not to ignore what had happened between them. She could be just as direct as he. "I have come to a decision on that particular topic. While I still believe you need help, you will not get it from me. At least not until I can trust you to behave like a gentleman. That was terribly crude yesterday, and I don't wonder that gentlewomen run away from you."

His eyebrows rose and his mouth rounded. "Oh? I don't recall your running away."

"That is only because you caught me off guard. I never expected . . ." Amanda's flush deepened. She had no intention of describing what she never expected. "Be that as it may, we have other things to talk about."

163

"More's the pity."

Amanda wished she had taken the time to perfect her mother's impatient "humph." She did her best with an explosion of air and a sharp tilt to her nose. "That is precisely why you are in such an unfortunate position. However, we shall not discuss it." He refused to look properly chagrined, so she added, "Though it would serve you right if you had to marry some tradesman's daughter who will not mind churlish manners." She recalled his stated preference in a fiancée. "And I hope she has impossibly thick legs."

He guffawed. "When it comes to that, I am sure you will help me find someone suitable."

She had been right to declare the topic hopeless. "In my distraction yesterday I neglected to ask you the most important question."

"An oversight I am certain you will remedy immediately." He settled against the back of his chair and rested one ankle on the opposite knee, pulling his breeches taut on both calves.

"Who hired you?"

"As I understand it, you did."

She gave his answer the impatient wave it deserved. "Not yesterday. Before. Who were you working for?"

"Ahhh. Now there we have a slight problem."

Amanda tensed. "It is a simple question."

He lowered his foot to the ground and leaned forward with his hands folded between his knees. "But one with significant implications. I don't recall ever admitting to working for anyone."

"But yesterday you said—"

"No. You said. You said I was impoverished. You said I had come here to kidnap your birds, and you said I had to be working for someone."

"But you didn't deny it."

"Would you have believed me if I had?"

"No."

"So there." He sat back. "You have me guilty and convicted. But I have never been willing to confess my transgressions, and you cannot expect me to humble myself now."

Amanda frowned. "You are playing with words." Men did think such funny things where their pride was involved. "I am not asking you to confess to anything. Merely to give me a name."

He shook his head. "I cannot do that without admitting to being the wretch you think me."

Amanda still could not perceive the difference, though the tight line of his mouth suggested she would not move him easily. "But what am I to think?"

He smiled and looked directly at her with mischievous eyes. "You have never had the slightest difficulty in deciding what to think. May I make a suggestion which might solve your problem?"

"Please do."

"Now, I am confessing to nothing, mind you, but if I have been hired as you suspect, a breeder wealthy enough to pay for my services would scarcely approach me directly. He would hire somebody named Bonecruncher or something like that to draw me aside in a dark alley and present his proposition. I would never know who hired me and could never expose him."

"Are you saying that is what happened?"

He gave a dismissive wave with his right hand. "I am not confessing to anything, remember? Merely saying that is what might have happened."

She narrowed her eyes and regarded him suspiciously. "And where would you collect your money?"

"In the same dark alley. Say, two days after I accomplished my task."

She resented his refusal to be straightforward, but the suggestion of an intermediary made sense. "How can I be sure of your loyalty if you will not give me a name?"

She thought she saw a hint of compassion in his eyes, instantly replaced by his roguish smile. "Not *will not. Cannot.*" He turned his palms up. "I gave you Bonecruncher. I swear that is the best I can do."

Her eyes narrowed. Perhaps a threat would serve where polite questions failed. "And if I say I cannot let you stay if you do not tell me who hired you?"

His jaw tensed and he spoke in a cool tone. "There will be nothing more I can do. I have told you all I can." He let the silence linger, and Amanda refused to break it. A dry leaf tumbled across the flagstones between them. "I must remind you," he said at last, "if you send me away, you have no way of knowing who might follow. A band of ruffians. A delivery man from the village. You might never spot the threat in time." He smiled. "A foreign prince. An Indian rope climber. A—"

"Enough. You have made your point."

"And?" He rose and took three firm steps across the distance that separated them.

She spoke quickly before he could come near enough to urge a commitment she was not ready to make. "And I don't know."

He stopped in front of her and looked down directly into her eyes. "Then know this. I have no wish to harm either you or your birds. I swear it on my life." He spoke so slowly, his eyes so unguarded, Amanda could not bring herself to doubt his sincerity.

Without conscious thought, Amanda found herself placing her hand into his extended palm. He drew her to her feet so close to him she could feel his warm breath on her face. The breeze carried his heavy masculine scent mixed with the smell of roses from the terrace. He lifted her chin with his index finger so she had no choice but to look directly into his eyes. "I don't believe you want me to go," he said.

She watched his lips form every word, conscious of the way they would feel on her own and how much more subtle their movements could be. Her breath quickened, but the immovable chair prevented a retreat.

"Say it. You don't want me to go, do you?"

"No," she whispered.

His fingers still held her chin, and he reached up and flicked her lower lip with his thumb. "Good."

166

She put her hand on his chest to keep him from bending forward with the kiss she feared and wanted. "I don't want you to go." She spoke so softly she could barely hear her own words. "But I don't trust you either."

"Good." Now his thumb traced her lower lip.

Her chin tingled.

"If you had not chosen such a wretched place to meet, I would show you another reason for not trusting me. As it is, this is the best I can do." He increased the pressure of his thumb, circling her lips in a kiss that was not a kiss.

Amanda's knees weakened with the same surrender she recognized from the previous day. If they were alone . . . If . . . Involuntarily her hand rose to imitate his gesture. The faint roughness of his chin tickled against her index finger. Her thumb found his lower lip, soft, pliant, and alive under her touch. His upper lip closed, trapping it. His tongue darted forward, wetting the tip of her finger in a shockingly intimate gesture.

"Ummm. That's nice." He formed the words around her finger, drenching her hand with hot breath. His words carried the echo of a dim room and far more passionate contact. His fingers trailed promises across her throat.

"I must be crazy," Amanda thought, but still she did not withdraw her hand. Instead she let her tongue play over the roughened ridges of his thumb.

Footsteps slapped against the stone. "Miss Langley."

Rexford drew his hand from her mouth, but reached up to hold her fingers against his lips for a final fluttering kiss before releasing it and stepping back.

Abel, the groom, came into view. "Miss Langley, come quick and see what's happening in the stable!"

Chapter Ten

Amanda glanced at the sky over the stable. She grasped her skirt and took a single running step toward the structure.

Rexford clasped a restraining hand around her upper arm. "I am sure it is nothing to be alarmed about."

She shook off his grasp. "What is it, Abel? What's the matter?"

"Two men, miss. Big men with two of the prettiest horses you ever saw. They said they was gonna stay here. But you didn't tell us nothin' so I thought I better come and get you quick."

"I told you it was nothing to be alarmed about." Something in Rexford's tone made her turn and study him. Whatever was going on, he knew more about it than she did.

"Rexford!" How do you accuse a man who has just been sucking on your thumb of . . . She didn't even know what to accuse him of. Of renting out part of her stable? "Rexford, what do you know of this?"

"I told you it was nothing to be alarmed about."

Abel shuffled his feet and looked back over his shoulder. "Are you coming, miss? I think you oughta come now."

"Quiet, Abel." Amanda tightened her jaw, then turned and backed up three full paces to give Rexford the full effect of her glare. "What is going on?"

"The horses belong to me. I arranged to have them delivered this morning." He absently drew out his watch. "Right on time, I see."

"You—you—" Amanda sputtered. "You arranged to have horses delivered without my permission. I . . ."

"Not exactly without your permission." Rexford came forward and gave her arm several patronizing pats. "Yesterday you insisted I stay on. Not that I mean to make any criticism of the stable you keep, but surely you did not expect I could make do with the sorry goers you keep here. All three of your riding horses are several years past praying for, if you will forgive me for saying so."

Amanda backed out of reach. "I know. Mother's last husband had no interest in—I cannot believe I am apologizing to you for the horses we keep. You can just send your fancy creatures back wherever they came from. They cannot stay here."

"Of course they can," he said in a patronizing tone. "I have explored the stable. You have six extra stalls and two rooms above where the grooms can stay."

"The grooms!" Amanda rolled her eyes toward the sky. "You expect the grooms to stay as well?"

"Naturally. Abel here certainly would not want to take on the extra work, would you, Abel?"

"No, yer lordship." Abel shot a hasty glance at Amanda and took in her expression. "I mean, yes, miss." He looked back at Rexford and again at Amanda. "I mean no if yer don' want me to, and yes if yer do. Whatever either of yer wants me to say is fine with me."

Rexford brushed his hands together. "I guess that settles it. I shall go and see them settled in."

"You will do no such thing. Nothing is settled."

"Of course it is." Rexford shifted his gaze to the open-mouthed groom. "Run along, Abel. I will join you in a minute."

Abel doffed a nonexistent cap and hurried away.

Rexford waited until the groom was well out of earshot, and even then spoke in a confidential tone. "It was a little embarrassing to mention it in front of a servant, but you said yourself we must watch the expense. I am merely following your orders. It will be much less costly keeping the horses here."

"I meant you watch your expense. Not—"

He grinned. "I intend to do that as well. I have made a mental note to eat less and plan to cancel my most recent order with my tailor." He stepped forward, halving the distance she had so carefully created.

"You are impossible." Amanda took another step back lest he reach for her chin again. She weakened. She had known since the moment he first suggested staying that an earl did not visit like an ordinary mortal. Perhaps she should be grateful his entourage had not arrived days ago. Two horses would not present a significant problem, and the grooms certainly could not be any more trouble than their master.

"Think of the rides we can have together."

Amanda thought of all the secluded places they might ride to—places where he could make her forget everything but how she felt when he stood so close she could feel his breath on her face. "In that case, I think I had better send for several more grooms," she said. "I would not want to ride with you with less than seven grooms and three maids as chaperones." She turned and stomped toward the house, aware she had given permission for him not only to stay, but to keep his horses.

He always did seem to get his way.

The following morning Rexford paced his room, planning his campaign as carefully as any battlefield maneuver. He had been selected for this job because of his ability to analyze information, and he did not need to be a genius to know he was in trouble. If Tag's father said time was running out, time was running out, regardless of the reports of gay soirees and balls in Brussels.

To secure Amanda's cooperation he would have to make the war as real for her as it was for him. He immediately discarded his first plan. It would not be a particularly good idea to drag Amanda to the Continent and let her sit on a hill where she could look down on the massing armies and listen to the sound of cannoneers practicing their aim.

But she needed something like that. Amanda lived in the present and found reality in things she could see. Rexford rotated his shoulder. The newly formed scar tugged slightly. Something real she could see and touch. He let his mind linger on the last word, and conjured up some singularly pleasant realities, but refused to let his mind drift further in that direction. Her mother might object if he stripped off his shirt in the drawing room to display his evidence of war.

Hands clasped behind his back, he lowered his head and resumed pacing. He found little inspiration in the gleaming wood floor. He had already heard Amanda's opinion of the newspaper accounts. "More fuss about that wretched Napoleon. We just put him away once, and he was emperor then."

Half of the people in Brussels refused to believe Napoleon could amass an army large enough to threaten the world in the few months he had been free. The documents from the Continent dealt more with the gay social life of all the English tourists in Brussels than with the fact the city might be torn apart by war in a matter of days.

Rexford shrugged. For artillery he would have only his own words. He rarely talked about his experiences on the Peninsula, but he would do precisely that if he had to. Somehow he would convince her that men he knew and cared about might die without her help.

Amanda had agreed to ride with him at one o'clock. If she did not carry out her threat to bring seven grooms and three maids, he should have the perfect opportunity to do some serious convincing, if he could keep his mind above his waist.

He glanced at the clock. Exactly ten minutes to think of men he cared about. Ten minutes to give his voice the proper note of intensity. The task took precisely fourteen seconds. Faces and voices tumbled through his head, until he finally stopped at a picture of Tag's father with his arm thrown around his son's shoulder, both lifting a glass to drink to "God, country, and a room full of women."

"Ready," he said aloud, and realized he had straightened his shoulders just as he did at the first note of a bugle.

Amanda pulled her mare to a stop atop the grassy hill and circled so she could look back over the valley. A stiff breeze had blown away the early morning clouds, leaving only a few feathery patches of white in an azure sky. The same breeze set the young leaves of the trees below to dancing and bent the early grasses in a playful bow. White and lavender wildflowers formed a patchwork quilt of color. She loved the view, and never more than in late spring.

Never more than today in the company of her disreputable earl.

The mare shied and Amanda looked down. Rexford had dismounted and stood next to her with one hand extended and the other barely touching the reins. His grooms had already proven themselves as much of a nuisance as she had anticipated, buzzing around and treating him like the master of the house. Fortunately, she had Abel and Lily to frustrate any plan he had to unsettle her.

She ignored him, and waited until both the groom and maid crested the rise on their slower mounts, then unhooked her leg to dismount. Before she could move, he reached up, circled her waist with his hands, and effortlessly lifted her down. His hands lingered a fraction of a second too long for strict propriety, but several fractions too short for a woman who had gone to sleep remembering his mind-numbing touch.

She put off inhaling, knowing the air would carry his masculine scent. She could not afford to close her eyes to savor it. "Thank you." If the words came out slightly breathless,

172

the final canter up the hill could explain that and the warm flush that burned her cheeks. When she finally drew a breath, the fresh spring air carried the tangy crispness of pine-scented soap, and a touch of something else that could only be defined as healthy male animal.

The mare at her back blocked her retreat.

"A beautiful spot, Amanda." He smiled, not even turning to admire the panoramic view.

Remembering her determination to be perverse, she ignored the echo of his words through her thoughts. "We did not come here to admire the day."

She put her hand on his shoulder and shifted him aside, surprised she had never before realized how easily she could do that. "Over here, Abel," she said to the groom, who had already begun unhitching the crate strapped to the back of his saddle.

Abel carried the crate over and set it on the ground next to Amanda. Amanda's hands shook as she reached in and lifted out the small bundle of feathers Jeb had unimaginatively christened Whitey.

Rexford watched. "You said you just flew him the other day. Why weren't you nervous then?"

"He was with a whole flock then. Even the youngest bird will follow a flock home. Today is the real test." Her hand tightened, and she had to fight the irrational impulse to return Whitey to the carrying cage. "I may never see him again."

"I thought you said they always come home unless . . ."

"The old ones, yes. But the young ones—some do and some don't."

"Some get lost?"

"Possibly." Amanda smiled, and the wind lifted the errant tendrils of hair that had escaped her hat and blew them against her cheek. Her spirit lifted with the exhilarating fantasy of being carried aloft by that wind. "I prefer to think some choose the endless freedom to security. I would if I were a bird."

He looked at her, an unreadable but soft expression in his

dark eyes. "Only if someone were unwise enough to let you go off alone."

Amanda drew her arm back for the underhand toss. Without a break she swung it forward. At the height of the arc she released the white bird.

A heartbeat later the rapid snap of wings filled the air. She and Rexford watched Whitey rise toward the blue sky. The bird circled. Amanda held her breath, conscious that beside her Rexford was doing the same. Twice more the white form circled overhead, then shot off in a straight line, back in the direction from which they had come. Air whooshed from Rexford's lungs.

She bent, lifted out the next bird.

Ten minutes later the last bird became a tiny speck and disappeared against the blue sky. Abel had already loaded the crate onto the waiting horse and stood poised to leave. He usually started down first, but had sense enough this time to wait for orders.

Rexford looked from him to Amanda and back to Abel again. "You may go ahead, Abel. I will see Miss Langley safely home."

"Not on your life, Rexford," Amanda said. She raised her voice so the two servants could hear her. "Abel, I will let you and Lily know when we are ready to leave."

Rexford gave a faint nod. "A wise precaution, but in this case unnecessary."

"After yesterday, I would not say—"

A hint of color appeared on Rexford's cheekbones, but he met her gaze without flinching. "I admit I let things get a bit out of hand yesterday, but in general, I do not seduce innocents."

His nearness and the memory of his hand caressing her breast made Amanda feel like anything but an innocent. His eyes softened, and continued to stare into hers until she became conscious of the blood rushing through her veins. Her tongue darted out to lick her suddenly dry lips.

"I . . . I don't seduce innocents unless they look at me like that," he murmured. He stepped back and looked toward the chatting servants. "Perhaps you are wise to have them remain. I am only a man, after all."

Amanda recognized the way his tone quickened her heartbeat. She wondered what it would be like to be kissed at the top of the world with the sun on her face, though his look warned he would not stop with a kiss. She would have to think about that.

She looked out over the serene valley and managed to slow her breathing. At least she could enjoy a few relaxed moments in his company. "I usually linger a while after I release the birds," she said.

He offered his arm and led her to the precise patch of grass she usually chose when she came here alone.

She eased down to sit, running her fingers through the warm grass.

"I assume you have something you want to talk about," he said. He dropped down beside her.

"Why would you assume that?"

He stretched out comfortably on his side, resting his head on one elbow. "Because you usually do." He smiled. "As often as not it is one of my faults that needs correcting. I have come to quite look forward to our conversations, lest I go through life with any illusions."

The warm sun gentled Amanda's mood, and the soft breeze wafted away any desire to bicker. She studied his languid form, and thought how comfortable she felt with him in this mood. As if she could say anything and he would accept her without listing the dozen ways she should be different. "Am I really so hard on you?"

He gave his head a gentle shake. "This week you are the only good thing in my life. You keep me from thinking too much. Otherwise I might have gone mad."

Mad. The word shocked Amanda. He seemed to regard life as a huge game. "Thinking about what?" she asked. "Surely not money. I said—"

"The war."

"What—" Amanda almost said *What war,* then remembered Napoleon had escaped and there was a lot of talk about

175

more fighting. "The war is far away. A small thing."

He sat up, and seemed to look straight into her soul. "To you perhaps. Not to me. You forget I was a soldier. I was with Wellington on the Peninsula. I saw horrors no one should have to face." He closed his eyes, and deep pain lines appeared on his forehead and around the corners of his eyes.

Amanda checked the impulse to smooth the lines away. More than that, she wanted to put her hand over his mouth and silence him. But he had never talked to her of this. Perhaps he was offering an important part of himself. "Tell me about it," she said softly.

Rexford talked. With his gaze on a distant rock he spoke of riding for endless hours through driving rain, chilled to the bone, of watching friends cut from their horses and being unable to help, of men carrying comrades for hours, knowing they wouldn't live until noon, then carrying them for miles after they died.

His voice went on and on. Amanda knew even when he looked that he wasn't seeing her. He was seeing friends whose lonely deaths still haunted him.

"I'm sorry," she said softly every time he paused. Any other words seemed meaningless and inadequate.

Finally he stopped speaking. A leaf rustled. A bird chirped. Still, he didn't speak again.

Amanda allowed herself a silent sigh of relief. She did not want to hear any more. She sought for words to drive the lonely look from his eyes. "I am sorry. It must have been terrible. But at least it's over."

"Hardly. It has begun all over again. Even now, in France . . . All my friends—"

She gasped. "But Napoleon has just escaped. No one . . ."

He shook his head. "You just don't believe it because you don't know anyone there. I do. Some of my closest friends might be dying right now while we're enjoying a patch of sunshine." His jaw tightened, and he looked at her as if it were her fault. "Do you want to hear about them? Would you like to know there are real people over there?"

No, Amanda's mind screamed. She did not want to hear

any more, but nodded, giving him silent permission to continue.

"The Earl of Elmgrove, my best friend's father. You would like him."

Good, Amanda thought, they could talk about the Earl of Elmgrove. Not about war and dying. Just about a man. "How do you know I would like him?"

Rexford smiled, and for the first time in a long while really seemed to see her. "Because you don't tolerate fools gladly, and Elmgrove's no fool. He would match you word for word, then laugh with you if you bested him. He can outdrink, outsing, outlaugh any man I know. I would have traded my soul to have him as a father. He knows that and treats me like a son." His wistful look turned into a wary grin. "At least when he's not trying to swindle me out of my shirt."

Amanda returned his smile. "You are right. I would like him. Certainly if he can best you at anything."

Rexford's face hardened. "Then you better be quick to like him. You may not have much time."

"Why?"

"He is over there now. Supposed to be in uniform doing reconnaissance work, which isn't too dangerous. If they catch him, he will be a prisoner of war and eventually exchanged. But Ta—my friend suspects the earl is running about behind the lines out of uniform. If they catch him, they'll hang him for that."

"Oh, dear." Unconsciously Amanda put her hands to her throat. "Your friend suspects he might be out of uniform? What do you think?"

Rexford gave a humorless laugh. "Me? I know he is. Elmgrove never in his life went after anything except at full tilt and devil take the consequences."

"I see." Amanda could not think of anything consoling to say, so she let the silence linger, surprised to note the day had not darkened at all. The chill came from the words not the still warm wind.

Eventually she drew her legs under her in preparation for rising. She put her hand over Rexford's clenched fingers. "I am sorry for your worries. You do have a way of making the war seem very real.'' She stood and walked toward the servants and the horses.

Rexford's voice came from beside her. "I'm glad. I wish I could do the same for all the civilians here. That way more of them might be willing to help when asked.''

Something in his tone caused Amanda to snap her head sideways and look at him questioningly. A false note? A warning he had manipulated her again? She studied his impassive expression. His eyes held no hint of the smoldering look that would suggest he hoped to take advantage of her newly awakened sympathy.

She shrugged the feeling aside. "Thank you for a lovely afternoon, Rexford. I hope I understand you a little better now.''

Rexford turned from his position at the library window. "Dammit, Tag, do what you want."

Tag lowered the paper he had been holding and stood. "That's it, Marc, we have to do something about you. And we have to do it today.''

"About me? You're the one asking the stupid questions. What do I care whether you send that on to London or burn it? You decide.''

"And you're the one who has been snapping my head off three times an hour for the past two days. I keep waiting for the servants to ask me if my name really is *Dammittag*. If ever I saw a man who needed a woman, you do. What do you say we go to the village right now? I swear, that little Betsy at the inn is not only willing but very accomplished.''

Rexford cursed again, but inaudibly so Tag couldn't claim it as a name. He didn't need a woman. He knew that because the first time Tag had suggested Betsy he had seriously considered the idea, actually pictured himself at the inn undressing a willing woman. The idea had left him cold. "I don't need a woman.''

Tag laughed. "No. Of course not. You'd rather prowl

around growling like a caged bear and alienate the only friend you have left.''

Rexford forced his muscles to relax, starting with his fingertips. "Sorry, Tag." He got as far as his shoulders before his fingers tightened again. He needed to do something, and there wasn't a damn thing he could do. He was trapped in a house with a woman he wanted to tumble to the floor every time she walked into a room. A woman he shouldn't even think of touching.

She would do no more than take his arm to walk in to dinner, and his mind would explode with fantasies of drawing her into his arms and kissing her. Worse, with every day that passed, he became less confident he could stop with a kiss. His hands tingled with the memory of the soft curve of her buttocks under his fingers.

Rexford gave a wry laugh and considered confessing to Tag that *Don't seduce your hostess* had replaced *Dammit* as his favorite mental expression. "Bah, the waiting is just getting to me. Are we about finished here? Maybe I will go for a walk."

"Sure. I'll take care of these last few things." Tag grinned. "Keep your eyes open. Maybe you will find your charming personality somewhere. I know you lost it on the grounds here."

Rexford slipped out the side door without a reply. Outside he unconsciously searched for Amanda, even though he knew she had gone upstairs for a rest. He decided to stroll in the direction of the cote and practice identifying the birds, the only thing he did excel at nowadays.

Even before the buildings came into view, he heard the scratchy sound of Jeb's rake and the tuneless whistle that always accompanied the interminable task of cleaning out the loft.

"Afternoon, Jeb," he called.

Jeb looked up with a jerky bounce to his head. His gaze passed over Rexford as rapidly as it did the barren earth between them. "Where's Miss Langley?" Jeb asked. He leaned forward on his rake and shifted his head from side to side as if Rexford were deliberately blocking his view. "Where is she?"

"She's resting in the house." Jeb did not seem nearly as happy to see him come as Tag had been to see him go. Fortunately, as Earl of Rexford, he did not have to depend on his charm to make his way in the world.

"She's gotta be here." Jeb kept looking and tapped the ground impatiently with his rake. "It's important." His chest swelled and he gripped the rake in what seemed to Rexford a fair parody of a military sentry. "It's important. We got a message."

"A message?"

Jeb dug the small cylinder out of a pocket in his loose breeches. "A message." Not only did he not mind Rexford's slow-witted response, but seemed content to prolong the conversation. "We got a message."

Rexford made an effort to clear lingering thoughts of Amanda from his brain. Only an important message would justify using one of the precious few Langley birds in Brussels. Perhaps the start of the war. It shouldn't take five minutes to just establish that a message had arrived. "From whom, Jeb?" Rexford asked brusquely.

Jeb stood his ground, still searching behind Rexford for Amanda. "I think it's one of Mr. Gully's birds. Not Mr. Gully's birds. Miss Langley's birds that she sent to Mr. Gully. But Mr. Gully's birds because it comes from—"

"I understand. I will take the message." He strode across the clearing and held out his hand.

"I think you should get Miss Langley. Messages are always for Miss Langley." Jeb planted his feet like blocks of stone.

Rexford debated his alternatives. Violence could do serious damage to some of his favorite body parts, and even then he might not succeed. To say nothing of annoying the hell out of his already suspicious hostess. A bribe? All the banks in London probably did not contain enough money to shake Jeb's conviction that messages belonged to Amanda.

He opted for reason. "Miss Langley is very tired, Jeb. She

asked me to come out and take care of things today. I think that means messages too."

"I don' know." Jeb hand clenched almost tight enough to wring water from the light metal container. "She lets you take care of a lot of things, but I don' know if messages is a thing like that. Do you think?"

Rexford held out his hand until Jeb's curled fingers actually touched his palm. "Oh, I'm sure." He held his breath and watched the sausage-sized fingers begin to relax. "Thank you, Jeb," He felt the warm metal drop into his palm. "I will take this to Miss Langley."

Jeb continued to stare uncertainly at the fist Rexford had closed around the message. "You be sure to tell her you said I was supposed to give it to you."

"I will." Rexford ignored the feeling that Jeb begrudged him every step, and hurried from the clearing. He waited until he knew the trees sheltered him from view, then stopped to examine the metal cylinder. He immediately recognized the special design, identical to the ones on Amanda's shelf except for the secret compartment, scarcely noticeable unless one measured the depth or knew to look for the hairline joint at the base. Definitely a critical message from the Continent.

He opened the regular compartment first and pulled out the diversionary letter from Gully. Uncurling the thin, transparent paper he read, *My Dear Amanda.*

His dear Amanda, indeed. The man had the nerve of a parvenu. Rexford started to put the letter aside. He had no legitimate business reading any further. The pair had been corresponding long enough that if she chose to let Gully address her as his dear Amanda, she had the right.

She should certainly have more pride. Stupid name, Gully.

He rubbed the paper between his thumb and forefinger. He wouldn't read it. His resolution lasted exactly a second and a half. Possibly it contained information relevant to the war. He didn't really believe that, but it made this breach of etiquette almost acceptable.

He smoothed the paper with his forefinger. *My Dear Amanda, I trust you are looking as forward to the coming race as I am. I have been having great success with* . . . He carried on with a list of names of birds he was having great success with, names of birds he was not having great success with, and hopes that Amanda was having great success with . . .

A thoroughly tedious letter.

Rexford continued to mutter criticisms as he skimmed the page. "Pompous windbag." He slowed only when he came to the final paragraph. *I still thrill to the memory of the glorious night we spent in the storm. I wish every day could contain the same excitement and gratifying conclusion. In the sincere hopes that this year we may repeat the same satisfying performance without the wretched anxiety, I remain* . . .

"You will remain a corpse if I ever get my hands on you, you unctuous bastard." Rexford cursed some more, read the paragraph again, and used up the rest of his vocabulary. He crumpled the thin page and tossed it to the ground. Turning, he stomped off ten paces. Now he had a fair idea where the well-chaperoned Miss Langley learned such a devastatingly effective kissing technique.

He turned and stomped off another ten paces, eyeing the offending letter. On his fourth circuit he bent and picked it up.

He still might have to deliver it if he could not think of some way to convince Jeb not to mention it. Raising his knee, he tried to smooth the creases. Maybe she wouldn't notice. Maybe she would decide Gully was a sloven as well as a bastard.

After two minutes he managed to bring himself under control. Amanda was twenty-five, old enough to decide where she wanted to dispense her favors. So Gully had been there first. So it made worry about offending her with his desire a little ludicrous, and presented some very interesting possibilities.

He began casting about for something to do with the letter. The metal edge of the casing cut into his palm. Of course. He uncurled his fingers.

The war.

Bloody hell, he had forgotten the damned war. With the haste of an uneasy conscience he pried the rimmed bottom from the cylinder and dug with a fingernail at the wadded paper inside. The message had to be from the Continent and had to be important.

He tucked Gully's page in his pocket and smoothed the smaller sheet on his raised knee. Small neat block letters filled the page. His gaze traveled to the signature at the bottom, a cramped but stylized *E* tucked in the corner. Elmgrove.

Rexford supported his back against a tree and read the message. In concise words Elmgrove summarized the opinion he had developed over the past week. Despite all evidence to the contrary, Napoleon would not stop at the Franco-Belgian border. The fortifications there were makeshift in too many places. French soldiers talked with too much knowledge of the terrain between the border and Brussels. Napoleon would march straight past the border, perhaps to Brussels itself. And he would do it soon.

Rexford paused in his reading and frowned. Important information, critical perhaps, but something that could wait until Elmgrove returned to headquarters. The plan had been for intelligence officers to carry the birds, but to use them only for information that could not be gotten out any other way. That meant . . .

Rexford's thumb and forefinger tightened on the page in an effort to quash the thought.

He ran his gaze to the final paragraph. *Forgive a personal note to spare my family the pain of an unexplained disappearance. I was regrettably captured out of uniform. Ironically I am being held at the Perpignan farmhouse, where I played as a boy. I assume the French will deal with me in their usual efficient manner at dawn. Warmest regards to my son.*

Blood drained from Rexford's head. He turned and clutched the tree for support, his fingernails digging into the soft bark. "Tag," he whispered, and heard his own agony in the word.

He continued to grip the tree until his knees promised to support him. Even then he did not start directly for the house. He would need strength to face Tag. He dug for it, and found only a quivering weakness in his stomach. He drew his shoulders back. "Fake it, Rexford," he said aloud. "You're a soldier. Tag's a soldier." He stepped out toward the house with a precise military stride.

He entered his room to find Tag sprawled on the bed, his boots black against the green coverlet. Tag nodded without glancing up from the worn book of Greek tragedies. "I am not even going to look at you until you assure me the walk improved your disposition," Tag said.

"Tag." Rexford hated the scratchy sound of his own voice and the fact he couldn't think what to say next.

Tag glanced up. "Blazing hell! What happened to you?" He bounced to his feet directly from the prone position and crossed the room in two strides. His fingers circled Rexford's upper arm in a tight supportive grip.

"Not me, Tag. You." For all his resolution Rexford found he could not put words to the news. He held out the letter, waited until Tag started to read, then walked to the window to give his friend the dignity of dealing with the shock in private. Seconds passed. Minutes? Tag would tell him when to turn.

"Dammit, Marc—"

Rexford turned.

Tag's face was the color of the paper he still held only inches from his chin. His eyes glistened with naked pain. "Do you think . . . ? Is there any hope . . . ? I must . . ." Frantically he looked about.

Rexford crossed the room and gripped his friend's shoulders. "I'm sorry, Tag. So sorry." In spite of the haunted eyes, Tag stood firm under his grip.

"We have to do something. This . . ." Tag shook the letter. "This just came today. He is still alive. I can . . ." He looked toward the door, poised to run all the way to Brussels.

Rexford tightened his grip. "It would take you two days." He shook his head slowly. "Do you want a drink?"

"I can't just sit here. Not all night." His expression anticipated the endless night. "We can't just sit and wait for the sun to rise." The paper fluttered to the floor.

Rexford could not say "I'm sorry" again, but he couldn't think of anything else to say. He walked over, poured a glass of brandy, and held it out.

Tag waved it aside. "No. He wouldn't give up on me." He paced across the room. His boots made a solid, falsely reassuring sound on the wood floor. "He's still alive over there. I know the farmhouse. I spent enough summers there as a boy."

Rexford froze in place. "You could describe how to get there?"

"Of course. I am standing here seeing myself running up the path. I know how to get there. I just can't do it."

Hope flared. Rexford's mind raced with an idea. He pictured soldiers slipping through the night to an indifferently guarded farmhouse. "You can't, but others can. The 95th Regiment is in Brussels. Half of those men would shovel out Hell itself to get your father back—and consider themselves well paid if he sat and drank with them until dawn. They just have to know he needs them."

Tag gave a defeated shrug. "And we can't tell them."

"Of course we can. A bird got the message here. A bird can get a message back to Gully's place and whoever is there can pass it on to headquarters." He crossed to the window. "We still have enough light. The flight takes two hours. Maybe three. We have at least five or six hours before it is completely dark."

Tag's face burned with a fierce light, then once again sagged into hopelessness. "The birds are for emergencies."

Rexford's jaw hardened. "What is this? A walk in the park? Dammit, it's your father." He clenched his fist to rein in the emotion. "Not just your father. One of England's most important agents. In his head he carries more information about the people and terrain between Paris and Brussels than

185

all the rest of the agents put together will collect in a year.'' He straightened. "This time I am not speaking as a friend, I'm talking as a soldier. Think how many lives his knowledge might save."

"But even if we could get a message through, the French would have guards. . . ." Tag's voice trailed off, begging Rexford to counter the objection.

Rexford smiled. "Sloppy ones, I'd say, if they let your father keep the bird in the first place."

Tag shook his head with an affectionate and admiring smile. "Knowing my father, he convinced them to let him keep his beloved pet for company on his last ni . . . Do you think we could do it, Marc? Do you really think there's any hope?"

"I know there is."

"But Amanda—"

"Damn Amanda! We'll gag her and put her in the attic if we have to." Rexford's spirits soared with the thought of any action, but he forced himself to lean against the wall and think. Perhaps the moment had finally come to risk the truth and trust Amanda's good sense. "I don't think we'll have to tie her. I've been telling her war stories for the past three days. Half of them about your father. Hell, by now she knows him almost as well as we do. She will help us."

Tag was already at the door. "Come on then. You can talk to her, just let me listen. I swear if she says no, I am going to tie a message on every one of her birds and let them all go."

Rexford learned from Prescott that Amanda was in the sitting room where he had kissed her. He approached the room with a firm step, conscious of Tag hard on his heels. At the door he paused and turned to Tag. "Wait here."

Amanda looked up when he entered. She sat stiff in her chair, a pink letter in her lap. "Ahhh, Rexford. Just the person I wanted to see."

"Not now, Amanda. I need to talk to you about something. I need to talk to you about the war."

She gave an artificial smile. "What a coincidence. I want to talk to you about the same thing."

"About the Earl of Elmgrove, he needs—"

"Oh yes. The Earl of Elmgrove." She nodded, her body stiff, her tone more bitter than he had ever heard. "Your incomparable Earl of Elmgrove. Slinking about in France. Hiding in abandoned barns. Eating kernels of corn left by the chickens. Are you looking for more sympathy for all your friend is suffering?"

Rexford's mouth dropped open. "Amanda, I don't understand. I need—"

"You can need all the way to hell and gone." She rose. "Here's your precious Earl of Elmgrove in a letter just come by post from my cousin Emily in Brussels." She flung the letter at him. The pages fluttered to the floor midway between them. "Devil take me if I ever believe another word you say."

She brushed Tag from the doorway as she sailed out of the room.

Chapter Eleven

Rexford took a single broken step toward the door and checked the impulse to physically support his friend. Tag's ashen face had frozen in open-mouthed disbelief. His fingers rested against the door frame, but bore no weight. "I . . ." His voice cracked. He stiffened for a renewed effort, looking directly into Rexford's eyes. "I presume the lady has chosen not to help." Somewhere he had found the cool, dry tone Rexford had heard only once before, when a drunk but notorious swordsman had challenged Tag to meet him at dawn.

"I'm sorry, Tag. I have no idea. . . ." He bent to pick up the paper at his feet, knowing he would soon know more than he wanted to. It turned out to be not one paper, but three sheets of elegant feminine handwriting.

One word told Rexford everything. *Brussels.* Somehow Amanda had gotten a letter from Brussels and she didn't like the contents. Rexford read.

The content was as feminine as the script. Shopping, bonnets, lengths of ribbon. Morning calls. He said . . . She said . . . *Get on with it,* he thought impatiently. An entire page about one gentleman whose name Rexford had never heard.

188

Finally, on the last page, underlined—*The Shocking Incident at the Ball*.

The Earl of Elmgrove kissed one young miss on the terrace. The Earl of Elmgrove kissed a matron in an alcove. The Earl of Elmgrove complained to his hostess that if he married every woman he kissed he would have his own army and attack the French himself. The Earl of Elmgrove then kissed his hostess in full view of everyone and marched out.

Rexford let out a long breath and looked at his friend. "I am afraid your father's privations do not quite match the picture I painted for Amanda. She probably thinks she has caught me in another clanker."

"But what . . ."

Rexford didn't bother handing him the pages. "Your father was at a ball. As usual, people noticed."

"I don't see what that has to do with—"

"Civilian view, Tag. If they send you off to war, you damn well better stay there. Soldiers are supposed to stand in front of firing guns twenty-four hours a day until everyone gets tired and goes home. I never considered disabusing Amanda of that notion, and now . . ." Rexford shrugged.

"And now what are we supposed to do?"

"We steal a bird."

Like Amanda a moment before, Rexford brushed past Tag, though he did it so he would not have to look at the naked gratitude that flared in his friend's eyes. He marched directly to the library to compose the note the bird would carry.

The sound of footsteps behind him told him Tag had followed. "I think the last part of your father's letter speaks for itself. We need only be certain it gets in the right hands." Rexford wrote. *Gully; Please deliver the attached letter immediately to* . . . He paused. He could think of a dozen men capable of the action necessary, but if the one he chose could not be located within the hour, all might be lost.

He crumpled the sheet and began again. *Gully: Please deliver the attached letter immediately to the most competent senior officer available. It goes without saying, a life and possibly the war effort may depend on your efficient action.*

He signed the note and rolled it with the message he had retrieved from Tag. "When we get to the cote, Tag, I will ask Jeb to show you to the stable. Keep him there a few moments and I will have this off."

Rexford spoke with more confidence than he felt. He moved toward the door leading to the terrace planning his actions. The storage shed for a container. Insert the documents. Select a bird. Attach the container and throw the bird toward Brussels. What could go wrong?

Nothing, he assured himself fiercely, because Elmgrove's slim chance for life depended on it.

Moments later Rexford watched Jeb and Tag walk away. He felt a fierce admiration for his friend. Whatever Tag's feelings, he was chatting amiably to Jeb as they walked. So like his father. Whatever the outcome of the afternoon, Tag would have made a new friend in Jeb.

They disappeared from sight, and Rexford acted with the precision he had defined in his mind. Locating the container and inserting the documents took only seconds. He entered the aviary. Ooze squished under his boots. Grace fluttered to his shoulder. Rexford resisted the impulse to brush her away. No one would see, but she wasn't to blame for his tense state. "I wish I could return your affection, old girl."

In the partitioned area he searched for the bird he wanted—the white one who should have a funny tilt to her head but didn't. He remembered her best because he often tilt his own head when he looked at her, trying to get her to produce the quizzical look he had first seen.

After the initial flurry she settled almost at his feet. She scurried away. He resisted the temptation to lunge and waited. After a moment she bobbed her way back. He reached slowly this time, and captured her in his palm.

Attaching the container proved easier than he anticipated, and a moment later he divested himself of Grace and stepped from the aviary. With the fencing safely between them, he even turned and winked at Grace. "I love you too, my dear. But ours must be an unrequited love." Gully's bird sat quietly in his palm.

190

Still not believing the scheme would work, Rexford took three long strides into the clearing. The bird looked ready for a nap. He drew back his arm in the underhanded throw he had seen Amanda use and released the bird. For a fraction of a second nothing happened, then she snapped her wings once, again. She rose toward the sky.

Rexford held his breath, certain she would circle and return. She flew higher and circled directly overhead. "Go," he whispered. She circled again, still higher, then chose a path and flew. Rexford watched until she was only a tiny speck, then nothing.

He exhaled. He'd done it. He looked about, poised for action, and realized he could think of nothing to do but stand about and practice looking innocent. He did that for about two minutes, then joined Tag in the stable.

Jeb saw him first. "I'm glad you've come," he said with an uneasy expression. "I showed him here, but he kept standin' askin' me questions. I haf ta get ba—"

"It's all right. I'll take over." Rexford spoke to Jeb, but he saw the unspoken question on Tag's face and nodded.

Jeb lumbered off before Rexford finished speaking.

Tag's shoulders rounded, and even from twelve feet away Rexford could hear the whoosh of air he exhaled. "Thank—"

"Don't say it, Tag. It was the right thing to do." He could not accept Tag's relief without a warning. "It may not help."

"At least we tried. Now we wait." Tag's color was better, and he forced a smile. "It might have been the right thing, but now you have to figure out how you're going to explain it to your lady friend."

Rexford laughed. "I have been thinking about that. I decided to borrow a page from Wellington's strategy book."

Tag raised his brows. "I doubt you can expect her to stand still while you pound her with artillery for three days."

"Tempting as that is, I have decided on an opening salvo and a temporary strategic withdrawal."

"Splendid. At least the withdrawal part. My only questions are, how far can we retreat and how long can we stay in hiding?"

191

"Probably not as far and long as either of us might wish." Rexford clapped Tag on the shoulder. "Come along. I will show you." Before leaving the stable, Rexford paused for a word with Abel. "Have my grooms bring my horses around immediately."

Fifteen minutes later Rexford and Tag descended the stairs. Rexford had a maid summon Prescott. When the butler appeared, he placed the metal container with Gully's message into the man's hand. "See that Miss Langley gets this." He started to turn away, and then added with what he hoped was a note of casual indifference, "And tell her she need not trouble to respond this afternoon. I have already sent a bird to Gully to tell him his courier arrived safely."

Rexford figured he had a full three minutes before Amanda set the house to quaking with her response to that plumper. He used three seconds of those minutes to hasten Tag out the front door. A little extra distance between them and the lady's wrath couldn't hurt. "And now to the village, where I trust we will both drink ourselves into oblivion. Perhaps if we are fortunate, the sun will forget to come up tomorrow and I won't have to face her."

At noon the next day, Rexford stood at the window of his room and awaited the summons he knew would come. At dawn he had kept a silent vigil with Tag. By unspoken consent, neither of them had mentioned the hope and fear that kept their eyes glued to the fiery red globe as it emerged from behind the distant hill.

After a few hours sleep, Rexford had risen to wrestle again with the question of what to say to Amanda. With noon approaching he still had not come up with anything better than the rather flimsy lie about saving her the trouble of responding. Even if she chose to believe it, rather than suspect he had begun kidnapping her pigeons one at a time, she would be angry. Beautiful, with her cheeks flushed and her eyes flashing, but angry.

No innocent looks would convince her he didn't know she would not approve of anyone releasing one of her birds without her permission. So long as she was merely angry and not suspicious, he could probably survive.

He smiled with the faint hope she might discover some new and interesting character flaw in him, which would explain his odd behavior. Being Amanda, she would probably also have a plan for dealing with that flaw. If only he could keep silent long enough to—

A discreet knock at the door announced the hour had come. "Miss Langley would like you to join her in the yellow sitting room, Lord Rexford," Prescott said.

Rexford squared his shoulders and marched to meet his fate.

He paused at the door of the sitting room to assess Amanda's mood.

She sat stiffly in a winged armchair, her hands neatly folded, her face impassive. Her hair, pulled into the tight knot she had worn during the first days of his visit, provided another clue to her mood. "Come in, Rexford."

"Good morning, Amanda." He walked in and smiled down at her, wondering if she would offer her hand.

She kept her hands clasped tightly in her lap. "Sit over there." She nodded to a nearby chair.

He sat where she indicated, managed to produce a casual expression, and waited.

"You stole one of my birds."

"Stole?" He produced the wide-eyed expression he had practiced all morning. "What a shocking thing to say."

"You would call it something else?"

"I would hardly call it stealing. Stealing is where you creep in and take something secretly. I sent a message telling you exactly what I did." He sat back as if he had just given a perfectly reasonable explanation. Looked at the ceiling, as if it had never occurred to him she might not want someone sending off her birds.

"You sent off a bird you thought would go to Brussels. Without permission. Tell me again why you did a thing like that."

He preferred her usual barrage of words to the sharp

clipped tone she was using. Without much hope, he tried a flank attack, a personal comment. "I will, if you will try to stop talking as if your mouth is made out of ice. You are so much more attractive when you smile."

She glared. "Rexford, this time you will not distract me. Just explain."

"Very well. When I last saw you, you had just swept out of the room to go and have the vapors or the megrims or whatever it is women have when they sweep out of rooms."

"I never had either, though I vow I shall if . . . My health is not the subject of this discussion. Please get on with it."

A reasonable tone, Rexford reminded himself, as if any perfectly reasonable gentleman would read her mail and answer it. God, he hated lies. "You were indisposed. Gully's message arrived. I knew he would be concerned and want to know that the bird arrived safely." With a sick feeling he deliberately did not add, *So I read the very personal message.* "I saw no reason to disturb you. I was only trying to help." He waited for her face to reflect his own disgust.

He saw only the mild annoyance of a patient tutor. "You did it deliberately to make me angry."

Rexford felt a flare of hope. Perhaps she did have a more reasonable explanation than he. "I did? Why would I do a wretched thing like that?"

"Because I discovered the truth about all your heroic tales. You get very snippy when I uncover one of your schemes."

Given he had spent the last five minutes avoiding the ugly names he could put to his behavior, snippy seemed a very mild character flaw indeed. He still didn't understand, but he relaxed slightly. She would explain. "I don't understand—"

"A schoolboy prank, Rexford. Because I uncovered your lies about the war."

Rexford considered the alternative. She might have become suspicious enough to tell him to leave, or at least deny him access to the birds. He might not like it, but he could accept the accusation.

Still, she would expect a protest. "Why would I lie about the war?"

"The war stories were another of your schemes?"

He nodded as if he understood completely. "I was scheming to . . . If I pretend not to know, are you going to tell me what I was scheming to do?"

Her cheeks colored. "I believe you know."

He knew why he had told her about the war. But she had called them lies . . . which meant . . . which meant he didn't know. "I am afraid you are going to have to explain," he said.

She stood, took several steps across the room, and turned to face him, her skirts swirling around her. "It makes no sense to be coy about this. Something changed between us the day you kissed me. You cannot deny you want to do it again. More than kiss me. I see it in your eyes every time we are alone."

"I admit I want to, but—"

"But you have not kissed me again. So I can only assume . . ."

"Assume that I would find it very difficult to kiss you as thoroughly as I want and walk away."

"Exactly. So you exaggerated those stories." She took a few more steps and turned to face him. "I am not as naive as you think, Rexford. I know about women who give their favors to soldiers because—"

Rexford shot to his feet. "You think I made up those stories to seduce you! You think—Damn it, Amanda." He had been prepared to accept any accusation. But to lure an innocent into bed with lies . . . "Damn it—"

"You may stop swearing. And you needn't be quite so indignant." She lifted her chin, and the sun through the window caught flashes of fire in her hair. "Perhaps if you had just asked nicely—"

"I told you, I do not seduce innocents." He remembered Gully's letter, her fiery response to his kiss. In her defiant pose she looked like anything but an innocent.

He crossed the room until he stood only a few inches away

from her. In spite of his intention to deny any scheme to seduce her, he could not avoid focusing on the throbbing pulse in her neck. "I do not need lies to take a woman to bed."

She met his gaze directly, her eyes glistening with a softness that belonged in a bedroom. "Tell me you don't want—"

His body stirred to her breathy voice. "Want yes. But I don't . . . Young women—"

"I'm twenty-five, Rexford."

"This is a very dangerous conversation."

"Would you stop acting as if I am some seventeen-year-old schoolgirl? At my age I should know . . ."

He took her shoulders. He could tell her why it was dangerous, or he could show her. The silence hung between them, giving her a chance to retreat. If he kissed her, it would not be a gentle chaste kiss. He breathed in the hint of lilac. "Do you know how dangerous?" he asked.

He bent and kissed her, not fiercely as he expected, but slowly, in a kiss that would last until she understood he would not need lies to take her to bed.

Her lips softened against his, proving her readiness. Her hands slid around his neck, and he drew her to him until he could feel her breasts against his chest. The back of his neck prickled with the realization that they stood in full view of the open door. If he intended this as a warning, it would be a good one. "Excuse me."

He released her and crossed the room to close the door.

He turned to face her again. She had retreated to rest one hand on the back of the sofa. Crimson circles of color highlighted her cheekbones, and her eyes drew him like a magnet, but he forced himself to cross the room very slowly. "Now is the time to say no, because I am going to kiss you again."

Just before he reached her, her tongue darted out to moisten her lower lip. "I know," she said in the husky voice he associated with his erotic fantasies. Without urging she moved into his arms, her fingers sliding up his chest until her hands rested on his shoulders. He bent again to the strawberry taste of her lips.

For a long time he savored the softness, until that was no longer enough. Slowly he eased her lips apart and let his tongue dart in just for a second. Her response shuddered through her body, and he tightened his arms around her, allowing one hand to stroke from her shoulder to her waist.

Her tongue mimicked his in a flicker so brief he recognized it only from the sudden stirring deep inside him. The time for restraint had passed, and he opened her lips with his. Hot breath poured into his mouth as she welcomed him. Even as his tongue probed her mouth, he knew a kiss would not be enough, he had to feel her against him.

He dropped his hands to her buttocks and drew her in to his hips, disappointed to feel layers of petticoats beneath the thin muslin skirt. With the layers between them, he could only let his tongue tell her what he wanted to do. Tentatively at first, he felt her body respond as she stirred against his hands and his thighs.

He hardened until he knew she could feel him searching for her softness even through the barriers. "I warned you it was dangerous."

"It's intoxicating."

"Not delicious enough." He continued to kiss her, still probing with his tongue, but more slowly.

He had to stand between her legs, just for a minute.

He traced the curve of her backside, feeling soft woman through the layers of cotton fabric. Still holding her against him, he turned so he could lower himself to half sit against the back of the sofa that had supported her moments earlier. "You are right," he whispered, "I want you."

He lowed his lips to kiss her neck, and felt her thighs melt against his. With his hands on her buttocks, he lifted her so she came to rest exactly where he wanted her, soft against his hardness. He closed his eyes. This should be enough. In a minute he would release her.

She stirred against him, her body promising exactly what he sought. He could . . . he would . . .

He would not seduce his hostess.

He lifted his head from her neck and drew several long deep breaths. "I suggest you stay very, very still, or I will forget that a gentleman does not put his hand under a lady's skirt."

She looked up in alarm. The movement of her lower body sent rivers of fire through him. "Am I hurting you?" she asked.

He bit his lower lip, knowing if he raised her skirt he might not be able to stop himself from taking her right here against the sofa. "Unbelievably. I am only a man, after all. And right now, not a very comfortable one."

"Do you want me to . . ."

"I don't want you to. But I think that would be best."

She pushed her hands against his chest and slid off him. The movement almost shattered his fragile control. She left an acre of emptiness behind her.

He stared at the ceiling and counted to fifty. From across the room he could hear her ragged breathing. "I am sorry," he said. "I did not mean to take that quite that far. I only meant to illustrate why I find it difficult to give you a brief chaste kiss."

She stood across the room smoothing her dress along her thighs.

Rexford counted to fifty again to avoid thinking of the long legs under that dress, and what he might have done if he had parted those legs so she straddled him.

Cheeks still flushed, she raised her chin defiantly. "And I merely wanted to illustrate that you don't need all those lies. Women like honesty in these matters."

His gaze met hers across the room. "So do men. And before you have any more to say on the subject, I suggest you think very carefully. There are limits to my control."

"I believe we have said enough for now." She gave a small shudder. "I think I will go for a walk."

He started toward her, as much the gallant gentleman as he could manage with the ache in his groin. "I will be pleased to accompany you."

Amanda stayed him with a hand gesture. "I would like to walk alone today. I need some time to think, and I suspect you do too. Use the time to consider how you might make yourself more agreeable if you were a little less determined always to arrange everything."

He almost laughed aloud. If he had arranged everything, they would be upstairs in bed right now. "I certainly shall. And I thank you for being much more understanding about the bird than I probably deserve."

"Of course." She started toward the door, then turned back to face him. "I admit I might not have been if you had actually taken one of Albert's birds. We go to a great deal of trouble to ship them from Brussels. But since——"

His body stiffened. "What are you saying?"

Amanda tossed her head and laughed. "The bird you sent off belongs to a neighbor."

Ice chilled every nerve. He must have heard wrong. "The bird did go to Brussels, didn't it?" Only his mouth moved. The rest of his face felt carved out of marble.

"No. It . . ." Amanda looked at him with the suspicion he had dreaded earlier. "It does not matter why. Suffice to say, you did no harm."

His exhaled air had a broken sound. "Nor any good," he said in a half whisper. He forced himself to bow again. The practiced movement seemed to require conscious effort. He needed to be alone. "As you say, I need some time to think."

Rexford forced himself to stand until the last corner of Amanda's skirt disappeared from the doorway, then staggered back the two steps to the chair behind him. He dropped into it, still consciously controlling his breathing. "Oh, God." He covered his face with his hands and doubled over as if that would control the sick feeling in his stomach.

For immeasurable moments, he couldn't think, just felt an overwhelming grief. Gradually conscious thought returned, and with it the knowledge he would have to tell Tag. Where would he find the courage to do that again?

He stood and paced the small room, his slow steps finally bringing him to the window to look out on the splendid day

199

and the sun Elmgrove must have dreaded to see.

That sun had taunted him from the moment he comprehended Amanda's words, *The bird belongs to a neighbor.* Only rigid training had frozen him in place. He wanted to rail against the revelation, shake her until she took the words back. What would her face have looked like if he'd told her that her schemes had already cost a good man his life?

He shrugged hopelessly. What good would it do? Minutes ticked by while he sought the courage to go on from here.

Prescott appeared in the doorway. "Lady Harriet would like to see you in the drawing room."

"I will be there in a moment." He would be there and listen to her latest plan to tie him to her daughter, but only because it would give him a few more minutes to compose himself before he had to face Tag.

He paused at the threshold of the drawing room to set his face into a polite mask.

Lady Harriet offered her perpetually bright smile. "Come in, Lord Rexford. I want you to meet Margaret Sheridan. I am sure you have heard Amanda speak of her." She indicated a seated, dark-haired woman with intelligent eyes. Her straight back made Lady Harriet's socially correct posture seem positively relaxed.

Rexford crossed the room and bowed. "Miss Langley speaks of you frequently. With great admiration, I might add."

Despite the compliment, Margaret looked more like an annoyed duchess than the loving guardian Amanda had described. "I am sure she does."

Lady Harriet smiled. "I have been telling Margaret she will not believe the change in Amanda since you arrived. Why, this morning she had on the loveliest yellow . . . Well, you will see for yourself, Margaret."

"I am sure I shall." Margaret kept her penetrating gaze on Rexford. "But right now I am more interested in Lord Rexford. Will you sit down, my lord." She gave orders in exactly the same no-nonsense tone as Amanda.

Rexford sat. Despite Margaret's imposing presence, he had

a hard time focusing on what promised to be a tedious conversation. He longed to be either alone with his own pain or with Tag. The mocking sun continued to stream through the side windows. "Lovely day," he commented, intensely aware of the irony of the words.

Margaret chose not even to respond to the banality. "As you may know, Lord Rexford, I was responsible for Amanda for much of her life and will always be concerned about her."

"Miss Langley is most fortunat—"

Again Margaret, with her slight Scottish burr, demonstrated limited tolerance for pointless interruptions. "That explains why I feel I have the right to inquire about your motives first in coming here, and second in remaining so long."

Rexford's neck almost snapped with his start at the unexpected attack. A dozen glib explanations sprang to his lips. He offered a polite "I see" to allow some time to sift through them. Pride made him reluctant to present himself to this no-nonsense woman as an impoverished earl who had hired himself out as a pigeon-napper. "I . . . I . . ."

"Before you continue with whatever you are about to say, it might help you to know what brought me here. I came in response to a message I received from you yesterday—the one addressed to Albert Gully in Brussels."

Rexford's sickness at the memory of his failure returned, but with it came a curious relief. He had hated every minute of this masquerade. The woman's unflinching stare told him she would accept nothing but the truth. "If you read the message, you probably guessed my intent. I had hoped that bird might save the Earl of Elmgrove's life. As it is . . ." He broke off to close his eyes as a new wave of grief washed over him.

Margaret's face softened. "I am sorry. I should have reassured you at once."

"Reassured?" A spark of hope flared.

"I happened to be feeding my birds when the letter arrived. I read it immediately. Naturally, I had no idea why I had received it when it was clearly intended for Albert, but since it was so obviously critical I sent it on at once.''

Whatever else she might have said Rexford lost in the rush of blood to his head and the tangle of emotions that swept over him. He curled his fingers into his palms, praying he had not misheard her. ''You sent it on? To Gully?'' His blood pounded the message *Please say yes.*

Margaret held out a warning hand. ''Please. I cannot promise you anything.''

''Any small hope is enough.'' Just for a second he let his face rest in his palms.

''Please. The only bird of Albert's I had was old. Amanda had given him to me because he was sick.'' Despite her forbidding appearance she was a compassionate woman. Every phrase spoke of her reluctance to rob him of his slim hope. ''He seemed better, but . . . I would never have started a bird for Brussels so late in the day, but . . .''

''But you sent the message on? For now that means everything.'' None of her reluctant warnings counted if he did not have to face Tag with the news the bird had not flown at all.

She nodded. ''This man is important to you? Not just to the war. But to you personally?''

''Very. He is—'' Rexford stood and paced before he explained in unmanly words his feelings for Elmgrove. He drew several deep breaths, and felt composed enough to turn and face the two women. ''He is my valet—my closest friend's—father.''

''Your valet is the son of an earl?'' Lady Harriet smiled. ''How curious. That nice young man I see with you?''

Rexford felt he had grown several inches. His strength returned. He should be devastated at being unmasked, but he felt only a wild happiness both at Elmgrove's chance for life and the end to the lies. He walked over, took Margaret's hand, and looked directly into her eyes. ''Thank you. Whatever happens, thank you.''

''You may not be so eager to thank me by the time we have finished our talk.'' The gentle squeeze she gave his hand before releasing it belied her harsh words. "I believe you still have some explaining to do."

Succinctly and still standing as if reporting to a commanding officer, Rexford summarized his mission. He began with Amanda's fierce behavior toward the first emissary, and ended with his role as impoverished earl now currently allied with her against the villains.

Lady Harriet had peppered his tales with exclamations. "My goodness," she said, "you seem like such a respectable gentleman. I find it hard to imagine you coming up with such outlandish tales. An impoverished earl!"

Rexford chuckled. "Frankly, madam, that was one of my favorites. Though I am afraid I cannot take all the credit."

"Then who—" Lady Harriet asked.

"Amanda." Margaret said. She echoed Rexford's laugh.

"Precisely," he said. "I have found the easiest way of explaining anything to Amanda is to wait and let her explain. She is so much more creative than I." He gave an exaggerated wince. "I am still smarting from the peal she rang over my head for stealing the bird I sent to you."

Margaret's possessive smile banished forever Rexford's image of a cold dowager. "She explained that for you, did she?"

"Quite adequately. An immature ploy on my part to repay her for not appreciating my war stories." He suppressed another chuckle. "Perhaps it is a good thing I will be leaving. I would have no illusions left about myself."

"Leaving?" Lady Harriet exclaimed. "Margaret, we must not let him do that."

"Hush, Harriet. Tell me, Lord Rexford, what are your plans?"

"I had intended to tell Amanda the truth soon in any case. Now you can help me convince—"

"Excuse me, but I believe you have misinterpreted my role. I came here to assure myself you meant Amanda no harm. Now that I have done so—"

"But . . . she trusts you. You can—"

"I have spent years teaching Amanda to be independent.

I am scarcely going to start telling her what to do now.''

"But . . .''

"But nothing. You're on your own, young man. Now perhaps we can get back to the fascinating conversation you began about the weather.'' Her teasing smile, so like Amanda's, softened the sharp words. "I agree it is a lovely day.''

Less than five minutes later, the familiar click of heels drew Rexford's attention to the door. Amanda stood there in a yellow gown, her cinnamon hair tangled by the wind, her cheeks flushed. "Margaret!'' Her delighted exclamation danced through the air. "I am so glad you're here.''

Margaret rose, and the two women embraced in the center of the room.

Rexford waited until they untangled themselves and sat side by side on the sofa. "I trust you ladies have much to talk about, so if you will excuse me?'' He bowed to Lady Harriet and to the two who had almost forgotten his presence. "Mrs. Sheridan, we will talk again.''

Margaret nodded. "I will look forward to it.''

He walked to the door, but could not resist turning for one final look at Amanda's sparkling eyes. His gaze found the throbbing pulse in her throat. His body tightened with the memory of that pulse under his lips. With a twinge of guilt he wondered if that pulse was the reason he had not pressed harder for Margaret's support. He did not want to leave Langwood. Not just yet.

Chapter Twelve

Late in the afternoon, Amanda watched the coach bearing her mother and Margaret pull away. On any other day, she would have considered Margaret's visit far too short. Today, she had repeatedly found herself avoiding the questioning look in those penetrating eyes.

She needed to think, and she needed to be alone. For once she had a problem she could not talk over with Margaret. As it had all day, her body heated with the memory of the encounter in the sitting room.

She could solve the problem easily by following her mother's suggestion and sending for Aunt Charlotte. Mother, in her newfound enthusiasm for husband-hunting, had instantly accepted Margaret's invitation to help entertain the baron Margaret's husband, Rodney, would bring down from London tomorrow. However, she had shown one of her rare bursts of insight by insisting Amanda invite Aunt Charlotte to chaperone during her absence.

Unlike Mother, who went to sleep early with her laudanum drops, slept late in the mornings, and spent most of her afternoons visiting, Charlotte would take her duties very seriously. Charlotte would hover. Charlotte would have walked into the sitting room this morning—and not survived the day.

With a brusque gesture Amanda brushed aside the suggestion. At her age, she would chaperone herself or not as she chose. With characteristic honesty, Amanda admitted that with that gesture she had already chosen.

She wanted to kiss Rexford again.

All day long her body had insisted there was more than what she had experienced. His hoarse words, ''A gentleman doesn't put his hands under a lady's skirt,'' had echoed in her mind. A shocking suggestion, but one which weakened her knees every time she thought of it.

At twenty-five, she was unlikely ever to marry. She would be cheating no one if, just once, she let herself experience what his words suggested. Her face burned with the thought.

Perhaps he would not even have to put his hands under her skirt. Perhaps with fewer petticoats, just his closeness would ease the hunger his kiss created. She knew now she could trust him not to force himself on her.

Perhaps tonight . . . after dinner . . .

Relieved that the interminable meal had ended, Amanda rose from the table. For the first time since the day he arrived, Amanda had felt awkward with Rexford, struggling to find things to say to fill long silences in the conversation. They had eaten alone before when Mother dined with friends, but never had the room been so filled with tension. Never had she been so conscious of his eyes—eyes that seemed to never to leave her.

He had watched every forkful of food she brought to her mouth as if he envied it, though a tight knot in her throat made it impossible to eat more than a few bites. Instead she had studied his hands and remembered how they felt on her body. His lips would taste of the claret wine that made them glisten in the candlelight.

''Since we are dining informally tonight, perhaps you would prefer to take your brandy in the sitting room with me.'' She managed to keep her words steady enough, but the tightness in her throat gave them a husky sound.

He stood as etiquette demanded, but held her immobile with his heated gaze across the flickering candles. "I am not certain that would be a good idea."

Damn him, he intended to treat her as a green girl after making her feel like a woman all day. "Why is that?"

"I am not completely convinced you know what you are doing."

"Offering you a brandy? I believe that is quite customary." For just a moment Amanda felt as sophisticated as she wanted him to believe she was.

He circled the table and stood looking down at her with eyes that seared like a candle brought too close. "In that gown, with the messages you have been sending me all night, a brandy is not all you are offering."

A more experienced woman might have laughed and teased him. Amanda couldn't. "Can you deny that you have thought about what happened between us this morning?"

"I have thought of little else all day. Your offer of *a brandy*"—he moistened lips with his tongue—"is power-fully tempting."

"Then I fail to see what the problem is. I am not inviting you into my bed, merely—"

"One thing frequently leads to another."

"Don't you think that should be my problem?"

Rexford forced himself to breathe slowly. He should never have stood up. Should never have permitted himself to look down at the enticing curve of those creamy breasts straining at the low neckline of her cream gown. He had known from the minute she walked into the room he would have trouble putting two coherent thoughts together.

She had entered like a goddess, tussore silk dress shim-mering about her like sunshine on a river. His experienced eye told him she wore no more than one petticoat, if that. Loose curls the color of fire tumbled about her shoulders, inviting him to run his fingers through her gleaming hair. Even now his fingers itched to brush back the coil that con-cealed the pulse in her neck. "If I could be certain . . ."

If he could be certain she knew what she was about, he would tumble her right here on the dining room table. He temporized. She was twenty-five. Had been to London. The one letter from Gully suggested she had known at least one night of wild abandon with a man.

None of that mattered.

What mattered was that he would go mad if he could not hold her against him one more time. He could exercise restraint, but he had to hold her again. "If you are certain, Amanda, I would be delighted to share a . . . a brandy." He did not offer his arm, but placed his hand on the small of her back to guide her from the room.

A few moments later, Prescott placed the tray with the crystal brandy decanter and two glasses on the small table next to the sofa.

"That will be all, Prescott. Lord Rexford will pour."

Prescott gave a hint of a bow and left. Amanda had not suggested he close the door, and Rexford rose immediately to remedy the oversight. He turned from the door and paused to consider the illusion that he might merely drink a glass of brandy and bid her good night. No power on earth could have kept him from crossing the room.

Deliberately, he removed his coat and tossed it over the back of a chair. She could have no doubt of his intentions when he came to a stop before her chair.

Her hands twisted nervously in her lap. An uneasy expression flitted across her face, and disappeared immediately. "Do you want a glass of brandy?"

Rexford glanced at the decanter and shook his head. He wanted nothing to dull his senses. Without a word he took both of her hands in his and drew her to her feet. She would have come directly into his arms, but he would settle for nothing less than what he had sacrificed this morning.

He led her around until he stood with his back to the sofa, so he could use that to support his weight if the moment demanded it. "I believe this is where we left off this morning." He folded his arms around her, content for the moment just to hold her and savor the scent of lilacs that had lingered

with him all day. "You are beautiful tonight. Beautiful."
Wisps of her hair danced with his breath and tickled his nose.

"Rexford, I—"

"That is the first thing we must change."

"What?" She looked up at him.

He resisted the temptation to capture her lips immediately.
"My name. My closest friends"—his hands moved over the
cool silk on her back and pulled her closer—"call me Marcus."

"Marcus." She tested the name in the soft, breathy voice
of his fantasies.

Tonight she would say his name as he had imagined it so
often, urging him closer. He tilted her chin up. "You have the
most sensuous voice of any woman I ever met. Tonight you
need to tell me what you want. Say, 'Marcus, I want . . .' "
Her lips were so close she could not speak without his feeling
the words.

"Marcus I want . . ." Her lips touched his. He felt the
breath and the vibration of the words. "Marcus, I want you
to . . . kiss me." She was already kissing him, speaking, and
opening *his* mouth with lips that tasted of wine. "Marc . . ."

The half word left her mouth open inviting his tongue. He
lowered his hands to her hips. The silk gown slid like water
through his fingers. Such a fragile barrier. He could feel her
thighs all along his. "That's it. Let yourself feel it."

Her lips parted even more. "Marcus."

He touched his tongue to hers. "Come to me." He slipped
one foot between her feet and shuffled them apart, so he
could stand between them. Did she know how badly he
needed her to open her legs to him? Where was the restraint
he promised to exercise? It didn't matter. He would kiss her
until she begged him to stop. Or begged him not to.

"Oh, Marcus. Ohhh." She drew her head back, the movement arching her against him.

He rested his weight against the sofa, slipping his legs
more firmly between hers, then bent to trail kisses down her
neck. Her skirt glided over her body under his hands. He
could raise it so easily, but not until he had touched his

209

tongue to the curve of her breasts. Sacrificing his grip on her buttocks, he drew one hand up to cup her breast.

She gasped, shuddered against him, and breathed his name like fire. "Marcus."

With his other hand, he drew her up so she stood on tiptoe, her dress so thin he could almost imagine her naked against him. He kissed the curve of her breast and played his thumb over the nipple.

She whimpered and shifted so he stood almost between her thighs. "That feels so . . . I have wanted . . . Oh . . ."

"Dammit." Rexford cursed the tight gown that prevented him from freeing her breast and tasting its softness. At least the skirt would not present such an impenetrable barrier. Using both hands on the outside of her thighs, he slid it upward, drawing the petticoat with it. "Ahhh." His hand touched the silken flesh of her thighs. A little more fumbling and he had both garments above her waist and could grip her buttocks through the thin film of her chemise. He lifted her completely off her feet, and her legs slipped so she straddled him, vulnerable and soft against his hardness.

"You know what I am going to do now, don't you?"

"What?"

"Dammit, Amanda. I want you. Now." With both hands he held her against him, let her feel the throbbing, lest she have any question what he intended.

She looked uneasily around the room. "I . . . I don't think that's a good idea."

Rexford bit his lip. "Of course it's not a good idea. I warned you this was dangerous." He forced himself to gentle his tone. "If you are going to change your mind, you need to do it quickly, before I undo these buttons."

"I don't think . . . I need time to think . . . You are the most attractive man I know, but . . ."

"Dammit." His hand hovered. She was so responsive, he could change her mind with a touch. *Dammit, Dammit, Dammit.* He could remind her, he had warned her. He could . . .

He could do nothing, because she was right. He had never intended to take things this far. "If this is over, then I suggest you be very careful how you move. I don't have a great deal of control right now.''

''I . . . I do,'' she said, reaching the floor with her toes and walking backwards until she stood safely away from him. She brushed her skirt into place.

Rexford straightened. ''Thank you.'' He reached out and took her shoulders in both hands.

She stiffened.

''Don't worry,'' he said, pulling her toward him, ''I just want to hold you for a minute.'' He drew her toward him, wrapped his arms around her, and rested his chin on her hair. ''Tomorrow I will thank you for your good sense. Right now I think it would be a good idea if you left me alone for a few minutes.''

''Will you be all right?''

He laughed. ''I will probably put my fist through that window and drink most of that brandy. But after that, I'll be fine.''

''I'm sorry . . . I . . .''

''Don't be. Once I can breathe again, I am sure I will look back on this as a very pleasant episode.'' He kissed her forehead. ''Go now.''

''I . . .'' She turned and started from the room.

''Wait,'' he said more sharply than he intended. ''You said you need to think. Know there is something unfinished between us. By tomorrow, I hope you will have done your thinking.''

Three hours and three glasses of brandy later, Rexford was still awake. He tossed restlessly in the darkness. No woman had the right to leave him in this state. Not even Amanda.

Footsteps thundered in the corridor outside his room. Rexford leapt from bed and cursed himself for sleeping naked. Someone pounded on his door. He ignored his nakedness and crossed the darkened room to fling it open.

''There's a fire in the cote,'' Brownley, the lieutenant he'd disguised as a groom to guard the birds, shouted.

Rexford turned, took two steps, and slapped his palm

against the door to his dressing room. "Tag! Fire!" The open door provided enough light from the corridor for Rexford to find his discarded pantaloons. He drew them on and stuffed his bare feet into his boots.

Tag poked his sleepy head through the door. "What?"

"There's a fire near the cote. Let's go." Rexford bounded for the corridor.

He took two steps, and almost collided with Amanda as she came out her door. He gripped her shoulders to prevent tumbling them both to the floor. "Fire," he explained, and felt her straining to follow Brownley. He looked down, even in the crisis aware of every inch of naked flesh beneath the transparent nightgown. "Go put some clothes on."

He launched himself into a full run, taking the stairs three at a time. At the side door he bent long enough to snatch up a light rug from the floor. Perhaps the fire would still be small enough to beat out.

He ran across the grass and through the wooded section, urged on by the flickering glow in the distance. He reached the clearing and almost shouted with relief.

The fire was not in the cote itself, but in one of the wooden buildings Amanda used to house supplies, a good thirty feet from the birds. His "grooms" were beating at the flames with horse blankets. He joined them, automatically assessing the situation.

They would lose the storage building but, if they could keep the flames from spreading to the cote, the birds should be safe enough. Abel, Amanda's groom, arrived carrying two buckets of water, which he pulled back to toss on the burning shed.

"No," Rexford shouted, "over there." He pointed to the adjoining shed. They had to keep that from igniting.

Abel dumped the water as directed, and turned to race back to the river for more.

Rexford continued to swat at the leaping tongues of fire, but only to keep them contained. From the corner of his eye he saw Amanda arrive. He thought she would come to fight the fire, but she didn't. She headed directly to the stone cote.

She flung open the door and entered. Agitated birds fluttered at her head and milled at her feet. "Keep the smoke away from here. It will kill the birds."

Just like Amanda. She didn't hesitate to give a command just because it was impossible. The smoke would go where the wind took it, and all her orders would not change that. Rexford snapped his rug at the air above his head. "Stay away from the birds, dammit." The movement caused the smoke to swirl. Fortunately, there was little wind, so the smoke merely rose and hovered.

Two more men arrived with buckets of water. He directed them to drench the vulnerable building while he continued to beat at the sparks that threatened to jump across the narrow space separating that structure from the flames.

He looked toward Amanda. She was standing on something struggling with the ropes that secured the netting over the aviary. "Don't let the birds go yet," he said, "I think we might be all right here."

"I just want to be ready." She tugged at more ropes, but did not roll back the overhead netting.

Men came and went with buckets of water, and finally, the crackle of flames diminished. The fire had all but devoured the shed, and now seemed content to lap at the few jagged boards remaining. Rexford stepped back and noticed Tag across the blackened earth and glowing embers. "Nice of you to join us."

"I've been here. You were just too busy pointing at where you wanted me to dump water to remember my name. I expect we will be all right now. I will watch if you want to go and help Miss Langley." He pointed to where Amanda stood in the shadow of the cote, wide-eyed and waiting.

"Thank you." Rexford crossed the clearing to the open door of the aviary. Amanda stood just inside. "Are the birds all right?" he asked.

"I think so. I am getting only a little bit of the smoke here. They are frightened, but not hurt."

He studied the open space where she had loosened the netting. "What were you going to do?"

"I was going to let them go. I think I would have had to go around waking them up and shooing them out. But it is a clear night and most of them might have had sense enough to roost in the trees. We might have lost some, but it would have been better than letting them all just sit there and die from the smoke."

Rexford pointed at the open netting. "Come on. I will help you fasten that cover." He stepped inside and they worked together for a few minutes.

She stepped back, looked up at the newly secured covering, and brushed the flecks of dirt and twine from her hands. "For the second time I have to thank you for saving my birds."

"My pleasure." Rexford felt his good humor returning. Life certainly had not been dull since he came to spend a few quiet days in the country. "Just let me go and speak to Tag and I will walk you to the house."

Rexford returned to where Tag stood with Brownley and Wolfe. "No new problems?"

"I don't believe so," Tag said. "I sent Miss Langley's men to bed, but I will stay with these two, just in case."

Rexford walked to the house with Amanda in silence. Every step made it easier to replace the memory of the fire with the awareness of the woman at his side. So much a woman, ready to battle a fire or a flood, or turn to liquid fire under a man's hands. Perhaps their unfinished business would not have to wait until morning.

He half expected to find the house glowing with light when they reached the side door leading to the library, but evidently the commotion had not been loud enough to wake the servants on the third floor. At the door, he paused to remove his soot-covered boots.

He entered, hurried across the room, lit a lamp, and threw two logs on the glowing coals in the fireplace. He looked toward where Amanda stood indecisively just inside the door, and wondered if she'd smile if he offered her a brandy. He shivered.

Amanda looked at Rexford standing half naked before the

fire and saw him shiver. He had to be thoroughly chilled. The night air had left her teeth chattering, and she at least had some covering. She crossed the room to the decanter always kept behind the desk, poured a glass of brandy, and carried it to him. "Here, drink this."

He accepted the glass and smiled down at her. "Thank you, but I thought we decided it was not a good idea for you to offer me a glass of 'brandy.' Or have you reconsidered?"

"This is different."

"Not so different." He took her hand, and drew her over so she stood directly in front of the fire. He took three steps back and stood looking at her with eyes that warmed her front as the fire did her back. "Do you have any idea how you look right now?"

"A fright." She reached up and touched her hair.

"Like a woman who just got out of bed. Your hair is tangled in a way that drives men wild. And that wrapper you obligingly put on conceals nothing." He took a long sip of brandy and exhaled. "If you have any more thinking to do, I think it might be wise to leave now." He stepped forward, holding out the glass he held cupped in his right hand. "Unless you want to share this brandy."

Automatically she reached out and accepted the glass. She had not done any thinking. She had lain awake for hours, but every time she tried to think of what she should not let him do, her body had throbbed with the memory of what he had done.

One of the logs in the fireplace snapped. Her hand shook as she tasted the brandy. A single sip could not have caused the heat that surged through her. A drop of the liquid hovered on her lip and slid slowly toward her chin. He reached out, caught it with his thumb, then slowly sucked it from his finger.

Unable to tear her gaze away, she watched the slow movement, remembering how his lips had felt around her thumb on the terrace.

"You look lovely in firelight," he said. "Your hair is the color of sunset."

"Perhaps I should not be here. I should—" She should be able to think, but couldn't.

He took a long sip of the amber liquid, reached across her shoulder, and put the glass on the mantel. His returning fingers curled around the back of her neck. "You should come here and talk to me." He drew her to him.

"Please, I have never—"

"You have never drunk brandy from a man's lips?" So slowly it seemed to take him an eternity to move, he bent toward her. "Taste this."

One small kiss and she would leave. She reached up to hold him off, and her hands encountered his naked chest. So warm but hard under her fingers. Automatically her hands moved across it. She could feel the small hairs crackle under her palms. Her next breath drew in the lingering smell of smoke from the fire and the more powerful essence of man she remembered, stronger now as if it emanated from every pore of his exposed flesh. Then his lips were on hers and she tasted the brandy. His hands on her back drew her in to him until she felt his thighs against hers.

She had to stop this or she would lose herself to him as she had earlier. "Noooo," she whispered. But her mouth rounded and the word ended as a muffled moan. Her whole body softening, she began to respond. Unable to stop herself, she slid her hands up to cup the warmth of his shoulders.

He continued kissing her until she felt her body seeking his. Even when he relaxed the pressure of his hands holding her against him, she continued to cling to his neck, arching toward him. His hair tickled against the back of her hands, and she yielded to the temptation to touch it, letting the black rivers tickle at the webbing between her fingers.

Slipping a hand between them, he fumbled with the tie of her robe, then pushed it back from her shoulders. Only then did he surrender her lips and seek the place in her neck that had set her shuddering earlier.

Her lips touched his naked shoulder, and she tasted the salt of his skin. Her tongue flicked his collarbone, and she heard him groan. Every sensation seemed wondrously magic, as if the drama of night and the fire had intensified them a hundredfold.

He felt it too, because he moaned. "Ahh, Amanda, I love it when you kiss me." The words moistened her shoulder with his warm breath and set her blood pounding.

"Yes. Yes." But she had vowed not to do this again without considering. "But you have to stop. I can't think when you're holding me like this. Ohhh. I can't think. . . ." She couldn't think of anything but the fact she never wanted him to stop. "But . . . we have to talk."

"Yes, we have to talk. I have to hear you say my name. Say, 'Marcus, I want you.' " He traced his tongue over her neck, and she began to tremble.

"Marcus, I want you to . . ." She said the words, but discovered the naked skin of his back. She clutched her hands along the warm flesh. He could not have moved from her if he wanted to.

She struggled for control. "Marcus, I want you to . . ." Her mind said *stop,* but the word was lost as his tongue invaded her mouth again.

"Just a minute, my love." His voice sounded unbelievably hoarse. With both hands he slipped her wrapper from her shoulders, pinioning her arms against her body for an angry minute so she could not touch him.

"Marcus . . ." The robe slid to the floor at her feet.

"That's better." He began to trail kisses toward the loose neckline of her nightgown.

"Ohhhh . . . Ohhhh, yes. No, don't . . . don't stop."

He slid one thin strap off her shoulder. "Do you want me to stop this?" He inserted a hand between their bodies and reached for her breast to roll the nipple between his fingers. "Do you want me to stop? Or do you want me to kiss you here?"

She gave a hungry moan. "Kiss me. Then—ohhhh."

As he sucked her breast, he put one arm behind her knees, the other under her neck, and lifted her. He knelt, taking her with him to the rug at his knees, the firelight flickering over his face as he stretched out beside her.

She struggled to rise. "I can't . . ."

Rising on one elbow, he cupped her exposed breast, stroking at the tip with his finger. "Say my name," he said. "Let me hear you say my name."

"Marcus." She didn't say his name, she exhaled it, bit her lip, shook her head from side to side, and exhaled it again. "Marcus."

He eased the other strap from her shoulder, and then simply ran his hands over both breasts, creating a fire between her legs. She had no breath to protest. He rolled over so he straddled her, supporting his weight on his elbows and a leg on either side of her. Bending his head, he kissed each breast, toyed with and teased one with his tongue while caressing the other with his hand. She began writhing beneath him.

He no longer had to tell her to say his name. Her head rolled from side to side and she breathed it out. "Marcus, Marcus, Marcus." She strained towards him, stroking his bare back. Her hands tightened in the small of his back, and she fought to pull him toward her.

"Not like that, my love. Not like that tonight." He rolled off her and reached with his hand to where her gown tangled at her knees. Slowly he stroked the back of her knee, then up her thigh. This was what he meant about a hand under her gown. How could she have known it would feel like this?

The gown rode up on his arm. He shimmied it up all the way to her waist. She should . . . In a minute she would . . . For now she could do nothing but surrender to his stroking hand. With each stroke he moved higher up her thigh, as if he knew where she longed for his touch and was teasing her.

Her legs tensed. He bent to suckle a breast, stroking his hand between her legs, each stroke bringing him closer. Each stroke opening her legs a little wider. "That's it. Let yourself feel it." His fingers brushed the hair at the juncture of her thighs. He retreated immediately.

She strained toward his hand with a whimper.

"That's it. You're telling me what you want." His tongue toyed with her swollen nipple. "Is this what you want?" He let his hand slide up again, this time to linger and search. "Say yes. Say yes, Marcus."

"Yes. Oh, yes." She closed her eyes and bit into her lip, knowing she should stop him, knowing she would die if she did.

Finally his hand found the ache between her legs and stayed there. This was what she needed, what she'd wanted all day. She strained toward his fingers. "Umm."

Suddenly he was gone.

"No." She protested the loss.

"Shhhh. Just for a moment. I'll be right back."

She opened her eyes and saw him struggling with his pants, and realized what he intended. "Oh." She gasped.

"Shhh. I'm back." He settled himself between her legs, using his hands to spread them wider apart.

"Marc—"

His fiery kiss cut off the protest. He rubbed again between her legs. Not with his hands, because they held her head when she tried to twist from his kiss. *Oh, no.* In spite of the protest her mind cried, her hips arched toward the fullness between her legs. Waves of sensation rolled through her.

His tongue continued to plunder her mouth as he rubbed himself against her in a rhythm that matched her own searching.

Gradually her tension eased. Nothing mattered but the stroking between her legs.

"That's it. Come with me." He grabbed her hips in both hands and raised her toward him.

Pain! "Owww." Pain tore through the white curtain of wonderful sensations that had enveloped Amanda. "Stop. You're hurting me." He was still hurting her, causing jagged shards of pain to shoot upward from that tender place between her legs. "Owww."

The cry and the realization shot through Rexford at the same time, too late to stop the heat from pouring out of him.

"Dammit. Dammit. Dammit." He lay very still. His clenched jaw rested against Amanda's shoulder.

She moved beneath him, tried to free herself from his weight. She gasped.

"Dammit, don't move. It will hurt less if you don't move. Dammit, I can't . . . Just lie still." He began to curse more creatively, and some of the tension drained from his rigid body with the words. His muscles began to relax and his breathing become more even.

"Get off me," she said.

"I will. I just need a minute." He raised himself on his elbows and drew back.

Amanda exhaled.

Rexford rose to his knees and found his pantaloons.

She gasped again and closed her eyes.

Still with his jaw clenched, he turned his back and drew his pantaloons over his buttocks. He turned back, knowing he had to face her.

She sat up.

Rexford clenched his hands into fists, blood throbbing at his temples. "Dammit, Amanda, why didn't you tell me?"

She crossed her arms over her breasts. "Will you stop cursing? You hurt me. If anybody has a right to curse, I do. You hurt me."

"I know I did. Why didn't you tell me you were a virgin? Why did you let me—" He whirled, took three impatient paces across the room, and turned to look down at her again. "Why did you let me—why didn't you tell me?"

"I tried . . . I . . . Why did you kiss me like that when you knew I couldn't think? I kept saying no."

"You didn't keep saying . . . Why didn't you just tell me you were a virgin?" He turned and paced again.

"I'm telling you now."

"Well, you're not now, so it doesn't—" His eyes really focused on her for the first time since he had left her. "Do you have any idea how you look?" Even now she was the most intensely desirable woman he had ever seen. "Your hair, your . . ." In spite of everything, he felt himself begin to harden. What a monster. "Even now I want to . . . to . . . Dammit, Amanda, pull your gown up." His gaze shifted to her thighs. "I mean down. I mean pull your gown up and down."

She grabbed for the neckline of her gown and pulled it up over her breasts. The lower half of her gown was bunched about her waist, and she tried to smooth that over her legs. She could only get it as far as her knees. "You can stop looking like that. You hurt me."

"Only the first time." He stepped closer. "If you let me—" He shook his whole body. "If you had let me, I might have—dammit, I can't talk to you while you look like that. Get up." He held out his hand to help her up.

She shrank back. "I prefer—"

"Get up." He shook his hand insistently. "Don't worry. I won't—not that I don't want to, but I won't." He stood reaching toward her.

Amanda wanted to sit there forever. Anything so she didn't have to look into his blazing eyes. Instead she let him pull her to her feet.

He walked across the room and stood at the window looking out. This gave her time to slip her arms through the straps of her gown and shake the skirt to the floor. She was fumbling with the tie of her wrapper when he turned. His look drove all thought of further repairs from her mind.

His hands clenched into fists at his sides. "Well, you have succeeded in getting me to compromise you." His eyes blazed with fury and his jaw trembled so the words came out with a quivering sound. "I hope you are satisfied."

Anger surged through Amanda. "I? I got you to—? I don't remember throwing myself on the floor and tearing off my clothes. My only other crime is letting you come within fifty feet of me. I-I-I . . ." She looked for something to throw, heedless of wrapper that gaped open when she released it.

"What about all your experience? What about the letter from Gully?"

"What letter from Gully?"

He took two long steps, cutting in half the distance that separated them. "The letter that arrived with the birds. The letter that talked of a glorious night in a storm. If you didn't do this''—he pointed to the floor, leaving no doubt what *this* referred to—''what did you do?''

''You read my letter from Albert? How dare you!''

He took another step forward, his face suffused with crimson, a purple vein throbbing in his temple. ''That's not important now. What did you do in the storm with your precious Albert?''

''We waited for two birds to come home. Through the lightning. With trees crashing all around us. It was thrilling when they landed just as if—I can't believe we are talking about Albert. You are insane. You . . .''

''You are coming out of that gown. Let me tie that for you.''

''You would like that, wouldn't you? I let you close enough to touch me and in a minute''—Amanda's face flushed with the memory of lying on the floor under him—''you would have me on the floor—''

''I only want to talk to you without thinking of—'' He reached for the tie dangling from the wrapper and made a neat knot.

In spite of herself, Amanda shuddered under his touch. Gooseflesh broke out on her shoulders and down her arms.

Rexford traced a line upward along her neck. ''You really are susceptible, aren't you?'' His tone had a touch of awe.

Amanda jerked away from him and turned to face him. ''Stay away from me. Just don't touch me.''

''Unfortunately, it is too late for that.'' He pointed to the small red stain on the rug. ''Whether it was your fault or mine, the result is the same.'' He took a step, eating up the distance she had just created, a resolute look on his face. ''I will marry you, Amanda.'' He put a hand on her shoulder. ''I am not even sure how much I will mind.'' His hand glided across her chest so his fingers hovered at the still-loose open neck of her robe. ''At the moment all I can think of is finishing properly what we began.''

Fury gave Amanda strength to reel away from his touch. She stormed across the room and whirled. ''You will marry me, Lord Rexford. How kind. And then we will do more of that.'' She pointed a hand trembling with rage at the floor. ''I hate to disappoint you, but if you do any marrying, or any more of . . . of that . . . it will be by yourself, because I don't even want to be in the same room with you.''

''Now calm down, Amanda. I said I didn't mind. I admit it takes getting used to, but I am sure—''

''You said you didn't mind. How splendid. But you forgot to ask me if I mind. And I mind very much.''

''Mind marrying me?'' He tilted his straight nose toward the ceiling, his posture and tone saying quite clearly that earls married where they would and expected gratitude. ''Why, women . . . mothers—''

''I am aware. Women and their mothers spend their lives scheming to shackle you. Well, I will say once more, for all the times you didn't listen. I have no intention of marrying. Specifically, I have no intention of marrying you.''

He looked at her in astonishment. ''Unfortunately, neither of us has a choice in the matter.''

With him safely across the room and angry rather than smoldering, Amanda found she could think quite clearly. They had indeed gone far beyond anything she intended, but since she never intended to marry, she had not deprived some nebulous future husband of anything. The only serious repercussion of the incident would be a rather unpleasant memory. ''Please, Rexford, don't make more of this''—she darted a fleeting look at the stain on the rug—''unfortunate incident than necessary.''

''Bah.'' Rexford's breath exploded with what might have been a word. ''Unfortunate incident . . . Don't make more of . . . Do you have any idea . . .'' He sputtered to a halt.

His frustration strengthened Amanda. ''I have a very clear idea. And I am not going to let one minor error in judgment ruin my entire life. So you can take your 'I don't minds' and your 'I am willing to marry yous' straight upstairs and start packing. I am going to bed, and in the morning I expect you to be gone.'' With a thrust of her shoulder, she headed across

223

the room to end the unpalatable discussion with a dignified exit.

Rexford moved faster than she, and planted himself in front of the closed door. His expression warned her she would not pass him without moving him aside.

Too well Amanda remembered the devastating consequences of any physical contact. His implacable stance informed her this encounter was far from over.

Chapter Thirteen

Rexford firmly planted his back against the door. He could not let Amanda leave like this. She sailed toward him, her face flushed with color but her chin high and her eyes flashing anger. He felt a burst of pride for the woman he planned to make his wife. They would deal well together.

He could identify the precise moment when the sacrificial proposal society demanded had turned into his own driving need. He had been fixing the tie on her wrapper and felt her begin to tremble beneath his fingers. He'd had to clench his fists to keep from drawing her back against his aching hardness. He might still have taken her again if she had not torn herself away from him.

In the instant when she whirled to face him, he knew he wanted her. Not just once more on the floor, but in his bed every night. Even now, with her eyes alive with fury, he wanted nothing more than to slip his hand into the loose neckline of her gown and set her to breathing his name and straining against him. She must have read his ravenous thoughts because she checked her step and even backed up a pace.

Rexford forced himself to breathe slowly, and infused his voice with a coolness that denied the throbbing in his groin. "You cannot simply dismiss this as an 'unfortunate incident.' It is not that simple. Neither of us has a choice."

She gave him a withering glance. "I have a choice, and I choose to go upstairs. Now if you will please move . . ."

"You cannot just march out of here. There are consequences."

"Only if one of us should ever be foolish enough ever to mention this night again. Now please . . ." She leaned forward to brush him aside, as if she might so casually dismiss the entire incident.

He remained rooted in place. "I should not have to explain the most important consequence."

"Nothing you can explain will keep me in this room a moment longer."

"A child."

She drew a long shuddering breath. "I am not a . . ." Awareness dawned on her face. "A child? Surely not . . ." She glanced back over her shoulder. "Is that . . . Oh, dear." She studied his face as if he might deny her thoughts, then winced at the memory of the pain. "Why would anyone ever have more than one?"

In spite of himself, Rexford almost laughed aloud. Leave it to Amanda. He had just told he her he had probably ruined both their lives, and she wanted to know why it wasn't more fun. Yes, they would deal well together. She would always come at him from where he least expected, and he would very probably follow her down that path.

At least he would now.

"Again, let me explain. I left you with a very wrong impression." He stepped toward her and took her shoulders.

She shuddered and tried to shake off his hands.

"The pain was only a momentary thing. If you had—"

Amanda reared back. Her jaw trembled as she tried to speak. "Of course you would say that. A man feels no pain. I woke up this morning and said, 'No one has hurt me re-

cently. I do hope Lord Rexford has some time tonight.' ''
She spun away from him and stormed across the room.

Rexford bit his lip to control his rising anger. He had never
deliberately hurt a woman in his life. "Stop it. I am sorry I
hurt you, but I have told you it will never hurt again."

"You have told me many things. Very few of them true."

He exhaled a long shuddering breath and waited a long
moment before speaking again. "I suppose I deserve that."
He gave his head an incredulous shake. "Before I came here
my word would have been enough for anyone in England.
Now . . ." He shrugged. "I cannot do anything about that,
but about the pain I am speaking the truth. Has your mother
never told you—"

"Of course not. Mother is so eager to see me married,
why would she . . . ?" Amanda's eyes widened. "No wonder
young girls must remain virgins. If they knew . . ." She
looked toward the place where they had lain and shuddered.

His thoughts raced with the memory, and his body
throbbed with the temptation not to explain but to show. A
moment to unbutton himself, raise that clinging gown, lift,
and slide her down onto him. He despised himself for his
thoughts. "Dammit, Amanda, "Take my word for it. It
would not—" He reminded himself there would be another
time. "Will not hurt the next time."

"I will never—" Her face paled. "You said a child.
Could I . . . ?"

Privately Rexford admitted he didn't know. Her cry and
the knowledge of what he'd done had inhibited his outpour-
ing, but he had no idea how much of his seed had escaped.
Or how much was enough. "Could you have my child?
Yes."

She backed to a chair and sat. "And you would marry me
because . . ."

"Yes." A lie. He would marry her because he would carry
to his grave the picture of the way she looked when he turned
from the window. She had sat there with her hair tangled,
her lips swollen from his kiss. He had never seen a more

desirable woman. That was how she would look rising from his bed.

She looked up at him with troubled eyes. "It doesn't always happen, does it? We could wait and see. Then if—"

"Then two months from now I will marry you and we will joyously wait for the early arrival of our child and the censure of everyone who would know I waited to marry you until I was sure I had to. I would not wish that for you. And I will not accept it for myself."

Her shoulders slumped and she cupped her chin in her hands. She straightened, pleading with him with her eyes. "Is there no other way?"

"I will get a special license tomorrow. We will marry within the week."

"Very well." She nodded and rose, drawing her dignity about her like a shroud. "If that is all . . ."

Rexford tried to think of something to banish the despair from her eyes. Words seemed too empty and any physical approach too unwelcome. She needed time.

As she headed toward the door, he walked to the mantel, picked up the discarded brandy glass, and smashed it against the hearth. Taking a jagged shard he sliced it across the outside of his palm.

Gasping, she halted. "You are insane."

"Just thorough." He walked over and let his blood drip onto the rug to mingle with hers. "In the morning you can have the servants deal with that. Tell them I had a slight accident."

She nodded slowly, and left without looking back at him.

Rexford walked to the fire, a betrothed man and not the least bit unhappy about it.

She would not be the first bride to come to her marriage bed apprehensively. He smiled. She would shed those apprehensions more quickly than most. For several long moments he stared into the blaze and pictured her hair spread out on a pillow beneath him, her body arching for his. So many things he would teach her. So many ways he would make her say his name in that throaty, hungry voice.

For the first time he understood why men married. The thought of any other man ever running his lips along her neck made the fire in front of him seem cold in comparison to his blazing rage. He remembered her whispering to Batterton, his hand holding hers. Rexford clenched his fists.

The thought of that man and his interest in the birds finally drew Rexford's attention from the persistent ache in his groin. He had yet another reason not to regret this latest development. With Amanda came the birds. He would accomplish his mission with no more lies.

With a laugh he realized he had no idea what she thought of him at this point. If she still considered him an impoverished earl, she should brighten considerably when she realized he could lay three prosperous estates at her feet. He glanced at the window with the vague hope of hastening the dawn. The new day promised to be very bright indeed.

Amanda dragged herself through her morning routine, every movement heavy. She selected a gray gown to match her mood. The dress had a high neck, and she had Lily draw her hair back into a tight bun. She might have to marry Rexford, but she did not have to encourage his attentions. What a fool she had been.

She put her hand to her abdomen where even now she might be carrying his child, a child who would trap her into surrendering everything she valued. Her freedom, her fortune, even her right to sleep alone. For as long as Rexford lived he would have the right to come into her bed, make her incoherent with his touches, and then hurt her as he had last night.

She had lain awake until dawn searching for a solution. She could go away from everything she loved, bear the child someplace where no one knew she had no husband. And then . . . That was where any solution broke down. Living alone, away from her birds, would be as bad as being married to him.

Perhaps he would be content to live in London and leave her here.

She gave a deep sigh and rose. He had sent a message an hour ago saying he wished to see her before he went out. She would have to face him sometime. As she walked, the tight ache between her legs unnecessarily reminded her of her grim mistake.

She entered the sitting room, and Rexford rose to meet her. His features relaxed into a wide smile. "Ahhh, Amanda. I thought you might keep me waiting until sunset." He took her hand. "Please, do not look so wretched. We are planning a wedding, not an execution."

She withdrew her hand and stepped back to increase the distance between them. "I had hoped you might have thought of another solution. Perhaps we could . . ." She waited.

He merely looked at her with curious amusement.

"Please," she said impatiently, "finish that sentence for me."

"You mean suggest a plan?" He laughed. "This is the first time I have found you not bubbling with some new plan."

"This is serious."

"Of course. But I thought of the only possible plan last night. And then spent several hours meditating on its merits." His heated gaze traveled over her like a touch. "Though I must say, that dress does not display the merits quite as well as the nightgown I fell asleep remembering."

"You are being offensive."

"Perhaps I am just being an eager bridegroom." He put a finger under her chin. "I don't suppose—" He drew his hand back before she could yield to the temptation to throw his hand back at him. "No. From your look I very much don't suppose I can tempt you to take up where we left off." He took her hand and drew her toward the sofa. "Come and sit. I have some things to tell you which should make our situation more agreeable."

She yielded to his insistent pull. Except for the quick flare

230

of anger at his undisguised lust, nothing could cut through the curtain of despair that surrounded her. She sat and he settled next to her. He retained possession of her hand.

"We cannot marry with any misconceptions between us. You will be glad to know I am not a pockets-to-let earl. My fortune is quite sufficient to support us both comfortably for longer than either of us will live. Nor am I some kind of rogue for hire to anyone with a few guineas to spare. I admit I have misled you on a few minor points. But I shall clear those up immediately."

"Please do." Amanda found it difficult to care. Anything he might say seemed insignificant next to the fact she must now marry him. Men did tend to confide in women they were attracted to. But in this case the price had been too high. She waited.

"I told you I am a soldier. I was ordered to come here. And you were right. I am interested in your birds. In fact, as soon as we are wed, I shall have to take them to Brussels. The army needs them to carry messages. I will . . ."

Amanda lost whatever followed. Her mouth dropped open. She felt a pulse begin to throb in her temple. Rexford continued to regard her with the same bland expression as if she should be nodding yes to whatever he said. "You—" Her lips moved, but she could not put words to her thoughts until she untangled them in her mind. She struggled to rephrase what he said. "You are a soldier. You came here to bed me and steal my birds, but you are certain I won't mind because you will do me the honor of marrying me first." She yanked her hand out of his, and then had to clasp it with the other one in her lap to keep from striking him.

"Now, Amanda. I had no orders to bed—make love to you. That was—"

"That was your own splendid idea."

His jaw got that tight, angry look, and his face suffused with a crimson color at least as bright as the flush that burned her own cheeks. "If I remember, you were no shrinking miss—I'm sorry. That is not what we are supposed to be discussing. I admit I have not been completely honest with you. I—''

Amanda sprang to her feet, walked toward the door, and whirled to look down at him. ''Completely honest! Rexford, have you ever said a truthful word in your life?'' She stormed across the room and pointed to the door. ''I want you out of here now.''

He stood, fists clenched, but wearing a man's patronizing expression. ''Now, Amanda, I knew you might be upset. But sit and we will discuss—''

''I won't sit. And I won't discuss. And God knows, I won't marry you.''

''You must. The child.'' He glared at her across the too small room. ''We discussed this.''

''You discussed it. The way you discuss everything else— with yourself.'' She folded her arms across her chest. ''Well, I don't have to do anything. I sure as blazes don't have to marry you.''

''Yes, you do. You don't seduce an earl and just walk off carrying his heir. Not in my world you don't.'' He curled his hands into fists so tightly his arms shook.

''For all I know this is another of your lies. Can you swear I am carrying your child?''

''Of course not. But—''

''Then go.'' She pointed to the door again. ''If there is a babe, I will deal with it. I will go . . . I will . . . I don't know what I will do, but whatever it takes so I will not be saying, 'Yes, Lord Rexford, as you wish, Lord Rexford,' for the rest of my life.'' She tightened her grip on her arms and stood motionless, determined not to move until he left or the walls came tumbling down. She did not much care which happened.

He stood immobile as a tree and matched her angry stare.

Footsteps sounded in the hall. Someone stood just outside the door. From her position against the wall Amanda could not see who.

''Marc, I've got some news. I think you need to come.''

Amanda recognized the voice of Rexford's valet, calling him Marc and sounding very unlike a servant.

"Not now, Tag." Rexford looked from the door to Amanda.

"But Marc, Brownley caught one of the men who was here last night. Found him in the village. The blighter had not even bothered to change his shirt. I told Brownley to hold him in the stable until you could get there."

Rexford gave an exasperated sigh. "You may as well come in, Tag. Miss Langley and I are just having a discussion."

"Oh, sorry." Tag stepped into the room. He looked from Rexford to Amanda and back to Rexford.

Rexford nodded to Amanda. "This is Taggart Elmgrove, my friend, the son of the Earl of Elmgrove, and right now not the sharpest man in the world." He smiled at the younger man. "It is all right, Tag. Miss Langley and I have just been discussing our betrothal. We may need a few more minutes to straighten things out."

Tag's face registered astonishment, then unadulterated delight. He stamped over and pounded Rexford on the shoulder. "My heartiest congratulations." With a huge grin and a wink he turned to Amanda. "I am certain you could have done better, Miss Langley, but he has potential."

Amanda refused to respond to his smile. "Actually, we were discussing his leaving. Immediately."

Tag raised his brows and looked back at Rexford. "I see what you mean about a few more details to discuss. I will wait for you in the stable."

Rexford put out a restraining hand. "But before you go, tell me, did you learn anything from the man?"

"Frankly, not much. He definitely set the fire. We can still smell smoke on his clothes, but he either can't or won't say who hired him."

"Very good. I will join you directly."

Tag nodded at Amanda. "Go easy on him, Miss Langley. Basically he's a good man, if a bit of a rascal." He left.

Rexford spoke in a carefully modulated tone. "I think you

233

had better come and sit down. That news illustrates rather vividly why I can't leave.''

Amanda backed up a step so her open palms rested against the wall. ''That rather charming young man changes nothing. I can stand, and you can leave.''

''Not if you want your birds to survive the week. Without my guards here, you would have lost them all last night.''

Amanda's knees weakened. With everything else she had all but forgotten the fire. ''What . . . ?''

Rexford came over and took her hand. For the second time that morning she allowed him to lead her to the sofa. ''Whatever you have thought until today, the army needs birds capable of flying from Brussels, and the French are equally determined we shall not have them. They have destroyed two lofts already. The French, not foreign breeders. And I can guarantee your birds will be next.''

''I can take care of my own . . .'' Even to her own ears her voice sounded weak. The dryness in her mouth made it difficult to speak.

''Two guards were killed in one of those attacks. Do you want to expose Jeb or possibly yourself to that kind of danger? My men are professionals.''

''I see. And if you leave—''

''I will take my men with me.'' He stood and paced around the room giving her time to digest his words. Coming to a halt in front of her, he looked down, his body rigid, his chin set. ''Believe me on this. You will have me and your birds or you will have neither of us.''

''And if you stay?''

''I will stay here until you marry me and let me take the birds to Brussels. I don't care which you agree to first. But you will do both.''

Amanda reeled before the force of his speech. She needed time to think and she could not do it with him towering over her. She summoned up will she didn't know she had to sound as determined as he. ''You have made yourself very clear. Now suppose you join your men. I will let you know what I decide.''

*   *   *

Amanda had the rest of the long day to do her deciding. Rexford returned from the stable only long enough to tell her he would be away for most of the day getting a special license. Tag and the others would watch over the birds.

For Amanda the process of deciding what to do consisted primarily of saying *no* followed by whatever thought happened to be utmost in her mind.

No, she did not have to marry him. No, he could not carry her birds off to Brussels. No, he did not have to stay. And most emphatically no, she would never repeat the wretched experience of last night.

In the middle of the afternoon, unable to sit for more than three minutes, she sought solace where she usually did, with the birds. The blackened remains of the shed and the lingering smell of smoke vividly reminded her how close she had come to losing them. Jeb might never have discovered the fire in time, and she and Jeb could never have battled it alone. Grace leapt into her palm, and no turned to yes.

She could never leave these trusting creatures unguarded. If she had to pay for Rexford's guards by tolerating his presence, she would do so. "I will never let anything happen to you, dear," she promised.

Even if Rexford did do his worst and simply walked off with the birds he wanted, he would take only the less able birds. Jeb still had her prize racers hidden. The meager victory seemed small consolation in the light of all that had happened.

Lucifer flew past her head and landed on the ground. Grace hopped down to join him, pecking at the ground and pretending not even to notice when he strutted past. On any other day Amanda might have made plans to breed the two. Today the idea seemed like a betrayal. "I would never do that to you," she said to Grace, and trudged back to continue pacing in her room.

That evening she sent a message she would dine in her room. She spent the rest of the night grappling with the possibility of a child. She conjured up a quiet seaside village and a kindly old woman who would care for her and the infant.

It seemed an almost acceptable plan until she fell asleep and dreamed of an insufferable toddler who strutted about the cottage with Rexford's self-assured step and pointed an accusing finger at her.

The next morning brought a renewed encounter with Rexford, very much the arrogant earl with his *I presume* and *I assure you.*

"I presume you are prepared to be more reasonable this morning," he said as she entered the impossibly cheerful sitting room.

"I am always reasonable."

"Splendid. I obtained the license. I suggest we marry immediately—in whatever kind of ceremony you wish. I must be off as soon as possible. I have made financial arrangements in case . . . We must both face the possibility I will not return."

"Nothing would please me more."

He stiffened. "Unfortunately, we do not have time for recriminations. If I return . . . When I return we will discuss details such as where we shall live and—"

"Thank you, Lord Rexford. I have listened to your version of reasonable. Now you will hear mine. You may take your special license and your financial arrangements and burn them. If there are any consequences of . . ." Amanda's face flamed, whether with anger or the vivid memory of lying spread beneath him she neither knew nor cared. "If there are any consequences, I will deal with them—"

"I assure you, I—" With both hands he started to push himself from his chair. In a moment he would be towering over her, using his size to intimidate her.

"Sit, Rexford." Amanda liked the tone she achieved. If she kept a dog she might have used exactly that voice.

He exhaled an exasperated gust of air, but sat.

"As to your remaining here, you may stay until I can arrange adequate guards, and at the moment I am not certain

236

where to find persons who could do the job without endangering themselves. However—''

''My men are perfectly—''

''If you will let me finish. However, it has occurred to me you might simply select the birds you believe you want and walk off with them. I must warn you, if you do, you will only injure both of us. Foolish as I have been, I did have sense enough to mislead you about the abilities of the birds. The ones you would choose would never make it back from the Continent. They would be lost to me, but you would also fail.''

''I see.'' His eyes narrowed and drew together. ''And this gives you some satisfaction?''

''Not much, because I would grieve for the birds I lost. But I am hoping your knowledge of this will prevent you from taking such a step.''

''And if I don't believe you?''

''Then you will test my word and we will both suffer.'' Amanda stood as Marie Antoinette must have stood after they discussed the details of her execution. ''I believe that is all we have to say to each other.''

He rose with her and gave a tight-lipped nod. ''It is not. But I agree, now is not the time.''

That evening after an uncomfortable dinner marked by long silences, Amanda rose from the table. ''If you will excuse me, Lord Rexford, I believe I will retire early. I am exhausted.''

Rexford sprang from his chair, and circled the table. ''Stay a moment, Amanda.'' He put a restraining hand on her arm. ''I would like to apologize for being unforgivably brusque this morning.''

She resisted the temptation to ignore the request. He would remain at Langwood until she could think of a better solution, and she would continue to encounter him unless she took to her room with a permanent attack of the vapors. ''Very well. I cannot imagine we have much more to say to each other." With a nod she indicated he should accompany her into the sitting room. "You may speak your piece one final time."

In the small yellow room, he coughed and waited until she sat on the edge of a chair. "As I said, I was incredibly brusque this morning." He drew a chair over and sat so close their knees almost touched. "It has since occurred to me you are a woman."

Amanda's mouth tightened. "I believe that occurred to you two nights ago."

He flushed. "Not in that way, though I admit—" He shook his head, banishing a warm expression that made Amanda nervous in spite of her determination to ignore the rapid heartbeat his nearness and such looks produced. "I realize women regard marriage differently than men." He cleared his throat. "I have failed to assure you of my regard. A proper proposal, if you like . . ." He shifted uncomfortably and darted a glance about the room. "On my knees, if you—" He took her hand.

"That won't be necessary."

"Very well." He took a deep breath. "Amanda, please do me the honor of becoming my wife. I assure you I hold you in the highest regard—"

"You have already said that."

"I hold you in the highest esteem and you would make me the happiest of men if—"

"Enough, I beg you. You sound like you borrowed those words from half a dozen different books."

"I admit I am not very good at speeches, but—"

"But you will make a speech anyway, because it suits you. Can't you just once be honest and admit you are trapped into a marriage neither of us wants because of a regrettable incident?"

He bolted from the chair, stomped across the room, and whirled to face her. "Honest! Do you want honest?" His face turned a livid crimson and veins throbbed at both temples. "What you term a regrettable incident was some kind of a miracle. I have been with hundreds of women—"

238

"Certainly something to make your future wife proud."

His fist clenched. "You asked for honesty. Don't turn missish when you get it." His jaw trembled. "I have been with hundreds of women. Some of them I took to my bed while still trying to decide what to wear the next day. Nothing has ever happened to me like the other night. I felt . . . I felt . . . I don't know what I felt."

He threw his hands in the air and shook his head. "I didn't make love to you because you happened to be convenient. Or because . . . I made love to you because I can't keep my hands off you. Dammit, I wake up wanting you. I go to sleep wanting you. I . . ." He took a breath. "When something like that happens between a man and a woman, they belong together."

"So I am supposed to marry you because you cannot keep your hands off me?"

"Yes. I mean, no. It is so much more than that. I know I won't say this right if I couldn't even say the other."

"Try." His bewildered expression made it impossible to infuse her voice with the proper coldness.

He paced a moment, then came and sat. Leaning forward with his hands between his knees, he studied her face. "I don't just want to make love to you. I want be in the same room with you even if I am not touching you." He gave a quick bemused smile. "I am not saying you don't make me angry." He curled the fingers of one hand. "Sometimes you make me so angry I feel I could crush rocks. But still . . ."

His brows knitted together in a frown and he cocked his head. "Do you know the first thing I do when I wake up in the morning? I look at the clock and try to guess how many hours before I will see you. I can recognize the sound of your footstep from three rooms away."

He circled the room and came to a stop in front of her. "I can't wait to see your face, hear what new role you've cast me in, or just try to make you smile. Dammit, I have no idea when you became so important to me. But you did."

Amanda steeled herself against the appeal in his eyes.

"That is all very well, but I don't see what it has to do with—"

He gave an impatient sigh. "It has everything to do with it. If I have to go away, I want to be damn sure you will be here when I come back." He stood again and crossed the room. When he turned, he thought a minute before he spoke. "One other thing. I have never been jealous of a woman in my life, but . . . but the thought of you ever saying another man's name the way you said mine the other night makes me insane."

He gave a mirthless laugh. "Don't mind me. This whole thing has made me a little insane." He came over, sat, and took her hand, folding it between his. His face softened into a smile. "I am sure I will recover if you say you will marry me."

Even after everything that had happened, Amanda's heart still quickened at his touch. His words had sounded so earnest. She understood at least the part about listening for footsteps. She would listen for his long after he was gone.

It would be so easy to look into his eyes and surrender. She looked away. A bird flew past her window, and she remembered how easily he could convince her of anything. He always got his way.

Not this time, she vowed.

She snatched her hand away. "Enough, Rexford. You are wasting your pretty speeches. A woman might pretend to believe them if marriage could offer some advantage. But I have no need for either your title or your fortune, if indeed you have one. I am quite content with my life here, or I was before you threw everything into such turmoil."

A cold mask replaced his vulnerable expression. He stood. "I see you are still not prepared to be reasonable. We will talk again." He made a formal bow. "Now, if you will excuse me, I believe I will go for a walk." He turned and retreated out the door leading to the terrace before Amanda could speak.

Rexford cursed. He cursed silently, he cursed aloud. He

mentally thought of several new ways to call himself a fool, muttered those to the disinterested air. Then he cursed his fumbling words and inadequate vocabulary.

For almost a mile in the gathering twilight, his feet pounded with bone-jarring force on the hard ground. He clenched his hands into fists to keep from shaking the nearby trees with a force that would strip them of every leaf.

The woman had no sense, but he'd known that. He had sense enough for both of them. Dammit, earls were born with sense. They were invented to tell other people what to do.

Nobody simply dismissed an earl. Except Amanda. Amanda.

He slowed his pace and tried to think. They had to get married. Surely she could see that. He felt himself tighten with the ache that had been almost constant for forty-eight hours, and he let himself think of the reasons they had to marry.

Not simply the possibility of a babe. Their union had been so brief that was unlikely. They had to get married because she had sat on the floor with her gown tangled around her waist, looked at him with eyes aching and bewildered, and captured his soul.

Yesterday he had left the village blackguard to Tag and spent six hours getting a special license because he could not imagine riding away from here and never seeing her again. Surely that should have some meaning.

Rexford clenched his teeth together until his jaw muscles ached. They had to get married because it would give him the right to kill any man who even thought about touching her. They had to get married and she didn't even understand why.

They had both had a glimpse of the woman she could become. It had thrilled him and terrified her. With time and tenderness he could bring her to appreciate the wonder of it, but the war left him no time. The war had pressured him into becoming the babbling oaf he'd been today.

He needed . . . Affectionate thoughts of Amanda slowed

his step. What he needed was a plan. In his place Amanda would have had a plan before she walked three steps.

He discarded the obvious heavy-handed strategies of kidnapping her or arranging to be caught in a compromising situation. In either case it would be embarrassing if she decided to stand in front of a clergyman and say, ''No, I don't believe so.''

The memory of her icy look suggested reason would not be any more effective, even if he could hope to be any more than a blithering idiot in her presence.

With a smile he developed his plan. Admittedly one which left him with one very small ethical problem.

He had never seduced a woman for her own good before. He wrestled with that for about thirty seconds, failed to fix on the proper rationale, and decided he'd already condemned himself to Hell three or four times already. The devil shouldn't even notice another minor transgression.

She was rejecting him because her only experience has been so wretched. Once she came to see the magic they could share, she would be as eager to marry as he. He had to make love to her again as much for her as for himself. Surely, in this case, it mattered that he only wanted to make her happy.

The decision made, he turned and looked back in the direction from which he had come. Darkness made it impossible to tell how far he had come. He smiled with the realization he had three or four miles to walk and think about the ways he would make her happy. Her breast cupped in his hand, her . . .

Bang. The loud sound dragged Amanda from an exhausted sleep. *Bang*. A gunshot. Definitely a gunshot. She sat up, her heart pounding in the darkness.

Bang. Bang.

She jumped from bed. Before she reached the window, two more shots rang out. She shuffled the curtain aside, but could see only darkness. Stumbling, she made her way across the room, and had taken three steps along the corridor before she remembered her flimsy nightgown. Rexford might have brought his war to Langwood but she would not fight it half-dressed. Not again.

Back in her room she pulled on the heaviest, most unattractive wrapper she owned. Nor would she face him again without a chaperone. "Lily." She pounded on her maid's door. "Lily, wake up."

Lily staggered into the hall.

"Come with me." Amanda ran to the library, actually got to the side door that led to the terrace, and stopped. In the distance she heard the shouts of masculine voices, then another shot.

Only a fool would rush blindly into that fracas. She turned to look for a weapon.

Lily grabbed her arm. "What's happening, miss?"

"Go wake Rexford. He should be here."

Lily ran back the way they had come and Amanda stood at the open door. Another shout startled her into slamming it closed, only to discover she could hear nothing. She cracked it open again, straining for every sound. "Dammit, Rexford, hurry."

"He ain't there, miss." Lily gasped the breathless words from the hall, then came to stand clutching Amanda's shoulder. "Maybe we shouldn't stand so close." She tried to draw Amanda back.

Amanda had fallen asleep still angry at Rexford. Now her stomach clenched into a tight knot. One of those shots might have been . . . Even now he might be . . . Again she fought the impulse to rush blindly into the darkness. "Hush, Lily. I can't hear. And stop pulling on me." Behind her Amanda sensed other people coming into the room.

She turned to see Prescott in an impossible red-and-white-striped nightshirt. His thinning gray hair stood straight up and his bare toes curled oddly. A thoroughly ludicrous picture except for the black pistol he waved awkwardly.

"What is it, miss? Do you . . . do you want me to go out and see?"

"I think Lord Rexford is there. Stay with us until—"

The disembodied voice of Rexford's valet sliced through the darkness. "Curse it, Marc, slow down before you bleed to death."

Chapter Fourteen

Amanda took a single step out the door and strained to see the two men.

"Curse it, Marc, let me help you."

"Stop fussing. You make me feel like somebody's grandmother." Two shapes appeared in the darkness, came closer.

Amanda recognized Rexford's purposeful stride as he moved onto the terrace. The knot in her stomach uncoiled, though her heart continued to pound wildly. She stepped back and threw open the door. "What happened?"

"Amanda, get back inside," Rexford commanded. "I should have known you would hear gunshots and frame yourself in light just in case somebody needed a target."

Amanda resisted the impulse to run to him. If he could snarl like that, he could help himself across the terrace. "What happened?"

"It's over. He's hurt." Tag said, walking with an awkward step so he could keep a hand on Rexford's shoulder. "Though I am hoping the injury is more to his disposition than his person. Slow down, Marc, before you bleed to death."

Light from the room spilled onto the terrace. "It's nothing." Rexford moved into the light, one arm stretched across his body, his hand clutching the opposite shoulder.

The two men entered together. Both were fully dressed in white shirts and dark breeches. Rexford had an empty scabbard at his waist. Crimson blood drenched the sleeve of his shirt. He winked at Amanda. "I would have done this days ago if I thought it would make you look at me like that." His injured arm moved a few inches as if he might touch her, but dropped to his side again. "Inside." he said. "The excitement is over." He stepped past her.

Amanda stood covering her mouth for a second, then jumped to follow the men. "Here, I will—"

Lily stepped in front of Amanda and indicated a straight-backed chair. "Sit here." She looked quickly across the room at the butler. "Prescott can you get—" The butler padded out the door.

Rexford sat and smiled at the three of them hovering over him. "You can all stop fussing. I said it was nothing."

"Excuse me, sir." Lily eased Tag aside. Raised on a farm with a horde of younger brothers and sisters, she might not deal well with the sound of gunshots, but she considered minor injuries her own special province. At a nod from Rexford, she tore at his sodden shirt. "You need to move your hand so's I can see. And I hope you will try not to bleed on the rug. My sister'll only have to scrub it all again."

"Yes, ma'am." Rexford winked at her and drew his hand aside. His warmer smile to Amanda brought a flush to her cheeks and the memory of his blood mingling with hers on the same rug.

Lily dabbed at the wound again. "You are the bleedenest man I ever seen." Prescott appeared at her side with a basin of water and several spotless white napkins. "This is gonna sting some," she said to Rexford. She washed the cut several times, turning the water in the ivory-colored porcelain bowl a sickening shade of red.

Amanda summoned the anxious-looking footman, who

had appeared with Prescott. "James, I think you better go for—"

Lily·shook her head. "No need to send for a doctor, miss. He'd only keep us up half the night and want to take some of his man-sized stitches in this little cut. I vow, he'd make it look a whole lot worse than it is." She looked at Rexford. "If you was my brother, I'd tell you ta let me tie it up, and then I'd warn you don't never do whatever you was doin' again." She dabbed again and studied the blood that welled to the surface. "Though if you like, I can take a few tiny tucks—"

"Just release me, Lily." Rexford glanced at his hand, which she held firmly tucked in her armpit. "I have no desire to—"

Lily smiled knowingly at Amanda. "Just like a man. No matter how big they get, you start talking about a needle and thread and they get fine in a hurry." With sure moves she folded a fresh napkin and tied it in place with another. "That should hold you till morning."

With the blood safely concealed, Amanda's stomach settled and she realized she still had no idea why they were all standing here watching Rexford bleed. "What happened? Are the birds—"

"Your birds are fine." Rexford offered a smile exclusively for Amanda. "I will take it as a good sign you waited to be certain I wouldn't die before asking."

"Would have been nobody's fault but your own if you did." Tag looked at Amanda. "He's too modest to tell you, but he took on three of those blighters all by himself to save your birds." He pointed at a nick just below Rexford's hairline that Amanda hadn't seen. "If you notice the new way he's got his hair parted, you can guess it was none too bright a thing to do. Thought he'd use a bullet instead of a comb."

Amanda's knees weakened and the room wavered. Blood might have been pouring from Rexford's head instead of his arm.

Tag tucked a chair behind her knees. "Sit. His color is a lot better than yours."

Amanda sank into it gratefully. "But you . . . Why didn't you help?" she asked Tag.

"He will tell you it's because he's smarter than the rest of us."

"I am." Rexford grinned at his friend. The grin turned into a warning look. "I am also smart enough not to frighten the ladies with—"

"They fired off those guns as a diversion. The rest of us went chasing off after that. He"—Tag angled his head to indicate Rexford—"figured they wanted the birds and went to the cote. By the time the rest of us got there, he had two of them running into our arms and was doing some rather unpleasant things to your friend Batterton."

Amanda pictured the darkness. A bullet. Rexford's head . . . his smile . . . Emptiness opened up around her. To fill the emptiness she reframed Tag's words in her mind. Three men. Running away. Batterton. Lord Batterton? Her brow furrowed. "Lord Batterton was here? I . . ."

"I should have told you." The good humor left Rexford's face. His voice gentled. "He wanted your birds. That is why he was here."

Amanda welcomed the confusion to replace the icy darkness of her imagination. "My birds? I don't understand. He has no use for the birds. We used to talk . . ."

"I don't know what else he used to do," Rexford said coldly, "but we have suspected him of working for the French for years. Nothing dramatic and nothing we could ever prove, but . . ." He shrugged and winced as the muscle under the bandage tightened. "His mother was French. He still has property there."

"I see." Amanda stood. Her knees quivered, but tightened under her determined effort. With a few minutes to think she would see. Batterton was French. He wanted the birds because Rexford wanted them, because there was a war. Incredible, but if Batterton wanted something he would take it. For the same reason she knew Rexford wouldn't, she knew Batterton would. She walked a few paces just to prove she could. "How did you know he would come tonight?"

Rexford's voice had a hard edge. "I have been expecting him. Tag let it be known in the village we would be moving some birds out tomorrow. We figured that would provoke an attack and we were waiting for him." His intense gaze never left Amanda's face. "Does that distress you very much?"

Distress. A mild word for the picture of a bullet slamming into his temple. Three armed men. "Why you alone? Why didn't you wait for the others?"

His face softened. "The birds. They would have gotten to the birds if I waited."

The birds. Of course. Always the birds, from the first day he came. Always his duty. Amanda stiffened. She studied his face. "But . . . ? But you knew those birds were useless." She steadied herself with a hand on the back of the chair she had just left.

His face softened with tenderness. "Not useless. I knew you loved them."

"But three armed men—"

"I drew those men here. That was the only way I could say how sorry—" He wrenched his gaze from her face to look first at Tag and then at the hovering servants in the room. He laughed. "Tag, I don't mean to be rude but there are far too many people in this room. Including yourself. If you don't mind . . ."

"Splendid night, ladies and gentlemen. Thank you for coming." Tag's sweeping gestures portrayed an ebullient host ushering his guests toward the door.

"Stop." Tag already had the servants in the hall, but they halted at Amanda's firm command.

Rexford smiled and lowered his voice so only Amanda could hear. "I suppose you are going to say that was a little obvious of me."

"Very."

"I thought we might—"

"We will talk in the morning. In the meantime . . ." Amanda raised her voice. "Prescott, James, could you please wait and see if Lord Rexford needs any help getting to bed?"

She sailed from the room, refusing to even notice Rexford's exaggerated disappointment.

Amanda climbed into bed certain she had the rest of the night to untangle everything that had occurred.

She awoke to brilliant sunshine streaming into her room and an irrational desire to see Rexford. She had so many unanswered questions, but honesty forced her to admit she did not want to see him for answers. She just wanted to see him alive and well.

She missed the anger he usually raised in her. Instead, she kept remembering the tenderness in his face when he confessed he had risked his life to protect the birds she loved. Birds he could barely think about without a shudder.

Naturally, being Rexford, he had immediately found a self-serving use for the dramatic gesture. What would have happened if she had been fool enough to remain in the room with him?

She didn't have to wonder. She knew.

He would have touched her—anywhere. She would have begun trembling. No matter how rationally she knew she should leave, she would have stayed and surrendered to him.

Perhaps in the revealing light of day she would stop seeing the blood on his sleeve and remember all his manipulations. With an effort, she dismissed the disturbing image.

Lily chattered away about him while she brushed Amanda's hair.

An insistent voice from the chamber doorway startled both of them. Kitty, the young parlor maid, stood there. Her face betrayed her excitement. "Miss, miss, you better come quick. There's men in the hall."

Amanda jumped up, tossing her loose hair back over her shoulders. "What is it, Kitty?" She started for the door without waiting for a reply.

"I don't know, miss. Soldiers, I think. Prescott told me to come and get you quick. He wouldn't let me stay and see anything."

From the head of the stairs Amanda heard the commotion

in the hall, masculine voices. She hurried down, but stopped at the foot of the stairs. Two soldiers in green uniforms stood there with a litter stretched between them. Amanda could see only the head of the man they carried. He appeared deathly pale, and she could not tell if he was alive or dead.

"Don't keep us standing here, my good man," the soldier closest to Amanda said to Prescott, "just show us where we should put him."

"Put me down, you blockheads, I don't go calling on my back."

The man at the back end of the litter looked affectionately at the reclining figure. "You wouldn't be half so heavy if you'd stop jostling about." He looked at Prescott. "Where?"

Prescott hesitated, then looked up to see Amanda. "Miss?" He might have been politely inquiring where to serve tea.

"Rexford!" Amanda clamped her lips shut, realizing she had raised her voice. Whatever was going on, Rexford was responsible. He did not even need to be in the same room to make her lose all sense of decorum.

She turned to Kitty who hovered at her shoulder. "Fetch Lord Rexford."

Before Kitty could move, the solid thump of masculine footsteps signaled Rexford's arrival. He and Tag appeared from the library. Both froze, staring at the reclining form. Tag turned visibly pale. His face twisted in anguish.

Rexford's features turned to solid granite. His fingers curled around Tag's shoulder in a grip that had to hurt.

Tag did not seem even to notice. He stood rooted in place, staring at the litter.

"Put me down and I'll fetch my son and his misbegotten friend myself."

Dawn never brought a light like the one that broke over the faces of the two statue-still men. Muscles relaxed. Rexford released his grip and replaced it with an encouraging slap.

Tag took a step forward, then stopped again to work his facial muscles into an indifferent mask. After three tries he seemed satisfied. Four more steps brought him to the litter. He held out his hand. "Good to see you, sir. I was beginning to think I might have to start behaving like an earl. Marc said it would be just my luck to have you show up." The tears in his eyes belied his casual tone. He gripped the reclining man's hand in both of his.

"You won't be an earl for another hundred years yet, boy. Unless you leave me in the care of these simpletons for another five minutes."

The blond man at the head of the stretcher grinned. "He'll be dying from a fall if you don't let us put him down."

Tag dragged his eyes from his father long enough to look anxiously at the man who spoke. "How is he?"

The man gave an indifferent shrug. "Not as well as he thinks he is, but from the look on your face, not as bad as you think. He'll probably live to bother us all another few years."

Rexford eased over to stand next to Amanda. "It is Tag's father. Perhaps you could . . . ?"

With a start she realized Tag's emotion had paralyzed her. She had forgotten her role. "Of course. Prescott, show these gentlemen to the blue room."

She started to follow the group upstairs, but Rexford put a restraining hand on her arm. "Tag and his father are very close. It might be a good idea to give them a few minutes."

"Excellent. That will give you time to explain why I have another half a dozen people in my house. If I give you time enough, you will invite all of London to stay."

He smiled down at her gently. "This one you deserve, my dragon, since your birds are the reason he is still alive. At least part of the reason. Come, I will explain." He turned her toward the sitting room with his hand still on her shoulder.

"Send for a doctor," Tag called from the top of the stairs. "Two if the village can produce them."

Amanda paused long enough to speak to Kitty, who had missed the nighttime excitement but would probably hover in the hall all day. "Send James, and we may need Mrs. Carter as well."

In the small sitting room Rexford explained about the message from Elmgrove and Margaret's help in sending the reply. "Until Elmgrove spoke, neither of us dared hope . . . Even when we saw the litter, we thought he might be dead."

"That was the Earl of Elmgrove, the one in Edith's letter? At the ball. Kissing the matron's . . ."

"That sounds like Elmgrove. That's why I could not imagine him cocking up his toes just because he was surrounded by the whole French army."

"Then all your war stories—"

"Were true."

"But Brussels sounds so gay. So many people I know from London are there—Lady Caroline Lamb, Charlotte Waddie, Georgiana Lennox—"

"Do not deceive yourself. Brussels is a city getting ready for war even if all the people there want to pretend that isn't true." Rexford looked at her directly, his message unmistakably clear. "Your birds could save a lot more than one life when this thing gets started over there. Whole battalions."

Amanda's mind peopled the room with haunted faces of wives, mothers, and children. Remembering Tag's anguished expression, she added a few grown sons. "It would have to be my racing birds," she said in a voice scarcely more than a whisper.

"I know," Rexford said, his eyes soft. He held out a hand, but didn't touch her.

Amanda tried twice to speak, but could not form the words that would sacrifice her birds. In her mind she pictured which birds she would send, knowing they might never return.

Her mother bustled in, still in her bonnet and shawl. "Kitty tells me we have another earl. Can you believe it. I almost didn't come home from Margaret's today. Thank God that impossible baron of hers kept falling asleep in his soup. Imagine, all these years not a one, and now it is practically raining earls."

Amanda smiled, grateful for any interruption that would

put off the dreadful commitment. "The Earl of Elmgrove. I suspected you would be pleased."

"Kitty said he is quite old, but being the goosecap that she is, she had no idea whether he is married."

Amanda darted a quick look at Rexford before she had to confess to being as thoroughly inadequate as Kitty.

Rexford grinned. "Unless Elmgrove has been a lot more busy than I suspect in the last few weeks, he is currently unmarried." He finished with a dubious look. "Though I feel obliged to warn you, he has never impressed me as particularly good husband material."

The older woman nodded in satisfaction, giving a quick pat to her hair. "I am aware of that possibility, Lord Rexford. But when the gods see fit to drop an earl on your doorstep, a person can at least be obliging enough to look him over." She stood. "I believe I will go and welcome him. Coming, Amanda?"

Amanda rose as well. "No. I must go and spend some time with the birds." She turned to Rexford. "I will let you know what I decide."

He held out a hand that might have brushed her cheek if she stood closer. His eyes softened as they looked into hers. "I have never had any question how you would decide once you understood." His voice held no hint of triumph.

She turned to leave.

"Wait." He took a step toward her. "I . . . I will be making plans to leave in the morning. I believe we should take care of that other matter this afternoon."

Amanda looked over her shoulder to be certain her mother had gone tripping off to view her new earl. "Rexford, I live for the day when you discover you don't get everything you want simply because you want it." That did not seem like enough, so when she reached the door she turned. "And I suggest you don't bother dressing for a wedding."

That afternoon Amanda spent an hour with Lord Elmgrove, unnecessarily confirming what she already knew. He described the massing of troops, making the sights he had seen come alive in his deep rumbling voice. He not only believed there would be a major battle, but that it might be only days away.

Somebody had obviously briefed him on her reluctance to part with her birds, because he finished with an impassioned plea. "When the war comes it is going to be the damnedest mess you ever saw. Four or five hundred thousand troops all running about with no idea where anyone else is. That is why we need somebody well out of it to coordinate things. We will have to get messages to someplace we can be sure will not be overrun by the French army."

"Someplace like here, you mean."

He nodded. "My message got through. The system will work. But they'll need more birds over there than they have now. There is no telling how long this war will go on."

"Is that why you came here? To convince me?"

"Not entirely. I did have to get out of France in a hurry. But once we got to Dover, I knew I wasn't going to be going back to Brussels any time soon, so I figured I might help out here."

Automatically Amanda's gaze traveled to his injured leg. "But the extra travel . . . You should have stayed—"

"A few extra miles wasn't going to do any harm. And I had all those letters from my son saying it was going to take a little more convincing before they could send any more birds." He gave a boyish grin. "I figured between me and my leg, I could be just about one of the best convincers you ever met."

"I see." The phrase sounded distant and cold after what he must have suffered on the journey. She softened it with a smile. "You certainly are that."

"Good. Now let's talk about something a little more pleasant." He brightened as if getting ready to invite her to a gala ball. "Suppose you tell me what that fool doctor and my son were saying about my leg. They stood over there"—he pointed to the corner—"whispering as if the leg belonged to them and they were only letting me borrow it for a while."

Amanda looked away, not prepared for the question or the uncompromising blue eyes he fixed on her.

He laughed. "You don't do much lying, do you, girl? You told me already, so you may as well go ahead and say the words."

Amanda hesitated. After all it was his leg, and he had a right to know. "The doctor said the next few days will tell whether you will be able to keep it. The wound is festering."

"And that's what all the whispering was?" He shook his head in disbelief. "I don't know why some people figure if you get shot in the leg your brains just slide out through the hole. I've see enough sour wounds to figure that out." He angled his head and studied her intensely. "You swear they are not going to give me a nice drink of something and slip back in here and lop it off?"

Amanda looked at the untouched water and tea on the table next to the bed. He had talked so casually, all the while fearing he might fall asleep and wake up without his leg. She drew her chair closer and took his hand. "I can't speak for your son or the doctor, but you can put your faith in Mrs. Carter."

"The crosspatch who's been standing guard over me all day?"

"She's a country woman and will make no bones about telling you what you have to do and expecting you to do it. But she'll be honest with you."

"Good." Elmgrove released her hand and reached for the water. "Good, because I intend to keep my leg." He laughed indulgently. "That lady who claims to be your mother appears to have some interesting plans. I expect I shall need both my legs."

Amanda returned his laugh. "For running away? You disappoint me, Lord Elmgrove."

"On the contrary, my dear. I am already planning to do some pretty fair chasing, if my son and that fool doctor agree to keep me whole." His intent expression returned. "Though you have my word, I would gladly sacrifice the leg if that is what it would take to convince you they must have your birds in Brussels.''

He seemed pleased with the thought of such a noble sacrifice. Amanda did not bother to point out it would make no logical sense. She rose. ''That will not be necessary. Rest now, and trust Mrs. Carter.''

By the time Amanda reached the first floor she had her plans fully formed, and derived some small satisfaction from the fact they might not totally match Rexford's.

In the library, Rexford blotted the last document and settled back to wait for Amanda. Being human, he allowed himself to indulge in a satisfying fantasy of the kind of farewell she should give him. Soft tears melting the starch on his shirt. Whispered pleas that he stay just a moment longer. She would let him go long enough for him to walk across the room, then choke out his name, causing him to turn and permit her to run into his arms again.

No. A fantasy should at least be a proper one. She would slip into his room tonight, her hair loose around her shoulders, her translucent shift clinging to every curve. Trembling under his touch, she would beg him to give her one last night to remember. He would have until dawn to imprint every inch of her body with a memory of him. Then, in the faint light of dawn, they could have the tears and the whispered pleas.

Women had been sending soldiers off to war with those memories for thousands of years. Amanda could at least make an effort.

The sound of approaching footsteps forced him to surrender the fantasy. He straightened in his chair. A moment later Amanda appeared in the doorway wearing a severe gray gown that concealed even the upper half of her neck. Silently, he sighed in resignation. She had obviously not come to act out his fantasy.

''Rexford.'' Her tone, cool and curt now, confirmed his wisdom in not suggesting they go upstairs so she could change into something with fewer layers—and fewer buttons.

He rose with a silent curse for the war, which had robbed him of any option but matching her guarded manner. "Amanda, come in. I gather from your dress that I am not to be married this afternoon." As soon as he spoke he regretted his cool tone. Years of training obliged him to pretend indifference when things mattered most. Women were supposed to help men overcome that.

"If you had paid more attention, you might have gathered the same thing from my words this morning," she said, coming in and sitting at the table where he had studied bird books in another lifetime.

He drew his chair around so at least the table did not separate them. The whisper of her scent assailed him, and made it possible for him to make one more attempt to break through her shield of reserve. "Amanda, I don't know what you want from me. I am willing to—"

"From the day you came I have never wanted anything from you. I am here simply to discuss what will happen from now on."

Rexford gave an exasperated sigh. "Very well. I have been working on it most of the afternoon."

"And now, I presume you are going to tell me."

Something in her tone warned him he should not continue. He studied her frozen face for a clue. Finding none, he lifted the papers from the table. "As you wish. We will postpone our wedding until I return. However, we must both face the fact I may not." He paused, debated whether to remind her she should have produced a horrified gasp, then decided a gasp would lose its charm if you had to ask for it.

"I believe these papers will all be legally binding. Kitty cannot read, but she has witnessed my signature." He held out the first. "This is a letter to my family introducing you as my affianced and asking that you be treated accordingly." He waited until she accepted the first paper, then held out the second letter. "In this I have settled a sizable sum on you. I simply chose an amount. If you think it is not enough . . .''

She accepted the paper and glanced at it. This time she did gasp. "That is a great deal of money for one night!"

"That is an ugly tone. It makes you sound like a . . . Amanda, please be civil about this. We haven't much time."

"Very well. You may have your say."

He picked up the final paper. "This . . ." A flush colored his cheeks. It seemed so impossible to relate this cold creature to the woman who had strained toward him so hungrily. "If you should . . . If you do bear a male child, this names him as my heir. I know it will be difficult for you, but it is the best I can do if you persist in refusing to marry me today."

She accepted the paper, but set it down on the table without looking at it. "None of this is necessary."

"I agree. I plan to return and when I do, we will marry quite properly."

"We will not—" For the first time her voice held some passion.

He held up a hand to stifle her protest. "I will even court you properly if you insist. I will spend however long you like making up for the dreadful mare's nest I have made of things. But we will marry." Much as she might resent the tone, he could not leave any doubt as to his intentions.

She nodded compliantly. "I see. Tell me what else you have worked out." Her voice held a sarcastic edge softened by a faint smile.

"That is all that deals directly with us. But we must talk about the morning. Am I correct in assuming you now agree the birds must go to Brussels?"

"Yes."

"Good. And can you have them packed and ready as soon as possible after dawn? Dover is not far, but I may have some trouble finding a boat."

"They will be ready."

"Splendid. Then I guess that settles everything. Unless . . .'' He stood and drew her to her feet. She came willingly enough and stood inches from him, staring into his eyes with a cool look he knew he could turn to fire. He softened his voice with the passion that smoldered every time he came within thirty feet of her. "Unless you would like to make some suggestions about how we might spend our last night together?"

He cupped her chin and ran his thumb over her lips to part them in preparation for his own suggestion as to how they might spend the night.

She put her hands on his shoulders. "I would not presume to suggest. It appears you already have your own ideas about that as well."

Rexford exhaled. Hope flared with the rush of blood through his veins. Just as he tightened his grip to draw her lips to his, her hands pushed against his shoulders, not back but down, forcing him into his chair. He sat and looked up at her, not sure he liked the newest development.

Amanda took three steps back and stopped with her hands folded across her chest. "Now we can talk, Rexford. You appear ready to listen for a change."

"I always listen." He knew he didn't like the latest development.

"You have just presented a rather long list of how you expect things to be. Now you will listen to my equally long summary of how things will *not* be." Her head angled and her eyes flashed a challenge. "Do you have any preference as to the order of my list?"

In spite of his apprehension, Rexford felt his body stir in response to her barely suppressed anger. Until he met Amanda he had not realized how powerful an aphrodisiac anger could be. "Any way you like." His mercurial mind suggested several ways he liked.

"On the subject of tonight. However each of us chooses to spend it, we will *not* spend it together. I will *not* go to your family with a letter introducing myself as your betrothed. I will *not* accept a comfortable sum as payment for a rather foolish mistake."

Rexford rose to protest. "That was not a payment. How dare you even suggest . . . That was—"

Amanda waved him back. "I listened very politely to you. Now you will show me the same courtesy. I will *not* present your illegitimate son as your heir. If it becomes necessary I will . . . I don't know what I will do, but whether you are alive or dead, I will *not* follow your casual orders. And if you do decide to come back I will *not* marry you. Are you beginning to understand now?"

Rexford studied her and shook his head. "I am hearing you, but I definitely do not understand. I have no idea why you are so angry."

She blew out an impatient puff of air and her face assumed an almost accepting expression. "I believe you, Rexford. Maybe it is not just you. Maybe all earls think a title gives them the right to walk into a private house and start giving orders."

"Most people like . . . The army is built on following orders. Somebody has to give them." He realized from her tightening jaw that that wasn't the response she was hoping for. "I am sorry if I sounded like I was giving orders. Things are just so much neater when everybody understands—" The bumbled explanation had at least given Rexford time to think. He was being wrongly accused. "I have not merely given you orders. I distinctly remember *asking* you to marry me at least three or four times."

Amanda gave a fierce shake of her head. "To my recollection you *asked* once and ordered me five or six times." She dismissed the question with a wave. "Besides, it is not an issue any more. By the time we have dealt with this war marriage will probably not even be necessary."

Rexford ground his teeth to cut off the rising impatience. "It will be necessary in any case." He spoke quietly and rose. "However, if you are not prepared to be reasonable, I suggest we postpone any further discussion. I have things to do before morning." A tactical retreat would keep him from saying things he might regret. "Now, if you will excuse me . . ."

"I suggest you don't go just yet. You will save yourself a nasty shock."

"I doubt you could shock me further."

She laughed. "I wish you were in a mood to make a small wager on that. You have not heard my final *not*."

Her tone stopped Rexford. "I doubt you have anything left to refuse me."

"The birds."

Her words prickled along Rexford's skin. "What about the birds?"

She spoke very quietly. "You are *not* taking the birds to Brussels."

"But you said . . . you cannot change your mind about something like that simply because you are angry with me."

She straightened her shoulders. "I am not changing my mind. I said the birds will go to Brussels in the morning. I never said you would take them."

"Then who—?" Rexford refused even to let the suspicion form in his mind.

"I will."

"That's insane."

"I had planned to take them to Antwerp at the end of a month. Brussels is only a few miles away. I merely have to move my plans forward a few weeks."

"Dammit, Amanda. That was before Napoleon decided to turn the entire continent into a battlefield. You are not going!"

She smiled. "I knew you would respond like this. Listen to yourself giving orders. I am not going. But, of course, you can."

The difference seemed so obvious he felt like a fool stating it. "You are a woman. I am a man. A soldier."

She laughed, and he realized she was thoroughly enjoying herself. "You forgot to mention a whole lot of other things that make it perfectly reasonable for you to give orders. You are a man. You are a soldier. You are an earl and a thoroughly annoying person. But none of that means you may take my birds to Brussels. You read my cousin's letter. Half of fashionable London is in Brussels with far less reason to be there than I will have.''

Rexford ran his fingers through his hair and half rose from his chair. ''You cannot go waltzing into a war just because you are angry with me.''

Her tight jaw relaxed. ''Much as it will satisfy me to deprive you of something you want, that is not my sole reason. The birds do not travel well. They will be upset and bewildered. You are not likely to get them to Brussels alive.''

''I beg to differ with you. I have fed them. I have watered them. Dammit, I have even talked to the blasted creatures. What more will they want?''

''They will need gentleness. Someone who cares. They will need me.''

In spite of every resolution to be reasonable, Rexford let the words explode. ''You are not going!''

Amanda simply walked to the door and turned to face him with one hand on the frame. ''I can see this discussion going on until midnight. If you truly believe I am not going, I suggest you be in front of the house at dawn to watch me leave.''

Chapter Fifteen

Naturally, Rexford stormed and protested. Amanda sent a message stating she had too much to do to prepare for her journey in the morning for any more discussion, so he turned to anyone in the house who would listen.

Lady Harriet, probably besotted at the possibility of sole custody of the Earl of Elmgrove, would not hear of any danger. Fully half of her correspondence came from Brussels. The city sounded so gay. She rattled on about how she had actually considered going there herself until ... Until, of course, the gift of her own private earl.

Tag had heard too much of the formidable Miss Langley to be any help in changing her mind.

That left only the Earl of Elmgrove, older, wiser, and certainly a reasonable ally. Unfortunately, he thought the idea a splendid one. "She knows much more about those creatures than you do, Marcus. Sensible girl, too. I'm sure she will be just the thing, and probably have herself a bang-up time too."

"But the danger ..."

"I doubt there is much danger to the civilians."

"But Napoleon . . ."

"Napoleon needs all the allies he can get right now. I assure you, he will be more concerned with enthralling the civilians than with—"

"But we need her here."

"No buts. I can take care of things on this end. With me here, both you and Tag can go. I am sure the two of you can take care of one female."

"But you can't . . ."

"Can't what? Even if I lose my leg, I won't lose my eyes or my mouth. I am sure I will see that the correspondence gets where it must. Now go off with you. I would like some time to contemplate the next few weeks with the rather interesting Lady Harriet."

In the end Rexford had no choice but to meet his reluctant fiancée and her maid in the front hall at dawn the next day. "Since we are going the same place, Amanda, I trust you have no objection if I accompany you."

"None whatsoever." She produced her coolest look, "So long as it remains perfectly clear who is accompanying whom."

Rexford's sulk lasted all the way to Dover. There, in a foul mood, he prayed for a crossing rough enough to teach Amanda the meaning of mal de mer. The sea gods heard his prayer with one mischievous twist. She spent the voyage entertaining the captain with tales of life at Langwood. He spent the same hours at the rail disposing of everything he had eaten in the past two weeks.

By the time they finally landed in Ostend, he decided he had punished Amanda enough for her independent ways. He would spend the remainder of the journey helping her learn to appreciate him more. Certainly, she could not appreciate him less.

Two days later, they arrived at the Hôtel d'Angleterre on Rue de la Madeline in Brussels. Rexford had been pleasantly surprised riding through the city. Prepared for chaos, even panic, he found only the normal afternoon bustle. He dismounted, sent Tag into the hotel, and went to help Amanda from the coach.

She stepped down and stared at the stately building. "The Duke of Wellington is here?"

Rexford repressed a sigh. As he expected, she had planned to breeze into military headquarters, personally carrying two crates of birds. His mind flashed a quick picture of her reaction if he told her a war room was no place for a woman. Perhaps she wouldn't notice if he just went alone. "This is a hotel. We can rest here. After I have changed into my uniform I will go to the Duke and inform him we have arrived with the birds."

An hour later Rexford followed Amanda into British Headquarters on Rue Royale.

Amanda hesitated and looked around the large room. She had expected stiff posture and crisp military dress. Instead she saw men draped everywhere, casually perched on the corners of tables, spilling out of chairs, and leaning against walls. One man balanced his chair back on two legs, his booted feet crumpling a map spread on his desk. Most were in dressed in uniform, but very carelessly. Sashes were missing, frock coats were open, and a tall man in the corner had eliminated his coat altogether.

With a lurch, the precariously balanced man swung his feet the floor. "Rexford, nice of you to come. We thought you had decided to skip this one entirely."

Rexford's laugh came from behind Amanda. "I had—until they told me you needed some help over here." He circled Amanda, met the man halfway across the room, and began pounding him on the back. The other men in the room surrounded the pair.

"Thought it wasn't like you to hide under the bed in—Brighton, was it?"

"Close enough," Rexford said.

"Somebody send a message to Napoleon. We can start now, Rexford's come."

Pride surged through Amanda. Not only was Rexford the

handsomest man in the room in his flawless uniform, but the entire atmosphere had lightened with his entrance.

The men liked and respected him.

Eventually, Rexford stepped back from the still-teasing officers and walked over to study a map on the wall. "What is the news?"

The man who had greeted him first followed. "Depends on what day you ask. Yesterday, we rather thought we might march out and look for Napoleon sometime toward the end of the month. Today"—he shrugged—"we might have to fight him right here in this room."

Rexford half turned and regarded him seriously. "You think he is marching? I saw no sign of it in the city."

"You won't. Nobody out there has time for a war. Too many parties to go to. Been out myself every night for two weeks."

"I had no idea you knew anybody in Brussels."

"Don't have to know anybody in Brussels. Everybody you ever knew in London either has been here, is here now, or will show up tomorrow. Damnedest war I ever saw." The disheveled officer gulped and looked toward Amanda, the first sign anyone had noticed her. "Sorry, ma'am."

Rexford hurried to her side. "Sorry," he said in a tone only she could hear. He turned and addressed the room in general. "Gentlemen, this is Miss Langley. She needs to see the Duke."

"I am afraid that may take some time." The man who had greeted Rexford so familiarly dragged over a chair. "Would you like some tea?"

"No, thank you." Amanda sat and watched Rexford move comfortably about the room. He studied maps, picked up documents, and paused frequently to enjoy the company of obviously close friends.

After a few minutes Rexford approached the tall man in the corner and stood with his back to Amanda. Something in the casual way he moved or the way he lowered his voice captured Amanda's attention. Pretending to look out the window, she strained forward in her chair to catch the hushed words.

"So, Evan, what do you think?"

"Finally decided to ask me, did you, Marc?"

Rexford clasped his hands behind his back and rested his weight on one foot. "You knew I would. You never were one to dress up what you know in wishful thinking. Will the French come?"

"They'll come."

Rexford's hands tightened. "How soon?"

The tall man shrugged. "Tomorrow. The next day. Definitely no more than a week."

"You're sure?"

"Would you have asked me if I wasn't?"

Rexford laughed. "I wouldn't even have spoken to you except that you looked so damn lonely. That pretty wife of yours had the good sense to throw you out yet?"

Though the two men spoke louder, Amanda lost track of the conversation. *Tomorrow or the next day.* Tomorrow or the next day the men in this room might be marching toward firing cannons. They should be . . . She didn't know what they should be doing, but certainly not chatting so casually.

Young men came and went through a door that apparently led to the Duke of Wellington. After about an hour, one of the exiting men stopped and spoke softly to Rexford.

Rexford nodded to Amanda. She rose and permitted him to shepherd her, with a hand on the small of her back, toward the adjoining room.

They entered. The Duke glanced up from behind a long table cluttered with maps and documents. Like the men in the anteroom, he looked past her. "About time you arrived, Rexford." His angular face, narrow chin, and crisp black hair made him look years younger than Amanda had expected. She had anticipated white hair and a grizzled appearance, but the man who faced her appeared to be in his mid-forties. Naturally, she recognized the nose, a favorite of cartoonists.

"I assume you have brought the birds," the Duke said. "Took you long enough."

Rexford gave Amanda a small nod of surrender. "I have brought Miss Langley. She has brought the pigeons."

"Miss Langley. The lady who owns the birds?" He hesitated just long enough for Rexford to contradict him. "Splendid." He circled the table and bowed to Amanda. "Sit down. You have no idea how badly I need you here."

"Miss Langley is returning to England in the morning."

Flattered by the Duke's enthusiasm, Amanda did not even dignify Rexford's statement with a response. She sat.

The Duke returned to his chair, leaving Rexford to stand with his hand on the back of Amanda's chair.

"I am happy to help any way I can, Your Grace," Amanda said.

"Know how to take care of those creatures, do you?" The Duke rustled a paper to the far side of the table.

"Of course."

"Capital. The man we had here, Gilly—"

"Gully." Only Amanda heard Rexford's soft correction.

"—just walked off one day and never returned."

"Albert would never leave his birds at a time like this," Amanda said.

"A friend of yours, is he?" The Duke's face softened. "I should have been a bit more gentle. I am sorry. My men say he left about noon two days ago to deliver a ham to his mother. No one has seen him since."

"You—your men, did they speak to his mother?"

"She never received the ham." The Duke's eyes hardened and his jaw tightened, giving Amanda a glimpse of the rigid discipline the commander was famous for. "Unfortunately, war attracts all kinds of scoundrels. There are probably a thousand men in the area who would kill a man for a piece of bacon. Never mind a whole ham. We may never know what happened to him."

He waved the matter aside. "In any case, my men have been caring for the birds, probably feeding them gin and hard rolls. You will report to Gilly's place immediately and do whatever is necessary to keep those birds flying."

Rexford's grip tightened so, Amanda's chair shuddered.

"Miss Langley only came to deliver the birds. I have made arrangements for her to leave for England in the—"

"Sit down, Rexford. You make me nervous standing there like a defending archangel." The Duke looked back at Amanda with a sheepish smile. "Though he did succeed in reminding me that you are a civilian. I am supposed to ask, not order."

Still standing, Rexford spoke from behind Amanda's chair. "If you will forgive me, sir. I have just spent two weeks learning about caring for pigeons. I am sure I could—"

Amanda tightened her lips to hold back the temptation to inform the Duke his valiant subordinate flinched every time a bird flew overhead. Rexford deserved whatever rebuke she could give him in private. He did not deserve to be embarrassed in front of his commanding officer. She smiled sweetly. "Yes. Sit down, Lord Rexford. I am sure you want to hear what His Grace has to say."

Rexford drew over a chair, then proved he could protest as well sitting as standing. "Sir, as I understand it, Miss Langley's birds are critical because there is a strong possibility Gully's place may be overrun the minute fighting breaks out."

"Not necessarily. There is still a strong possibility Napoleon will attack on the right and cut us off from the Channel. If that happens, birds might well be our only communication." He picked up a crisp sheet of ivory paper. "This communication suggests Napoleon may come straight at us. But I still plan to leave the Netherlands' Prince Frederick where he is to keep the route to the Channel open."

"Sound strategy, sir. But it still does not address the fact you may be sending Miss Langley into danger. I saw Gully's place on the map out there. Halfway between you and the whole French army."

"A short distance from here and to the east," the Duke snapped. He paused and looked at Amanda. "Though I admit there is some danger, Miss Langley. We have no certain idea which way the French will come—if they come. I will leave some men with you. They will get you to the rear if it turns out you are in the wrong place.''

Rexford muttered a comment that might have been either a protest or a curse.

The Duke shot him a black look and directed his intent gaze to Amanda. ''You must know, in a battle knowledge is everything. It can help predict an attack or, more important, distinguish between a deceptive feint and the full thrust. Every hour you can keep an aerial communication site open may save thousands of lives.'' His eyes challenged her to volunteer. ''I can move a hundred thousand men around, but it seems I can't move one miserable pen of birds.''

''I see.'' Amanda tried to imagine being in the middle of a battle. She could think only of noise and smoke. The idea of not knowing which way to run terrified her. Her hands were in her lap, below the level of the table, so perhaps the Duke could not see the way she clenched them to stop the shaking. ''Naturally, I will help in any way I can.''

''Amanda.'' Rexford said her name with a snap, then shrugged and addressed the Duke. ''You mentioned leaving some men with her, sir. May I request to be one of those men?''

''Aha.'' The Duke looked from one to the other of them. ''Like that, is it?''

''Yes,'' Rexford said.

''No,'' Amanda said.

Amanda gave a sigh of exasperation. If Rexford did not stop announcing his claim on her to everyone they met, she would volunteer him to lead a solo attack against the French. ''No,'' she repeated. ''Lord Rexford presumes—''

''A little problem on your hands, Rexford?'' Wellington laughed. ''I understand why you volunteered for the duty. Unfortunately, I need you here. Except for the men you saw out there''—he gestured to the door—''half the ninnyhammers they sent me from London wouldn't know a musket from a candle.''

The Duke pushed his chair back. ''You have my permission to spend your off-duty time anywhere you want, but I expect you here first thing tomorrow."

"But—"

Wellington stood. "That's all, Rexford."

Amanda rose, and felt Rexford spring to his feet beside her. His hand shook as he guided her to the door.

"Rexford, wait," the Duke called.

Rexford turned, and Amanda checked her own step.

"The Duchess of Richmond is planning a ball the night after tomorrow. I will secure invitations for both of you."

The Duke may have thought the words some consolation. They did nothing to clear the dark clouds from Rexford's face. "Thank you, sir," he said through lips that scarcely moved.

"Did someone tell me Elmgrove's son came with you?"

"Yes, sir."

"I'll miss Elmgrove. He'd joust with the devil himself and have both of them laughing about it. Hope the boy is half the man his father is."

"You will not be disappointed, sir."

"Good. Make certain he shows up at the ball. We may have to fight a war, but we don't want to disappoint any of the ladies while we go about it."

The carriage carrying Amanda and a very silent Rexford passed through some of the loveliest countryside Amanda had ever seen. Tall forests of beech trees yielded to sprawling meadows of rustling green grasses. The mid-June breeze felt soft against her face and carried the heady aroma of rich loam. She waved to farmers who stood in front of quaint cottages admiring the late afternoon sunshine and the sprouting crops.

Just east of the small village of Waterloo, she looked at Rexford and wished the whole war could be some tall tale he invented just to annoy her. "You can't have a war in a place like this. Look there." She pointed to a tall field of rye undulating in the breeze. "It's too..." *Peaceful? Lovely?* She didn't know, just too unwarlike.

"Where would you have us schedule one?"

"I don't know. On some ugly plain someplace. Far away."

He smiled sadly. "I know. It seems so wrong. But armies have been marching through this countryside for hundreds of years. I guess nature forgets."

Less than two hours after leaving Brussels, they pulled up in front of the serene chateau Albert had described so often. The brown stone manor house seemed almost to grow out of the fertile farmland. Behind the main house, Amanda could see the rounded stone tower of the dovecote and several barns and outbuildings. No wonder Albert had spoken of his home with such pride. She hoped he was alive and would someday return.

Four soldiers in uniforms that looked as if they had put them on in September hurried to the carriage. Rexford stepped out, and they snapped to attention. "Take care of those." He pointed to the two crates of birds lashed to the back, and helped Amanda down.

"Take care," she called, her mind filled with images of the careless men simply tossing the boxes to the ground.

"Crimminy, Joe, look what we got here," the soldier already fumbling with the ropes called to his friend. "Just what we need. More birds."

"I don't suppose we could just leave 'em." The bearded man darted a quick glance at Rexford, and reached for the crate more quickly than had been his original intention. "I'll take that, though I'm dashed if I know what we'll do with 'em."

"Just take them to the cote," Amanda said sharply. "And do it carefully, please."

"We know where to take them," the man addressed as Joe said sullenly. "We just don't know what to do after that."

Rexford scowled. "This time you know what to do. Just leave them and report to me. I suspect we have some talking to do."

"Yes, sir."

Rexford offered his arm to Amanda and led her up the stone walk between the neatly clipped carpets of grass.

Inside, a stalwart-looking farm lad hurried for the housekeeper. She appeared with slapping steps on oversized feet, which formed a perfect V when she came to a stop. Dressed in white, her body looked like the cook might have just fashioned it from dough.

Rexford spoke to her in French too rapid for Amanda to follow. The nervous woman nodded and said, *"Trés bien,"* every time he paused for breath. She smiled with a final *"Bien,"* and retreated to the back of the house.

Rexford turned to Amanda. "Most of the servants have left. She is glad you have come and hopes you will keep the soldiers in order." He laughed. "I assured her you would." He looked around at the rooms, already beginning to show signs of neglect. "I am sorry I cannot stay and help you here. I must make arrangements in Brussels. I doubt if I will be back until very late."

Amanda was too exhausted to do more than unpack her prize flyers and see that Albert's birds got minimal care.

That night, as she had every night for weeks, she lay in bed thinking of Rexford. He had changed since they arrived in Brussels. She understood why he walked so proudly. It had nothing to do with his title, and everything to do with the kind of man he was. A strong man. A man people respected and wanted near them in times of danger.

No wonder she had intuitively trusted him, in spite of every lie she'd uncovered. He was a man who trusted himself and expected everybody else to do the same.

As she drifted closer to sleep, she admitted that none of that had anything to do with the way she felt about him. Hero or scoundrel, whether he laughed with her or fought with her, she wanted to be near him. She had from the moment he smiled at her from the wide guest bed and announced she would like him better than his gamekeeper.

The days they had just spent traveling had been the happiest of her life. He had bribed Lily to ride with the driver, and they had been alone in the coach most of the way. After

Amanda had threatened to get out and walk all the way to Brussels if he mentioned marriage one more time, they had talked of everything else. Talked all day and never run out of things to say. She wondered if any of the men she had met in the Duke's headquarters knew what a lonely child he had been. How hard he had tried to please a father who would never stop mourning the loss of an older, favorite son.

The soft touch of the coverlet against her body reminded her of the other moments of the journey. The times when Rexford had laid his hand on her in what at first seemed a casual touch. Though every touch burned, she had responded only once. She had begun to fall asleep, and he'd slipped his arm round her shoulder so his hand hovered over her breast.

How feather-light his caress had been when he first began to stroke her. How quickly she had forgotten everything and surrendered to his touch. Only the horn announcing the approach of the next town had prevented her from permitting him to make love to her again.

Someday . . . She fell asleep knowing someday she would admit how much she wanted him to.

Amanda rose at dawn and hurried to the cote. The four soldiers of the day before were waiting for her, bright-eyed and much neater. A chat with Rexford must have vastly improved their attitudes. She set them to cleaning the loft, but reserved for herself the job of grooming and hand-feeding the birds.

Rexford joined her soon after the sun cleared the horizon. He came into the enclosure with his customary the-birds-are-going-to-land-on-my-head walk. Amanda smiled and shooed him outside. Even at her most malicious, she would not want anything to spoil his spotless uniform.

"I am off," he said. "I will send someone out with Lily as soon as I can. These soldiers will not give you any trouble." He indicated the raking men and raised his voice. "If these men do not cooperate completely, send a message to Wellington's headquarters. I assume he will have them shot."

For a moment Amanda felt in perfect harmony with her

handsome, elegant soldier. Then he took her chin in his hand. "I am afraid it would be unseemly for me to kiss you here, so you will just have to imagine I did." He let his gaze linger on her face long enough for her to imagine she had been thoroughly and completely kissed.

She took a moment to catch her breath and remember she needed respect from the men who would be working with her. "Rexford, don't you ever give up?"

He smiled, but did not release her. "Give up? This is merely the best I can do with an audience." He offered a lingering smile. "Though if you insist on throwing your arms around me and begging me to come back, there would be little I could about it."

"There are several things I could do, but they would probably ruin your reputation in front of your men."

He laughed. "Then we both have some things we should save until we are alone. I guarantee you will like mine better."

For just a minute Amanda had to fight the temptation to draw him to her and whisper impossible words. Instead she tilted her chin beyond his reach. "Go."

"I will be back." He teased her with a feather brush of his fingers across her cheeks. "Tonight, if I can possibly manage it."

Amanda spent most of the day in the cote. Albert had been gone only a few days, but all the birds needed grooming and most were hungry for attention.

Just after noontime, Amanda's maid arrived, accompanied by the ugliest man Amanda had ever seen. His small, round head grew from a body that might have formed one wall of a small building. A black patch covered one eye, and three livid red scars marked one cheek. "My name is Lucky," he announced from the doorway of the room where Amanda sat. "Lord Rexford told me to tell you, if it comes time to get out of here, you was to come with me."

Amanda's lips tightened. Someday Rexford would stop giving orders, and then she might just barely tolerate him.

"I see. Did Lord Rexford say who would decide when it was time to leave?"

"Not hardly. I think he figured you would put on a face like that, 'cause he said if I decided it was time to leave, I was to pick you up and take you whether you wanted to go or not."

He looked capable of carrying off not only her, but the rest of the household. "That sounds like Rexford. I don't suppose—"

"Don't even bother to suppose. Rexford is gentleman enough, but when he gives an order, a body had better obey him." He waved a huge hand. "But don't you worry about it. I won't bother you none unless it gets time to leave. If it does, I'll know and we'll go. Until then I'll be in the kitchen." He turned and left.

Amanda spent the rest of the day listening for the sound of guns. "Today or tomorrow," the man in Wellington's headquarters had said. The war might have started. Rexford might already be lying bleeding someplace.

She refused even to consider the thought, only to find herself listening again for a boom in the distance.

Amanda sat up late that night. Not waiting for Rexford, she told herself, just waiting for news. At eleven she finally heard the hoofbeats of an approaching horse. She jumped to her feet, but before she could see anything from the window the front door opened and slammed shut.

The sounds but not the words of a brief masculine conversation came from the hall. Amanda turned from the window and ran. She met Rexford halfway across the room.

Without conscious thought she threw herself into his arms.

He bent his head and kissed her briefly. "Now that's the kind of homecoming a man can look forward to."

Amanda eased back, afraid to move too quickly. He looked so drained a sudden movement might unbalance him "I didn't mean . . ."

He smiled wearily. "Don't worry, right now I want no more than just to hold you." He drew her to him, resting his face against hers. His cheek carried the coolness of the damp night, and he smelled of horses and sweat.

After a long time Amanda put her hands against his chest and leaned back. "Have you eaten?"

"About noon, I think."

She helped him out of his frock coat, then slipped her arm around his waist and guided him to the sofa. "Let me order you some food." Stepping to the door, she asked the waiting Lucky to bring whatever food he could find. She returned to sit beside Rexford and asked the question that had tortured her all day. "What about the French? Will they come?"

With a sigh he tilted his head back and rested it against the high back of the sofa. "It depends on who you believe. Some still say no."

"What do you believe?"

"They will come. Soon. I have been riding since I left here. Sometimes with Wellington, sometimes with messages for him. Everywhere there was someone who had seen the armies moving forward." His eyes held ineffable sadness.

"You seem more sad than afraid."

"Fear is something a soldier lives with, but I never have been able to get used to sight of the young men, some of them no more than sixteen or seventeen. So proud. Everywhere talking of how they can't wait for it to begin." He bent his head and covered his face with his hands. "They have no idea."

Amanda reached up, took his hands in hers, and just held them. Nothing she could say would make the pictures of the young men go away.

Eventually, he shook himself and brushed the back of her cheek with his fingers. "I am glad you are here. I hate myself for not keeping you safe, but even that cannot keep me from wanting you here. All day long, mixed in with the images of what I know will happen, were thoughts of coming back to you. Of sitting like this." He put his arms around her again and sat silently holding her.

Lucky entered with a tray. He set the tray down discreetly looking every place but at Rexford and Amanda.

"Thank you, Lucky," Rexford said to the man's disappearing back. He looked at Amanda. "I am too tired to eat. Too tired to do anything."

This, at least, Amanda could do. "You will eat and then you will sleep." She held his gaze until the protest died in his eyes.

Within minutes he had eaten everything but a few ragged crusts of bread. He smiled and sat back, the deep lines between his brows much less defined. "Thank you." He grinned. "I knew you were good for me. Now, let us talk about tomorrow. Will you come to the ball with me?"

Amanda looked quickly at the tray to see if it contained anything that might have sapped his senses. "A ball? We have just been talking of being overrun by the entire French army and you want to go to a ball?"

"Not want to, have to. The Duke has ordered all his officers to attend. He invited you too, if you remember—the Duchess of Richmond's ball." He laughed and took her hand. "Unlike me, the Duke had the wisdom not to order you to do anything, so I thought you might choose to attend."

Amanda considered and shook her head. "I may do many unconventional things, Rexford, but dancing to welcome a war will not be one of them. Besides, you might use the occasion to do something dreadful"—she looked at their entwined hands—"like announcing I have to marry you because I find myself touching you every time we are alone."

"I just might," he confessed.

"You will not, because I will stay right here."

"I was afraid you might say that. Perhaps it is just as well. I would probably start my own private war with any officer who thought himself good enough to dance with you."

He rose and drew her with him. "Come, let us go to bed."

She flushed and stepped back sharply, struggling to ignore the flood of excitement his words. "You—"

He tightened his grip on her hands. "Don't retreat on me now." In spite of his words, he relaxed his arms, permitting Amanda to take another step backward.

They stood facing each other, hands still joined, but a wide space between them.

"You asked for honesty between us, Amanda. If ever there was a time for total honesty, it is now." His eyes seemed almost liquid-soft in the candlelight. He lowered his voice almost to a whisper. "I never wanted a woman more than I want you now."

"I don't think . . ." Her stomach quivered. Her dry lips refused to form the words.

"Wait." He took a step toward her and, raised their joined hands between them. "I could seduce you. Lord knows I want to. All I would have to do is touch you here." He released one of her hands and let his fingers hover so close to her neck she could feel their heat, but not their touch.

Amanda knew his touch would set her trembling. She would step forward and lose herself in his kiss. She would not have to think, or fear. Just surrender. Every nerve cried out for him to touch her. Her tongue darted to moisten her lips.

"But tonight that's not good enough. I need you to come to me because you choose to. Do you understand? Not because of a physical response, but because you want me." He released her hand and stepped away from her. Leaving her incredibly alone.

He walked across the room and turned to wait for her decision. The hand that had almost touched her trembled at his side.

Amanda thought of the consequences. Thought of the pain when he entered her. None of that mattered. Nothing mattered but that tonight she wanted to be closer to him than she had ever been to anyone. "Yes," she whispered. "Yes, Marcus, I want you."

Trembling, she took his hand and let him lead her from the room.

Chapter Sixteen

Upstairs, in the room Amanda had selected for Rexford, she clung to his hand as he placed the branch of candles on the bureau. If she released her hold she might change her mind and flee.

He turned toward, his gaze burning and hungry. "And now . . ."

Panic surged through her. What would he want her to do? "I don't know . . ." She would have to undress. "Should you leave me alone while I . . . I can send for Lily . . . I . . ."

He smiled and put his index finger to her lip. "Shhh. Trust me, you don't need Lily tonight." With both hands he reached around and began drawing the pins from her hair. One by one he placed them on the bureau. When he finished, he ran his fingers through her hair drawing it out to let it float to her shoulders.

She watched his face, calm, intent, and wonderfully strong.

"Now this." He reached to the first button at the neck of her muslin gown. "I have wanted to undo these buttons all night. Slowly." After the first two buttons, he eased several fingers inside the gown, but held the material away from her so she could scarcely feel his touch.

"Here. I can do that faster."

He brushed her hands away. "Not tonight. Tonight we will do everything slowly and savor every minute." After an eternity he reached the last button just below her waist, then reached up and slid the gown from her shoulders. It pooled on the floor at her feet. Just as slowly he undid the ribbon on her petticoat.

When Amanda saw how long he lingered over the simple bow, she realized he was deliberately torturing her. She waited until the petticoat glided to the floor, then put her hands on his chest and pushed him back, so she could step out of both garments. "Two can play at that game, my lord."

A spark of approval flared in his eyes.

With the same excruciating care he had used, she began to unbutton his shirt. Unlike him, when she finished, she let her hands run freely over the flesh she exposed, savoring the warmth under her palms.

"Ummm." He bit his lip and arched his neck back. "Your hands feel so cool. I love it when you touch me." He struggled out of the sleeves of the shirt. "Well done, my love. But now let us see how you like a bit of the same." He put his thumbs under the shoulder straps of her chemise and slipped them from her shoulders.

Amanda gasped at her sudden nakedness. In the challenge of besting him she had forgotten what was to come. Automatically, she crossed her arms over her breasts.

He grabbed her wrists and drew her hands away. "Don't bother, my love. Do you think I haven't already seen everything you have? The picture is branded into my brain. I will go to sleep picturing you naked when I am eighty." He placed his hands on her waist and eased her completely out of her chemise.

Amanda resisted the temptation to cringe again, and stood watching his face while his burning gaze seared every exposed inch.

"Now," he said, placing his hands on her hips, "my turn

to touch." He ran his hands up her body, his palms just brushing her breasts.

In spite of a resolution to control her reaction, Amanda began to quiver and strain toward his touch.

He drew his hands back and pointed to the turned-down bed. "I think you better climb into bed, before I forget my promise to do everything slowly tonight."

Amanda hurriedly obeyed. With the coverlet pulled up to her chin she watched him finish undressing. She had never seen a naked man before. She yielded to the temptation to see what had hurt her so that night in the library.

He turned his back to strip off his breeches.

If she could have spoken she would have chided him about modesty. At that moment, he turned. She gasped. "Oh, my. So big. No wonder . . ."

He laughed, slipped in beside her, and turned on his side to face her. "Don't worry. I promise it will not hurt tonight." He put his hand on her hip and stroked up toward her breast.

"It doesn't matter if it does. Tonight is for you. But could you . . ."

"Could I what, love?"

"Could you kiss me first?"

He laughed. "First, last, and a hundred times in between. Come here." He slid a hand under her shoulders and rolled her toward him.

To keep from tumbling over him, she braced herself with her bent knee across his legs. The inside of her thigh touched his. Instinctively, she drew back from the monstrous thing she had seen.

Just then he captured her mouth with the kiss she remembered. She tried to close her lips to him. If she felt his tongue she would let him . . .

He did not seem to mind her sudden tightening. He kissed her closed lips and stroked his hand along the side of her body, making soothing sounds that had no words. His tongue flicked at her lips.

No, she thought. If her lips parted, even a little bit, she

283

would ... "I ..." She wanted to tell him she was afraid. "Marc—"

He seized on the opening. His tongue was in her mouth. Searching. Demanding.

"That's right," he whispered, speaking with their joined lips.

His kiss had the same fire she remembered, sending waves of warmth to the place he had hurt. The place that did not remember the pain, only the hunger.

His hand found her breast and she was lost.

She opened her mouth to accept his plunging tongue. When his tongue retreated, hers followed, knowing she had to have more. He drew away from the kiss. She whimpered, only to feel his lips, soft and teasing against her neck. The trembling began in her shoulders. Gooseflesh skittered down her spine and up her chin.

"That's it, my love. Give yourself to it." He rolled her onto her back and took her breast in his mouth.

Waves of pleasure shot through her. If only this could be all. If only she could just enjoy this without ... If only she could not let him ...

His hand began to stroke her thigh.

In spite of her need to keep her legs together, she began to relax under his tantalizing fondling. Every time his tongue touched her nipple she strained toward his hand, wanting his touch more than she feared it.

Finally, his fingers found the center of the fire his kiss had started.

"Marcus ... Yes, Marcus ... Please."

He rolled over so he lay between her legs.

She steeled herself for the pain she knew would come.

His lips captured hers. His tongue plunged in an insistent rhythm.

In spite of all she knew, her hips strained toward the thing that would hurt her, hungry for any contact.

Still kissing her, he slipped a hand between their bodies and touched her in a way that sent wave after wave of sensation surging through her. Nothing mattered. Nothing but the feeling.

Suddenly she felt that hardness between his legs. He plunged into her. She waited for the tearing pain. Instead, she found only a sense of fullness. She opened her eyes to find him watching her with a tender, concerned expression. "What . . ."

"Are you all right?"

"I . . . what . . . is it over?"

"Not quite. Are you all right?"

"It doesn't hurt yet."

He smiled at her and kissed her on the nose.

She moved with the kiss and felt a ripple of sensation. "Oh!" She moved again. "Oh."

"Yes, oh." His smile widened. Then he bent for a deeper kiss. He began to move. Slowly at first, then faster.

She moved with him. The world turned white. Then every muscle tensed to release in wave after wave of pleasure.

He continued for two more strokes, arched back, and dropped to rest his head against her shoulder, supporting most of his weight on his elbows. For several long seconds he lay there, his deeply drawn breaths matching hers. Finally, he lifted his head and looked at her questioningly.

"Oh, my. Why didn't you tell me it would be like that?"

"I couldn't."

"Is it always like that?"

He shrugged one shoulder. "I don't know. It has never been quite 'like that' for me either." He rolled off her, and she missed his comforting weight, but only for a moment. He reached over and drew her to rest against his shoulder. "I have imagined you like this a thousand times. In my bed, with your hair tumbling over me."

"That was quite wonderful, you know. Can we . . . ?" Amanda felt her face grow warm with a flush.

He laughed. "Are you going to ask can we do it again?"

Amanda could feel his continuing chuckle along her whole body. She refused to look at him, and answered the question with the softest "Yes."

He put a hand under her chin and tilted her chin up so he could place a very soft kiss on her lips. "I think we can arrange that."

There was so much she didn't know. But if she didn't have the courage to ask, she might never know. "How soon?" She viciously drove off the chilling thought that, after tomorrow, she might never have to know.

He laughed and traced his hand over the curve of her hip. "The way I am feeling right now, probably about fifteen minutes."

Amanda lay against his shoulder, content just to hold him. After a time the soft movement of his hand against her flesh became more insistent. They didn't have to wait fifteen minutes after all.

Later that night, she woke to find him touching her again, and she learned a person can make long sleepy love. She fell asleep trying to decide which she liked best and anxious for the morning to see what else she might learn.

She woke well before the sun rose to the crashing disappointment of being alone in the huge bed. Anxiously she called his name. Their only night could not be over yet.

It was.

She jumped from bed, dressed, and went to search for him.

She found him standing in the kitchen with Lucky sharing some hard bread and cutting off large wedges of yellow cheese.

He looked up and smiled when she entered. "You saved me the trouble of waking you." He put a small message cylinder in her hand. "The Duke wanted you to send this to England at dawn."

She closed her fingers around the warm metal. "You might have given it to me last night and saved yourself from rising so early."

He grinned, all trace of the previous night's exhaustion gone. "I might, but this way I insured that I would see you before I left."

Her knees weakened. "You are going so soon? You only just . . ."

He put a hand under her elbow and smiled. "For a moment you looked like you cared. I like that." A grave look replaced the twinkle. "I have no choice. I doubt that I will get back today, though I will try." He raised his other hand so he held her by both elbows, and looked deeply into her eyes. "I fear this thing may come sooner than anyone expects. Promise me you will listen to Lucky and leave if he tells you to. Any one of the soldiers can stay here and wait for messages."

She considered and almost promised, then remembered a frightened bird that would not have landed without her whistle. Whatever she felt, she would be as strong as he. "Like you, Rexford, I will do what I have to. So don't bother sending any messengers with your orders."

He opened his mouth to protest, then shrugged. "I don't know why I expected anything else. At least you can cooperate a little bit and give me an appropriate farewell." His fingers tightened on her arms.

Amanda shook herself free. She had vowed not to feel this growing uneasiness. "You are going to a ball, Rexford, not a firing squad. I am sure you will find some willing miss to drape herself over your uniform."

He laughed, kissed her anyway, and left with one parting salvo. "That is, if I can stop thinking of kissing you long enough to remember the way."

Amanda stood in the hall clutching the message container, still warm from his hand. In a few moments she would not even have that. She shook off her thoughts and hurried to the birds.

The day passed slowly. Late in the morning a messenger arrived from the Duke requesting two of her birds, which he could use to send messages to England. She sent them, and later gave three of Albert's birds to three soldiers who would only tell her they were going south.

By nine that night she began to suspect Rexford would not come, but still she flitted to the window to check on every imagined sound. She went to bed at midnight.

The sound of thumping footsteps roused her from a light

sleep. She glanced toward the window. It was still dark, but the kind of gray dark that promised morning would come. She jumped from bed, threw on a wrapper, and opened her door to find Rexford with his hand poised to knock.

He held a branch of candles in his hand. The yellowing light flickered over the shadows on his face. "The French have come," he said simply and brushed past her into her room. Pausing to light a lamp, he turned to face her.

"Where are they?" Amanda asked. Her chest pounding, she looked toward the window as if she might actually see the army.

"South of here. I cannot stay. I have just come from the ball and have to change out of this fancy uniform and into something I can fight in. Come with me." Still carrying the candles, he turned to go to his own room.

Amanda followed, her temper rising. He had wasted hours at a ball. Hours they might have shared. "If you knew the French were coming, why did you go to a ball?"

He lit the lamp in his own room and turned to grin at her. "Wellington's idea of not alarming the civilian population. He ordered us all to go and say nothing. You have to admire the man. He certainly picked the damnedest way anyone ever saw to announce a war."

"He actually made the announcement there?" Amanda tried to picture the man she had met calmly stopping the music and announcing he had decided on a war instead of a waltz.

"Not precisely. But by eleven o'clock the ball was a shambles. Even a blind man would have noticed. Messengers kept slipping in quietly and the soldiers began to disappear. It was too much to expect some of the young ones to go without at least a hint. Pretty soon there wasn't a corner left for a woman to cry in." He had stripped off his coat and shirt while he talked, but his movements were sure and precise rather than seductive.

He donned a fresh shirt and was holding out a different scarlet coat. "Will you help me on with this?" He gave a self-conscious smile. "I may have to marry you just to have a valet. I seem to keep losing mine."

Amanda took the offered coat and held it while he struggled into it. Her hands lingered to brush imaginary dust motes from the shoulders. The material had a softer feel than the one he removed, and the looser sleeves allowed more freedom of motion.

He turned to face her. "I must go now to carry a message to Blücher. Later I will meet Wellington at Quatre Bras. After that"—he raised his hands in a hopeless gesture—"I have no way of knowing where I will be. I will come to you when I can."

A thousand protests rose to Amanda's lips. She recalled his casual mention of women crying in corners. He would not find any weakness in her. "I will be here."

"I wish you would go with Lucky tonight. Now."

Amanda stiffened to protest.

He curbed the words by curling his fingers around her neck. "I know. I have finally learned. You will do what you must." He bent and brushed her lips with his. "But know—" His eyes took on a defeated look. "You know all the things I want to say. Everything but one. I did not come back tonight to change into a new uniform." He caught his lower lip between his teeth until the lip paled. For a long time he did not speak. Then he drew a long breath. "I have never said this to a woman." His voice tightened. "I came to tell you I love you."

"Rexford . . ." Amanda started to speak and realized she had no idea what word should come next. She knew she wanted him to stay. She would listen for the sound of his horse every minute he was gone, but she could not say the words that would bind her to him forever. "Rexford, I don't know—"

He put his finger over her lips. "Don't say anything. I just wanted you to know." He gave a mischievous smile. "I also want you to know this." He bent and kissed her, not the gentle kiss of earlier, but the fierce hungry kiss that robbed her of the will to do anything but surrender to him.

His hands slid under her loose robe and drew her to him. "That is what I want you to remember. That and the fact I will be back." He turned to leave.

She started to follow him.

He paused at the door and turned. "Don't come with me. This is as good a place as any to say good-bye. Stay so I can be thinking of you here."

Rexford stood peering into the smoky night, knowing he could do nothing more. The men who stood next to him when darkness had silenced the last shot were alive. Wellington was alive, or had been two hours ago. Other than that, Rexford knew nothing. Could do nothing but stand and try not to relive horrors he knew would trouble him in nightmares for years to come.

The day had passed in a blur of interminable waiting and desperate fighting. Despite every effort, the pictures came, one in particular. He had lost his horse and taken refuge in a square just before a French cavalry attack. The horde came at them, and some instinct warned him that the trembling man next to him was about to throw down his musket and run, causing a general panic.

With the road to the north at his back, Rexford had thought of Amanda. The French would not reach that road while he could still stand. He felt again the ice that had filled his veins and his voice when he said without turning, "If you drop that musket, you will be the first man I kill." Neither of them questioned that he meant precisely what he said.

Only when the French retreated did he turn and discover the "man" had been no more than seventeen. He had finally dropped the musket when a lance pierced his neck. He never heard Rexford's muttered apology.

No apology would bring back the men who had died holding the small crossroads at Quatre Bras. Rexford turned his back on the flickering French fires, the lingering smell of powder, and the stench of death. He walked north to find Wellington.

On the way he passed men he knew, always recognizing

a reaction that mirrored his own relieved surprise. The experienced campaigners quickly covered the unguarded expression with a neutral greeting. Somehow it seemed wrong to congratulate a man on simply being alive when darkness fell. Most stopped long enough to exchange hushed inquiries about comrades. No one had seen Tag.

About a mile back from the front, Rexford commandeered a horse. He arrived at Wellington's temporary headquarters at Genappe just before eleven.

The Duke looked up with the veteran's glad-you're-alive facial expression. "Rexford, about time you showed up."

"Little trouble with my horse, sir."

"I saw that. Missed you after he went down." Wellington waved an indifferent hand over the papers spread before him on a makeshift table. "You may as well get what sleep you can. I will have dispatches, but I cannot decide anything until I hear what happened with Blücher. Last I heard he was taking a frightful pounding at Ligny."

"I will be outside, sir." Rexford paused at the door and turned. Pride forced him to keep the anxiety out of his voice. "Don't know where I might find Elmgrove's son, do you?"

The Duke's eyes softened with understanding. "I sent him to the east with an order late this afternoon. I don't expect he will be back tonight."

Rexford slept outside. He wakened at four to curse the rising sun, and the cruel destiny that had planned the upcoming battle for one of the longest days of the year. Too many hours for more men to die.

Wellington still had no definitive news of the Prussians. Without any promise of support on his left, he had no choice but to order a retreat from Quatre Bras. Rexford shared the helpless rage of the other survivors. So many lives lost to defend a position they would now simply hand over to the French. He kept his opinions to himself. Throughout the afternoon, battling the torrential rains that began about two, he rode with Lord Uxbridge to protect the retreating army.

At seven, two hours before full darkness with its promise of food and rest, a messenger from Wellington found him.

He was to report immediately to the Duke's headquarters. Willingly Rexford hunched forward against the driving rain and rode the three miles back from the front lines to the small village of Waterloo. If he could accomplish the Duke's commission quickly, he should be able to ride to Gully's place and be certain Lucky had heard of the retreat and gotten Amanda safely back to Brussels.

The Duke stopped his pacing when Rexford entered. "Those birds are finally going to be worth something, Rexford. I heard from the Prussians." He held up two pieces of damp paper.

The pause seemed to call for a response. "Excellent, sir."

"Not excellent. This one"—Wellington held out the paper in his right hand—"says the army is in full retreat and won't stop until they get to Prussia."

"Damn."

"My response precisely. However, this one"—he dropped the offending paper so he held only one—"says Blücher will pull the army together at Wavre and move in with some support for our left flank late tomorrow."

"Have you confirmed either?"

"You've seen what it's like out there. Even without half the French army between us, a courier would have to be half fish to get through. So far I've sent out four different messengers and can't even be sure they got through."

Rexford nodded. "Just now, it took me almost two hours to come three miles from the front."

The Duke's black look cursed the rain and the roads. "I am aware of that. But if you take the birds, you only have to get through one way. They can fly back with your report while you're still scraping mud off your boots."

"The birds won't fly at night."

Wellington frowned, and again Rexford wanted to apologize for a fact of nature he hadn't created. "Dawn will be soon enough," the Duke said. "I can't move an army in this mess anyhow. They do fly in rain, don't they?"

"Yes, sir."

"Good. I will postpone my decision until I hear from you. Sit down."

Wellington sat, and Rexford pulled over a three-legged stool. "With Blücher's help I can defeat the French, or at least hold them here. Without it"—he allowed a defeated sigh—"I must retreat or risk losing the whole army." Though he had just sat, Wellington bounded up, walked three paces, and turned on his heel to face Rexford again. "I will not risk the entire army."

Rexford's heart thudded with the enormity of what he had just heard. "You would retreat? You would give the French . . . ?"

"Brussels."

"But the people . . . The civilians . . ."

"The civilians are already in a panic. This will just confirm what they already believe."

"But—"

"That will be all. Rexford."

Rexford stood, aghast, but trusting Wellington enough not to have made this decision lightly. "Yes, sir?"

"Take two birds with you. One to come back here and one to go to England. They need to know my decision as soon as possible. I have worded two different messages. Take them both. When you have confirmed Blücher's plans be sure you send the right one here and to England."

"Yes, sir." Rexford turned to leave.

"Oh, Rexford, Elmgrove is here. Last I heard he was bellowing at the surgeon who wanted to send him to the rear."

The relief that washed over Rexford would have made it impossible for him to speak even if the Duke had not continued talking.

"From what I gather he can still ride, so take him with you."

"To Wavre?"

"No. Just as far as that bird man's place. He can wait for your message and either bring it himself or see that somebody else does. Now let's not stand here wasting time."

Rexford found Tag a few minutes later. He sat chatting

with a prone soldier, who had a bandage on his head. Tag's right arm was strapped to his body, but the injury had not affected his voice.

Rexford stopped long enough to compose his face and drink in the sight of his friend. "I might have known a little thing like a war wouldn't quiet you for long."

Tag bounded to his feet, staggered slightly to regain his balance, and reached Rexford with an awkward run. With his good arm he alternately embraced Rexford and pounded him on the back. Somebody had forgotten to tell him about dignified restraint.

"Can you ride?" Rexford asked.

"Better than you. Even with one arm."

"Come on, then. We'll talk on the way."

The road to Gully's place was in far better condition than the one churned to a thick mire by the retreating army. Despite the rain, Rexford and Tag made the four-mile journey in less than two hours.

Half a mile from the chateau a black-garbed pedestrian hailed them from the shadows. "How much further to the army?"

"Several miles, and the road gets worse as you go. You are not likely to make it before dawn."

The man stepped into the road. "Oh, dear. I have been walking for hours. I am a clergyman, Allan Dubois, and I heard they might need me."

"You might be better off resting until morning," Tag said.

"By Jove, a clergyman," Rexford interjected. "You might be a gift from the gods if a certain young lady is not a whole lot better at following orders than I believe she is."

"Not planning to bury your Miss Langley, are you?" Tag asked.

Rexford ignored him. "Come with us now, Reverend. At the very least we can lend you a horse and you will get where you are going a hell—a whole lot faster than slogging through this mud."

With a bit more conversation, Rexford offered a stirrup and the reverend mounted behind him. Ten minutes later the three of them reined in their horses in front of the stone house.

"I suggest you don't dismount, gentlemen, until we have had time to talk." The slow words, heavy with a threat, came from the bushes at the corner of the house.

"Dammit, I thought so," Rexford said, forgetting for the moment the hovering presence of the clergyman. "Lucky, is that you? What the hell are you still doing here?"

"Lord Rexford, who is with you?"

"Friends of mine. I wish I could believe you are fixing to tell me Miss Langley is in Brussels."

"Well, my lord, we did have a little problem." Lucky spoke, but still did not appear from behind his cover. "She insisted on waiting here until she heard from you. By the time I made up my mind to move her off as you said, the rains had come and I began getting reports the roads were so full of murderous riffraff I had to agree we'd be better off here. At least we could set up a defense."

Rexford cursed again, but under his breath so the reverend probably missed all but the mildest parts. He looked around. "You're good, Lucky, but even you can't hit much in the darkness from as far away as you are. What is to stop us from riding right through this defense of yours?"

"Not a thing, my lord, so long as you don't mind having your chests opened up by the three muskets behind you." Lucky stepped from the shadows and raised his voice. "It's all right, boys. This is Lord Rexford, and he probably ain't gonna do more than talk us all to death." Lucky sloshed over and nodded to Rexford. "Good to see you, sir. I hear it was a little sticky out there the last two days."

Rexford kicked his foot from the stirrup to give Reverend Dubois a chance to dismount.

Lucky held up a staying hand. "You might not want to do that just yet, sir. Not till I wave. If I know your lady, she's got a pistol pointed at your head from one of them windows."

Rexford laughed. "Well, she'll have to put it down now. No proper young lady wants to get married holding a gun."

Chapter Seventeen

Amanda stood at the darkened window, clutching the pistol in both hands. She leaned forward, straining to see the mounted figures faintly illuminated by the light from the downstairs window. All day long Lucky had been warning that the French might come. She had sensed his conflict between telling her enough to intimidate her into retreating to Brussels, and sparing her things he thought a woman should never know.

As if a woman were not born with an awareness of her vulnerability.

A dozen times, with the sounds of the guns' endless booming in her head, she had almost agreed to turn and run. But each time she'd thought of the few birds that would refuse to land without her patient coaxing. And she'd thought of Rexford, who wouldn't leave until it was over.

A single bird, he had said, might save thousands of lives. How could she leave when one of those lives might be his?

She had stayed until even Lucky agreed they might be safer here than on the road with the wounded and half-crazed men retreating to Brussels. Foraging soldiers had begun to appear searching for food or anything they could burn.

So far only Allied soldiers had come. Seeing their hollow eyes and desperate faces, Amanda had given them everything but a few meager scraps. If the French did come, a few hoarded bags of flour would not buy safety.

The men below were the first in hours. Amanda waited. After what seemed like an eternity, Lucky stepped into the light, turned toward the house, and waved.

Amanda exhaled her tension. A tall lanky man dismounted first from the horse carrying two riders, and then . . . And then the second man to dismount took a step—a step Amanda would have recognized from two hundred yards. "Rexford!"

Whirling from the window, she raced across the room. She threw the pistol on the bed as she ran, then skidded to a halt. The gun might have gone off. Did a gun go off when you threw it? She looked nervously toward the bed.

What a fool. Rexford would think her totally defenseless. Tentatively, she walked over and picked the pistol up, careful to point it away from her and shake it in case it still might fire.

She had discovered one thing today. She did not like guns.

With the pistol firmly in hand she ran to the head of the stairs, then slowed. The sight of Rexford's red uniform in the hall below defeated any hope of a dignified entrance. She ran as fast as the steep stairs, her long skirts, and the dangling gun would permit.

He stood looking up, with his arms wide and a grin as broad as the planet. Without thought or hesitation she flung herself into his arms. He embraced her with only one arm, and used his other hand to gently take the gun from her and hand it to Tag before giving her the embrace she had dreamed of all day. "Glad to see me, are you?" he whispered in her ear.

"Oh, God, you're safe. You're safe." She thought she'd never stop saying those words. "Thank God, you're safe."

For a long time he held her trembling body against his

chest. "You didn't honestly think you would get rid of me that easily?"

She pushed herself away and looked up into his red-rimmed eyes. "Is it over?"

"Not yet, but soon." He smiled down. "Now perhaps we could save the rest of this for—"

With a start, Amanda realized she was standing in a room full of men. "I am sorry, gentlemen. Please—" For the first time she noticed Tag's arm bound to his body. "Tag, you are hurt."

"Not a bit." Despite the etched lines around his eyes and the glistening black smudge on his wet face, he offered his easy grin. "My arm just got tired swinging a sword all day, and I thought I'd rest it."

All day reminded Amanda how exhausted the men must be. "Please come and sit. I will have tea in a minute." With a silent apology to the missing Albert, she led the dripping men into the comfortable sitting room.

They followed, leaving patches of mud and trails of water. Both her dress and the furniture would dry. How wonderful to worry about such a minor thing. The four men sat, sharing none of her concern about the furniture.

"I am afraid we don't have time for tea," Rexford said. He shifted uncomfortably. "Reverend Dubois—this is Reverend Dubois." He pointed to the cadaver-thin man, holding a round black hat. "He has to be on his way, but he is going to do us a favor first."

Amanda looked at him curiously. "What is that?"

"I am really not sure," the clergyman said, looking at Rexford and giving a Gallic shrug.

"Something I should have done a week ago," Rexford said. He took a quick gulp of air and went on too quickly. "He's going to marry us."

"I see." Amanda looked from Rexford to the clergyman and back to Rexford. She was practically being ordered to her wedding. Suddenly, she realized it didn't matter. Sometime in the endlessness of the past two days, she had decided if Rexford returned and asked again, she would marry him.

298

Right now it seemed a small price to pay for keeping him with her and safely away from the battlefield. "Very well."

Relief flooded Rexford's face. He stood. "Let's get on with it."

Amanda laughed and looked at her sodden gown. "Perhaps not quite so fast. In the morning—"

"I am afraid Reverend Dubois cannot wait until morning." Rexford held out his hand. "If you are ready . . ."

Amanda looked at her prospective bridegroom. War or no war, some things were outside of enough. "I have never been excessively fastidious, Rexford, but I could not help noticing you smell like a cross between a stable fire and a mud slide. Surely the reverend can wait an hour while we both clean up a bit?"

Rexford's fingers curled into fists. "I hesitate to impose even for that long."

The clergyman waved the protest aside. "You need not concern yourself. I am sure I can do nothing before mor—"

Rexford's jaw tightened with the stubborn look Amanda knew so well. "We will do it now." He jerked his extended arm, a clear order for her to reach out and take his hand.

A cold thought chilled Amanda's spine. "Tell me, Rexford, is Reverend Dubois the only one with something else to do tonight?"

Silence.

"Am I going to get to spend the night with my bridegroom?" She looked around the room. Lucky and the clergyman looked confused. Tag looked at the ceiling. "Am I?"

Rexford shifted uncomfortably. "I do have one message to deliver."

One message to deliver. Such a benign phrase. A walk across the park. A card or a note left for a friend. Such an easy thing. Tag's determined fascination with the ceiling left no doubt she should ask Rexford precisely what he planned to do. "Is your almost-wife allowed to ask where this message is to go?"

"It is not important."

"Perhaps it is to me."

"A short distance. To the east."

The east. Amanda struggled to remember. The fighting had been to the west and south. That was good. If she had heard anything about the east, she could not remember. "Lucky, what is to the east?"

"Nothing unless . . . nothing was this morning." The one-eyed man showed every sign of being the most incompetent liar Amanda had ever seen. "I think you'd better ask him." He jerked his thumb in Rexford's direction.

"Who is the message to, Rexford?"

He gave her a resigned look and answered calmly. "General Blücher may be regrouping at Wavre."

Amanda glanced at Lucky, her best source of information. "General Blücher is Prussian. Did we hear the French were chasing the Prussians? Where does that put the French, Lucky?"

"I don't think anybody knows, miss."

"But if you had to guess, would somebody delivering a message to General Blücher have to pass through the whole French army?"

Lucky looked desperately at Rexford. "I wouldn't say the whole army. Maybe a few—"

"Dammit, Amanda, this is not—"

"Mind your language." She glanced at the clergyman, who did not look upset. She was upset. She was upset at the bone-chilling realization that Rexford planned to make her a wife now, and probably a widow before dawn. "I don't think we need to waste any more of Reverend Dubois' time."

"Dammit, Amanda—"

Amanda ignored Rexford's flushed face and turned to the clergyman. "Thank you very much for coming—" To the side she saw Rexford's lips move to speak. She whirled on him. "And don't you say 'Dammit, Amanda' again."

"I'll say anything I please." He snapped his gaze toward the seated clergyman. "Dammit, we have to get married now." He fished into his pocket and drew out a paper. "I

300

have a license. I've been carrying it for a week. Tell her she must marry me.''

He stormed across the room and turned. ''Or better yet, just marry us. Just say the words. Someday she may wish she had married me and everybody in this room will swear she did. Won't you?''

It seemed every man in the room had discovered Tag's secret of staring at the ceiling. The clergyman improved on the notion. He stared at the ceiling and shook his head.

Tag finally took the situation in hand. ''I think we need to leave these two to sort this out. Shall we see what we can find in the kitchen?'' The others rose with the speed of cannonballs leaving the cannon.

Rexford waited until the three men were well out of the room, reached down, took Amanda's hand, and pulled her into his arms. In spite of knowing what she must do, Amanda could not find the strength to tear herself from his embrace. She needed distance to resist him, but she needed the feel of him holding her even more.

''Dammit, Amanda. You know why we have to get married. This may be our only chance.''

The words finally gave her strength to pull herself away and put a solid six feet of space between them. ''But you had no intention of telling me that. You breezed in here as if this were just an extremely convenient time to get married, instead of your last chance to do your duty by me.''

''It is not like that.''

''Of course not. How long were you going to let me be married before you told me you had done your duty here and were now free to go off and do your other duty?''

Bitterness at the incredible waste of war built with her words. ''You could die for your country then. You could die knowing, as usual, you had done exactly what you wanted. How long before you were going to tell me that?''

''I said it was not like that.'' He took three steps toward her. She backed away, and instead of touching her, he circled the room, running his fingers through his rain-slicked hair.

"Suppose you tell me what it was like. Tell me about today."

"The war, you mean? The guns? The screaming, the smells?" His face twisted in pain. "Fortunately, I don't even remember most of it. The thing I remember is thinking of you. Knowing there weren't guns enough in the world to stop me from getting back here to marry you. You have to believe that. You have to marry me now. This may be our only chance."

His words pounded into Amanda's heart like nails. She longed to throw herself into his arms and confirm that he had survived. Tell him he could have anything he wanted. If she did, she would lose everything. She backed further away until the palms of her hands touched the smooth wood of the wall. "I do believe you. That is precisely why I won't marry you."

He smacked his hand against his forehead. "What kind of convoluted logic is that?"

"You always get what you want, Rexford. I have known that from the first minute I met you. Well, this time I won't make it easy for you. If you want to marry me, you will have to want it bad enough to live and come back here and do it right."

"That is the most beetle-headed thing I have ever heard you say."

Naturally, being the Earl of Rexford, he said a lot more than that. He stomped the room, convinced that if he said the same thing often enough and loud enough, she and the rest of the world would fall into line.

Ignoring his insults to her logic, his impassioned pleas, and his barked orders, she clung to her obsessive belief. He would come back if he wanted to badly enough.

Eventually, he began to punctuate his arguments with impatient glances at the window. "This is ridiculous. I have to go."

"Go then. And come back when you can stay."

He threw his hands in the air, looked at her with his lips moving as if he might begin the entire discussion all over again, then turned and stomped from the room.

"Don't go," Amanda whispered to the achingly empty room. She sat down to wait. He would say whatever he needed to the others, but surely he would not leave without saying good-bye.

Less than five minutes later, Rexford reappeared, no longer the frustrated lover, but a curt professional soldier in a grimy uniform. "I need some birds. I am sorry about the rain, but you will have to help me get them."

"Of course." She rose, donned a heavy cloak, and led him to the cote.

On the way he explained. He needed one that would fly back here and one that could carry the same message to England. "Tag will wait here with you. I expect to send off the messages at dawn. He will arrange to get the message to Wellington. Depending on what it says, Tag will decide whether you will be safer here or if he should try to get you back to Brussels." His face softened in the flickering lantern light. "Please, don't make it difficult for him. He is young and has been through a lot."

Amanda selected one of Albert's best birds, then turned her back to lift Grace from her the roost. Holding the sleepy bird gently, she rubbed the soft feathers against her cheek. "Take care of him, Grace," she whispered, then eased her into the bag Rexford would carry.

She followed him to the stables, where he saddled a fresh horse. He traded the lantern for a bag of birds, and used his other hand to tilt her chin toward him. "You win, Amanda. I will come back." With a whisper-soft kiss, he turned and mounted.

Outside, the rain had diminished to a silken mist. He rode into the darkness, obviously not totally resigned to her decision. Even after he disappeared from the circle of light, his muttered words reached her. "Dammit, Amanda."

She returned to the house to wait for the dawn. Tag kept the endless vigil with her.

Until that night Amanda had thought all hours were composed of minutes. Some, she now discovered, had hours within hours. She sat, vowing not to look at the clock or walk again to the window. After mindlessly allowing what had to be at least an hour to pass, she would surrender and cross the room to check for the first sign of light. Seeing only the unrelieved darkness, she would turn her impatient gaze to the clock and discover scarcely fifteen minutes had passed.

Tag seemed to follow a similar routine, only he circled the room three, five, or fifteen times before seeking out the window and the clock. Occasionally he tried to talk. He would begin stories of adventures with Rexford that should have fascinated her. Only, like hers, his attention would wander and he would drift off in mid-sentence to peer out the window again.

Finally, just before four, the sky lightened with the soft gray light of morning. Amanda waited another eternal fifteen minutes before shifting her vigil to the cote. Tag followed, and sat on a sheltered tree stump while she tended to the waking birds.

For the first time in her life, the insistent creatures failed to hold her attention. She turned constantly to search the brightening sky for the first distant speck that would tell her Rexford had made it through the French lines and survived the night. The rain continued. At least there would be no grinning sun to taunt them with the fact that dawn had come and not brought the promised message.

Finally, Amanda gave up all pretense of interest in the birds and simply watched the sky. Birds, the wrong birds, began to sing in the nearby trees.

There. Amanda's trained eye discerned a tiny speck in the sky. It disappeared almost immediately, but she trusted herself enough to know what she had seen. She waited. It appeared again, larger this time. She willed it toward her.

A long minute later it hovered over the sloped roof of the stone cote, then veered off to settle on a nearby tree. Amanda borrowed Rexford's *dammit* to curse the fact she had not known Albert's birds well enough to select one that would scurry through the one-way door without coaxing.

Tag jumped to his feet.

Amanda motioned him back and put her index finger to her lips to demand silence. She whistled the seven notes she used to call her own birds, hoping it would be similar enough to Albert's call. The slate-gray bird swept from the tree, circled, hovered, and landed on the roof. She repeated the whistle and rattled some grain in a metal container. With a slapping sound the bird dropped to the landing platform and waddled through the trapdoor.

Amanda fought the impulse to pounce on the bird. Instead, she picked up the strutting creature as gently as she always did. With trembling fingers she removed the weightless container with the message that would mean victory or defeat. She handed it to Tag. The message meant far less than the fact Rexford had been alive to send it. She continued to stroke the bird as if that might somehow connect her to the man she had worried about all night.

"Good news," Tag said with a smile. "The Prussians will come. I will deliver this myself. Wellington won't let me anywhere near the fighting, so I can be here in an hour if things go badly." He put an arm around her shoulder and guided her into the sun just beginning to break from behind the clouds. "But I think this means victory. You should be safe enough."

"You are injured, Tag. Let somebody else go."

He jumped back as if struck. "Oh, no. You won't trap me like that again. After last night I know women have the harder part in a war. Nothing is worse than waiting."

His words echoed in Amanda's mind throughout the long day. Nothing was worse than waiting. Repeatedly she made the short walk to stare hungrily down the road to the east. Rexford would come from there. She pictured him rounding the curve, perhaps slumped forward with weariness and straightening when he saw her waiting.

About noon the awful guns began again. At times the noise seemed to surround her, but Lucky assured her they were still miles away. A few birds arrived with messages, and a few new soldiers appeared to replace those who had delivered the small containers to the Duke.

Unbelievably, Amanda fell asleep for a few hours in the afternoon, only to startle to full wakefulness with the realization she had not checked the road since the sun had been high overhead.

At five the housekeeper chided her for not eating, and she choked down a few slices of bread and cheese. At six she would have set out to find Rexford if she had any idea which direction to take. Any way but north, she decided, but could never choose among the remaining three.

At seven o'clock, a ragged boy, no older than sixteen, arrived with a scribbled note. *It is over. I am well. I will come when I can. Rexford.* She bowed her head in her hands and sat on the stone steps leading to the house because her flaccid knees refused to support her. It would take hours to sob out all the pent-up anguish. She refused to surrender to the temptation. "Where is he?"

"Back there." The boy pointed back down the road leading to Waterloo. "About four miles. At the crossroads."

She stood, clenching her teeth to tighten her jaw and look thoroughly in command. "Take me to him."

"I can't, ma'am. He specially said I was ta say no if you asked. Said he'd kill me if I did."

The words reassured her more than anything had all day. They sounded so like Rexford. She almost laughed, but that would spoil the effect. "Then your problem is quite simple. He will kill you later if you do. I will kill you now if you don't." She looked past the boy at Lucky, who had picked up Rexford's note after it had fluttered from her hand. "Lucky, let me borrow your musket to shoot this cretin."

Lucky stepped forward and asked the boy several rapid-fire questions. He determined that Rexford was well behind the lines, helping see to the wounded.

"Lots of people there from Brussels," the boy said. "Ladies too." He spoke rapidly to the older soldier, obviously eager to hand the decision on to someone who would mind less being killed.

"Like yourself, miss," Lucky said, "I am a little tired of all this waiting around. I will go with you."

"He said to have someone bring water. Lots," the boy said.

"That's right," Lucky agreed. "They always need it. I'll hitch up something. You start filling everything that will hold water."

All day Amanda had dreamed of leaping on a horse and galloping to Rexford. Instead they traveled the long miles in a ponderously slow carriage accompanied by the sounds of water sloshing. But, as Tag had said, anything was better than waiting. When they reached the crossroads from Brussels, the slow progress diminished to no progress. People with anxious faces clogged the road, searching and calling for loved ones.

Without waiting for Lucky's consent, Amanda climbed down and ordered the boy to accompany her. Lucky stopped him and studied the throng of men, women, and children. All of them seemed more intent on searching for someone than doing harm. "Go with her, boy. I will stay with the carriage. But take care of her, if you value your life." The boy leapt down and led Amanda to the clearing where he had last seen Rexford.

She searched the sea of faces and spied him crouched down, offering a drink to a man with a bloody bandage on his head. "Rexford." She thought her cry would be lost in the hubbub, but Rexford stood. His eyes began raking the crowd as hers had a moment earlier.

She ran, heedless of the fact she had to circle or leap over prone bodies to reach him.

"Dammit, Amanda." His words carried, but his arms spread wide and the welcoming grin on his face made them a caress instead of a curse.

With a meaningless exultant cry, Amanda buried herself in the welcoming arms of the scruffiest man she had ever seen. "Dammit, yourself," she whispered when she controlled her quivering enough to speak. Hungry for any sensation of his presence, she rubbed her cheek against his

307

three-day growth of beard. It scratched, but nicely so, with just a hint of bending softness. She rubbed his cheek again, then pushed herself away to see that he was truly there and well.

Blood drained from her face at the sight of large rusty splotches of blood on his uniform. Tentatively her hand reached out to probe for a wound beneath the filthy coat.

"Not mine." He grabbed her hand before she could touch the stained material. "God help me, I came through with only the smallest scratch." His eyes clouded with pain. "That is why I had to stay and help here." He closed his eyes and shook his head.

Amanda clenched his hand. For the first time she fully appreciated the tortured moans that had been background noise of her search for him. Her eyes filled with tears for him and for all the men surrounding him. Tears would help no one. She straightened and looked him in the eye with all the starch she could muster. "Then we had better get busy. Lucky has a carriage of water over there." She pointed.

Evening turned into night as Amanda moved from one wounded soldier to another, always aware of Rexford only a few feet from her. They offered water, adjusted bandages, and scribbled messages to parents and wives from men who would never deliver them.

About midnight, Rexford appeared at her side dragging a clergyman. Not the gangling Reverend Dubois, but a short fat man who would have looked jolly except for the agonized compassion in his eyes. There in the flickering firelight, with the wounded men as witnesses, Amanda clutched Rexford's hand and whispered the words that would bind her to him for life.

Shortly before dawn Rexford came to her again, this time leading a horse. "We can do no more here." Without waiting for her nod, he climbed into the saddle. "It is a long way. You will be more comfortable behind me."

With darkness to conceal her skewed skirts, Amanda rode astride behind her new husband. She lay her head against his strong back, heedless of the smells of death and war that clung to him. She cared only about the man beneath the ugliness.

The sun she had waited so eagerly for twenty-four hours ago had just crested the same hill when he helped her down. Aware of how heavily his tired arm lay across her shoulder, she led him across the yard and directly to the room they had shared once before.

He closed the door and turned to her, his eyes little more than slits, his expression a mixture of exhaustion and dismay. "Heaven help me, this is my wedding night. I—"

Her fingers moved to the stained buttons on his coat. "Relax, Rexford, I will tell you when it's your wedding night." She helped him out of his coat. "Now sit down. I will help you off with your boots."

He sat on the bed, made a weak attempt to remove one boot, and fell back against the pillows. "Oh, the hell with them." He was asleep before she had tugged the second boot from his foot.

Amanda removed her own gown, poured water from a waiting pitcher, washed, and slipped into her nightgown. Too exhausted to think of anything but sleep, she dropped onto the bed beside him.

She woke once during the day, stirred at the novel sensation of a warm body beside her, and drifted back to sleep. When she opened her eyes again, the red glow of the setting sun filled the room. Memory flooded back. She turned over to confirm she had spent the day in bed with her new husband.

He lay next to her, his eyes wide open, his head propped on his elbow, and a soft smile on his face. "I thought you would never wake up," he said. He had traded his blood-stained shirt for a blue silk robe. She inhaled and detected no hint of the smells of war.

"Don't you have something to tell me?" he asked.

"I . . . what . . ." His nearness made it hard to think of anything.

"I remember a promise to discuss a wedding night." His eyes suggested it would not be a long discussion.

Her stomach fluttered. A woman needed time to think, to prepare. She edged away from him. "I need time to plan. . . ."

He reached out and stopped her with a hand on her waist. Not a still hand, but one that moved along her body in a most intimate way. "You plan while I do this."

After a very few minutes, Amanda made what was for her a momentous decision. Sometimes she preferred his plans to hers.

A Stolen Rose

CORAL SMITH SAXE

Bestselling Author Of *Enchantment*

Feared by all Englishmen and known only as the Blackbird, the infamous highwayman is really the stunning Morgana Bracewell. And though she is an aristocrat who has lost her name and family, nothing has prepared the well-bred thief for her most charming victim. Even as she robs Lord Phillip Greyfriars blind, she knows his roving eye has seen through her rogue's disguise—and into her heart. Now, the wickedly handsome peer will stop at nothing to possess her, and it will take all Morgana's cunning not to surrender to a man who will accept no ransom for her love.

_3843-9 $5.50 US/$7.50 CAN

Dorchester Publishing Co., Inc.
P.O. Box 6640
Wayne, PA 19087-8640

Please add $1.75 for shipping and handling for the first book and $.50 for each book thereafter. NY, NYC, and PA residents, please add appropriate sales tax. No cash, stamps, or C.O.D.s. All orders shipped within 6 weeks via postal service book rate. Canadian orders require $2.00 extra postage and must be paid in U.S. dollars through a U.S. banking facility.

Name_____
Address_____
City_____ State_____ Zip_____
I have enclosed $_____ in payment for the checked book(s).
Payment <u>must</u> accompany all orders. ❑ Please send a free catalog.

The Rose of Ravenscrag

PATRICIA PHILLIPS

Bestselling Author Of *The Constant Flame*

The daughter of a nobleman and a common peasant, Rosamund believes she is doomed to marry a simple swineherd. Then a desperate ruse sweeps the feisty lass from her rustic English village to a faraway castle. And even as Rosamund poses as the betrothed of a wealthy lord, she cannot deny the desire he rouses in her soul. A warrior in battle, and a conqueror in love, Henry of Ravenscrag is all she has ever dreamed of in a husband. But the more Rosamund's passion flares for the gallant who has captured her spirited heart, the more she dreads he will cast her aside if he ever discovers the truth about her.

_3905-2 $4.99 US/$6.99 CAN

Dorchester Publishing Co., Inc.
P.O. Box 6640
Wayne, PA 19087-8640

Please add $1.75 for shipping and handling for the first book and $.50 for each book thereafter. NY, NYC, and PA residents, please add appropriate sales tax. No cash, stamps, or C.O.D.s. All orders shipped within 6 weeks via postal service book rate. Canadian orders require $2.00 extra postage and must be paid in U.S. dollars through a U.S. banking facility.

Name_____
Address_____
City_____ State_____ Zip_____
I have enclosed $_____ in payment for the checked book(s).
Payment <u>must</u> accompany all orders. ❑ Please send a free catalog.

PASSIONATE ROMANCE BY LEISURE'S LEADING LADIES OF LOVE!

Noble & Ivy by Carole Howey. Ivy has long since given up dreams of marrying her childhood beau, and bears a secret sorrow that haunts her past. Now, as the two reunite in a quest to save their siblings, Ivy burns to coax the embers to life and melt in the passion she swears they once shared. But before that can happen, Noble and Ivy will have to reconcile their past and learn that noble intentions mean nothing without everlasting love.

_4118-9 $5.50 US/$6.50 CAN

Lord Savage by Debra Dier. Elizabeth Barrington is sent to Colorado to find the Marquess of Angelstone, the grandson of an English Duke. But the only thing she discovers is Ash MacGregor, a bounty-hunting rogue who takes great pleasure residing in the back of a bawdy house. Convinced that his rugged good looks resemble those of the noble family, Elizabeth vows she will prove to him that aristocratic blood does pulse through his veins. But the more she tries to show him which fork to use or how to help a lady into her carriage, the more she yearns to be caressed by Lord Savage.

_4119-7 $4.99 US/$5.99 CAN

Dorchester Publishing Co., Inc.
P.O. Box 6640
Wayne, PA 19087-8640

Please add $1.75 for shipping and handling for the first book and $.50 for each book thereafter. NY, NYC, and PA residents, please add appropriate sales tax. No cash, stamps, or C.O.D.s. All orders shipped within 6 weeks via postal service book rate. Canadian orders require $2.00 extra postage and must be paid in U.S. dollars through a U.S. banking facility.

Name_____
Address_____
City_____State_____Zip_____
I have enclosed $_____ in payment for the checked book(s).
Payment <u>must</u> accompany all orders. ❑ Please send a free catalog.

THE HIDDEN JEWEL

VIOLET IVANESCU

Dominique Chantal is already in mortal danger. She has been entrusted with the delivery of a precious medallion to a group planning to overthrow Napoleon. But her plight only increases when her carriage is ambushed, the medallion taken, and the lonely beauty captured by the emperor's henchmen. To her dismay, she soon discovers that her sentence is a sham marriage to Andre Montville, Napoleon's best spy.

They make a deal—no questions and no touching—but it isn't an easy pact to uphold. And as Andre saves Dominique time and again from danger, she yearns to know more about his past and his true loyalties—and aches to know the pleasure of his forbidden caress. But she soon finds that she will have to sacrifice more than her body and her innocence in order to lure from Andre...the hidden jewel.

___4291-6 $4.99 US/$5.99 CAN

Dorchester Publishing Co., Inc.
P.O. Box 6640
Wayne, PA 19087-8640

Please add $1.75 for shipping and handling for the first book and $.50 for each book thereafter. NY, NYC, and PA residents, please add appropriate sales tax. No cash, stamps, or C.O.D.s. All orders shipped within 6 weeks via postal service book rate. Canadian orders require $2.00 extra postage and must be paid in U.S. dollars through a U.S. banking facility.

Name_____
Address_____
City_____State_____Zip_____
I have enclosed $_____ in payment for the checked book(s).
Payment <u>must</u> accompany all orders. ☐ Please send a free catalog.

DON'T MISS OTHER LOVE SPELL TIME-TRAVEL ROMANCES!

Tempest in Time by Eugenia Riley. When assertive, independent businesswoman Missy Monroe and timid Victorian virgin Melissa Montgomery accidentally trade places and partners on their wedding day, each finds herself in a bewildering new time, married to a husband she doesn't know. Now, each woman will have to decide whether she is part of an odd couple or a match made in heaven.

_52154-7 $5.50 US/$6.50 CAN

Miracle of Love by Victoria Chancellor. When Erina O'Shea's son is born too early, doctors tell the lovely immigrant there is little they can do to save young Colin's life. Not in 1896 Texas. But then she and Colin are hurtled one hundred years into the future and into the strong arms of Grant Kirby. He's handsome, powerful, wealthy, and doesn't believe a word of her story. However, united in their efforts to save the baby, Erina and Grant struggle to recognize that love is the greatest miracle of all.

_52144-X $5.50 US/$6.50 CAN

Dorchester Publishing Co., Inc.
P.O. Box 6640
Wayne, PA 19087-8640

Please add $1.75 for shipping and handling for the first book and $.50 for each book thereafter. NY, NYC, and PA residents, please add appropriate sales tax. No cash, stamps, or C.O.D.s. All orders shipped within 6 weeks via postal service book rate. Canadian orders require $2.00 extra postage and must be paid in U.S. dollars through a U.S. banking facility.

Name_____
Address_____
City_____State_____Zip_____
I have enclosed $_____ in payment for the checked book(s).
Payment <u>must</u> accompany all orders. ❑ Please send a free catalog.

Heart's Magic

Flora Speer

Bestselling author of *ROSE RED*

In the year 1122, Mirielle senses change is coming to Wroxley Castle. Then, from out of the fog, two strangers ride into Lincolnshire. Mirielle believes the first man to be honest. But the second, Giles, is hiding something–even as he stirs her heart and awakens her deepest desires. And as Mirielle seeks the truth about her mysterious guest, she uncovers the castle's secrets and learns she must stop a treachery which threatens all she holds dear. Only then can she be in the arms of her only love, the man who has awakened her own heart's magic.

___52204-7 $5.99 US/$6.99 CAN

Dorchester Publishing Co., Inc.
P.O. Box 6640
Wayne, PA 19087-8640

Please add $1.75 for shipping and handling for the first book and $.50 for each book thereafter. NY, NYC, and PA residents, please add appropriate sales tax. No cash, stamps, or C.O.D.s. All orders shipped within 6 weeks via postal service book rate. Canadian orders require $2.00 extra postage and must be paid in U.S. dollars through a U.S. banking facility.

Name_____

Address_____

City_____ State_____ Zip_____

I have enclosed $_____ in payment for the checked book(s).

Payment <u>must</u> accompany all orders. ❑ Please send a free catalog.

FLORA SPEER

Bestselling Author Of *Love Just In Time*

Falsely accused of murder, Sir Alain vows to move heaven and earth to clear his name and claim the sweet rose named Joanna. But in a world of deception and intrigue, the virile knight faces enemies who will do anything to thwart his quest of the heart.

From the sceptered isle of England to the sun-drenched shores of Sicily, the star-crossed lovers will weather a winter of discontent. And before they can share a glorious summer of passion, they will have to risk their reputations, their happiness, and their lives for love and honor.

__3816-1 $4.99 US/$5.99 CAN

Dorchester Publishing Co., Inc.
P.O. Box 6640
Wayne, PA 19087-8640

Please add $1.75 for shipping and handling for the first book and $.50 for each book thereafter. NY, NYC, and PA residents, please add appropriate sales tax. No cash, stamps, or C.O.D.s. All orders shipped within 6 weeks via postal service book rate. Canadian orders require $2.00 extra postage and must be paid in U.S. dollars through a U.S. banking facility.

Name_____
Address_____
City_____State_____Zip_____
I have enclosed $_____ in payment for the checked book(s).
Payment <u>must</u> accompany all orders. ❏ Please send a free catalog.

Pure Temptation

Connie Mason

"Each new Connie Mason book is a prize!"
—Heather Graham

Spirits can be so bloody unpredictable, and the specter of Lady Amelia is the worst of all. Just when one of her ne'er-do-well descendents thought he could go astray in peace, the phantom lady always appears to change his wicked ways.

A rogue without peer, Jackson Graystoke wants to make gaming and carousing in London society his life's work. And the penniless baronet would gladly curse himself with wine and women—if Lady Amelia would give him a ghost of a chance.

Fresh off the boat from Ireland, Moira O'Toole isn't fool enough to believe in legends or naive enough to trust a rake. Yet after an accident lands her in Graystoke Manor, she finds herself haunted, harried, and hopelessly charmed by Black Jack Graystoke and his exquisite promise of pure temptation.

_4041-7 $5.99 US/$6.99 CAN

Dorchester Publishing Co., Inc.
P.O. Box 6640
Wayne, PA 19087-8640

Please add $1.75 for shipping and handling for the first book and $.50 for each book thereafter. NY, NYC, and PA residents, please add appropriate sales tax. No cash, stamps, or C.O.D.s. All orders shipped within 6 weeks via postal service book rate. Canadian orders require $2.00 extra postage and must be paid in U.S. dollars through a U.S. banking facility.

Name_____
Address_____
City_____ State_____ Zip_____
I have enclosed $_____ in payment for the checked book(s).
Payment <u>must</u> accompany all orders. ❑ Please send a free catalog.

THE LION'S BRIDE
CONNIE MASON

Winner of the *Romantic Times* Storyteller Of The Year Award!

Lord Lyon of Normandy has saved William the Conqueror from certain death on the battlefield, yet neither his strength nor his skill can defend him against the defiant beauty the king chooses for his wife.

Ariana of Cragmere has lost her lands and her virtue to the mighty warrior, but the willful beauty swears never to surrender her heart.

Saxon countess and Norman knight, Ariana and Lyon are born enemies. And in a land rent asunder by bloody wars and shifting loyalties, they are doomed to misery unless they can vanquish the hatred that divides them—and unite in glorious love.

_3884-6 $5.99 US/$7.99 CAN

Dorchester Publishing Co., Inc.
P.O. Box 6640
Wayne, PA 19087-8640

Please add $1.75 for shipping and handling for the first book and $.50 for each book thereafter. NY, NYC, and PA residents, please add appropriate sales tax. No cash, stamps, or C.O.D.s. All orders shipped within 6 weeks via postal service book rate. Canadian orders require $2.00 extra postage and must be paid in U.S. dollars through a U.S. banking facility.

Name_____
Address_____
City_____ State_____ Zip_____
I have enclosed $_____ in payment for the checked book(s).
Payment <u>must</u> accompany all orders. ☐ Please send a free catalog.

ATTENTION ROMANCE CUSTOMERS!

SPECIAL TOLL-FREE NUMBER
1-800-481-9191

Call Monday through Friday
12 noon to 10 p.m.
Eastern Time
Get a free catalogue,
join the Romance Book Club,
and order books using your
Visa, MasterCard,
or Discover[®]*.*

Leisure
Books